# THE MIDNIGHT CONSPIRACY

David Leadbeater has published more than fifty novels and is a million-copy ebook bestseller. His books include the chart-topping Matt Drake series and the Relic Hunters series, which won the inaugural Amazon Kindle Storyteller award in 2017.

www.davidleadbeater.com

D0988007

# DAVID LEADBEATER

# THE
# MIDNIGHT
# CONSPIRACY

avon.

HarperCollins*Publishers* Ltd
1 London Bridge Street,
London SE1 9GF

www.harpercollins.co.uk

HarperCollins*Publishers*
Macken House,
39/40 Mayor Street Upper,
Dublin 1
D01 C9W8

First published by HarperCollins*Publishers* 2023
1
Copyright © David Leadbeater 2023

David Leadbeater asserts the moral right to
be identified as the author of this work

A catalogue record for this book is available from the British Library

ISBN: 978-0-00-854510-9

Typeset in Sabon by Palimpsest Book Production Limited,
Falkirk, Stirlingshire

Printed and bound in the UK using 100% Renewable Electricity
by CPI Group (UK) Ltd

# THE
# MIDNIGHT
# CONSPIRACY

# Chapter 1

The plan for the heist had been prepared with pinpoint accuracy, right down to the amount of fuel they'd need for the helicopter, the number of spare ammo mags, the weight they'd add to backpacks and the chances of needing a medic and what supplies he should carry . . . everything. Johann could not remember a better-planned mission.

Of course, their mysterious employer had made the consequences of failure pretty bloody clear.

'If you fail, I will hire a team tasked specifically with the job of nailing your entrails to the highest tree, and then hanging you with them. I will see to it that your families burn, that—' Johann blocked out the rest of the speech. Their employer had to be either downright stupid or incredibly powerful to threaten an ex-military crew that way. Johann and all the others believed the man was the latter.

Thus, a job planned with expert precision.

Johann travelled in the back of one of two black Range Rovers, his Heckler & Koch MP5 sub-machine gun, with its retractable stock, laid carefully across his lap. The Range Rovers negotiated the swooping twists and turns of the lush English countryside with ease, driving at speed, about ten feet apart, gradually closing on their prey. Johann focused on the job ahead.

They were a tight, highly skilled team, a product of war that had survived years of action and reinvented itself as a practised, motivated unit. They operated where the money was, usually in military hot spots, but today they were in rainy rural England, where they'd been offered a ridiculous sum of money to obtain a particular object.

'Make no mistake, they will perceive you all as hostiles,' their mysterious employer had told them. 'Leave no one alive. Everyone except you who handles my treasure must die.'

It all left a bitter aftertaste in Johann's mouth, like burned coffee. In a war zone you could justify almost anything, you could assault an enemy convoy, kill everyone and still come away with a sense of satisfaction. But here . . . passing through sleepy old villages and country churches, past Grandma and Grandad tootling down to the local post office, seeing babies being pushed in their prams and hearing schoolchildren hollering in their playgrounds . . . it didn't sit right. This was home. This was what you fought to preserve. You didn't bring the war back here.

Unless the money was particularly good.

Johann sighed inwardly. He was a soldier. If his commanding officer told him to kill, he would kill. The three other members of his team would do the same. Following orders was how they stayed alive, how they eventually returned to a normal world that they no longer felt part of. Johann much preferred a strident war zone to an anarchic Sainsbury's. His colleagues felt the same. Johann had found that the downtime between missions hurt their team equilibrium far more than an intense firefight or a close call. And the men he sat alongside now, the men he fought with, were all that mattered. He would go to hell and back with them.

The Range Rovers plunged through twisty English backroads, rows of trees on either side. The rising sun disappeared, blocked out by the density of overhanging branches. Johann steadied his weapon as potholes rocked the suspension, listening to the interplay between the boss in the front seat and the helicopter that travelled above.

'Maintain airspeed,' the boss said. 'Target is six minutes out.'

'Understood,' came the reply. 'With you every step of the way.'

'Stay in constant contact, Air One.'

'Understood, Ground One.' Johann looked up through the Range Rover's smoky panoramic roof. The helicopter tracking them was a highly versatile multipurpose Augusta Westland, rented anonymously from a Northumbrian airfield just a day ago, that had an extended cabin and could carry up to seven passengers in addition to two pilots in relative luxury. It was an integral part of the plan.

They would hit their targets where they were most vulnerable.

'Four minutes to impact,' the boss said.

Close to the start of this long journey, when they were still negotiating the country lanes of Northumberland, well before they reached the A1 and major roads south, Johann and the other members of his team would attack the unmarked van that carried an unknown treasure. They would take everything, including the other team's lives. The heist would have to be clean, anonymous, speedy and clinical.

'Two minutes,' the boss said.

Johann blinked as the car passed through a tree tunnel, his face dappled by intermittent bursts of sunlight, and then raised his gun and placed his finger over the trigger, a familiar caress. He smelled oil and metal and leather. He heard the roar of the engine and the clump of the helicopter and the sound of blood rushing in his ears.

Ahead, the white van that was their ultimate target appeared.

# Chapter 2

Joe Mason longed for a punchbag. He hadn't hit the gym in weeks. Hadn't hit anything in weeks. Following their last mission where they had found the hidden Creed that belonged to the Amori after serpentine slogs through ancient catacombs and a damaging assault on their enemy's secret stronghold, Mason had come away with broken ribs, a broken index finger and a black eye. And Mason, along with Quaid, had been the relatively lucky ones. Roxy and Hassell had fared far worse.

Six weeks had passed. Wounds from the explosion were healing or had healed. Mason's ribs remained a little tender. But his index finger was as good as new.

As for the rest of the team: Quaid's bruising and headache had vanished within a few days. Hassell's broken arm, concussion and facial lacerations had mended almost perfectly. The only lasting scars were two narrow tramlines that crossed his right cheek, tramlines he found it hard not to track with his fingers on a regular basis. And then there was Roxy . . .

The raven-haired American had suffered scorching and scoring along her shoulders and arms, puncture wounds across much of her body, and skin torn from her face. The private doctors that Sally employed had done a great job of fixing Roxy's wounds, however. Now, apart from some redness, Mason found it hard to see where the damage had occurred. Not that he looked too closely. He didn't want to get on Roxy's bad side.

Sally had used the time for their convalescence well. True to her word, she had created a company called Quest Investigations, named them all as employees and set up a headquarters. It was based in the old rambling house her father had left after his murder, the event that started Sally and Mason and the others in their initial quest for the Vatican Book of Secrets. Sally had outfitted a large room with computers, added an oversized wall monitor, more telephones and wireless chargers than they would ever need, several light-oak desks, a food-making station, a fridge-freezer, coffee- and tea-making facilities and, finally, a comfortable L-shaped sofa that faced a flourishing and verdant section of the garden.

'That'll do for now,' she'd said on completion, leaving Mason to wonder just what the hell else she could possibly fit in there.

Sally had taken her time. They had time to kill due to their injuries. She had made contact with just a few trusted friends, and then their good contacts at the Vatican, asking for endorsements, validations that they could use as seals of approval for their new company. She had built a website, ordered business cards and stationery and even rented a company car. Most important of all, she had secured them a weapons permit.

The hardest part was convincing the authorities that they would need guns to track down a dusty old relic. But they had experience to draw on, and they had another justification that Quaid had come up with. 'We could offer an additional service,' he'd said. 'Simple enough, and one that could be quite lucrative. With our personnel we're easily equipped to transport precious items between places.'

His suggestion swung it in favour of the weapons permit. They'd installed a state-of-the-art gun safe in Sally's home. The next idea was to build a shooting range, but there hadn't been time for that yet. In addition, Sally had voiced a desire to learn how to fight and defend herself. She understood it would take a while, but she'd spent enough time cowering in a corner as the others fought; she wanted to make more of a difference and felt that she had the right people around her to make that happen.

The six-week convalescence was a good time to start.

Sally spent the rest of her time cultivating contacts. In typical style, she had ignored her father's old networks – affluent, arrogant men who still badgered her for investments – and instead targeted influential museums, historians and experienced professors. She intended to work only with the best, and to take on only what she deemed to be the most interesting archaeological quests. She saw no point in rushing anything.

Mason and the others had been staying in Sally's house for the most part during this period. At first, Mason hadn't fancied making the hectic journey back to his London apartment, due to his slowly healing ribs, which meant he hadn't needed a gym to frequent. Sally had promised to install a punchbag in the garage, but he was still waiting for that to materialise.

Eventually, Sally's house became the easiest alternative for everyone. The team were able to stay out of each other's way when they needed to, and were on hand when the situation required. Mason found that Professor Rusk's old, sprawling, irregular house had more rooms and attics and basements than he cared to explore and just enough modern touches to make it habitable.

Early on, they determined to stay together for as long as it took Sally to create her new business, which would be at least as long as their wounds would take to heal.

It was a hard time for Mason. Even harder for Roxy. Mason thrived on moving forward, turning his experiences into history, but Roxy needed them. She told him about the old wounds that crisscrossed her body, the daunting network a constant reminder of a terrible old life that she needed to leave behind. The new scars were more prominent than her old ones due to their freshness, but did they speak to her of the future . . . or of the past?

Mason hadn't found the right moment to ask her, to get into a deep conversation. It didn't seem appropriate whilst most people's wounds were still on the mend. The events that transpired at Boneyard Bay, the final battle and Marduk's explosion, the atrocities carried out by the murderous thief Cassadaga and his companion, Ivana, had affected them all deeply and required a certain amount of distance. Mason found he couldn't deal with them head on, at least not yet.

Probably because he already had deep-seated, unresolved issues.

Mason shrugged, purposely derailing his own train of thought. He was currently alone, standing in one of Sally's garages and wondering how much junk they'd have to get rid of to install a decent boxing-based mini-gym inside. The roof was high and sturdy, the walls constructed from thick breezeblock, but every square inch of space was taken up by an assortment of detritus that numbed Mason's mind with the thought of getting it all cleared away.

'Hey.' Roxy was standing at the door, her shadow blotting out the mid-April sunshine. 'You ready to go, Babyface?'

'You still calling me that?'

'If the face fits . . .' Roxy shrugged. 'Embrace it.'

Mason started walking towards her. 'There are worse nicknames, I guess.'

'Oh, believe me, there are a lot worse, and I would be happy to apply them.'

'Let's stick with Babyface, shall we?'

Mason was blessed with blond hair, blue eyes and a face that – no matter what hell he'd been through – never changed. Due to his clean looks, people often underestimated him.

He caught up with Roxy and accompanied her around to the front of the house.

'How are you feeling this morning?' he asked. This was their first mission since the day of the explosion.

'Antsy,' she said. 'The room's too full of me when I'm the only one in it.'

Surprisingly, Mason knew exactly what she meant. He wouldn't tell her – he didn't want to admit he was on the same wavelength as Roxy Banks – but both of them had heads full of demons to exorcise and neither of them wanted to be inactive for too long. Inactivity allowed the past to creep up on you. It used hard, skeletal fingers to drag you back to its deadly lair where old mistakes, errors of judgement and poisonous memories lay waiting to enfold you in unbearable pain.

'It will be good to get back to work,' he said simply.

'I'm not sure today classifies as work.'

'What? You'd rather be getting shot at? Chased?'

'Whatever builds a wall,' Roxy said. 'You know what I'm looking for.'

Mason did. Roxy was essentially trying to find the woman she could have become if an undercover agency hadn't taken twelve years of her life and trained her to be an assassin. Only then would she feel worthy enough to reclaim the love her parents so longed to give her.

'The last two missions must have helped,' he said. 'The Vatican Book of Secrets and then the hidden Creed. Marduk's lair. Saving the world twice. Or at least, the Catholic world. Do you remember how grateful Cardinal Vallini was?'

Roxy slowed as they approached the hire car that was parked out front of Sally's house. 'I do, and that's great. But Joe' – she turned to him – 'it's not happening fast enough. It feels a little slow. I'm worried.' She turned away and put a hand on the door of the car. 'Worried for all of us.'

Mason watched her climb into the back seat with Hassell and Sally. Slow? Just hearing her words made him apprehensive about her state of mind. For him, there had been nothing slow about the last two missions. Was Roxy seeking something she would never find? Would she try so hard that the effort would get her killed?

Quaid, sitting in the driver's seat, waved at him, drawing him away from dark thoughts. Mason shrugged the melancholy away and climbed into the front passenger seat, greeting his friends as he closed the door. Despite Roxy's claims of tedium, he was looking forward to this mission. It was their first time working for Sally, their first as an official new team, and their first for the new company.

'Are we ready to go now?' Quaid asked impatiently.

'When you are,' Mason said. 'Are you sure you can drive this thing? It's brand-new, you know.'

Quaid tried to look confident. 'It's a bloody auto,' he said. 'You point it, and it goes. What could possibly go wrong?'

'Sorry I couldn't get a saloon with a manual box,' Sally said from the back seat. 'I did try.'

Quaid nodded in appreciation. 'Well, we'll see how it goes. I have to get used to driving these things one day, I suppose.'

Mason buckled his seat belt, not overly happy with Quaid's description of driving them on a three-hundred-mile round trip today. But it was mid-April, and the sun was shining. It was 9.30 a.m., and they were about to embark on their first job.

'The first leg of the journey is to Coventry,' Sally said, reminding Mason of how she'd helped direct and guide them across the globe recently. 'Do you have everything you need?'

'Yes, Mother,' Roxy said.

Mason had his gun holstered at his waist, his permit and a bottle of water. For him, that was enough.

'I have all the papers,' Sally said.

Mason thought hard. He wanted this to go well. No matter what he was doing, if people were relying on him – he wanted it to go well.

'Maybe we should run through it one more time,' he said.

'Give me a break,' Roxy murmured. 'We ran through it twice last night.'

Quaid started the car, and they set off down the winding gravel-filled driveway towards the front gates. Mason slipped a pair of sunglasses on as a bright glare filled the windscreen. It was Hassell who decided to run them through the day's itinerary.

'First stop Coventry,' he said in his New York accent. 'We collect the valuable relic from a guy called Roger Beat. We don't examine it; we just take the box and leave. We then transport it to Poole, to where a second expert will sign for it and take it off our hands. The second guy's name is Professor Mark Evans. Basically, we're to act as security for a priceless item that's being transported from one specialist to another.'

Mason nodded. 'It's a start. Every business has to start somewhere.'

Sally shifted in the back seat. 'It didn't feel right accepting a job from one of my father's hoity-toity friends. But you're right, Joe, it does get us started. I'd rather have kept the privileged crowd out of our work, but Geoffrey was friendly, and he knows nothing about our recent exploits. I know it's not exactly relic hunting, not what we're used to, but it does get us out of the house.'

The last sentence was meant as a joke, Mason knew, but it rang true. The last six weeks had been increasingly hard for the team. A forced recuperation wasn't always the best way forward for mind and body. Not in Mason's case, and clearly not Roxy's. But at least he'd managed to overcome most of the boredom by starting to train Sally. Quaid had spent the time shipping any old valuables he still possessed into the country, items like Corgi die-cast models, bottles of wine and a precious case of old cassette tapes. Hassell had brooded for five out of the six weeks. The sixth week had been spent on exercise and brushing up on infiltration techniques – which was his job. Not that they'd need his services today.

Mason settled back as Quaid joined a main road and started them on the main part of their journey north. The miles rumbled beneath their wheels. A light drizzle coated the windscreen and side windows after about an hour, diffusing the sunlight that still tried valiantly to claim the day for itself, and the roads grew busier. They stopped briefly at a service station on the M1 and then started making their way through Coventry. Mason sat up straight as the satnav informed them that they were three minutes from their destination. Roger Beat had asked that they meet at St Mary's Guildhall, a dwelling that retained a seven-hundred-year history from medieval times to the present day and, good to his word, was standing outside the impressive old building when Mason and the others walked up.

'We're from Quest.' Sally stepped forward, presenting their papers. 'Come to transport your relic.'

Roger Beat handed over a small lockbox that he tugged out of a tight backpack. The box was approximately eighteen inches by twelve and covered with black velvet. The lock was gold and came with a golden key which Beat gave to Sally with a solemn nod.

'Keep it safe,' he said. 'Although it's one of two I'm studying, the relic inside that box is completely irreplaceable. Recently discovered and still going through the process . . .' He didn't explain himself further, but Mason just assumed he meant some kind of authentication procedure.

'That's our job,' Sally said a little proudly. 'We're the best at what we do.'

Mason took responsibility for the lockbox, slipping it into his own big backpack with ease. They'd been apprised of the item's dimensions before today and had determined the best way to transport something back to their car through the centre of town was by sturdy rucksack. The others would watch his back all the way and their everyday clothing ensured they wouldn't stand out from the crowd.

They returned to the car without incident, and headed out of town. Now for the long journey to Poole. Before they set off, Mason had made sure his backpack was safe and secure in the boot, tied down carefully with ratchet straps. If they stopped for any reason on the way, someone would stay with the car. If they needed to communicate, they had their phones. Mason had wanted to try out their new Bluetooth earbud comms system, but Sally had pointed out that, since they were essentially driving together all the way there and all the way back, they wouldn't really need it. Mason gave in gracefully, but still itched to try out the new comms.

From Coventry to Poole, the road held blessedly little traffic, the only problem they encountered being the bright glare of sunlight on the tarmac. Quaid got used to driving the car and didn't complain too much, though when he did once again mention the automatic gears Mason dived straight in and enlightened him on how the new paddleshift gearing was far superior to the old manual boxes. Quaid, of course, was having none of it, but that didn't stop Mason trying.

'You two will keep on having this argument 'til the cows come home,' Sally said with a laugh. 'Why don't you agree to disagree?'

'Because I'm right,' Quaid huffed.

'Not even close,' Mason said, and they started at it again.

Poole sits on the south coast, a large seaside town with a rich history. Quaid guided their car down the narrow streets and across busy junctions until the satnav warned them that they were two minutes from their destination. Everyone stretched and started taking note of what was outside the window.

'First job almost well done,' Sally said, and this time Mason could hear the pride in her voice. 'I think this will be a great new venture for us.'

'Yeah, so long as it gets a little more interesting,' Roxy complained lightly. 'I haven't come close to hitting anyone today.'

'Would you rather be crossing swords with Marduk again? Trying to reclaim the Book of Secrets or searching for the Creed? Battling that madman?' Hassell asked. 'Or fighting Cassadaga, that deranged thief who stole the Creed in the first place and was interested only in cold-blooded murder? And who, I might add, is still out there somewhere.'

Roxy didn't reply, and Mason knew the real answer was insanely complicated. It was a twisted mix of need and necessity. To change the subject, he pointed out the name of the road they were on and then started counting down the house numbers.

'So we're delivering to this guy's home?' Roxy asked, peering out the window. 'That's not exactly secure.'

'It's what the client wanted,' Sally said pragmatically. 'He'll probably take it to his museum office himself.'

Quaid pulled up at the kerb the moment the satnav announced their arrival. He let the car idle whilst pinpointing the house. 'To the right,' he said. 'Across the road. White gate.'

Mason had already spotted it and opened his door. He stepped out, felt a cold sea breeze and zipped up his leather jacket. He took a quick scan up and down the street, unable to help himself. This was something he'd been taught in the army; a habit that had become ingrained during those long, bloody days in Mosul and other Iraqi cities. Checking his surroundings had become intrinsic to him now, whether he was eating dinner in a restaurant or chasing down an enemy.

The street looked clear apart from an older man pushing a pram about a hundred feet down the hill and a woman painting a garden fence on the other side of the road. He opened the boot, released the backpack and shrugged it carefully across his shoulders. The others watched and then started walking towards the white gate alongside him. Roxy reached it first, unhooked the latch and pushed it open on a set of creaking hinges.

Mason paused, eagle eyes noticing that something wasn't quite right. Roxy saw it a split second later.

'Door's open,' she said carefully.

'Could be anything,' Sally said. 'He could have left it open for us.'

Mason was trained to look deeper than that in all ambiguous situations. 'It's better to be safe than sorry,' he said. 'Stay at the back.' She hadn't been training with them anywhere near long enough yet to face trouble head on.

Roxy and Mason, followed by Hassell and Quaid, walked carefully up the garden path to the slightly ajar front door. Their senses were attuned, their eyes searching every inch of the front window but unable to penetrate the reflections caused by the direct sunlight. Mason paused just a step from the door.

'I'll knock,' he said. 'Just be ready to—'

His words were abruptly cut off by a bloodcurdling scream. Something high-pitched and agonised, something that Mason had heard before when he'd come across soldiers and civilians in distress. It was the sound of torture.

'Help!' someone screamed inside the house. 'Help me!'

# Chapter 3

Johann watched the white van as it grew larger through the front window. A message came through their bespoke earbud comms system, ordering the heist team to make ready. The two Range Rovers tucked in behind the white van, ready to make their move.

Above them, the helicopter swooped just above the tree-tops, its rotor blades battering the air.

They were the only cars currently driving on this particular stretch of back road of Northumberland. Johann hadn't seen another car for ten minutes. The driver of the lead Range Rover must have thought the same, for he chose that moment to pull out and overtake the white van at speed using the opposite carriageway. When he was past, he swerved back in and matched the van's speed for a few moments.

The second Range Rover boxed the van in from behind. All three vehicles approached a wider part of the road.

'Now!'

The order lit up the comms and fired Johann's adrenalin at the same time. Their lead vehicle slammed on his brakes, forcing the white van to slow. At first it was a gradual process, taking them from fifty to forty and then thirty miles per hour, but then the frontrunner stepped hard on the brake pedal, bringing the whole convoy to a sudden stop.

The helicopter blasted overhead.

The front Range Rover's tailgate came up. Two men holding assault rifles jumped out. The rear doors also opened, disgorging more men with weapons. The men were masked, and wore armoured vests. Johann held on as their own car stopped, and then threw open his door. He hit the road with his boots, and brought his gun up to his shoulder, running at the rear of the white van. Three other men were at his side. They joined all but two of the men from the front vehicle.

The two that were left focused their guns through the front windscreen on the driver and passenger of the white van, gesturing that they should hold their hands above their heads. Johann lost sight of them as he approached the van's rear doors.

Two men fixed a small packet of explosive to the handle without checking to see if it was already unlocked. The explosive wasn't devastating – nobody wanted to destroy the van's precious cargo – but it would demolish any locking mechanisms and debilitate the guards inside.

Johann waited, gun aimed at the ground. Seconds had passed since they stopped the van. Watching the road, he was conscious of the passage of time but still saw no other traffic. The helicopter was back, now hovering over the scene, and reported that the road was clear as far as the pilot could see. One man produced a silver device and pressed a tiny red button. The explosives detonated with a dull thump. The rear doors buckled. White smoke plumed into the air. Two men grabbed a handle each and wrenched the rear doors wide open.

Johann stepped forward, weapon raised. 'Come out,' he shouted. 'Come out with your hands in the air.'

The smoke cleared. Johann saw four men staring back at him, all with their guns drawn.

'Stand back, man,' one of them shouted back. 'We're security. We won't hesitate to shoot.'

Johann took the words to heart. Without a second thought he opened fire. His bullets slammed into the shouter, stitching a line across his chest and then his face, throwing him back into the side of the van with a dull, wet thud. The man's weapon clattered to the floor.

Johann, conscious of a colleague backing him to the left and two more behind, aimed his gun at the three remaining men.

'Anyone else wanna die?'

'Don't shoot.' A tall man, dressed all in black, hunched over and scrambled forward, heading for the back of the van. All he effectively did though, was block Johann's view of the other two men inside the van.

'Get down,' Johann said.

Several things happened at once. The other two men dropped to their knees and reached for their sidearms at the same time. The man in black threw himself headlong. Johann found that his gun was sighted on nothing, just a spot where the other two men had been.

Shots rang out. Johann felt a blow to the chest that knocked him backwards, driving the air right out of him. Fire erupted from his ribcage. Even as he gasped, even as he understood that the Kevlar vest had saved his life, gunfire exploded to either side of him. Johann's colleagues coolly loosed well-placed shots at their opponents' centre masses. There was no emotion in their actions, no fear or rage or elation; it was a detached and practised reaction to being under fire.

Special armour-piercing bullets slammed into those who remained inside the van. Johann could tell the men inside weren't wearing bulletproof vests and, in a disconnected way, wondered why. The men dropped their guns and threw their arms out and staggered into the sides of the van before falling to their knees and breathing their last.

The man on the floor looked up. 'Don't shoot,' he whispered.

Johann took a deep breath. His ribs hurt. His colleagues sent him a quick glance of enquiry and he nodded.

'I'm fine.'

'Please don't shoot.'

Johann knew what was going to happen. With three men already dead in the back of the van there would now be no point leaving any living witnesses. The man in black, the driver and the passenger up front would be taken care of. Johann didn't think of his bosses as ruthless. They were simply practical; this was the way it had to be.

Johann took a deep breath, ignored the pain in his chest and aimed his gun at the man's face. One squeeze of the trigger took care of that loose end.

Other members of Johann's team scrambled up into the truck.

'Get a move on,' the team leader said through the comms. 'Find the prize and get the hell out of there.'

Johann stepped back, leaving them to it. They knew exactly what they were looking for: a small black lockbox, a mini-safe. The men were equipped to extract it from whatever physical security measure the dead team might have employed.

'It's right here on the seat,' came a bemused observation through his earpiece. 'These guys were useless, total amateurs.'

'Just get on with it,' the team leader growled.

Johann moved away from the door. He checked the road north and south. They had purposely executed the raid at this spot along this stretch of tarmac because the road was wider here. Much wider. There was sufficient space to allow the helicopter to land and afford the heist team a quick getaway.

'Chopper down,' the team leader said. 'Chopper down.'

'We have the box.' Johann saw his two colleagues jump out of the back of the van. 'Repeat: we have the treasure.'

Johann saw the small, nondescript lockbox clasped in the man's hand, the scarred metal container as unremarkable as a loaf of bread. He wondered what it might hold that could be so incredibly important to their client.

The roar of the helicopter filled his ears as it landed to the right. He looked across as the black bird touched down, its skids bouncing lightly off the road. There came the sound of heavy gunfire from the front of the van as the driver and passenger were both shot and killed. Johann started towards the chopper. The Range Rovers and the van would remain where they stood whilst the heist team made good their escape by helicopter.

'Move it.' The team leader's voice galvanised him to move faster despite the pain in his ribs.

Mission accomplished, Johann thought, and no witnesses left behind. He felt better about that. Despite wearing masks, a team could still sometimes be identified by their enemies due to their methods. This had all been a damn sight easier than the last time he was in Mosul. It was now time to deliver the treasure to their employer. A benefactor Johann had never heard of and secretly wanted nothing more to do with.

The mysterious Guild of Night.

# Chapter 4

As soon as he heard screams from inside the house, Mason kicked open the front door and reached for his weapon. The cool metal of the semi-automatic Glock 17, polymer-framed, seventeen-round handgun felt reassuring in his hand but even he balked a little at having to draw it on the first day of their new job.

Inside, Mason saw a narrow hallway that ran all the way to the back of the house and a wooden staircase to his right. Doors were open, left and right, along the hallway. Mason stepped over the threshold.

'At your back,' Roxy whispered.

Mason held his gun out and walked slowly forwards. Another scream rang out, filling the house. Mason guessed it came from one of the rooms ahead rather than upstairs. He reached the first open doorway and paused, taking a quick look back.

Roxy was at his shoulder, Quaid and Hassell behind her. All three of them had drawn their guns. Sally was standing outside the house, her expression a mixture of worry and disbelief. This wasn't how she'd expected their first job to go.

Mason stuck his head into the first room and then withdrew quickly. It was a dining room, complete with a long, oblong dark oak table and six upright plush chairs, and it was empty. He moved on. The next room, on the right, was a living room with a four-seater sofa, a small television and a black Persian rug over wooden herring-bone flooring. It, too, was empty.

Mason moved further down the hallway as another scream rang out.

Closer to the source of the screams, he could now also hear furious, taut whispers. The sound of someone without conscience questioning another man.

Mason paused outside the next doorway. He counted to three. Just as another scream rang out, he walked straight into the room, the others following him. The scene that met his eyes was enough to make him wince.

Four men stood around an older man who'd been tied to a chair. There was rope binding the older man's legs to the seat, and his hands were behind his back, probably secured. One individual stood over him, whispering in his ear, his mouth stretched into a wide grin. Three others stood around the room – a study – looking bored. Two held kitchen knives, and the other a small axe. The tied man already had four knives sticking out of the top of his legs from thigh to knee. Blood ran from the wounds and dripped to the floor. As Mason walked forward, holding his gun steady, the interrogator looked up and narrowed his eyes.

'Why are you here?'

'Mason,' Roxy said loudly, then nodded at a side window. Mason immediately saw the shape of another man stand-ing outside.

'Quaid, Hassell,' he said without taking his eyes off the interrogator. 'Go and watch out for Sally. Roxy, with me.'

He took another step, watching his enemies carefully. He saw fists clench over knife hilts, eyes grow even harder, mouths draw into tight, merciless lines.

'Stand down,' he said. 'No need to make this any worse than it already is. You, on the chair, can you speak?'

The captive's eyes were rolling in pain, but he inclined his head towards Mason and nodded. 'Are you Mark Evans?' Mason asked.

The figure nodded. This then was the man they had come to see, the would-be recipient of the black velvet lockbox that Mason carried in his backpack. But why the hell were these men torturing him?

'Stand down,' Mason said again. 'We'll let the police take care of this.'

The interrogator rose to his full height. Mason noticed that he appeared to favour his right foot. He was a thin individual with a sallow complexion and sunken cheek-bones. He wore a leather jacket that was too long in the sleeves. The other men were muscle, Mason thought, hard-faced goons with about as much going on in their brain boxes as a broken television.

'Walk away,' the interrogator said softly. 'I'll give you one chance.'

'We're the ones with the guns, asshole,' Roxy said in her inimitable style.

'You're gonna kill us in cold blood, are you, Roxy?' came the reply. 'I doubt that.'

Mason realised he'd made a slight error in mentioning their names, but couldn't dwell on that now. He moved his gun slightly up and down. 'Move away from the chair,' he said. 'The rest of you, on your knees.' He was acutely conscious that every passing second increased Mark Evans's suffering.

'He won't shoot,' one of the goons spoke up. 'He's no cop. We have what we came for. Just go.'

Mason noticed for the first time that, on the desk that stood behind the interrogator, a laptop sat open. It was swivelled around facing the interrogator, its screen filled by an image of a golden basin.

'Agreed,' the thin man said, his sickly facial appearance worsening as he smiled, most probably because the expression looked alien on him. 'Mason,' he said. 'Catch you later.'

As one, the four men broke for the back of the room, where an open door led to a small kitchen.

Mason was left with a quick decision to make and only one clear option.

'Stop.'

He ran for the third man in line, assuming Roxy would take care of the fourth. Maybe if these goons lost a couple of members, they'd capitulate. Mason's target was a bulky individual wearing a brown leather jacket and a beanie hat. When Mason closed in on him, he turned and struck out with his knife.

Mason twisted his body out of the path of the blade, then stepped in and smashed the barrel of the Glock across the man's head. The force of the impact staggered the man and drew blood from his temple. The man stumbled and crashed into the room's far wall. He put a hand to his head and examined the blood that coated his palm.

'Bastard,' he said in a thick voice. 'You're gonna pay for that.'

The man lunged, knife slashing left and right. Mason evaded the swings, still holding on to his gun. They were fighting to the right of the captive professor now. Out of his peripheral vision he saw the leader and the second man hesitate in the doorway that led to the kitchen and look back.

To his left, Roxy fought a similar battle with the fourth man. He thrust a knife at her, and she skipped away, chopping at his wrist. The man whistled through his teeth in pain but managed to hold on to the blade.

Mason remembered his training, both army and boxing. He breathed deeply and watched for an opening. He didn't rush in. The third man lunged, his knife held out like a short sword. Mason let it travel underneath his armpit, trapped the arm and then delivered three harsh punches to his opponent's face, two to the jaw and one to the eye socket. Mason felt the man's legs go to jelly and let him fall to the floor.

'Trent,' the second man said to the leader. 'Those boys will do no good in an interview room.'

Trent swore, raised his knife and loped back into the room, straight at Mason.

Professor Evans groaned, still in considerable pain, and clearly bleeding out. Mason had no idea how Quaid and Hassell were faring outside. Next time they'd use the comms system like he'd suggested. He had no more time to think as Trent closed in.

The leader of the torturous crew wielded a knife far better than the man Mason had already taken out. He held it properly, underhand, and slashed at Mason with small, conservative movements, sidestepping left and right to keep Mason guessing. In addition to that, the second man had now joined Trent and was prowling around the other side of Professor Evans, coming up on Mason's right side.

Behind him, he could hear Roxy tussling with the fourth man.

Mason fended off Trent's attack and chose to quickly thrust his gun into his waistband. He wasn't law enforcement, and there was no way he was just going to shoot these men in their stomachs. He spun away to upset Trent's rhythm and threw a spinning kick at the second man's head. The man threw a hand up at the last instant, blocked the kick but lost his grip on the knife. The weapon spun away through the air before clattering across the desk that held the laptop.

Trent ran at Mason, moving oddly because of his limp. Mason saw an opening, dropped and swept his opponent's legs away. Trent hit the floor hard but managed to hold on to his knife, and started slicing at Mason's shins.

Mason heard the rush of a body behind him. Before he could react, the second man took him around the waist in a flying tackle. Mason was lifted off his feet, carried three or four yards and then crashed into an unused fireplace. Mason's head hit the plastered flue, his left side struck the top of the fireplace and he learned that the rib he'd broken in their last battle against the Amori hadn't yet fully healed.

Pain flooded his system as he crashed down among the long-dead coals of the fireplace. His vision blurred. He expected an instant attack and drew his legs up into a foetal position, but when it didn't come put down his elbows and took a quick look around the room.

Trent had hold of the man Mason had felled earlier and was pulling him to his feet. The second man was shouting at Roxy's adversary, urging the guy to run. Tension and violence filled the air. Trent was limping worse than ever. No words passed between them, but each man and woman glared at each other with vicious intent.

Before Mason could climb to his feet, Trent and his team broke once more for the kitchen. Roxy's adversary just left her standing. They raced across the room, through the rear door and vanished. Mason used the fireplace to lean on as he struggled upright and put a hand gingerly to his ribs.

'You okay?' Roxy asked.

'Yeah, yeah, it's nothing. Phone an ambulance, and the police.'

Whilst Roxy made the calls Mason multitasked. He compartmentalised the pain in his ribs and ran towards the kitchen. At the same time, he called Quaid.

'Hey. We're safe,' the older man answered immediately.

'Watch your backs,' Mason said. 'They got away.'

The kitchen was empty. The back door was flung wide open. A quick glance out the window revealed nothing except a narrow garden with brick walls and a small green-

26

house. Mason wanted to give chase, but Professor Evans was the priority here.

Back in the room, Roxy was already bent over the professor, removing one blade at a time and binding the man's wounds. The professor's eyes were closed, his mouth open in a wide O of pain, his face pointed towards the ceiling. Mason made his way through the mess they'd caused to crouch at the man's side. The pain in his rib had already subsided. The professor's pained grunts filled the air. Mason could smell the sweat of fear and the pungent, metallic sharpness of blood. He knelt next to the professor's chair.

'Mark,' he said. 'Mark, an ambulance is on its way. You're going to be fine. Can you hear me?'

Roxy tied a small towel across two wounds, making the professor groan. Mason got his first good look at Roxy then since the battle ended.

'Are you okay?'

'Guy got a couple of good hits in.' She shrugged. 'Surprised me.'

'Must admit, I didn't enjoy being thrown into a fireplace,' Mason said drily.

'It's not my idea of fun either,' Roxy admitted.

Professor Evans groaned.

'If he's complaining, he's okay,' Roxy said pragmatically. 'Unless it's my joke he's complaining about. Then he's on thin ice.'

Mason laid a gentle hand on Professor Evans's shoulder. 'Sir,' he said. 'We've brought you the lockbox from Roger Beat, from Coventry. We're the security team. You're safe now. What were those men after?'

Evans's eyes flew open so fast Mason rocked back. Despite his pain, the man reached out with a shaking hand and grabbed hold of Mason's wrist.

'Keep them safe,' the professor grated between clenched teeth. 'It's up to you now. Keep them safe. One of . . . one

27

of seven basins of . . . of the Tabernacle. The Molten Sea. From the Holy of Holies. Use the Templar code. Do you see? The sacred vessels . . .' Evans swallowed drily as Mason heard sirens just outside the window. 'The clue . . . is around the edge. Do not let them take it.'

Mason didn't point out that the torturers had already seen, and no doubt photographed, the images on Evans's laptop. The professor would know that. In his pain, reality might have become fogged in his brain.

'What's he talking about?' The voice came from Mason's back.

He whirled, saw Sally, Quaid and Hassell and sighed in relief. He was about to answer when the professor's grip tightened painfully on his arm.

'You must listen to me. The basins and the Templars . . . the Tabernacle . . . the Molten—'

Professor Evans stopped talking as Roxy tied another towel around his wounds. The first had become soaked. Mason leaned in close to the man's face.

'I think he's fainted.'

Sally was already eyeing Mason's backpack and the item it held. 'What does he mean, "Tabernacle"?'

# Chapter 5

Mason and his team endured several hours of questioning by the police, but were eventually let go. They'd done nothing wrong. They'd probably saved a life. Professor Evans was taken to the nearest hospital for treatment, having not re-awakened after his fainting episode. The team were left with many unanswered questions and an undelivered backpack.

Their actions put them on a good footing with the police, though the officers offered no explanations as to who the criminal gang might be. Maybe they didn't know. Maybe they were playing it close to their chests. Mason wasn't sure, but he did know that – once they were released – Sally Rusk was going to pose several thorny questions.

By mid-afternoon they were out in the street, hunched against an uncomfortable drizzle, and about a twenty-minute walk from their car. Mason shouldered the backpack and started off, drawing the others along with him. The street outside the police station was thick with people and noisy, the road full of traffic, so they didn't speak again until they were settled inside their hire car.

'I find it interesting,' Mason said. 'That not one of us told the police the last words Professor Evans spoke before he fainted. Why do you think that was?'

It was a deep question, more profound than he'd intended. It spoke to inner character and entrenched behaviour. Mason hadn't mentioned the conversation with Evans because recent conflict with the Amori had made him highly suspicious of those in authority. He also believed the words had been meant solely for them and that they were best prepared to action Professor Evans's request.

*It's up to you now. Do not let them take it.*

Sally shifted in her seat as if itching to get hold of a laptop and start work. 'Professor Evans entrusted his secret to us,' she said. 'The police didn't even look at his laptop on the desk. They just took it for evidence. Yes, I know they will eventually get around to examining it, but that could take days. We have the lockbox and the key. We have the means to find out . . .' She paused. 'Evans actually said the words *It's up to you now*. Through Roger Beat and the man who gave us this job – he must have heard of our reputation.'

'Reputation?' Mason wondered.

'For finding things.' Sally shrugged. 'You know how a grapevine works, especially in the small circle that makes up the world of artefact retrieval.'

'What the hell he's talking about though?' Roxy asked.

'The poor man was obviously agitated. He was tortured for information. Clearly, it's of vital importance to someone.'

As if to underline her words, Sally's mobile started to ring. She fished the device out of a pocket and checked the screen.

'It's the company phone,' she said, holding it to one ear. 'Unknown number. Yes? Quest Investigations, can I help?'

Mason watched as Sally's face fell and took on an ashen quality. She didn't speak much, except to offer a few words of condolence before ending the call.

'Well,' she said. 'I didn't expect that. Do you remember the man we took possession of the lockbox from? Roger Beat?'

'The man we met in Coventry,' Mason said. 'Of course.'

'Someone attacked him. Tortured him. He's in hospital too.'

Mason felt a cold trickle of anticipation slide down his spine. 'I'm not going to even pretend that's a coincidence.'

'What state is he in?' Quaid asked. 'Maybe he's able to answer questions about the box.'

Sally shook her head. 'They don't know if he'll make it. They only called me as a courtesy because they know we're currently working for him. But . . .' she said. 'That does give me an idea.'

Mason waited whilst Sally worked on her phone. He turned the engine on to stay warm and drove them to a nearby bakery where they all ordered freshly made cheese and ham and chicken salad sandwiches and washed them down with bottles of water, Pepsi Max and lemonade. By the time they'd finished and wiped their mouths, Sally had made three phone calls.

'It's not much.' She stretched in her seat, rolling her neck from side to side. 'But it is a step forward. Apparently, according to people Roger Beat worked with, two of these basins have been found quite recently. They are made of gold, but I don't think that's the reason for the criminal attention. At least, I hope not.'

'Wait,' Quaid said. 'How did you get Beat's people to talk to you?'

'Weren't you listening? I told them I was Professor Rusk from Oxford, and that I too had been asked to look at the items recently. Which is, loosely, true. We run in the same circles. And a Professor Rusk is still on the lists at Oxford.'

'Of course.' Quaid nodded. 'Sorry.'

'The two golden basins – just like the one we saw on Professor Evans's laptop – were found in the collection of an old, wealthy couple, who recently died just weeks apart. They had several rare items in their basement, many that had been marked down as stolen and known

31

only to reside in secret, private collections. Several items were found in the couple's house including these two basins. Since then, they've been looked over by experts and then sent by experts to places where more experts can look at them. The usual process when ancient valuable relics are found. The difference here is . . . the secrecy involved. Roger Beat is normally very open about his processes. His staff say they've never seen him keep anything closer to his chest than what he discovered concerning these basins.'

'There are two?' Mason asked quickly and judiciously. 'And we have one. Where's the second one?'

Sally frowned. 'Due to the secrecy surrounding this particular collection, they weren't told. But Beat has been working on both in between their journeys to and from experts.'

Hassell, leaning with his head against the car window, looked at the backpack that Mason had wedged in between the front seats and the back. 'Do you think we should open it?'

'The lockbox?' Sally also turned her gaze to the backpack. 'Yes, I do. We need to look at the basin to know what we've gotten ourselves into this time.'

'Technically, we haven't gotten ourselves into anything,' Quaid reminded them all. 'We could just hand this off—'

'To whom?' Sally interjected. 'Experts at both sides of this delivery have been attacked and are in hospital. Evans asked us to handle it. Maybe we got this job through reputation after all.'

'What do you mean?' Roxy asked.

'I mean we've already helped the Vatican out twice. We've already located the Book of Secrets and the Creed. If someone we don't know hand-picked us for this job, we must see it through.'

'A job that seems innocuous on the surface, but has

underlying substance of real consequence,' Mason said. 'So they find out who's the hottest team in town . . .'

'Don't let them in on the secret, but use them,' Sally finished for him.

'We still don't have to go through with anything,' Quaid said.

'I feel obligated,' Sally said. 'All of this happened on our first mission, our watch. Evans told us it was up to us . . .'

'And that puts us in danger,' Mason said. 'There will be records leading back to the couriers. To us. That backpack isn't safe and neither are we until this whole thing gets sorted.'

'Years ago,' Quaid said quietly, 'as you know, I used to be an army officer. I left because I got sick of all the political shit, of sending good men and women to die fighting enemies that, a week later, became allies, all so one ponce in Whitehall could gain some political advantage. The stories I could tell you . . .' He shook his head. 'But that's for another day. What I am saying is . . . there's a chain of command. The courier – the messenger, shall we say – never ends up taking charge of the hot potato.'

Sally frowned at him. 'You're saying we should hand this over to one of the professor's teams? The people who work for him?'

'That's the logical next step in the chain of command, yes.'

'If we hold on to them,' Hassell said, 'it might be considered theft.'

'But you heard what Evans said.' Sally shook her head as if confused. '"Keep it safe." That's pretty clear, if you ask me. And who better to keep it safe than us? Also, he mentioned the Tabernacle and the fact that there are seven basins.' Her eyes shone.

Quaid sat forward, making his craggy face with its twinkling eyes, lustrous black hair and grey sideburns more prominent. In a lighter moment, Mason might have poked fun at Quaid, asking him if he dyed his hair, but this wasn't the right time.

'If you open that backpack,' he said. 'You're putting all the responsibility on us. On this company. I know something about sharing responsibility, about taking the burden and the blame. Did you ever see or hear a politician take the blame? No . . . Blame is a highly transferable commodity.'

Sally bit her lip. 'I understand,' she said. 'I do. And yes, I know a little bit about responsibility myself. I fought against the establishment if you remember. I fought against wealth and privilege and back-slapping. And I know when to put this company's name on the line, and when not to.'

'It is our first mission,' Hassell said.

'All the more reason to be as conscientious as if it were our thousandth,' Sally said. 'And don't you have a sense of adventure, Quaid?'

'A sense of . . .' Quaid looked surprised at the question. 'Do you remember Anya?'

Mason nodded along with the others. Anya was a full-blooded, knife-carrying millionairess who'd assisted them on previous missions, always clashing heads with Quaid. Sally nodded and Roxy gave a snort of laughter.

'My kinda woman,' she said.

'I met Anya after I left the army, during a dangerous mission to Venezuela for human rights purposes. We spent three trouble-filled days in Caracas . . . Don't ask me to explain. She flew me in and out of Yemen and, once, to the jungles of the Amazon delta. I think adventure finds me whether I want it to or not. And I'm sure you remember how we met.'

Quaid had been a procurer of necessary humanitarian goods for people who needed them, working in Bethlehem. Not dealing in strictly illegal goods, Quaid had operated in a grey area and kept his dealings under the radar. Over eight years his business got bigger and bigger until the name Quaid grew quite legendary among the locals.

'You help people,' Sally said. 'You can't help it. It's who you are.'

'I procure basic, crucial items for desperate people using my wealth of contacts. I help the needy. Or at least, I used to. I don't think this qualifies as quite the same thing.'

'But what if it did?' Sally said. 'I have a bad feeling about this basin, and its twin. Bad' – she then corrected herself – 'and, at the same time, exciting. Evans mentioned the Molten Sea, the Tabernacle, the sacred vessels and the Holy of Holies. Don't you know what that all means?'

Quaid blinked. Mason made a bemused face and Roxy looked blank. Hassell sat back and said nothing. Sally reached into the footwell for the backpack.

'We're doing this,' she said. 'Because I know how important the Tabernacle is. I know what it held and where it went. We're doing this because it might lead us to the most important treasure that's never been discovered.'

Mason briefly closed his eyes. There was no turning back now.

## Chapter 6

The artefact has been found, Murdock McCloud thought as he stood at the edge of the water.

But more precisely, two artefacts had been found, both incredibly similar. The two golden basins of the Molten Sea. Who could ever have imagined they'd been languishing in the dusty basement of some wealthy and bitter old couple for countless years? And before that? Passed between private collections, no doubt.

McCloud shrugged out of a towel and dived into the underground swimming pool that was a private feature of the newly renovated wing of his countryside castle in Scotland. The heated water engulfed him, wrapping him in a cocoon of silence as he swam to the bottom of the pool. Down here, he could sit in peace for a while, uninterrupted by the demands of everyday life, untroubled by the duties and obligations that came with being the Grand Master of the Guild of Night.

Not that McCloud didn't enjoy his status within the organisation. Running a secretive, hostile splinter group inside a wider, better-known outfit called the Freemasons was sometimes a discomfort, sometimes a joy, but always came with its own clandestine pleasures. McCloud's biggest challenge was keeping his other eleven group members in line. Too many of them were too hot-headed, despite their ages, and their decision to shun all electronic means of communication, whilst prudent, was highly impractical.

Still, it helped keep them safe.

McCloud pushed off from the bottom of the pool, broke the surface and wiped water from his eyes. He looked around. Reflections from the pool's surface glimmered and pulsed across the marble walls. The dark ambiance down here soothed his soul. Not only was it his place of recuperation, but it was also a place of healing.

McCloud sank to the bottom once again, wrapping himself in silence. The marble tiles beneath his feet were smooth, the roar in his ears welcome. He spent another ninety seconds down there before rising to tread water once again. McCloud repeated the process another four times before clambering out of the pool and wiping himself dry with a plush towel. He then placed the towel on a hot radiator because the last thing he wanted was his staff coming down here and traipsing through his sanctum of solace.

The teams should have completed their tasks by now. McCloud dressed and took an elevator straight back up to his study. The doors dinged and slid open, giving him a limited view of the familiar dark-oak panelling and thickly carpeted floor. His hair was still wet, and dripped persistently, but that didn't matter. The highest room in the castle was warm. McCloud crossed to his desk, ignoring the wide window view of the Scottish Highlands in front, and the steaming hot black mug of coffee that sat to the left. Of course, there was no sign of his staff. They knew when to be invisible.

McCloud eyed two silver-framed mobile phones that sat on his desk. Whilst the Guild of Night rejected all electronic devices in their own communications it was imperative that they used them for outside interaction. Their various dealings depended on such modern technology.

Even as he looked on, the nearest began to chime. McCloud scooped it up.

'Yes?'

'Bravo here, sir. We have the package. No issues whatsoever.'

McCloud nodded, having expected as much. 'Deliver it to the agreed location. Your money will be wired to you.'

'Sir,' the voice continued. 'If you need us for anything—'

'I will call when I need your services,' McCloud interrupted and then hung up the phone. He was pleased, some of the tension in his shoulders loosening. He took a seat and drank deeply from the hot mug of coffee. The bitter aroma smelled good to his nostrils, the heat stinging his tongue. He sat back in his well-padded leather chair and looked to his left, towards the windows and the wild country beyond.

It is an auspicious time to be leader.

But it was far more than that. This might be the grandest, most profound cycle of leadership the Guild of Night had even known.

McCloud considered the staggering and unbelievable events transpiring in the world right now as that important. The responsibilities he felt as Grand Master of the Guild hung over him like a demonic, razor-sharp shroud. If that shroud descended, it would flay the flesh from his bones.

He twitched as the second mobile phone started to ring. 'Yes?' he answered quickly.

'Team Charlie, sir,' a voice said. It was significant that he'd named the teams Bravo and Charlie because no team that worked for the Guild of Night – no matter how adept – would ever earn the moniker Alpha.

'Go on,' McCloud urged, sensing hesitation on the other end of the line.

'Well, it's good news and bad news,' the annoying voice said uncertainly. 'We met some stiff opposition.'

'The professor bested you and your team?' McCloud enjoyed bouts of caustic wit, no matter who was on the receiving end.

'No, sir. The professor wasn't a problem. It was the other team.'

McCloud's stomach did a double flip. 'The what? You're not making any sense, man.'

'We carried out all your orders. Only, the package wasn't there. It hadn't been delivered. We were too early. Thinking on our feet, we made the professor show us photographs he'd received of the package on his computer. We made photocopies and took pictures, and it's those that we have for you, sir.'

McCloud was angry. First, they'd moved too soon. And then they'd failed to secure the bowl. If they'd done that, at least, that would have given the Guild sole control over both items.

But . . . what was all this dross about another team?

McCloud didn't trust these men. They were paid mercenaries who would try any excuse to cover up a mistake. Was this an attempt at misdirection? Something to take the spotlight off their failure?

'Take the pictures and photos to the agreed location. That will conclude your input. You will still receive your money. But first, tell me more about this other team.'

'Of course. I have names . . .' The man reeled off five people McCloud had never heard of. 'They fought us to save the professor. They were good, not amateurs. Two women, three men. And they were armed, but they didn't use their guns.'

'Could they have been the security team tasked with delivering the package to the professor?' McCloud asked.

There was a moment's silence followed by a cough. 'Of course. They weren't there to protect the pro, they were there to meet him.'

McCloud sighed. 'And they interrupted you beating the old man half to death? No wonder they challenged you.' He hated mercenary stupidity.

'We have the pictures, sir,' the man said after a while. 'We'll get them dropped off.'

McCloud hung up without answering. It bothered him that this other team had managed to keep hold of the basin, but he didn't believe they'd done it intentionally. Were they something to worry about?

No. Because they are a simple security unit tasked with delivering one valuable item between professors. What will they do with their package?

It was hard to say. They couldn't exactly return it to Professor Roger Beat. McCloud had already ordered and paid for a Coventry-based gang to beat the man to death. Perhaps they would return it to the university, or offer it to Professor Evans's staff? McCloud was going to have to dig deeper.

The Guild of Night must be protected at all costs.

It had been the same ever since the Knights Templar first crossed swords with Saladin in the Holy Land. The crusades had brought great wealth to the west, not the least of which McCloud was searching for right now. The Guild had been born out of bitter vengeance; vengeance against a church that persecuted and tried to kill all of the living Knights. But some survived that fateful Friday the thirteenth, and made their way to Scotland with many of their greatest treasures.

And some of those treasures remained hidden to this day.

McCloud had lived with the rich history that mantled the Guild since he'd been indoctrinated into their way of life in his early years. Most importantly, he'd helped steer the Guild about its business. The Guild was the most powerful of secret sects, comprising twelve of the wealthiest people in the United Kingdom. They endured as a singular brutal and spiteful body within the wider organisation known as the Freemasons. And where the Freemasons chose integrity, respect, friendship and charity as their guiding principles, the small, hateful sect that existed inside their ranks embraced quite the opposite.

The Guild had been established through a hatred of the Church. That value persisted today; not only that. It was one of the Guild's guiding principles.

McCloud had always believed in the Guild, as much as he outwardly lived his life as a Freemason. His parents had been Guild members and had made sure he was aware of his duties to the Guild at a very young age. Thankfully, the Freemasons were a busy organisation, occupied with unity and equitability and sharing a sense of togetherness rather than considering that, for centuries, there had been a rat nesting inside their collective barrel. Not that McCloud considered the Guild to be the rat in any shape or form. Their mission, their objectives and duties far exceeded anything the Freemasons could ever hope to attain.

To destroy the Church in any way possible.

Was there a rival team out there chasing the basins?

McCloud didn't think such a thing would be true, but as Grand Master, he was forced to entertain every possibility. It shouldn't be too difficult to find out which security firm had been involved in delivering the basin to Professor Evans.

McCloud rose from his desk and padded across to a window. His castle overlooked a wild stretch of the Highlands and offered views that never failed to stir his soul. Sometimes they brought solace, sometimes they brought forth anger, depending on his mindset at the time. From his office he could see the castle keep and several walls, some of which were crumbling. The castle dated back to the fifteenth century and had been remodelled in the eighteenth, but that hadn't stopped the march of time.

Despite the great wealth that he'd inherited from his father's timber empire, McCloud preferred to maintain the image of a man struggling to maintain the building's upkeep. This castle had changed hands six times in its first three hundred years; it would not change hands again.

McCloud felt a surprising sense of peace wash over him. The fact was, they had access to both golden basins. They had researchers hard at work. Yes, the Poole-based team had failed, but they'd still managed to secure images. Nobody else in the world knew the significance of the golden basins, or that they had only recently been discovered after several centuries of being lost.

But that didn't mean the Guild could be complacent. The basins would lead the way to the Tabernacle and the Ark of the Covenant. Possession of those treasured items would not only validate the Guild's present and future narrative, the chronicle of their very existence, but would reunite them with their founders – the very Knights Templar who had hidden the items for future generations to find.

Their retrieval would also vindicate McCloud's life's work and cement him as the greatest leader the Guild had ever known.

McCloud knew he should be contacting his eleven fellow members, who were scattered the length and breadth of Scotland and England. They ought to be involved in every aspect of this. But, for now, he took a long moment. He was their Grand Master and the buck always stopped at him. He deserved time to bask in glory.

The golden basins were his and would lead to the greatest find imaginable once the clues that had been carved upon them were solved. A find that would put the world in shock and bring the Church to its knees, knowing that outsiders had discovered that which it held most dear. Perhaps the Guild would finally achieve exacting vengeance for what had been done to their ancestors, the Knights Templar, on Friday, 13 October 1307.

Nothing would stand in their way.

McCloud would bring all his resources to bear, and all his deadly accoutrements of torture and death, every ounce of his powerfully warped imagination, to make sure of it. Nobody on this Earth would be safe until the Guild of Night stood united over the bones of the Catholic Church.

# Chapter 7

'This Tabernacle you mention,' Hassell said to the others as they all sat in the car in Poole close to Professor Evans's house. 'Could you explain it a little more?'

Sally held up a hand, signalling that she was in the middle of something. 'I will,' she said. 'But there really is no point if we can't decipher this clue. And I believe we're sure that Roger Beat worked on both basins?'

Mason blinked at the quick-fire question he hadn't been expecting. 'Yes,' he said after dredging the information up from his memory. 'Professor Beat said he examined both basins.'

'Then remember that he will have photographs of the other basin in his office,' Sally said. 'That information may come in handy.' She was currently sitting with her shoulders bent forward, the faint blue tips of her hair hanging over her face. Mason had noticed but never mentioned how the shade of blue had faded ever since her father passed. Sally no longer needed to show him the depth of her rebelliousness.

She unbuckled the backpack. 'Hassell,' she said. 'Please go grab my laptop.'

Mason twisted around in his seat. 'Are you really going to remove the relic from its box?'

'I think we owe it to Professor Evans. You heard his words, Joe. You heard him tell us to keep it safe, to look for the clue around the edge. And this is but one of seven. You heard—'

'I don't think that's exactly what he said.' Mason raised his eyebrows.

'To me, it was.' Sally tugged the lockbox from the backpack and placed it on her knee. She ran her fingers across the soft velvet. She eyed the lock and then fitted the golden key into the mechanism before giving the others a quick look of appraisal, taking a deep breath and then opening the box.

'Hope it doesn't explode,' Quaid said drily into the silence.

Mason craned his neck to see as Sally opened the lid.

The golden basin nestled amid bubblewrap inside the black-lined container. Sally released it quickly, handling it with care. She put on her cold-weather gloves before handling the artefact. It was a good-sized bowl that could be held in one large hand and had several small carvings around its circumference. Its surface threw forth golden shafts of light wherever it reflected the sunshine. The base was a flat circle of metal. Sally studied it before turning it upside down and then looking inside.

'You checking for a hallmark?' Quaid asked, tongue in cheek.

'No,' Sally said seriously, lost in her research. 'Just examining the extent of the carvings before I look at the rim.'

Mason looked up as Hassell climbed back into the car, carrying Sally's laptop. The New Yorker placed it on the seat between them. Sally barely noticed.

'Here,' she said, holding the basin up to the light and slowly turning it. 'There are letters all around the edge. Someone grab a piece of paper and a pen whilst I read them out.'

Quaid reached into his jacket pocket. 'Always prepared,' he said. 'You won't find a bloody mobile phone in my pocket.'

'No, but you do occasionally have a Bluetooth communications system in your ear,' Hassell pointed out.

'Under duress,' Quaid assured him, plucking out a notebook and a pen. 'And for the good of the team.'

Sally read out seventeen letters, turning the basin as she did so. When she was finished, she placed the basin back in the box and looked expectantly at Quaid. 'What does it say?'

'Means nothing to me,' he replied, staring at his notes. 'Realigning art eden.'

Sally frowned and took the pad from him, glaring at the words as if she could force them to make sense. After a few minutes she shook her head.

'Doesn't mean anything to me either.'

'But wait,' Quaid said. 'Professor Evans didn't just mention the basins. He referenced the Tabernacle, the sacred vessels, the Templar code and the Holy of Holies. Also, the Molten Sea. What do we know about those?'

Sally reached for her laptop and placed her hands on its lid, speaking from knowledge and experience. 'The Molten Sea was a very large basin commissioned by King Solomon for ablution of the priests. It's mentioned in the Bible many times. The brim was like a lily blossom, its thickness a hand's breadth. To move it, they had to place it on the backs of twelve oxen; its water was brought in a conduit from Solomon's pools. It was made of brass or bronze that Solomon had taken from conquered enemies. These basins' – she nodded at the lockbox – 'are small representations of the Molten Sea.'

'I don't see how that helps us,' Roxy said bluntly. 'Apart from locking down the provenance of the basins.'

'That's true,' Sally said. 'Artist representations tell us what the Molten Sea once looked like, and this basin is an accurate depiction. I can only assume the other basin is similar until we get a look at Professor Beat's research. But, more importantly, the Molten Sea ties in rather spectacularly with the Tabernacle.'

'Aha,' Hassell said casually. 'I knew we'd come back around to this Tabernacle thing.'

'By that, I'm assuming you have no idea what it represents.' Sally tapped her fingers on the lid of the laptop in a tiny show of frustration. 'Basically, the Bible, mostly the Book of Exodus, tells us that the Tabernacle was the transportable worldly abode of the god of Israel. It's so important to the religion that you should know Moses himself was instructed at Mount Sinai to build and take the Tabernacle with the Israelites on their journey to the Promised Land. It is, quite literally, the dwelling place of God.'

'I still don't see how that helps us,' Roxy said.

'So far, neither do I,' Sally agreed. 'But it was Professor Evans who referenced the Tabernacle with the Molten Sea. I'm just revealing how they connect through history. And there's more. The inner sanctum of the Tabernacle was called the Holy of Holies.'

'So . . . everything revolves around the Tabernacle,' Mason said. 'It makes sense that the basins would hold clues as to its whereabouts.'

'Maybe,' Sally said. 'Maybe not. There are other greater treasures that link directly to the Tabernacle. Of course, any object that travelled inside would be considered a great treasure. According to Exodus there were gold lampstands, candlesticks, tables, oil lamps and a golden altar. Of course, the Tabernacle is also famous for ending up in the Temple of Solomon.'

Now Mason caught on. 'The Temple of Solomon?'

'Yes. Oh, it moved around a while before that. King Saul had it near his hometown and then it was moved to a hill shrine called Gibeon. Prior to David's moving the Ark to Jerusalem it was located in Kiriath Jearim, a city in Israel.'

'The Temple of Solomon was the first temple in Jerusalem,' Quaid said. 'Mega important. It stood for four centuries until the Babylonians destroyed it. Probably under directions of the Amori,' he added with a little anger in his voice.

Sally nodded. 'That wouldn't surprise me. The goal of the Amori had always been to bring down the Church ever since Jesus Christ stole the original copy of the Creed.'

'So this really could all be about the Temple of Solomon?' Roxy asked.

'Yes and no,' Sally said. 'When I knew the Tabernacle was involved, I had my suspicions. Did you know that it was believed the Knights Templar took the temple – or at least its main treasures – with them in 1307?'

'That's a switch,' Mason said. 'What happened in 1307?'

'I thought everyone knew,' Sally said. 'It's where the fable of Friday the thirteenth came from.'

'That's usually a bad day for me,' Roxy acknowledged. 'What happened to the Templars?'

'On Friday the thirteenth of October, 1307, French king Philip IV ordered the mass arrest of the Knights. It is said that the king owed them a large sum of money and chose to get rid of them – and cancel his loan – in an underhand manner. The arrested Templars were subjected to torture and eventually "confessed"' – Sally made speech marks in the air – 'to committing obscene rituals and spitting on the cross. This so-called proof then allowed the king to talk the Pope into arresting all the Templars in the world.'

'It was the end of their order?' Quaid asked.

'Yes. Even the Grand Master, Jacques de Molay, was burned at the stake. Of course, there are always rumours that then become legends that state some of the Templars escaped and made their lives elsewhere. Legends that tell of great treasures and riches being smuggled from the east to places such as Scotland, England and Wales, and several cities along the way.'

'One of those treasures being Solomon's Temple?' Hassell asked.

'According to certain fragments of folklore.' Sally nodded and then added, 'I'll know more by consulting the Rusk Notes.'

Mason recalled that Sally's father, Pierce Rusk, had scribbled down entire tomes of research in his long career before being murdered inside the Vatican, and that Sally had copied it all down into a set of coherent manuals she called the Rusk Notes. 'Did he study the Templars?' he asked.

'Didn't everyone?' Sally replied with half a smile. 'My father spent some time studying their connection to the Church. He studied most things connected to the Church, as you may recall.'

'Of course.' Mason remembered that Rusk had been one of the Vatican's preferred historians, allowed entry to the secret archives whenever necessary, though accompanied by Cardinal Vallini.

'Back to this clue then.' Quaid nodded at his pad of paper. 'Realigning art eden. Could it be a reference to a painting perhaps? The Garden of Eden? What did the words "realigning art" mean back then when the basins were created? I'm just thinking outside the box.'

'Always the best way to think.' Sally opened her laptop. Usually she carried all of her many reference books with her too, but today's mission hadn't really warranted any.

'There's one other thing Professor Evans said,' Mason remembered. 'He said: "Use the Templar code." I'm assuming that's important.'

'I'm on it,' Sally said. 'That's why I need the Rusk Notes.'

Mason took a few moments to stretch in the cramped surroundings of the car. It occurred to him that for the amount of time they'd been sitting here they could easily have driven to a more comfortable place such as a café or a service station. He pointed the fact out to Quaid who immediately put the car into drive. Sally yelled out as he started to move.

'Hey, I can't read this and get driven at the same time.'

'We can't sit here all day,' Quaid said.

It was true, of course. Sally reined in her enthusiasm until Quaid found them a quaint old café close to the sea front and then led them all through the front door. They found a corner table and ordered drinks all round. Mason ordered a hot black coffee, desperate for the caffeine kick.

Sally reopened her laptop and started her research as soon as the drinks had arrived.

'The Temple of Solomon was thought destroyed before Christ,' Quaid said as she worked. 'Its site in Jerusalem is still disputed. Are you saying that its material riches – the altar and all the rest – might have come into the possession of the Knights Templar and then been transported elsewhere?'

'The Knights Templar were hugely influential, incredibly rich. As rich as nations. That's why they were ultimately wiped out by a king and a pope. If anyone could have become the wardens of Solomon's riches – with or without the Church's knowledge – they could have.'

'What would those riches be worth today?' Roxy asked.

Sally glanced up at her, blinked and then narrowed her eyes. 'Of course,' she said. 'You don't know, do you? Yes, the relics from the Tabernacle and from King Solomon's Temple would carry limitless worth. They'd be invaluable. The greatest find imaginable, almost. But they are not the most famous item on the table here. Not even close.'

'Not even close?' Roxy echoed.

'It's why the first mention of the Tabernacle drew my attention,' Sally said. 'Because, according to the Bible, it was where they placed the Ark of the Covenant.'

Mason paused with his mug touching his lips. 'You have to be joking. The Ark of the bloody Covenant?'

Sally beamed. 'The Ark has long been associated with the Tabernacle and the Temple. If you find one, you might believe that you'd find the other. And it doesn't matter that the Tabernacle's construction is disputed among scholars. Was it a simple tent sanctuary, a pillared shelter or a building that they constructed every day? It doesn't matter. It's what was inside that counts. The items the Tabernacle was made to house.'

'The Ark ended up at King Solomon's Temple?' Mason asked.

'Along with the Tabernacle, yes. And, I might add, the Molten Sea, which is where these beauties come in.' She tapped her backpack indicating the basin within. 'Now do you think we should start solving the clues?'

'This Ark,' Hassell interrupted. 'I mean, I've heard of it but what the hell is it, and why's it so important?'

Sally looked at him. 'It's a most sacred chest built by the Israelites. Their greatest relic. It consisted of a gold-covered wooden chest with a decorative, extravagant lid called the Mercy Seat. It was said to contain the Ten Commandments. Created at the foot of Mount Sinai, it was carried by its crosspieces in front of the horde of marching people or in front of the vast Israelite army. God was said to speak to Moses through the two cherubim on the Ark's cover.'

'All right, so it's got provenance,' Hassell admitted drily. 'Why us though? I mean why is it so important that we do this? Why don't we just hand if off to someone?'

'To whom?' Sally said. 'The authorities? Do you really think they're going to put the same effort into this that we will? Do you think they'll care too much?'

'They might. If you explain how valuable these things are.'

'Think of all the time we would waste just doing that. But that's not all. We already know that there's at least one dangerous, deadly force looking for the Tabernacle. We've come up against it. Hitting this at a primal level, head on, is the only way to go.'

'Because you don't want the Tabernacle, the Temple and the Ark to fall into such dangerous hands?' Mason said.

'Exactly. And I'm sure, neither would you. Now, are we ready?'

# Chapter 8

'I wonder what happened to the other basin,' Sally ruminated as she worked. 'You know, the second one that was found?'

Mason thought it was a pretty good question. 'You have contacts,' he said to Quaid. 'Can you find out?'

The older man pursed his lips. 'I can try,' he said. 'But I blew a lot of bridges during our last mission. You remember Canterbury Cathedral?'

Mason winced. They'd pretended they were scouting a wedding for a minor movie star to locate a clue in the cathedral's depths and somehow drawn the full attention of the local constabulary. 'Do your best,' he said. 'If anyone can pull some strings using your history, you can.'

Sally again read out the clue that had been carved around the golden basin's edge. 'Realigning art eden. I wonder when the basins were fabricated? Perhaps it wasn't at the same time as the Molten Sea. It's one of the metal tests the professors will have been carrying out.'

Mason assumed she was merely cogitating out loud and didn't answer. His head still reeled from the revelation that the Ark of the Covenant might still be recoverable and, failing that, Solomon's Temple. He drank coffee, ate digestive biscuits and kept an eye on the café's front window.

Were they now targets? Of course they were. They had unknowingly interfered with someone else's operation, which had made them targets. And now that they knew this operation involved the Ark of the Covenant, they also knew they had no choice but to become properly immersed or let it fall into the wrong hands.

Of course, maybe they should assume they would be targeted even if they didn't pursue the Ark. They couldn't let violent men take control of such incredible wealth. The wrong hands were entirely evil when it came to such a priceless treasure. Sally was right. There was no telling which warmongering tyrant might get hold of it.

Clearly, a violent individual knew the stakes involved and was hell bent on taking possession of the two golden basins. Mason didn't think they'd been followed to the café but hadn't been checking closely, a fact that preyed heavily on his mind now. Guaranteeing their safety was his job. He couldn't blame himself for the attack on Professor Evans but everything after that fell squarely into his purview. Annoyed at himself, Mason rose, left the café and took a quick scout around. He didn't answer Roxy when she asked where he was going because he blamed himself for not looking after his team properly. This wasn't the time to chill out and sit back; this was the time to reconnoitre as if you knew the enemy was dug into a nearby hill.

'You listening to the Devil, Mason?' The voice next to his right ear made him flinch.

'Roxy? Shit, you sneak up quieter than the flu.'

'I saw the look on your face when you left the café. I know what that means by now.'

'I'm not sure that's a good thing.' Mason smiled to himself and then addressed her initial question. One of Roxy's mantras was burned deeply into his consciousness: don't listen when the Devil's calling – meaning that the malevolent inner voices, if listened to, could take you down to Hell.

'We need surveillance,' he said blandly. 'It's not impossible that we could be targeted next. And these evil bastards need stopping.'

'Targeted by whom?'

'I don't know. Whichever psycho sent a gang of thugs to torture an old man for a bloody relic.'

Roxy nodded, pulling a tentative face. 'This has nothing to do with Mosul?'

Mason stared at her. The woman held nothing back. He couldn't hide the damage even if he wanted to. 'I lost two friends. They were killed by an IED after entering a house I'd already checked. That's never gonna go away. I never thought I'd lead a team again, but here we are. That should tell you I've progressed more than I ever thought possible. The voices,' he said, 'are receding. But they're never going to go away.'

'You've come to terms with what happened? Stopped blaming yourself?'

Again, Mason was surprised by her direct insight. 'I want to rectify past mistakes,' he said. 'Working for Sally helps. But what about you, Roxy? Have you found the person you want to be?'

'Stop changing the subject.'

Mason laughed gently. 'Still fighting to raise those barriers then?'

'The new life is replacing the old life,' she said. 'That's all that matters for now.'

Together, they stood outside the café window, studying the street for shadows that shouldn't be there, warmed by a single shaft of sunlight that somehow found its way through the clouds and feeling the heat on their upturned faces. It was a distinct moment that lifted Mason's soul and made him feel closer to Roxy Banks than ever.

'You think we're doing the right thing?' he asked. 'For our humanity?'

'Who knows?' Roxy responded. 'I take every good minute I can get.'

A sudden rap on the glass interrupted them. Mason turned to see Hassell beckoning them both inside.

'You see anyone?' Roxy asked, straightening.

'Street's clear,' Mason said.

'Not even a sniper?' she said, ribbing him gently.

'Let's get back to your rum and coffee,' Mason countered. 'I'm seeing signs of withdrawal already.'

Roxy jabbed his arm. Mason opened the door, re-entered the café to the jangle of a discreet bell and walked back to their table. When their waitress reappeared, he ordered a crispy bacon sandwich.

'What is it?' He looked from Hassell to Sally. From their expressions, it was clear they had something to say.

'The Knights Templar,' Sally said.

'What about them?'

'Well, it occurred to me that they could be heavily involved in all this. Legend says that at one time they had possession of both Solomon's Temple and the Holy Grail. And then there's their persecution, and an understandable subsequent hatred of the Church. Of course they'd want to steal the Church's greatest treasure and keep it for themselves.'

'Those who survived the persecution,' Mason said.

'Exactly. And the Templars were masters in the art of cryptography. They had to be, of course, being heavily involved in mercantile transactions and the transfer of secret documents. It is said they had a secret alphabet.'

'Like the Freemasons?' Quaid asked. 'Weren't the Templars and the Freemasons connected?'

'The Templars were the forerunners of the Freemasons,' Sally said. 'Their organisation bears no similarity today, however, and is totally benign and charitable. But when the Templars exceeded their key function of supplying routes to the Holy Land they became creditors to the French royals. Systemisation was crucial.'

'There are many claims to secret alphabets,' Quaid said. 'Can we be sure this one is real?'

'Oh, three documents are known to exist that contain the alphabet, including one on display at the National Library of Paris. The alphabet was designed so that each letter resembles a piece of the cross of the Order of the Temple. And, whilst we're at it, let's not forget another thing that links the Knights to Solomon's Temple. Their name.'

'They knew of the Temple?' Hassell asked.

'In 1120 King Baldwin of Jerusalem granted the newly formed monastic order a headquarters in a wing of the royal palace on the Temple Mount, the very site believed to be the ruins of the Temple of Solomon. The new order took the name the Poor Knights of Christ and the Temple of Solomon, which eventually became shortened to the name you know so well today.'

'So they lived in the Temple?' Hassell said. 'A good way to learn how to infiltrate it if they ever needed to.'

'Typical of you to mention infiltration,' Sally went on.

'Have you ever done that, Hassell?' Roxy interrupted, looking interested. 'Lived in a place in order to infiltrate it?'

'I could tell you, but then I'd really have to kill you,' Hassell said with a grin.

'You could try,' Roxy muttered.

'Anyway,' Sally went on. 'The deciphering of the Templar alphabet was done using a medallion that bore a secret code and was hung around the necks of the chosen knights. I won't delve into that now, because we don't need it, though my father explained it in depth, it seems.'

Sally tapped the lid of her laptop, drawing Mason's eyes to the screen and the lines of odd symbols there. 'You found all this in the Rusk Notes?'

'The bulk of it, yes. Other stuff, I just know.'

Mason nodded respectfully. 'From writing up your father's work and your own studies.'

'The Templar code,' Sally said, 'is not just restricted to an alphabet. There are many different forms of coding. But, more importantly, they were very fond of anagrams.'

Mason studied the clue. Realigning art eden. 'You're kidding?'

'Not at all. If there are seven of these basins, and two that we know of, then the Templars would have encoded each one with clues very carefully. The reason why is obvious.'

'So all we need to do is reassemble the letters?' Roxy asked.

'I believe so,' Sally said. 'But nothing makes sense.'

'To be honest,' Quaid said. 'Seventeen letters isn't an awful lot to go on. Where could it possibly point to? Are you sure it's an anagram?'

'What else could it be? The bloody sentence makes no sense.'

Sally borrowed Quaid's notebook and pen once more and began making notes. The sheet was soon filled with scribbles. Mason saw no reason why she should be the only one tackling the anagram and sat down to help.

'I have the name "Reginald",' Quaid said. 'Does that help?'

Sally looked up. 'It might,' she said. 'Was he a Templar?'

Quaid looked blank. 'Is that what we're looking for?'

Sally shrugged. 'The remaining letters almost make "Argentina" but wait . . . Argentein was a popular medieval name. Let's try that.'

Mason sat back whilst Sally put her head down and worked. The little café bustled around them, full of bacon and coffee smells and the sounds of scraping plates, clinking mugs and erratic-sounding timers. The staff hurried around their stations and completed their tasks quickly, finding the time to talk to everyone and judiciously hustle across to close the outer door that patrons kept leaving open.

Mason waited for Sally to finish her work. When the brunette finally sat upright there was a wide smile on her face.

'Reginald Argentein,' she said, 'was a Templar who died in 1307, and was believed to be responsible for rebuilding the Church of St Mary at Baldock in Hertfordshire. It dates to the twelfth century and is a Grade 1 listed building. There are many items remaining inside, including the font, that date back to the original construction. The church was rebuilt by the Knights Hospitaller around 1330, after the Templars' well-documented suppression.'

'You think we should go to this church?' Mason asked.

Sally let out a deep breath. 'I think we have to. For the sake of the clue itself, for the sake of Professor Evans who trusted us with the knowledge. For Professor Beat. And to stop the Ark falling into a killer's hands. Can you imagine? They'd smash the place up for sure.'

Mason recalled chasing clues around the Middle East, hoping against hope that those who arrived before them wouldn't destroy ancient relics in their quest for glory. It had transpired that the Amori revered the relics as much as Sally and the Church did.

'It's high risk,' Mason said. 'Somebody else is clearly on the same trail.'

'It's risk versus reward,' Sally said. 'And there's no greater reward than the Ark of the Covenant.'

# Chapter 9

A few hours' drive after leaving the café in Poole, Mason stopped on a pavement that ran between two rows of shops either side of Church Street, and stared up at St Mary's Church. Occupied since prehistoric times, Baldock was a market town with a deep archaeological legacy. Now it was a busy little place, and the clamour and clatter of everyday life filled Mason's ears, passing pedestrians and random cars drawing his eyes. He inhaled the fresh, sugary scent of a nearby bakery as he stared at the church.

Roxy's hand fell on his shoulder. 'You okay?'

'Yeah. Just wondering what we're getting ourselves into this time.'

'As long as we're not crawling through crypts again. I hate crawling through crypts. It goes back to unfortunate incidents in my childhood. Did I tell you that?'

'About the crypts – many times, recently, even as we crawled through them.'

'Well, don't worry, Babyface. I'll look after you.'

Mason grunted.

The walls of St Mary's were cement grey in colour. A tall stained-glass window with strikingly colourful images stared across the street. The whole church and the tower had embattled parapets and the tower was topped by a lead spire and a golden weathervane in the shape of a cockerel. Roxy made her way towards the entrance, a wide metal gate that was currently closed. Sally hadn't stopped talking since they parked the car and locked it up.

'Baldock itself was founded by the Knights Templar,' she told them. 'A medieval market town around 1140. One assumes the original church was built around the same time.'

They crossed the road and approached the gates. Mason stayed vigilant but saw nothing except people going about their everyday business. Hassell and Quaid stayed at the back, walking several steps behind so that no one watching would assume they were a team. When they reached the gate, Sally and Mason pushed through first.

'What do we know about Reginald Argentein?' Mason asked as they trod the narrow path through gravestones.

'He was from a distinguished Norman family that came to England with William the Conqueror, and was the son and grandson of Knights Templar. He has a gravestone and a memorial here at St Mary's but still he is obscure. I wonder why they chose him – the inscribers of the basin, I mean.'

'Maybe that's the idea,' Mason said. 'If you didn't know, why would you ever look for a clue here?'

Sally nodded. 'Valid point. I think we should check out the memorial first.'

'Ya think?' Roxy said from just behind them. 'I mean rather than the grave. And if you try to drag me down any more catacombs this time someone's gonna be very sorry.'

'I think the grave could be the most likely place,' Sally said, 'since the memorial inside the church is basically a stone slab.'

Roxy sighed unhappily. 'I don't do catacombs. I don't do graves. In other news, I don't do vaults or sepulchres either. Burial chambers are basically out. I mean—'

'We're here,' Sally interrupted. 'Shall we go inside?'

Mason pushed at the door as a gust of wind blew through the graveyard. It was a heavy gust, soulless, and whistled bleakly between tree branches and around the concrete headstones, screeching across the pitted surfaces like nails dragging across a blackboard. It made the hairs on Mason's neck stand up.

Inside, Mason was faced with a wide oblong nave and a chancel at the far end. Rows of wooden pews stood to each side. A candlestick stood in the centre of the aisle and red carpeting led through the rood screen beyond the pews.

'Where do we go?' he asked, relieved to find the inside of the church empty.

'I don't know,' Sally admitted. 'There's no record of where the memorial slab might be.'

Mason guessed it was a case of looking around. It was then that he spied movement to his right and turned to look.

'Or we could just ask,' he said.

The vicar of St Mary's approached them with a smile and an offer of help. He was an older man with an odd contrast of sparkling blue eyes and yellowing teeth. When he approached, he did so with a grin, as if happy to walk away from a boring task.

'Can I help you?'

Sally stepped in, addressing the vicar. Mason was acutely aware of the distinction between this mission and their last. In Jerusalem and Paris and London they'd been moving between crowds, searching for a needle in a haystack, using their initiative and intelligence, whereas here in Hertfordshire they were asking a local for help in an empty old church. Of course, the more obscure the clue, the vaguer the answer.

'Reginald de Argentein,' the vicar repeated. 'Yes, of course. Follow me. Are you historians?'

Sally gave him the Oxford professor story – which wasn't a million miles from the truth – rather than try to explain that they were a new company, tracking and protecting relics the world over, and were currently seeking the Ark of the Covenant. Sally's made-up version was definitely the right way to go, Mason decided.

As they walked, Mason looked around at the others. Roxy was just a few steps behind and trying to look interested in their surroundings. Hassell and Quaid had remained outside, acting as lookouts. Mason wasn't sure exactly what to expect but had to accept that whoever ordered the theft of the golden basins knew how to crack a Templar anagram.

This time, they had Bluetooth earbuds in place, and carried concealed weapons. They were taking no chances.

The vicar talked as they walked. 'We don't get many asking about Reginald,' he said breezily. 'He was a baron, you know, summoned to parliament in 1283. He married the daughter of Hugh de Vere, the fourth earl of Oxford, and enjoyed a relatively quiet life compared to his father and grandfather, who were recognised as great knights. Oh, here we are.'

Mason slowed at the top of the nave in front of the chancel screen, allowing the vicar room to move away. Sally thanked him for his help and then bent to look down. Mason came up alongside her.

Sally looked up. 'No basin,' she said.

Mason nodded, seeing the memorial slab for himself. A single, rectangular chunk of limestone, it offered no clue other than the name of the Templar himself. Mason fought frustration. This mission had stalled before it had even begun. But then there was always the gravestone.

Mason studied the slab more closely. The inscription, according to Sally, was written in medieval French, which the vicar translated as: 'Here lies Reginald de Argentein who caused the chapel to be built. He was a champion of St Mary, to whom pray for the pardon of his soul.' Mason straightened. Sally rose with him and waited for the vicar to move even further away. 'I'm surprised,' she admitted. 'The clues have fitted together so perfectly until now.'

'Clues?' Roxy said. 'This is the first one.'

'No,' Sally said. 'I meant the golden basins being small representations of the Molten Sea. The obvious fact that someone wanted to steal them, the presence of the clues themselves. Although . . .' She coughed. 'We still haven't seen the other clue. Maybe you need that one to make sense of this one.'

'But there are seven basins,' Mason pointed out. 'If the clues don't point to their whereabouts, how would we find them?'

'A good point,' Sally said, bending down again. 'Let me take another look.'

Mason blinked then as Quaid's voice practically exploded in his ear. The earbuds were too loud. Mason tried to ignore the volume and focus on the man's words.

'A group coming in,' he said. 'Four. Two old guys and two bruisers that could well be bodyguards. Eyes up.'

Mason acted quickly. He caught Sally's arm and pulled her to her feet. For a moment, straightening in that position with the memorial slab directly beneath him, he found that he was staring straight at the chancel's stained-glass window, but then the moment was gone and he pulled Sally away from the area before the altar and to the more dimly lit sides of the church. With Roxy following, they moved quickly and quietly, staying low. Behind them came the sound of the church door opening.

'It's this way,' one man said loudly, his voice cracked with age.

'I know which way it is,' the other older guy retorted as if vexed. 'I just don't see how a memorial is going to help us.'

'It's not a memorial, Julian. It's a—'

'Yes, I know that, Justin. I simply feel we should utilise our time more effectively and search the outside first.'

'Oh, don't be an arse. We're here now.'

Mason put stone arches, pillars and pews between them, lurking on the far right of the church. It was the best he could do. The two older men came marching down the centre of the nave, ignoring the advances of the vicar. Their two bodyguards hung back a little, staying clear of the little spat and glaring around the entire church. Mason turned away. If the bodyguards saw them, they made no fuss about it.

'They must be working on the premise that other people will be nearby whilst they search,' Roxy said. 'If these men are connected to the thieves. We don't have to hide.'

'Agreed.' Mason took surreptitious glances at the older men as they made their way down the nave, arguing all the way. The vicar had given up and retreated from the two bodyguards. Mason knew that Roxy's first instinct was always to attack, even if it gave their position away. He had been forced to try to blunt that instinct more than once.

'Look,' Justin scoffed after stopping right next to Argentein's slab. 'As I said, it's useless.'

'But worth checking,' Julian answered petulantly. 'And Justin, you simply cannot say that an eight-hundred-year-old memorial slab is useless. It's history, for Pete's sake.'

'Oh, stop with your claptrap. You're—'

'Please keep your voices down,' one of the bodyguards told them. 'We are not alone in here.'

Mason now knew they'd been spotted. Both he and Roxy suddenly found a very interesting stone pillar to investigate whilst Sally stared up studiously at one of the stained-glass windows. Mason could tell that Roxy was champing at the bit.

'I wouldn't expect to be alone,' Justin snapped. 'This is a church, goddammit.' The old man burst out laughing as if blaspheming inside the old building was the greatest trick he'd ever pulled.

'Reginald's memorial,' Julian said, bending at the waist. 'Just as we deciphered.'

The man's words sent a trickle of expectation down Mason's spine. It was true then, confirmed here and now. Somebody else was searching for the seven golden basins, Solomon's Temple and the Ark. This kind of confirmation brought everything to the fore, the danger, the pressure, the anticipation.

'Please keep your voice down,' the bodyguard said.

'Oh, come, man. We're practically alone in here. Why don't you go out to the graveyard and wait for us?'

'The Grand Master said never to let you out of our sight.'

Mason clutched at that clue like it was newfound gold. The Grand Master? The Grand Master of what? He pretended to point something out to Roxy just on the off chance that they were being watched.

'The memorial slab was worth checking,' Julian said. 'And would have been a far easier objective than the gravestone. What are you going to do about the vicar?'

Mason assumed Julian was now addressing one of the guards, but refrained from checking. His blood ran cold when he heard the reply.

'The vicar is our problem, but he won't interfere. We'll just dig a deeper grave.'

'Is he being funny?' Justin asked Julian. 'I think he thinks he's being funny.'

'Whatever, I don't care,' Justin said. 'Kill him, don't kill him. Just get me to that gravestone.'

# Chapter 10

'Let them go,' Sally said.

'Not a chance,' Mason growled from the corner of his mouth. 'They just threatened the life of the vicar.'

'The vicar isn't outside,' Sally said. 'I saw him ducking into the sacristy a moment ago.'

'We shouldn't let them leave,' Mason insisted.

'You gonna fight 'em right here in the church?' Roxy pointed out. 'Among the pews? I know I'd like to.'

'But she has a point,' Quaid said unexpectedly through the comms, making Mason start. 'Plenty of room out here for a fight if we have to. And it's quite private too.'

'Make yourselves scarce,' Mason said. 'They're coming out.'

'Already done.'

Roxy turned her attention to Sally. 'You've figured something out, haven't you?'

'Maybe.' Sally waited for the main door to close before rushing back along a row of pews to the nave of the church. Then, with more reverence, she approached the memorial stone of Reginald de Argentein and looked down at it. 'The Purbeck limestone slab is early fourteenth century,' she mused. 'The floriated cross in the centre, with two small shields at the top. But when you rise from the stone what are you facing?'

Roxy tracked her movement. 'The window?'

'A beautiful stained-glass window. A fifteenth-century window that looks out over even older buildings from the fourteenth century that house traces of old windows, of shallow sinks called piscinas and seats made of stone called sedilia, which also date back to the original church. Maybe the window holds a clue.'

Mason was on his knees. He jammed his fingers in the minuscule gaps around the slab. 'I hope so,' he said. 'Because this isn't coming up without a jackhammer.'

'It would make more sense that the basin is buried in his grave,' Roxy said.

'I never leave a stone unturned,' Sally said. 'You should know that by now.'

Mason did. Sally was a hard-headed rebel who'd been born into money, but rejected every penny. She preferred to live rough and help out at soup kitchens rather than entertain suitors in lavish surroundings. She skipped hard-to-land internships and lucrative jobs she could have easily acquired because her father knew the boss. Her parents had been born into money, and had little empathy for the lesser fortunate. It had only been in the last few years that Sally realised she shared with her father a passion for history and archaeology. Only then had she sought to build bridges by working alongside him. It was shortly after their reconciliation that her father had been murdered in the Vatican.

'I yield to your expertise,' Roxy said.

Sally gave her a suspicious look, perhaps wondering if the infamous Roxy sarcasm was in play, before hurrying across the chancel, past the font. She then paused before the high stained-glass window. Facing east, it was essentially blue in colour with five main lights and some complex tracery above. As Sally stared at it, Mason pulled out his phone to take pictures.

Quaid's voice burst through the comms. 'They're roaming through the graveyard now, walking over graves and checking headstones. They don't appear to know where Reginald is buried.'

'Good,' Sally said. 'That gives us some time.'

She moved forward and started with the first light, studying every nuance of the glass. Mason glanced at Roxy and shrugged before starting at the other end and doing the same. He didn't know what he was looking for, but was sure he'd recognise it if he found it. 'Is there another reason we're spending time on this window?' he asked.

'Because the Templars loved their codes and this, my friend, may be a treasure trove of codes.'

'Interestingly,' a voice said at their back, 'this may be the only remaining part of the original chapel.'

Mason spun around a little too quickly to find the vicar standing behind them.

Sally also turned, frowning as she did so. 'Really? I assumed this was fifteenth-century, perhaps built by the Knights Hospitaller. You're saying the Templars built this part?'

The vicar nodded. 'The chancel in its eastern half contains the remains, the rubble, of an early church, dated to the twelfth century. The Black Death then hit in 1348, giving Baldock two hundred years of plague and pestilence to worry about.' The vicar sighed deeply and then looked Sally shrewdly in the eyes. 'What exactly are you looking for? Perhaps I can help.'

Sally couldn't help but smile. 'Of course. You want to help us?'

'I'd rather help you than those other gentlemen who came in.'

Roxy almost slapped him on the back but managed to refrain. 'Stick with us, Vic,' she said. 'You won't go wrong.'

Sally turned her attention back to the window. 'If this was built by the Templars,' she said, 'and lines up with Reginald de Argentein's memorial stone, then I guess we're looking for a basin.'

Mason frowned. 'You mean a picture of a basin?'

Sally shrugged at him. 'Nobody said the seven basins had to be actual basins.'

Mason nodded, impressed with Sally's mind, not only her intellect but her grasp on history in relation to code cracking. Thinking outside the box was the key.

'A basin?' the vicar pondered. 'Well, I believe what you're looking for is right there. Third light along in the very centre.'

Mason first double-checked that Roxy was keeping an eye on the main door in case their toxic friends returned, then switched his attention to the stained glass. What he saw astounded him. It defied belief that these secret representations could remain in full view centuries after they had first been imagined, scanned by countless eyes over the years, meaningless without the proper information. It was a testament to the Templars that their codes had lasted so long.

'I think that could be exactly what we're looking for,' Sally said. 'Thank you.'

The vicar murmured in acknowledgement. Mason studied the stained-glass representation that was about two feet above his eyeline. Still thinking about the mission, he made sure to take several photographs before examining the illustration with his bare eyes.

The basin was one-dimensional, about as large as a small plate, and perfectly matched the physical one that his team were still storing in Mason's backpack, which was currently back at the car. It was gold, with a flat base. Sally stood on tiptoe as she tried to read the inscription around the rim.

'It's faint,' she said. 'Have you taken a photo?'

Mason nodded. The vicar was also staring. 'What is it?' he asked.

'A portrayal of the Molten Sea,' Sally told him. 'From the Tabernacle.'

'Oh, really?' The vicar sounded interested. 'How do you know?'

But they didn't have time to explain their quest, their reasons for being here and, inevitably, what the 'gentlemen' outside were doing. Mason was glad when Roxy butted in with her unique grace.

'Sorry, Vic,' she said. 'Gotta go. I just realised the bakery on Main Street's probably getting busy. Can't do without my fresh afternoon coffee and muffin.'

Mason winced a little but used Roxy's lead to turn on the spot and walk away. That left Sally, who faced the vicar a bit more apologetically.

'It's a long story,' she said. 'But if you know the Tabernacle you know what's at stake. The Temple of Solomon. The Ark of the Covenant. Maybe you'll hear about it in the news someday but, until you do, keep it under your hat.'

Mason had been taught to keep everything close to the chest, to maintain the discipline of the mission by keeping it under wraps. Sally's openness grated on him. He beckoned her over, shaking his head.

'No need to explain,' he said, quietly. 'It makes our job harder and puts him in danger.'

The vicar heard him and blanched a little. Sally hurried back across to him with a shake of her head. 'Sorry,' she said, and then to Mason, 'Is that part of my training?'

'Yes, and we can examine the basin later,' Mason said.

'For now, let's get to safety,' Roxy said.

Mason wondered briefly if they should take the vicar with them. The poor guy had already been threatened, albeit indirectly. But when his deliberating gaze fell on him the vicar held up a hand.

'Don't worry,' he said. 'I know how to avoid a couple of ruffians.'

Mason wondered if they were underestimating their opponents, but reminded himself that until now they'd been fighting the Amori, a secret global society with an army of mercenaries. His perspectives might be somewhat awry. The more recent attacks on the professors had been carried out by local gangs, thugs, not mercenaries. Mason and his team had the authority to take on a few muggers and they could even state that this latest quest came under their purview of tracking down ancient relics. Also, they were guarding the golden basin. Mason was confident they could lawfully detain a couple of goons.

'We're coming outside.' Roxy thought to use the comms, something that hadn't occurred to Mason. 'Are we clear?'

'Just take it easy,' Quaid replied. 'Saunter away like you're meant to be there. We'll meet you at the gate.'

Roxy reached the door first, opening it outward. Mason zipped his leather jacket up as a chill wind rushed inside. Sally ducked behind him, shivering. Together, they left the church behind and went outside, squinting at the bright sun.

'Wait,' Quaid said through the comms. 'That doesn't look good.'

Mason hesitated, looking left and right. 'What do you see?'

'The original bodyguards are on their phone, talking, and four more rough-looking brutes have just entered through the front gate, also on their phones. It would appear they're looking for each other.'

Four more? Mason feared for the vicar if nothing else.

'That's kind of impolite,' Sally said. 'I mean they might just be—'

'I'm ex-army,' Quaid said quickly. 'I know a military man when I see one.'

'Still . . .'

Mason sent a nonchalant glance towards the gates and saw Roxy doing the same thing. 'What do you think?'

'I think they're part of the same team,' she said.

Mason agreed, but he still needed to verify their identity. He walked a few steps, and stopped to examine a gravestone. Sally and Roxy joined him, and they pretended to study the inscription.

The four newcomers made a beeline across several graves towards their colleagues. Mason could hear the two old men – Justin and Julian – arguing from here. They waited as the two groups merged and then Mason considered their new dilemma.

Six bodyguards and probably the two older men to deal with.

'We can't let them go back inside the church,' he said.

'And what if they start digging up the graveyard?' Hassell asked.

'We call the cops,' Roxy said.

'And risk sending a couple of local plods into a fight they can't win.' Mason sounded worried. 'The guards might even be armed. We can't just walk away from this.'

'What do you suggest?' Quaid asked.

'Follow my lead . . .' Mason said.

# Chapter 11

Mason needed to get closer.

'Hey,' he said, approaching the eight-strong group. 'We're the head groundsmen here. Can we help you find something?'

Sally had taken a position behind a large grave marker, not yet ready to stand alongside the others in what might turn out to be a bloody fight. Roxy stood by Mason's side. Mason had a big smile on his face and had asked Roxy to do the same but, somehow, the smile on her looked more like the grin of a crocodile preparing to strike.

'Go away,' Justin said. 'We're busy.'

Mason was as close as he needed to get. The four newcomers were carrying handguns; he could see the rectangular bulges under their tight jackets. The two original guards didn't have any bulky weapons that he could make out. His observations prompted him to recall that his team carried weapons of their own but, just like the events in Poole, did they really want a shootout in a sleepy English churchyard? He preferred to avoid that. The goons and the professors probably didn't care either way and stood staring at them now with unfriendly looks on their faces.

Speaking of their faces . . .

Mason stared now, examining one of the faces that hadn't registered properly until now. The man had changed; he'd never previously sported so many deep, carved lines on his face, or a head of hair, but it was definitely him.

'Johann?' he breathed.

The tall man blinked and then focused on him too. A look of recognition flashed across his features. 'Shit, Mason, is that you? Of all the places . . .'

Mason struggled to come to terms with what he was seeing, not only because Johann's face was a hard blast from the past, but because Johann reminded him of the worst time of his life. Johann had been in the war in Mosul. He'd been part of the backup unit that moved in when Zach and Harry had been killed.

'Johann . . .' he said again, unsure how to finish.

'What are you doing here, man?' Johann asked, his voice dangerously low. 'I hope you're not involved in this.'

Mason fought to remain focused. When Zach and Harry had been blown up in Mosul under his watch, life had changed. Everything had changed. He'd been struggling with self-reproach ever since, and battling survivor's guilt. It was why he'd ended up working with Patricia's security agency. And, after a long slog, he'd been finally succeeding, somehow managing to put the past behind him by immersing himself in the challenges of a new team, something he'd once thought would never happen.

But Johann . . . here now? That didn't compute. That couldn't be happening. Johann had been present at Mason's worst and constant nightmare, and the sight of that face stirred up feelings that Mason was trying to keep under wraps.

He believed he'd let Zach and Harry down badly, and Johann knew that.

'Don't tell me you're involved with the crowd chasing the basins,' he said.

'You need to let it go, Mason.'

'We've been through a lot of shit together, Johann. You know me. You know I can't do that.'

'You never could let Zach and Harry go either.'

Mason felt his teeth clench. He wasn't sure if Johann was simply commenting or trying to bait him. He didn't think it was the latter. He and Johann had generally been on good terms.

'This isn't about Zach and Harry.' He had trouble speaking their names. 'I'm trying to get past all that. This is about old soldiers.'

'Speak for yourself.' Johann attempted a little levity.

'I don't want to cross paths with you, Johann. We have a good history.'

Johann looked like he felt the same. There was a wistful, almost sorrowful, glint in his eye. 'I won't fight against you, Mason. But you gotta back down.'

'Yeah, get lost,' Julian said.

'Are you sure?' Mason stuck with the cover he knew was already blown, stalling, still trying to overcome his shock but also letting Roxy get into place and Quaid and Hassell creep closer using a series of gravestones.

'We don't need your help,' Julian said.

'What gravestone are you guys actually looking for?' Roxy drawled, continuing the deception despite everything, and took another step forward. 'Maybe we can help you. We get foreigners in here who don't know what they're doing all the time.'

Both Justin and Julian turned to glare at the American with hard eyes. Mason would have laughed at Roxy's idea of a joke but was still too shell-shocked. And then he realised that Roxy's comments might have gone a step too far. The professors – if that's what they were – didn't bat much of an eyelid, too lost in their own importance and rhetoric, but Mason noticed at least two bodyguards narrow their eyes at him. Johann didn't say a word, and Mason wasn't sure why – maybe it was sheer surprise or old battlefield respect. Maybe it was something else entirely.

'Shit,' Mason said.

'We don't want any trouble,' Quaid said, standing up from where he'd been squatting beside a nearby gravestone, distracting the guards.

Mason used the diversion to step in and tackle one of the armed guards, aware of Roxy at his side. He didn't draw his gun, but didn't hold back with his attack either, delivering two swift, hard jabs to the man's solar plexus. The man's face twisted in pain. His breath whistling through clenched teeth. Mason kicked him in the stomach and watched him fold.

Seconds had passed.

Roxy slammed a fist into her opponent's throat, making him lift his arms to protect himself before kicking him in the groin. Her opponent fell hard, turning from a tough foe to a groaning ball in milliseconds. Neither Roxy nor Mason had the time to stop and disarm their debilitated opponents.

Two armed men remained standing, and two more guards including Johann, in addition to the ones who had been guarding the professor. Quaid and Hassell took out their own guns, drawing the attention of these men.

'Stand down,' Hassell cried out. 'Stand down, now.'

Mason winced at the appearance of weapons and resolved to talk to the American later. It was no good to just assume you were all on the same page. Fortunately, there was no sign of Sally, who was still hidden behind the gravestone. The two armed guards reached slowly for their weapons.

'Stop!' Quaid yelled.

They didn't. Mason and Roxy were forced to attack before this confrontation turned into a shooting match. Mason grabbed the arm of the first man, twisting it. The man spun and threw a punch at Mason's face, catching him across the jaw. Mason felt an explosion of pain and staggered to the side, but held tightly on to the arm. He'd been hit much harder in the ring. When his opponent reached for his sidearm with his other hand Mason threw several hard punches, targeting kidneys and ribs, but received only a grunt and a grimace in return. This man too, it seemed, had been hit harder. With a great heave he threw Mason off and reached for his gun.

A mistake. Mason had seen many people make the exact same mistake in combat. Throwing away the advantage they'd made, losing precious seconds trying to grab a superior weapon when, if they'd pressed forward, they'd have stood a far better chance.

Mason struck back hard. He punched the midriff and then the face, targeting the man's eyes. The longer the fight continued the less chance there was of concluding it without bloodshed. Mason was distracted as both Justin and Julian started yelling and then, even more, as the vicar emerged from the church and shouted at them.

'What are you doing? Leave here at once or I will call the police.'

Events were shifting, worsening. What had at first seemed like a relatively simple takedown was mutating into an uncertain, violent incident.

Mason changed tack. It was time to incapacitate these guys for a long period, one at a time. Roxy, having already come to that conclusion, had broken ribs and given her assailant a black eye. Now, she grabbed hold of his neck and threw him into the nearest gravestone. There was a crack as his face rebounded off the thick concrete. He slithered to the ground.

Mason reversed the arm he was holding, thrusting it up behind the guy's back until it almost snapped. The man yelled out in pain. Mason threw punches into his ribs and kidneys with his spare hand, driving him to his knees. By now, Quaid and Hassell were confronting the two unarmed guards including Johann and the two gunmen they'd downed earlier were staring to rise. It was all flashing by too fast to dwell on anything, but having Johann here in this fight was truly surreal.

Mason saw knives flash: both Quaid and Hassell were now confronted with sharp military blades.

Mason's own opponent tried to strike back, but Mason increased the pressure on his arm, before forcing the man onto his stomach, face first. Mason then rendered him unconscious with two blows to the back of the head.

The two men they'd felled earlier were now back on their knees and reaching for their weapons. Mason moved fast, kicking one in the face, boot-slapping the man across the jaw. There was the sound of snapping bone. The man fell into oblivion.

Roxy was dealing with the other armed guard. Quaid and Hassell were engaged in combat with the knifemen. Mason knew that Hassell was untrained and Quaid hadn't fought hand-to-hand in over a decade.

Scanning the scene further, Mason saw that the two professors were taking advantage of the chaos to target the distraught vicar.

Make a decision.

He chose to rush to the aid of the vicar, who had looked terrified to see the professors hurrying towards him. Justin and Julian were yelling at the man to stay where he was. Mason sprinted to intercept them.

Justin whirled. Mason saw a small Glock in his right hand and ducked behind the nearest gravestone. The sharp report of a bullet cracked across the cemetery. The headstone shuddered, chunks of concrete exploding left and right. Mason stayed low and crawled to the next headstone as the professors turned once more to the vicar.

'Come here, pal,' one of them said. 'We have a few questions for you.'

Mason slipped from stone to stone in the direction of the church. He moved quickly, never staying still. Whoever had designed the churchyard had fitted the bodies close together. There was no shortage of closely packed cover for Mason to use to his advantage.

Finally, Mason reached the last line of gravestones and was faced with a narrow path and then the church building. He chanced a glimpse at what was happening.

The vicar was disappearing through the front door of his church. Justin and Julian broke out into a sprint as they tried to catch him up. Mason decided enough was enough.

He stepped out of hiding, drew his weapon and fired two low warning shots. The bullets slammed into the old wall, but Justin and Julian didn't know that. Like most citizens would, on hearing gunfire they flapped their arms, skidded to a halt and then ran for cover. Their protracted actions gave Mason the chance to race past them and follow the vicar through the front door of the church.

The darkness inside blurred his vision. Thankfully, his eyes adjusted quickly but not his brain. The calm aura inside was stunning compared to the madness he'd just left. 'Hey,' he shouted, seeing the vicar running ahead. 'I'm here to help. Stick with me.'

The vicar rushed on regardless.

Roxy threw her opponent to the ground, heard his spine hit the earth and then fell onto his chest with both knees. Judging by his face, he didn't like the treatment, so she pressed harder and started pummelling his face with both fists. The man's gun had already slipped away; now his consciousness was close to doing the same.

Roxy looked up. The two knifemen – one of them the man Mason had called Johann – were forcing Hassell and

80

Quaid to retreat through the headstones; they knew how to use their blades. She saw Sally's face briefly around a gravestone but then the woman thought better of getting involved and disappeared. Roxy was glad – she'd been training her and knew she wasn't ready. The unconscious gunmen remained so, at least for now. Roxy threw another three devastating punches before determining her opponent was sufficiently comatose and then rose to her feet.

Assessing the knifemen, she saw that their moves, their urgency, were preventing Quaid and Hassell from being able to use their weapons.

Roxy drew her gun. 'Drop the knives, boys,' she said. 'Or die screaming.'

It wasn't the best line she'd ever delivered, but it got the point across. The 'boys' however, didn't appear to believe she was serious. They ignored her and continued to harass Quaid and Hassell.

Roxy discharged one shot at a nearby headstone, apologising silently to its owner. 'Drop the knives,' she growled.

'Okay, okay!' Both men stopped advancing. 'Give us a second,' Johann said.

They turned, faces twisted with ferocity. 'She's not gonna shoot us,' one said. And then again, more loudly, 'You're not gonna shoot us, love.'

'You wanna gamble your balls on it?' Roxy shifted the focus of her aim.

Both men's eyebrows shot up. One dropped his knife instantly, the blade falling from nerveless fingers, but Johann narrowed his eyes and shook his head.

'No way she's gonna shoot us, man.'

Then Hassell and Quaid drew their own guns and aimed them at the knifemen's backs. 'Maybe she won't,' Hassell said. 'But after you just tried to kill me, I fucking will.'

Roxy grinned as Johann closed his eyes in defeat and then dropped his weapon.

# *Chapter 12*

Mason chased through the church after the vicar, finally catching up to him at the top of a narrow flight of stairs.

'Hey,' he shouted. 'Hey, I'm on your side.'

'They have guns,' the vicar muttered. 'Guns in my church-yard.'

Mason quickly holstered his own weapon after checking no one was following them. 'You can't go down there. You're trapping yourself.'

'They'll never get through,' the vicar said, mostly to himself. 'Never get through.'

Mason cursed silently. He could wait to ambush the two professors but felt as though he should accompany the vicar. There was no telling what the man was up to. The stairs were about four feet wide and steep, ending in a pool of darkness. The vicar stopped at the bottom, pushed open a door and then disappeared. Mason wasted no time following him.

And found himself inside a small storage room with a very small desk. Shelves were filled with all manner of objects and the floor space was reduced to just a few square feet by several large boxes. The vicar had a bronzed key in his hand.

Mason squeezed past him.

The vicar hauled on a thick wooden door, closed it and then locked it, effectively sealing them inside. 'It's old,' he said. 'Very old oak. It will easily stop a bullet. They won't get to us in here.'

Mason wondered exactly how the vicar knew that, or if he was just acting on faith, but decided a bit of backup would help and tapped his ear-based comms system.

'Can you hear me?' he asked. 'Roxy? Quaid? Hassell?'

The vicar turned to stare at him as if he'd just realised he was sharing his sanctuary with a madman. 'Who on earth are you talking to?'

Mason tapped his earbuds. 'Bluetooth,' he said.

'I don't have that,' the vicar said.

Mason chose not to comment. Roxy was in his ear. 'Where the hell are you?'

'Inside the church. First stairs on your right. Locked inside some kind of . . .'

'Vestry,' the vicar said.

'. . . storage room,' Mason finished anyway, thinking Roxy would find his description more helpful.

'Give us a few.'

Mason gritted his teeth, but there was nothing he could do. Roxy and the others had their own issues. Issues that included Johann. 'Both Justin and Julian have guns,' he said for information and then turned his attention to the door.

There were noises coming from outside.

'Open up.' Mason recognised Justin's voice. 'Open up now and we'll let you live.'

'Oh, yes,' came Julian's voice. 'All we want is Reginald de Argentein. The Templar and the basin. Give us that and you live.'

The vicar screwed his face up at Mason. 'Reginald? That's who you were asking about.'

Mason nodded. 'We didn't bring them here,' he said by way of apology. 'And it's a long story . . .'

'You're looking for the basin in the window?'

'Okay.' Mason blinked. 'Maybe it's not that long.'

'They're not coming out,' Julian said. 'We have guns,' he shouted. 'If you don't tell us what we want to hear we're going to shoot our way inside.'

The vicar looked smug. 'No way they can—'

A gunshot rang out, loud in the confined space. The vicar shrieked and fell to his knees as if struck, holding his hands over his ears. Mason was pleased to see the door didn't even shudder as the bullet struck it.

'Barely scratched the surface,' Julian said. 'Aim for the lock.'

'Wait,' Mason said. 'I wouldn't do that. You may get a ricochet.' He had no idea why he was giving these men advice. Something deep inside compelled him.

'He's right,' Justin said. 'Could happen. We could wait for the mercs.'

'Oh, shut up and shoot,' Julian said. 'You won't get hurt.'

'You shut up and shoot.' The men continued their argument as Mason pulled the vicar upright.

'Are you okay?'

'Yes, yes, that was a little loud for me. And, of course, I've never been shot at before.'

'Of course,' Mason said.

'Who are you anyway?' the vicar asked.

'We're a company who investigate and guard ancient relics,' he said.

'Been at it long?' the vicar asked.

'This is our first job,' Mason admitted. 'But none of this is our fault.'

They fell silent when the second gunshot rang out. This time, there was a metallic clang and an unbecoming shriek from one of the gunmen. The lock mechanism juddered but didn't break.

'Just keep firing,' Justin said.

The vicar had again fallen to his knees. 'No, no,' he cried. 'Not inside my church. Not here in the presence of God. Go to Argentein's slab. Beyond that you will see the basin in the window.'

'No,' Mason hissed. 'That won't help.'

But Justin and Julian had fallen silent. Mason heard footsteps as at least one of them made the journey back to the top of the stairs. He was about to speak further when three more gunshots exploded in the narrow space, shaking the whole door and the lock. The vicar screamed. Mason felt like firing back but knew the futility of doing so. Maybe one shot into the door itself would make their attackers think twice. Remind them that the prey they were hunting was also armed.

'Got it,' Julian's voice rang out. 'Leave them. Let's go.'

'You have it? That's surprising for you. But I think we should finish the job here.'

'Finish the job? You're a historian, for God's sake. Now let's get the hell out of here and find our mercenary friends. The clue is more important.'

Mason listened as Justin ran upstairs to join his colleague. Quickly, he jumped on the comms. 'Heads up,' he said. 'You have the two professors, armed, coming your way. Searching for their co-workers.'

With that he turned to the vicar and clapped him on the back. 'You were right,' he said. 'The door withstood the bullets. Let's hope the bloody lock did, too.'

Roxy looked up as Mason's voice rang in her ears. The front door of the church was currently vacant. The problem now was that the four unconscious gunmen were starting to wake, and the two knifemen were struggling. They hadn't been restrained, which meant that subduing what were about to become six violent mercenaries was no easy matter.

'C'mere,' she told both Quaid and Hassell. 'Keep your guns drawn.'

They'd already collected and hidden their enemies' weapons. Now, as the men rose, held their heads and nursed wounds, Roxy made sure they saw her gun.

'Stay calm,' she told them. 'I don't wanna have to perforate anyone.'

Quaid and Hassell paced to her side. Sally also came out from hiding. It was right then that the two professors came running out of the front door of the church, waving their hands, shouting and brandishing their weapons. As soon as they saw the scene ahead, they started shooting.

Roxy ducked behind the nearest headstone. Their captives yelled out warnings to the professors and scattered. Bullets flew among them, making errant, lethal patterns through the entire cemetery, patterns that outlined a person's life or death and hinged on chance.

Quaid and Hassell ducked behind more headstones. Sally fell to the ground. The professors fired off four and then five bullets each, locking down the graveyard as they ran towards the gate. Roxy heard only one pass relatively close as it gouged out a chunk of marble from a nearby mausoleum. She had her gun in her hand, but knew they weren't targets anymore.

All the mercs wanted now was to escape.

She kept her head low, eyes focused on the grave marker, nostrils filled with the scent of grass and soil. 'They're escaping,' she told Mason. 'It's gonna be better for this town if we let them go.'

'Agreed,' Mason came back in her ears. 'But they have the clue. The vicar blurted it out.'

Roxy cursed and took a quick glance around the corner of the headstone. The six mercenaries and two professors were at the gates, no longer looking back, but hurrying away. Their job here was done.

'Sally,' she said through the comms. 'We're gonna need a quick turnaround on this one. They got away.'

Sally emerged from her place of hiding and held up the strap of her laptop bag. 'Ready and willing.'

'Mason,' Roxy said. 'Hurry up and get your ass out here.'

# Chapter 13

They returned to their car, running most of the way whilst keeping an eye out for their enemies. The gunfight in the church grounds had produced remarkably little reaction out on the main road; perhaps anyone hearing them imagined they were backfires from boy racers' cars on a nearby street. Mason found it curiously fascinating how ordinary folk often convinced themselves that the simplest answer was probably the best. Through working with Patricia's security company, he'd found that even late at night, when there came the sound of a hand unmistakably trying your front door, a person would continue to lie in the darkness, dismissing the sound as wind and creaking and, perhaps, their own tired brain making assumptions.

Their car was sitting in the rear corner of a pay-on-exit parking area, the bright blue metal gleaming in the glare of the afternoon sun. As Quaid unlocked it using the remote key Mason went straight to the boot, opened it and checked on the backpack. He unstrapped and opened it and looked inside to be sure the golden basin was secure.

When he climbed inside the car Sally was sitting with her head in her hands. 'They would have killed the vicar if we hadn't been there. I've seen bad people in my time – I lived out on the street for a stint when I was rebelling and came across some of the worst – but a penchant for callous murder is hard to accept.'

Mason realised that, apart from the Johann moment, he'd taken the whole episode in his stride. Most other people wouldn't be able to. His own background had made him less sensitive to guns and killing than Sally, something he wasn't sure was healthy. It was one thing trying to come to terms with the death of his friends in battle, an event he might have been responsible for, but quite another to brush off cold-hearted murder in broad daylight in southern England.

'You're right,' he said and was about to say more when Sally continued.

'First, they sought out Reginald's memorial slab. Then his gravestone. And they mentioned a Grand Master. Do you remember that?'

'I do,' Roxy said. 'I also remember that they were competent. A lot of mercs these days couldn't find a bullet in an armoury.'

Quaid started the car. Sally looked up. 'Where are you going?'

'We can't stay here. Who knows what's been reported to the cops? Our enemies, whoever they are, are a step ahead of us. We should keep moving.'

Sally nodded as Quaid pulled out of the space and then stopped at the exit to pay the parking fee. Soon, they were following the road out of town.

'Maybe we should take a look at what we found,' Hassell suggested. 'Before we get too far away from the church.'

It was a good point. If they hadn't recently been in a life-or-death battle, it might have made Mason smile. Come to that, he wished he could make Hassell smile. Just once. But the man was wrestling with a horde of deeply buried, malevolent inner demons and appeared to gain new worry lines every day. Hassell was the baby of the team but sometimes looked Quaid's age. Mason was already dreading the day when Hassell's torments would surface.

And thinking of torments, Mason took a moment to evaluate what had happened back there with Johann. Clearly, his old acquaintance had been working for the other side and had fallen a long way since Mosul. Mason had no idea what had happened to the man but remembered him as a likeable, dependable character, someone you wouldn't mind having your back.

The shock of the encounter still stung Mason's brain.

Back then, Johann had turned up just fifteen minutes or so after the blast that took two of Mason's best friends out. Johann's face was indelibly associated with that life-changing incident and seeing it again made Mason regress. He couldn't shake the memory, the sights, the smells, the sounds, of that devastating explosion from his mind.

Sally dug her phone out of her pocket. 'I took a thousand photos,' she said absently. 'Let me check.'

Quaid negotiated the twisting roads, heading for the nearby A1(M), a major road that could take them easily north or south.

Sally squinted at her phone. 'Wish I had 20-20 vision,' she said with a sniff. 'As it is, I think all the screen-strain is ruining my eyes.'

'I have great eyesight,' Hassell said. 'Pass it here.'

Mason settled in the front passenger seat as those in the back seat studied the photographs, and he let their conversation divert his attention. They took their time, peering hard at the small screen and zooming in. After a while, Sally took out a notepad and pencil.

'The window's representation of the basin is clearly modelled upon the Molten Sea,' she mused out loud. 'The flat base is unmistakable. The edge is quite broad on this one. I think it has to be because of the writing that runs round it. Damn my eyes,' she swore and let Hassell lean in, angling the phone towards him.

'The more you zoom, the blurrier it becomes,' he said. 'I think a magnifying glass would help.'

Quaid stopped midway through the next town, citing the clear superiority of old tools over new. Hassell hopped out as the car idled, found a local newsagent and bought a plain black magnifying glass. Soon, they had restarted their journey. Mason was becoming impatient.

'Is it code?' he asked. 'Templar code? A secret language? We know how much they loved their ciphers.'

'Kind of.' Sally was scribbling on her pad. 'I'm not sure. It's tricky at this point.'

'You mentioned that the Templars formed the modern-day Freemasons,' Roxy said. 'Would we be better off enlisting the help of one? Would that help?'

Sally paused to look up. 'It's not so simple,' she said. 'Freemasonry was established over three hundred years after the Templars. They were separate organisations. The seed of Templars may have evolved into Freemasons, but both groups have their own unique heritage. The traditions of Freemasonry are made up of imagery, parable and comparisons inspired by the Temple of Solomon. And let's not forget, the Templar order spent nine whole years underground excavating the actual Temple of Solomon. The older Templars assign their incredible stonework and building skills to reverse engineering gained from that ancient site. Those skills eventually shone through in the work of the Freemasons.'

'So the Freemasons tried to distance themselves from the Templars?' Quaid asked.

'It's complicated,' Sally said. 'The Freemasons respect and cherish their historical connection to the Templars but they don't want to be associated with all the drama of it. They walk a fine line very astutely.'

Roxy stared at Sally with an unimpressed look on her face. 'Well, you didn't really answer my question, but I'll take it as a no.'

'It's a no,' Sally said.

'What do you have?' Quaid asked.

'Something about a painting, a village, some mills and hills.' Sally stared hard at her sheet of paper. 'It doesn't make sense.'

'Did you really expect it to?' Mason said.

'A good point,' Sally said. 'Let me get it in the right order first. All right . . .' She held up her pad and started turning it around before her eyes. 'As far as I can tell this is a riddle. A Templar riddle. This is what it says:

The Painting in the Preceptory hangs,
The village near Blackwater stands,
Mystery Cloth and Fulling Mills,
Among our green and verdant hills.'

Mason turned to face the front window. 'Yeah, that's a riddle all right.'

'And something else has just occurred to me,' Quaid said. 'Or maybe it occurred before but it's just taken on prominence in my mind. The other basin. You recall there were two at the beginning. Professor Roger Beat was working on both and then he ended up in hospital. He gave us one basin, but there was another.'

'I remember,' Sally looked up. 'And I think I know where you're going with this.'

'Two basins,' Mason agreed. 'They were working on two basins, both found quite recently.'

'Which means . . .' Quaid said. 'That we're missing another clue.'

'This one,' Sally said, pointing at the boot, 'was sent to Professor Evans. We don't know what happened to the other one.'

'Do you think you can find out what was written on the other basin?' Mason asked her.

'You're thinking that if Beat was working on both then some record of the other basin and its riddle must exist in his office?' Hassell said. 'That's fair.'

'I've already done it once,' Sally said. 'I remember the name of the guy I spoke to. It has to be worth a try.'

Quaid drove on as they put the riddle aside for now and concentrated on the clue they didn't have. Sally placed an exploratory call to a man named Masterson, a colleague of Beat's, who explained that the first basin had been stolen in a violent and daring heist somewhere along the northern coast of England. Those very words put Mason and his whole team on a new level of high alert.

'Whoever Johann and the other mercs are working for, they appear to have both basin clues and the Baldock one,' Mason said quietly.

'Probably think they're in charge of the whole situation,' Roxy said grumpily.

'They are in charge,' Mason pointed out.

'They think they are,' Roxy said. 'But they haven't met me yet.'

Mason grinned. She was right. He didn't say anything else as, at that moment, Sally started to speak.

'Mr Masterson, I am completely invested in these two basins right now. Professor Beat entrusted their safety to us. I am a qualified historian, and my father was one of the most renowned professors in Oxford's history. There is nothing I want more than to see these basins recovered and Professors Beat and Evans back to full health. Please, help me.'

Mason didn't hear Masterson's reply but knew from Sally's reaction that he was balking in some way.

'Please, sir . . .' Sally continued with her diplomacy.

Roxy leaned into Mason. 'She's being civil,' she whispered. 'That's not a good sign.'

Mason tended to agree in principle but also thought Masterson deserved respect. 'He's just doing his job,' he said. 'Imagine how he feels – knowing his boss has just been assaulted and at least one basin stolen.'

'You're too nice,' Roxy told him. 'Anyone ever told you that before, Babyface?'

'Only when I'm holding a gun on them.' Mason laughed but didn't feel humorous.

'Please . . .' Sally was saying. 'You may check our endorsements from the Vatican. We have worked for them twice already.'

'It's just a bunch of photos,' Roxy said with a shrug. 'He must know that. I mean, how many people at Oxford have already seen them?'

Sally looked up then with hope on her face. 'You will? That's wonderful. Thank you, Mr Masterson. Let me open that account so I can see when the email comes through.'

Mason widened his eyes as Sally muted the phone and addressed them.

'He's sending us the photographs that were taken of the other basin,' she said. 'Emailing them across.' Her face, strained, took on a lighter expression when a notification chimed softly on her phone. 'Got it.'

'Excellent,' Mason said. 'So now we have two clues to solve.'

'Let's stick to the one we got from Baldock for now,' Sally said. 'We know this Grand Master, whoever he is, will be trying to decipher it even as we speak.'

Mason repeated the riddle: 'The Painting in the Preceptory hangs, The village near Blackwater stands, Mystery Cloth and Fulling Mills, Among our green and verdant hills.'

Sally looked around expectantly. 'Any ideas?'

# Chapter 14

Luke Hassell ran his right index finger across two narrow tramline scars that crossed his right cheek. The mostly healed wounds were the only physical sign that the last two operations he'd carried out with this team had been fraught with danger. They'd almost killed him.

In more ways than one.

During the search for the Vatican Book of Secrets Hassell had joined Mason's team after leaving the employ of the criminal Gido. He'd belatedly discovered that Gido ordered the murder of his childhood sweetheart, and had been forced to face the terrifying fact that for four years he'd been working for the man who killed his Chloe. Not only that, Gido had engineered the whole scenario out of spite because Hassell used to be a cop. Hassell had ended up killing Gido but the revenge had proved to be anything but sweet. Hassell still hurt; hurt like every minute was the end of the world.

Where did he go from here?

And then, during their search for the hidden Creed, Hassell had been blown up by the madman Marduk. It had all happened very quickly, but after the blast hit and his brain started functioning again, Hassell had wondered if he were dead.

The sensation wasn't entirely unpleasant.

*You blame yourself for Chloe's murder. For your submission to Gido and the years you worked for him. Is the guilt so profound that you would welcome death?*

Hassell spent most of his time thinking. He was an expert infiltrator and so far on this mission his skills hadn't been called for. He didn't feel that he entirely fitted with Mason's crew, but then where else was he supposed to go? Because he had spent four years working for a crime kingpin of New York, many of the world's most dangerous criminals were looking for him. He had to keep a low profile. So the answer to the question 'Where do I go from here?' was pretty much: 'Nowhere.'

Running around the world chasing ancient relics wasn't a bad cover. But could he find the peace he was looking for whilst working alongside them? Hassell was trying to come to terms with the mistakes he made around and after Chloe's death – just trying to find a way forward. His future was shaping up in a way he'd never thought possible – running with the good guys and still able, occasionally, to use the skills he'd so far put to more nefarious uses. At the same time, he wanted to overcome all the demons that contact with Gido had possessed him with.

He liked the crew – Mason, Roxy and Quaid. He didn't mind putting himself on the line for them. Do you enjoy risking death or is it more of a friendship thing? The real answer was: both.

'Any ideas?' Sally asked then, drawing him out of his reverie. Hassell's mind snapped to the present. They were seated in the car, driving somewhere, trying to figure out a riddle that might lead them to a treasure coveted by the chivalric Knights Templar, sought for millennia and worth more than the combined debt of the entire world.

'A village near Blackwater,' Mason said. 'Do we have a map?'

Hassell was taken back, struck by a sudden memory of Chloe. At some point during their blissful years together they'd undertaken a road trip out of state. He'd driven and Chloe had taken charge of the map – a huge old paper thing that when opened out over four leaves took up the entire front windscreen of the car. When the map was open, you forgot about seeing where you were going. Hassell smiled to himself now as he remembered those times. Better times.

Roxy was seated beside him in the back of the car, Sally to their left. Hassell liked Roxy. She was a no-nonsense, rule-breaking, straight-talking slice of pure-blooded American. But Roxy had her own demons, and Hassell didn't want to get among all that. He preferred to stay aloof.

'You hanging in there, Hassell?' she asked, keeping her voice low.

'Is it that obvious? Are you a mind-reader as well as a bad ass?'

Roxy shrugged and grinned. 'I read people well. I see when Mason's brooding extra hard, and I give him a pep talk. Now I see you doing the same. And, hey, I'm not all bad.'

'I don't think a pep talk's what I need right now.'

'I get that. But I'm here if you ever need it. I make a good sounding board.'

Hassell nodded and listened to his companions' discussion around Blackwater, mystery cloth, fulling mills and a painting in a preceptory. Hassell enjoyed the hunt; it calmed the rushing wave of stress that constantly broke against his mind like a troubled surf. It gave him alternative focus.

'I get stained-glass windows and carvings,' he said aloud. 'I understand how these clues might still be there. But a painting in a preceptory? How long ago were these clues written?'

Sally turned towards him. 'A good question. And why? The original Molten Sea on which the basins are based hails from biblical times. The clues simply can't. The church we just visited in Baldock, for instance, dates back to the twelfth century. The clues would have to have been written some time after that.'

'Even so,' Hassell said, 'it's a long time for a painting to hang outside a museum.'

'You have a fair point,' Sally said. 'But we have to follow the clues. If the objects we're being led to are so important, we must believe they'll have been preserved.'

Hassell concurred with a nod. It was the only logical way to proceed. He tried to sort through the tangled mess of doubt and doom and blame that filled his mind. The right thing to do was to move forward, but Hassell doubted that he was likely to do the right thing. Moving on would dull the past. Just look at how Mason and Roxy got on with their lives . . .

But did they? Mason was struggling just as much as Roxy. Hassell could tell through snatches of conversation and the odd question he overheard. On top of that, Quaid hadn't come to terms with orders he'd been forced to execute whilst in the army. He still resisted the onslaught of a turbulent past. Sally, on the other hand, was fighting against her wealthy upbringing whilst inheriting more money than she could ever spend.

They were a proper bunch of misfits, a ragtag crew.

Hassell couldn't help but smile inwardly. They had come together by chance, dragged into a semblance of a team by accident and circumstance. Now, they were trying to make it work. Hassell needed to try harder and take a step forward.

'To me,' he said, 'Blackwater means a lake, or a river. We're looking for a village that stands near either of those.'

'Don't most villages stand near a river?' Roxy ribbed him gently.

'Maybe, but there are other clues too.'

'Plus, and just as important for me,' Sally said, 'the ancient British sites of the Knights Templar.'

'A great way of narrowing it down,' said Mason approvingly.

'Thank you. Of course, there are hundreds to go through.'

'Don't forget the fulling mills and mystery cloth,' Roxy said helpfully.

Sally glanced at her. 'Don't you have a phone you could use to lend a hand?'

'I do fists and fury, not phones. Sorry.'

'And I don't do these new-fangled mobile things,' Quaid said. 'Give me a rotary any day.'

Hassell accepted a small tablet from Sally and soon everyone except Roxy and Quaid was trawling through digital information. Sally stayed with her notes and knowledge, combining them with her father's writings, but soon said that their current riddle was outside her particular area of expertise.

'The Painting in the Preceptory hangs,' she mused. 'The village near Blackwater stands, Mystery Cloth and Fulling Mills, Among our green and verdant hills. This is pure gruntwork, nothing else.'

Hassell flicked through digital pages, running searches as Quaid drove the car steadily south. The older man followed no clear direction, but they seemed to require just a sense of travel to help spur them on. Standing still wasn't the answer.

'At least we're not being chased this time,' Roxy said.

'Don't count your bloody chickens,' Mason said. 'And don't jinx it.'

'Do you remember those days stood by the water cooler?' Roxy reminisced. 'In Patricia's office when we worked for her security firm? They called me a loose cannon and a jinx. They didn't even know me.'

'I never stood by the water cooler,' Mason said. 'In fact, I didn't know there was one, and rarely ventured into the office. I guess they didn't know me either.'

Hassell wondered how close you could get to someone to really know them. He'd been close to Chloe. He'd known what she'd loved and liked, what she was going to say next and how she moved in every situation. He didn't think you could get much closer to someone. What horrendous mischance had caused her death and how had he failed for so long to see who murdered her?

Hassell shrugged the demons off once more, but they dug in, clinging to his heart and soul with their clawed, blackened, twisted fingers. They would never let him go. He concentrated on the screen, tapping and sliding until two words leapt out at him.

River Blackwater.

It was a decent-sized river in Essex. Hassell spoke up. 'All right,' he said. 'There's a river Blackwater that veers east and south on its way to the Blackwater Estuary in Essex. It has two major tributaries, the Rivers Brain and Chelmer. Can we check to see—'

'Brain, as in Braintree?' Sally said quickly. 'Now that's interesting. I read something about Braintree a little while ago. It didn't mention the river, but it does say . . .' She paused. 'Oh, hang on.'

They all waited as Sally trawled through her research, finally clicking her tongue as she found the right page. 'Here we are. Right, well, the history of Braintree village began four thousand years ago, so we have a great heritage. In the twelfth century it became an important commercial site. It was a significant location for the wool trade and had fulling mills at the Rivers Brain and Blackwater.' She paused.

'What's a fulling mill?' Mason asked.

Sally had to Google it. 'Fulling was the first part of the cloth-making process to become mechanised,' she said. 'Records dating back to the twelfth century show a fulling mill at Temple Newsham in West Yorkshire and another near Temple Guiting in Gloucestershire. Now, the fulling mills processed the cloth made from the wool and so were important in the production of woollen cloth.'

'Wait,' Mason said. 'Do those town names mean what I think they mean?'

'I'm glad you picked up on that. Both these towns and their fulling mills were built by the Knights Templar.'

'So we're on the right track?' Hassell felt a little proud of himself.

'Not necessarily.' Sally quashed his enthusiasm. 'Braintree is not associated with the knights, and neither are its mills.'

'Then it's a different one near there,' Mason said. 'The coincidences are too numerous for it not to be. What else stands along the River Blackwater and is close to a fulling mill?'

'You may be right,' Sally said softly. 'The other part of the riddle – mystery cloth – is explained by the Braintree bailiffs when they state "The Art of Mystery of weaving woollen cloth" was also practised at the town around the same time. It relates back to the mills.'

'We're in the right area,' Mason said. 'But Braintree, as well as being a town, is also a district of Essex. We're not talking about a small area here.'

'That actually helps,' Sally said. 'But if we just look for Knights Templar settlements along the River Blackwater, we find . . .'

She lapsed into silence, now using the Rusk Notes since her father had conducted some research into the Knights and their influence over medieval England. 'Bear with me,' she said. 'My father loved his waffle.'

Hassell continued to consult the various resources he'd found across the Web, trying to match Templar sites with the district of Braintree in Essex. It wasn't long before he found something.

'Hey . . .' he began.

'I think I have it,' Sally said. 'Now, it's a little confusing due to the terrible things that happened on Friday the thirteenth. Do you remember?'

'The Church ordered the death of all Knights Templar,' Mason said.

'Exactly. But what I didn't tell you was that, after carrying out this act, the Church was obviously left with many unowned lands, titles, homes and places of worship. It's known that, throughout England at least, many of these things were simply given to the Knights Hospitaller, also known as the Order of Saint John, another religious society that fought in the crusades, escaped the persecutions of 1307 and became better known in recent times as the St John Ambulance brigade.'

'You're saying that the Templars' lands were handed over to the Hospitallers?' Hassell realised the information matched what he'd found too.

'Yes, that's right. And there's one town that leaps off the page,' Sally said. 'Little Maplestead, a village in the district of Braintree. It's relatively close to the River Blackwater and would have had the fulling mills all those years ago. It has a round parish church supposedly built by the Hospitallers but which could just as easily have been built by the Templars. You see, the round church design is a favourite of the Templars. They're based on the fourth-century rotunda of the Church of the Holy Sepulchre in Jerusalem, a place we do know a little about . . .' Sally paused and smiled as she referenced the earlier adventure. 'To be clear, the other round church in England is a Templar church – the one in London. I think Little Maplestead used to be a Templar stronghold.'

'So that's where we're going?' Quaid asked.

'Set a course,' Sally said grandly, 'to the next stage of our journey.'

# Chapter 15

Little Maplestead is a picturesque village in southern England, set among country lanes, surrounded by green fields and lush stands of trees. Its environs are festooned with footpaths and bridleways that members of the public can explore.

By the time Quaid was closing in on the village, Mason was starting to feel nauseous. The constant sweeping bends and turns of the English countryside weren't helping his equilibrium any and, judging by the silence coming from the back seat, it wasn't doing much for his colleagues either.

When Quaid parked up and switched the car off, Mason heaved a sigh of relief. 'I really don't fancy the journey back,' he said quietly.

All the way there, he'd been quietly struggling with the issue of whether or not they should go forward. Why couldn't they hand this off to the police now, or at least try? The answer, he'd decided, came in several forms. First, he knew Sally would want to continue; she was fully invested in the recovery of the basins and knew the value that would be placed on Solomon's Temple, the Tabernacle and the Ark of the Covenant. That kind of value couldn't be allowed to fall into the wrong hands.

Mason knew that . . . but he needed more.

A new urgency came from the appearance of Johann. Though Mason had known him in both better and worse times, and gotten along with him just fine, he knew what Johann was capable of, and the lengths to which he might go. Johann was a good soldier, but he was a world-class killer. And, Mason believed, if Johann was involved there was a far uglier criminal network behind all this than they had imagined. Mason wanted to look Johann in the face one more time and ask him 'Why?', 'Why?' a hundred times. Why are you here? Why are you working for criminals? After all the bad things you've seen, all the worst kinds of evil that men and women can do . . . why are you helping them?

They climbed out of the car into a mid-afternoon minor climate crisis. The weather really didn't know what it wanted to do. A bright sun presided over dark clouds that scudded across the sky at spectacular speed, throwing wayward, fast-moving shadows upon the land. Mason bent his head as a blast of drizzle struck him.

'So we're looking for a painting in a preceptory,' Roxy said. 'Where the hell's the preceptory?'

Sally took in the view. 'You know,' she said, 'it's not like we're being chased here, or on a tight clock. We should take advantage of that and just ask someone.'

Mason liked her thinking. Their previous missions had been laden with unrelenting danger. This time around, while they had already stumbled across an organisation willing to kill for the grand prize, they had so far managed to stay clear of any serious trouble.

What constitutes serious trouble?

Guns? Mercenaries? A death order? Johann? Mason shook his head, reflecting that his army days had moulded his understanding of what trouble entailed.

'What I'm saying is . . . We ask around,' Sally said. 'It's not like we have to sneak through a catacomb or anything.'

Roxy shuddered at the memory. 'I won't be doing that again in a hurry.'

Mason scraped his boots in the car park gravel. 'Your research not helping with this one?'

'According to my research,' Sally said, 'there is no preceptory.'

Mason grimaced. 'Maybe we're in the wrong place.'

'Let's poke around first.' Sally started off towards the little round church. She followed a narrow, gravel-strewn path that meandered its way across a lawn, and would lead eventually to the door at the front of the circular nave. As they approached, the door opened and a small, white-haired man wearing a short-sleeved shirt and clerical collar emerged, puffing his cheeks out against the bracing wind.

'Oh, hello,' he said. 'I was just about to leave. Are you here for the church?'

Mason imagined they got a fair number of visitors to one of England's last surviving medieval round churches.

'It is remarkable,' Sally said. 'And I'd love to examine it some day at leisure but, today, we're more interested in the preceptory . . .' She left the sentence hanging.

The vicar looked confused. 'The preceptory? I'm afraid to say that although the preceptory stood here for a long time, it stands no longer. Now, I really do have to go,' he fretted. 'It's time for little Maisie's walk, you know. She does rely on me.'

'There's no preceptory in Little Maplestead?' Hassell asked. 'Maybe we're at the wrong village.'

'Maybe . . .' Sally said. 'Was there—'

'There used to be a preceptory though,' the vicar said. 'Right there.' And he pointed beyond them, across the lawn that fronted the churchyard.

Mason turned to look. 'That's Maplestead Hall,' the vicar said. 'And stands close to the foundations of the old preceptory.'

Mason scratched his stubbly cheek. 'They built a new hall over the preceptory?'

The vicar nodded, hopping from toe to toe in his urgency. 'And a very good job they did too. Many of the original timbers were incorporated into the rebuild including the uprights and the tie beams. The staircase is from 1850. The doors, architraves and mouldings, 1870. Now, if you don't mind, I do have an obligation . . .'

'More important to us then,' Sally said in musing tones, 'is what happened to the items that the preceptory contained. Were they also incorporated into the new house?'

The vicar frowned at them. 'Why on earth would you be interested in those items?' He rubbed his cheeks, looking anxious, and then checked his watch. 'Little Maisie does rely on me, you know,' he repeated.

'Please, we're trying to track something down,' Sally said. 'For a family once associated with Little Maplestead that moved away.' She kept her explanation vague, but mostly truthful, hedging her bets.

'I see,' the vicar said. 'All of you?'

Mason tried not to wince. There was something about him and Roxy and probably Quaid too, he knew. Something about their bearings that spoke to civilians of trained professionals, something that set them on edge. It wasn't anything that Mason could ever change but it was a lesson for the future that they should learn when approaching the public, especially an anxious vicar like this one.

'It's quite valuable,' Sally ventured.

'Be that as it may,' the vicar said. 'I can't help you other than to say that all the preceptory's original items were dispersed. The Hall got some, the church got some, a few locals were also involved. I'd advise a visit to the local archives as it was all a matter of record. Go to the local County Records Office. You can visit these places, you know.' The vicar squinted at them as if assessing their determination. 'Now, look, I just came out to assess the weather. My little dog relies on me, and I won't let her down. Do excuse me.'

'Excellent,' Sally said a little tightly. 'We'll be sure to try.'

As the vicar went back inside, Mason watched him go, impressed with his loyalty to his little dog. Hassell let out a deep breath. 'And I thought chasing ancient artefacts would be relatively easy.'

'It's always been a matter of piecing all the evidence together,' Sally said. 'Just like history, actually. One step at a time, one event at a time. We just need to locate a County Records Office.'

'Don't they have an online presence?' Roxy asked.

'I'm sure they do,' Sally said. 'But not to this degree. I think we're hands-on with this one, I'm afraid.'

'Maybe we could just walk over to the Hall,' Mason suggested as they all turned away from the church and started to make their way out of the churchyard. 'Knocking on that door would be easier than going to this Records Office.'

'And say what?' Quaid affected a deep voice. 'Excuse me, man, can we take a look around your house?'

'Something like that,' Mason said defensively. 'Maybe Sally could try it alone.'

'I'm leaning towards the County Records Office,' Sally said. 'Research is what I do. Don't worry, if their records are good, we'll find the painting.'

Mason nodded and followed the others back to their car. At the back of the group, he slowed slightly to try and assess their surroundings. Were they being watched? Was anyone else searching Little Maplestead for a preceptory and a painting? It didn't feel like it. The day was quiet, the wind now gentle and the vicar was hurrying along the pavement with his dog pulling on a leash. If it wasn't for what they'd seen and overheard at Baldock he'd believe they were the only people searching for the seven golden basins of the Molten Sea.

As they reached their car, Sally paused and put a hand on the roof. 'Just a thought,' she said. 'We could always leave this clue for later. We still have another that needs solving.'

Mason recalled Professor Beat's people had emailed photographs of the other basin. Sally would have them by now.

'We're here now,' Quaid said. 'It makes more sense to see it through.'

'Agreed,' Sally said. 'But we're a team and I thought the team should decide.'

Mason and the others concurred. They would carry on. Quaid started the car and waited for Sally to pull up more information about the local Records Office.

'Got it,' she said after a while. 'There's a place called Halstead nearby. They have a small County Records Office which we could use.' She gave Mason a postcode that he could tap into the satnav.

Quaid set off along the country roads, following the satnav's directions with a shake of his head, determined not to harbour the thought that anything so technologically advanced could take the place of a good old-fashioned paper map. Mason was feeling deflated after the disappointment they'd met at the round church and couldn't even be bothered to start a sparring match with him.

'Cheer up,' Sally said, breaking the general malaise that filled the car. 'This is what normal relic hunting is all about. It's not all glamour and adventure, you know.'

Roxy raised an eyebrow. 'During the last mission we crawled through catacombs and a cemetery. Now, as you know, I'm a little claustrophobic and I don't see an awful lot of glamour there.'

'I'm sorry you had to do that,' Sally said. 'I know there was an incident in your childhood.'

108

'I got locked in a crypt by my friend when I was young,' Roxy told them, surprising Mason with her forthrightness. 'I don't recommend it.' Mason was glad to hear her speak of it; she was moving forward.

'You surely can't deny that you enjoyed the hunt,' Sally said.

'Oh, I really can,' Roxy said. 'Being up to my elbows in graveyard dust doesn't hold a great attraction for me.'

'Then we couldn't be more different,' Sally said. 'I love it.'

Mason listened. They all knew about Roxy's aversion to catacombs and underground tunnels. She'd mentioned it often enough. Despite that aversion, however, Roxy always came through when they needed her most. Sometimes too much. One of her other instincts was to attack first and ask questions later. It was all part of her determination to leave the old life behind and embrace the new, a need to raise the barriers faster and faster. It hit her out of the blue, just occasionally, and it could get them all killed. It served to distract her too, another dangerous trait. Mason believed it was why, back at the old office, she'd been known as a loose cannon.

The road ahead twisted and turned. They passed hedgerows and negotiated sharp bends, Quaid slowing and turning every few seconds.

It was only because Mason saw a flash of black in the wing mirror to this left that he realised two black shapes were quickly closing on them.

Range Rovers, he thought. Coming fast in tandem. The sight of them brought Johann once more to the centre of his mind. He watched them close in behind. He was about to say something when Quaid tapped the rear-view mirror.

'We've got company,' he said. 'And they don't look friendly.'

'Drive,' Sally said. 'Just drive.'

'Not a chance of outrunning them,' Quaid said. 'They're way more powerful.'

'The tight roads make it impossible for them to get past,' Mason said.

'Doesn't mean they can't run us off the road,' Quaid grated, grimacing and stamping on the accelerator.

Mason watched as the two large black cars loomed in the side mirror. He could see two vague faces in the front seats but little else. He discreetly took out his Glock 17. For the first time, he thought, he was going to need it.

'This feels different,' Roxy said. 'They're targeting us, not reacting.'

Mason knew exactly what she meant. The Range Rovers were inches from their back bumper. Their own car's engine roared as Quaid extracted every ounce of power he could whilst still safely negotiating the bends.

'This is gonna get messy,' Quaid yelled as a sharp bend approached.

The lead Range Rover smashed into their back end.

# Chapter 16

Mason winced as the crunch of colliding metal resounded through the car. Quaid held onto the wheel with grim determination, trying to correct the swerve. Mason saw that their pursuers hadn't pulled back and were closing in for another strike.

'We can't win this,' he said.

'And I'm counting at least ten men in those cars.' Roxy turned around in her seat. 'Can we win against that?'

'Give them something to worry about,' Mason said.

'With pleasure.'

Roxy lifted her Glock – they'd all been given the same model of weapon – and aimed at the driver of the following car. When he didn't react, she pulled the trigger. Their rear window shattered instantly, a cold gust of air blasting through. Mason had turned around in his own seat and closed his eyes as a few small fragments blasted back into the car, propelled by the wind.

When he opened his eyes again, he saw the front windscreen of the lead Range Rover crack. An impact crater opened up, the epicentre for a racing series of faultlines that suddenly covered the windscreen from side to side. Roxy opened fire again.

The Range Rover's nose dipped forward as its driver stamped on the brakes. The windscreen exploded.

Quaid put on as much speed as he dared. The second Range Rover narrowly avoided colliding with the first. A gap opened up between the pursued and the pursuers.

Mason felt brief elation. The country roads swung around sharp and sweeping bends, often between high hedgerows and past impenetrable stands of trees that threw shadows across the fleeing car. Mason heard a roar from behind as the Range Rovers sped up once more.

'Ideas?' Quaid shouted.

'Not many,' Roxy admitted.

'Keep them busy,' Mason said. 'And scared. Target their tyres too.'

Hassell unholstered his Glock and twisted in his seat to aim through the shattered rear window. Sally ducked, gripping her laptop bag like it was a life preserver. As the first Range Rover drew near, Hassell squeezed off three shots, aiming for the front tyres.

The bullets bounced off tarmac, missing their target completely. Mason wound down the window on his side, as one of the vehicles drew in even closer. He slipped his upper body out of the window and took aim.

The driver saw him and shifted to his right, taking that vehicle out of sight but exposing the second Range Rover.

Mason fired. His bullets bounced off tarmac to the left of the car's tyre. He hung on, thrown left and right by potholes, Quaid's driving and the direction of the road. Then he targeted perfectly on the Range Rover's tyre. Just as he fired, Quaid swung them around a left-hand bend, sending his carefully aimed bullet into bordering vegetation.

'Tell me when there's a straight,' Mason yelled.

'There are no straights,' Quaid yelled back. 'The English countryside doesn't do straight!'

Mason cursed. All he needed was one good shot. Roxy and Quaid were still taking potshots at the closest vehicle, which had decided to pull back.

Quaid cursed. 'Crap,' he said. 'There's a village coming up.'

Mason grimaced and locked eyes with Roxy for a second. 'We have to end this fast,' he said. If they took this fight through the village, then innocent bystanders would be harmed.

Roxy nodded. She aimed her gun once more at the driver of the lead car. Mason concentrated on the second Range Rover. They opened fire simultaneously.

But at that moment the occupants of the pursuing cars started firing back. Mason saw figures leaning out of the windows, saw their elbows and shoulders and heads; they were all holding guns. The men fired their weapons and Mason ducked back inside the car.

So far, there had been no sign of Johann.

Bullets pinged off the metalwork, some thudding into the boot, others glancing off the A frames. Mason flinched as the wing mirror on his side of the car was hit and then sheared off, knowing that if he'd stayed in position the bullet would have smashed through his face.

Quaid cursed as he was forced to speed up again.

They were on the outskirts of the village now, passing a few isolated houses. Mason turned around to look out the front window.

'Drive,' he said under his breath. 'Just drive.'

The road, narrow as it was, had to contend with another obstacle ahead. Villagers had parked their cars along one side of the road, contracting the available space even more dangerously. Quaid was clenching his teeth. Mason swivelled around again in his seat.

'Pin them back,' he said.

Both he and Roxy opened fire. Mason felt the car swerve

as Quaid pulled out into the opposite carriageway. Mason's mag clicked on empty. He dug into his pockets for a spare.

'There's more ammunition in the damn trunk,' Roxy growled as her own weapon ran out of bullets. 'In the bag.'

Mason eyed the back seat. He leaned out of the window and loosed off two shots. When he ducked back inside, he spoke quickly.

'Sally, Hassell, move across as far as you can. Roxy, pull that catch. The back seats split and fold down and you can crawl into the . . . the boot.'

'Why the hell am I always crawling through things?' Roxy moaned but started doing as Mason suggested.

Quaid was now driving fast along the wrong side of the road. The gap was narrow. Mason found that he couldn't lean out of the window for fear of getting swiped by parked cars. The proof of that came just seconds later as their speeding car hit a stationary wing mirror and smashed it away. The sound of screeching metal filled their car just as the Range Rovers loomed large behind them, blocking out the sun like vast eclipses.

'Shit.' Quaid jammed his boot even harder on the accelerator. Mason saw ahead that a van was threatening to drive towards them along the narrow corridor. It would effectively block them off. Fortunately, and perhaps because of Quaid's speed, the van decided to wait, flashing its headlights.

Quaid held on grimly to the steering wheel. Mason looked for a gap to stick his head out. The Range Rovers pushed them hard, almost touching their rear bumper. And Roxy crawled head first into the rear boot compartment.

'You see the backpack?' Mason shouted. 'Grab all the spares.'

'On it.'

Hassell was looking cramped in the back seats' remaining space with Sally. Mason felt an impact as their car sideswiped a parked vehicle, jerking them all to the right as it bounced off. Quaid managed to keep them relatively straight.

Mason took advantage of his colleagues' positions to fire through the smashed back window. His bullet entered the pursuing vehicle's front grille and hopefully broke something. His next bullet followed in exactly the same direction.

'And . . . clear . . .' Quaid threw the car back into the correct carriageway as they reached the end of the parked line of cars. 'Ah . . . bollocks.'

Mason didn't like the sound of that but couldn't take the time to turn around and look. 'Tell me.'

'Just another line of parked cars,' Quaid hissed. 'And a fucking school.'

'It's after home time,' Mason said, glancing at his watch. 'But still take it easy.'

His words might have sounded ridiculous, but Quaid took them to heart. Mason fired more bullets into the lead Range Rover's grille as Quaid slowed. Roxy shuffled backwards out of the boot. She dropped an armful of spare magazines in an untidy heap on the rear seat.

'Finally,' she said, changing mags.

Quaid took them past the school, the atmosphere in the car one of charged tension. The contrast of the slower pace and the looming danger was hard to reconcile, especially for Mason, who passed the school grounds with a gun in his hand. But Quaid soon came to the end of the school boundary, slipped past the last parked car and pulled them back into their own carriageway.

Ahead, the road opened up. Quaid floored it as they left the village. A few people out for a nice walk through the country shook their fists at the speeding vehicles, oblivious to what was really happening.

Quaid smashed his boot on the accelerator, temporarily pulling away from the pursuing cars. Mason heard the

Range Rovers' roaring engines and then saw them approach like giant predators.

Roxy opened fire through the shattered rear window. The pursuing cars weaved across the road. The passengers leaned out of their own windows, returning fire.

A flurry of shots sent both Mason and Roxy ducking back inside the car. The speedier vehicles took that opportunity to get closer. The lead Range Rover powered forward and crashed into their rear bumper.

The car swerved. Quaid fought with the wheel. Their car slewed slightly left and then hard right, veering into the other carriageway. Quaid couldn't hold on and cursed loudly. The car ran off the road to the right, striking the grass verge so hard it bounced. Mason got a look at high hedgerows and a steep slope and winced.

This wasn't going to end well.

'Shit, man, that's a big ditch,' Roxy said.

Quaid fought to keep control of the car. The grass verge had become a deep channel at the bottom of which was a dirty, turgid stream of water. The car raced towards it with the Range Rovers even now still following, travelling along the wrong side of the road with one set of wheels on the verge.

Quaid didn't slow. As the car tipped with the slope, he poured on the power. The back wheels skidded. The engine roared. The car scraped halfway down the ditch with its back end throwing up mud and grass. Quaid aimed the wheel at the top of the slope. The car glided forward at a sharp angle, the rear having slid lower down and now well below the front, tyres angrily trying to find a grip. Mason held on. Roxy yelled out and Hassell's eyes bulged. Mason couldn't see Sally properly but he did notice her laptop slide across the back seat.

Quaid finessed the steering wheel and feathered the accelerator pedal as their car tried to power its way out of the ditch. The Range Rovers were using their four-wheel drive system to motor sideways along the ditch and stay straight, slightly above Mason's car. Even now, men were leaning out of their windows and taking aim.

'Down!' Mason yelled.

Everyone except Quaid took cover. Bullets peppered the side of the car as it fought for traction and threw clouds of grass and mud from its spinning back wheels. Mason saw Quaid's teeth bared at the wheel.

Fight it, he thought.

Quaid was fighting it. His boot never stopped tapping the accelerator. His hands grappled with the barely manageable steering wheel. Bullets slammed into the car, the noise of the impact echoing around them. Mason heard the roar of the wind, the grinding of tyres and the scream of car engines. Against the G-force that drove him back into his seat he struggled up, pointed his gun out the window and opened fire.

Through luck more than skill, his shots struck one of their aggressors, making the man drop his gun and then slump through his open window. Blood poured down the side of his car. Mason didn't feel any sense of triumph, just relief at thinning out their enemies.

Quaid yelled at the top of his lungs as their back wheels caught solid ground. The sudden traction propelled the car up the slope at high speed, cutting across the front end of the first Range Rover. That driver took evasive action, missing an uncontrollable collision by inches, but sent his car barrelling towards the bottom of the ditch. The second Range Rover didn't fare much better. Its driver didn't react fast enough, and struck the other car side on.

Mason's eyes widened as the second Range Rover took to the air. It flew up and started to roll, several feet above the ground and on a course to land smack bang on top of the smaller car's roof. The shadow of the big vehicle fell over them. Mason felt his breath catch in his throat. The smell of earth and petrol filled the car. Mason held on tightly as Quaid kept his foot on the accelerator, making their car shoot from underneath the other one as it crashed to the ground.

The Range Rover hit hard, its roof glancing off their boot with a shriek of metal. Mason heard a shuddering crunch and looked out the back window.

Both Range Rovers were out of action. The ditch had claimed the first car – it was stuck nose-first in the narrow stream. Bad luck had neutralised the second car – it lay on its side, its occupants struggling to get free.

Quaid cheered as they reached the top of the ditch and their wheels gained traction on the tarmac. Without hesitation or a look back, he put his foot down and sped off along the narrow country road.

In the back seat, Roxy groaned.

'Are we there yet?'

# *Chapter 17*

'Move it,' Mason hissed. 'Let's get to Halstead quickly.'

Quaid looked over. 'We're still going?'

'They'll be out of action for a while,' Roxy said. 'As long as they don't have any backup, we're golden.'

'And there's nobody else following us along these roads,' Hassell put in.

Quaid took a long look through their rear-view mirror. 'Car's in a bit of a state,' he said.

Mason took the time to change the magazines in his Glock before secreting the weapon in his waistband. Roxy handed out spare mags so that they could zip them inside their jacket pockets. Quaid maintained the speed until a rectangular white signpost reading 'Halstead' came into view.

'All right,' Quaid muttered. 'Just remember – try to act like normal people who haven't just been in a car chase.'

Mason determined to do his best. His heart was still beating fast. Inside, though, he was calm.

'Slow down here,' he said. 'Stop.'

Quaid pulled into a pub parking area. The sudden absence of noise roared in Mason's ears. He shrugged it off and got out of the car. 'Nothing we can do about the damage,' he said. 'But we can leave Hassell here to warn us of any followers.' He turned to the New Yorker. 'You okay with that?'

'You want me to sit in a pub parking lot and drink beer?' Hassell looked pleased. 'Yeah, I think I can handle that.'

'Will the Bluetooth range carry that far?' Sally touched her ear.

'If it doesn't, use your phone.' Mason stated the obvious and climbed back inside the car. Quaid started it up again as Sally narrowed down their search for the County Records Office and gave him a street address.

'Four minutes to closing time,' she said.

Mason sat back and took several deep breaths. The minutes after action were always a challenge as you tried to readjust to normality. The damaged state of their car didn't help. Quaid drove it through the little town, stopping at a zebra crossing and then carrying on past a group of school-aged youths before slowing down.

'Hope we don't come across a copper,' he muttered.

'We won't,' Roxy said. 'You gotta have faith.'

Mason noticed that the pedestrians barely glanced at their car. It was after five p.m. now, still light since the clocks had sprung forward just a few weeks earlier. Mason wondered if the Records Office would still be open.

'Hurry,' Sally said as if sensing his concern.

Quaid found a car park. They left the broken vehicle behind and stepped into a cold but windless evening, the lowering sun shining right into their eyes. Mason hurried out of the parking area onto the main street of Halstead.

'There,' he said.

It was a small, oblong brick building with two UPVC windows and a broad front door. Mason saw the sign 'County Records Office' hanging unobtrusively in one of the windows rather than above the door. This was clearly a discreet satellite office.

Sally led the way forward as Mason turned swiftly to Roxy and Quaid.

'You two hang back,' he said. 'If we learned anything so far it's four's a crowd when it comes to civilian interaction.'

Sally tried the door, clearly wondering if it might be locked, found it open and pushed through. Mason was a step behind. The interior was minimal and dim because of the half-drawn blinds and the various window stickers. Mason saw a middle-aged woman with red hair sitting behind a desk.

Sally strode straight up to her and presented her credentials, something about a historian working for a team who were trying to track down an artefact. The woman's face brightened at the thought and at the idea of being involved. Sally checked the dates and then asked about the preceptory.

'I have no idea,' the woman admitted, dashing their hopes of finding a learned administrator. 'But I can certainly check the records for you.' She came up with a fee that Sally paid on her card.

Mason drifted to the only place where he could keep an eye on the outside, a clear spot on the window between a flyer for a local sports team and a note for an upcoming town gala. The streets outside were brushed in crimson by the setting sun, populated by dozens of people going about their daily business. Two lines of cars waited at a nearby pedestrian crossing. Mason saw no sign of enemies outside. He tested the comms to make sure they were active.

'How's the beer?'

There was no answer. Mason assumed they were out of range for the Bluetooth receivers, so he checked his phone which had a good signal and a good battery. Satisfied, he turned his attention back to the street outside.

The redhead returned five minutes later. 'All right,' she said. 'I have records right here for the old preceptory. Did you know it stood on the grounds of what is now Maplestead Hall?'

Sally smiled and said that she did know. The woman handed a thin folder across and told her to be careful with it. Sally looked around, but the woman only smiled.

'Sorry,' she said. 'We don't have a reception room, but you're welcome to stay right here. We close at half five today.'

Mason checked the time, seeing they had about ten minutes to find what they were looking for. He didn't want to have to spend the night in Halstead – he had nothing against the town, it was their enemies he was worried about. Sally opened the folder and started to scan its contents.

'Interesting,' she said aloud for Mason's benefit. 'The initial establishment of the preceptory took place in around 1186. It says right here in the histories that the preceptory belonged to a "farrye clark", whose business it was to officiate in divine things, and quotes a memorandum from the rental notes that' – she air-quoted – '"the vicar payeth by year to the Farrye Clark 40s or else the Farrye Clark may take the challis or the masse booke, the painting or any other ornament for his dewtie". And there's a long list of preceptors up to the date 1365.'

'I think we need to move forward in time,' Mason said gently.

Sally nodded absently, lost in her research. 'There's a long list of assets, a value of possessions and even expenses that were paid to various tradesmen. For instance, seven pounds was paid for wheat for baking bread, five pounds and four shillings for malt for brewing ale, a stipend for the chaplain and much more. Among the asset list are two paintings.'

'When was the preceptory destroyed?' Mason assumed that had to be the case.

'Not a clue.' Sally sifted through the meagre contents of the file.

As Sally searched Mason was assessing their recent encounter with the violent mercenaries and admitting to himself that the gloves were well and truly off now in their search for the golden basins. Whoever controlled the goons had decided Mason and his team were a threat. They must have tailed them to Little Maplestead earlier today. Mason realised he'd been too complacent in looking out for tails and resolved not to make that mistake again.

'How are we doing?' he asked Sally, acutely conscious of the passage of time.

'It is five twenty-five,' the redhead reminded them sharply.

Sally ignored them both, still leafing through history. It was only when Mason decided to get radical and call her on her mobile phone that she reacted.

'Oh, it's you,' she said, blinking and turning to him with the phone held at her face. 'What are you doing?'

'We need answers,' he said, giving her a grim smile. 'It was the only way to get through.'

'Can I photocopy this?' Sally held up a single sheet and waved it at the redhead.

'Of course. We're due to close in two minutes.'

Sally crossed over to a photocopier in the far corner of the room, dragging Mason along with her. When they were relatively alone, she started to speak.

'The preceptory's assets were divided up when it fell out of use,' she said quietly, head down. 'Books, ecclesiastical items, paintings, even pews and chairs. It was all shared out. All of the paintings went to the parish church.'

Mason frowned at her. 'Which is . . .?'

'The Church of St John the Baptist,' Sally affirmed. 'It's in Little Maplestead.'

Mason now closed his eyes briefly. 'You're kidding me,' he said. 'The little round church we've already been to?'

'The very same,' Sally finished her work, turned and gave the whole file back to the redhead. 'There you go,' she said. 'Bang on half-past five. You can go home now.'

'Thanks,' the woman said drily.

123

Mason didn't hear any of it. His mind was fielding thoughts like a sports player fields a non-stop procession of machine-fed balls. The worst of it all was that they would have to return the same way they'd come and that meant . . .

. . . passing the place where the Range Rovers had crashed.

Mason caught hold of Sally's arm. 'C'mon,' he said. 'Let's make this quick.'

# Chapter 18

The Range Rovers were gone, but the signs of the earlier car chase were evident. Mason had urged Quaid to drive slowly around the corner that overlooked the crash site but, when he saw the cars had disappeared, he told the older man to put his foot down.

'We have no idea who we're up against,' Roxy said, huddled in the back seat as they drove by the crash site. 'The depth of their reach.'

'You're referring to the Amori?' Mason asked. 'We wiped most of their network out during the last mission. But whoever our enemy is can clearly command large assets and has deep pockets.'

'Maybe we should capture one of those assets,' Roxy said. 'I could make them talk.'

Mason didn't doubt it. Roxy was an ex-asset herself, plucked from childhood to work for a questionable, unknown American agency for years before she found a way out. The ghosts of what she'd done for them still haunted her.

'Do you think this is wise?' Hassell said, also from the back seat. 'Sooner or later someone's gonna report this car, or a cop will see it.'

'Little Maplestead is just minutes away,' Mason said. 'We can't hit the pause button now. I think it's worth the risk.'

'It's a shame the vicar didn't know what was hanging in his own church,' Hassell said a little huffily.

'You can't blame him,' Sally said. 'It's a setback for us, yes, but he may not know the provenance of the church's assets. He might be relatively new. It's not like the history of each individual item is going to be passed down from priest to priest. And these missions don't always run smoothly.'

'I still know I could make one of them talk,' Roxy said quietly.

'And say what?' Mason sought to prove a point. 'If the man who hired them is even a little bit clever, he won't have told them the full plan; won't even have told them who or where he is. The hired help is usually clueless in my experience.'

'Yeah, like mushrooms, I get the idea. Kept in the dark and fed on shit.'

'And let's be clear.' Mason turned to look at her. 'Aren't you trying to distance yourself from the person you used to be?'

'I was trying to be useful.'

'Don't compromise yourself,' Mason said, hoping he wasn't about to see another flash of the loose cannon. He'd always found Roxy as dependable as they came, but there had been that one lone incident in the London cemetery where she'd well and truly lost it. She'd blamed it on too much introspection, too much addiction to raising those internal barriers.

'Don't worry,' Roxy said. 'I don't do compromise.'

That was more like it. Hassell was quiet and Quaid was concentrating on the road. Sally was peering around his seat, trying to see what was coming up ahead. Mason soon saw why. They were approaching Little Maplestead, less than two minutes away from the church.

The first thing he saw was the village park laid out to the right. It wasn't big, but there was a set of swings, a slide and a roundabout built upon rubber tiles for safety. There were some winding paths and a large green area where children were playing football as the sun went down.

'That is not good,' Hassell said.

He was referring to the small parking area where a black Range Rover currently sat. Mason bit his bottom lip.

'We can't engage them here,' he said. 'We just can't.'

'We might not have a lot of choice,' Roxy said as the Range Rover started to move.

'Keep driving,' Mason told Quaid. 'Lead them away from the park.'

'Have to admit,' Quaid said grudgingly. 'Driving at slow speeds is easier with an automatic box.'

Mason stared at him, as though he couldn't be sure this was an impostor in Quaid's place. Where had the technology-hating man gone?

'We don't need another car chase,' Hassell said, checking the map on his phone for a spot nearby where they could set up an ambush. 'There's a decent-sized parking area to the right. Hopefully, it will be empty.'

The Range Rover was already closing the gap. Mason saw now that its front end was slightly damaged, so definitely one of the vehicles that had been chasing them. He wondered where the second one had gone. More to the point, he wondered where Johann was. The last thing he wanted to do was go up against a former colleague. It wasn't right, the world throwing them together like this. There had to be a way around it, a way to avoid a confrontation with a man he'd always considered a close colleague.

As Quaid spied the parking area and turned towards it, Mason checked his gun.

'Take them out fast and clean,' he said, keeping his voice steady. 'And, Sally . . . stay low.'

'You should give me a gun,' she said. 'I'm learning to fight. Not there yet. But I definitely should have a gun.'

Quaid pulled into the car park, a small area that was currently empty but would normally hold about twenty vehicles. As he jolted up the irregular ramp on entry the Range Rover accelerated towards their back end.

Mason winced. There would be no quarter given then. The Range Rover struck their rear but Quaid managed to floor the accelerator just before the collision. Their car spurted forward, making the impact light. It barely shook them. Quaid continued into the car park and used the wide space to turn around so that their front end was facing the Range Rover.

'No,' Hassell said.

Quaid blipped the accelerator pedal, letting the engine roar.

'No,' Sally said.

Quaid gripped the steering wheel tightly with both hands.

'We don't play chicken with two tonnes of Solihull steel,' Mason said carefully.

'Who said anything about playing chicken?' Quaid let the car shoot forward several inches before applying the brake pedal once more.

'I say go for it,' Roxy sniffed, testing the strength of her seat belt by yanking on it.

'Then you don't know anything about cars. I do. They'll crush us,' Mason said. 'Quaid, you know this.'

'Trust me,' the ex-army man said between tightly drawn lips. 'I know what I'm doing.'

Mason held on to his next words by clenching his mouth shut. Quaid again blipped the car's throttle. The Range Rover suddenly shot forward.

Quaid floored his own accelerator pedal. Their car surged ahead, eating up the gap between them and their opponent.

Mason could see the other occupants' grinning faces and a jagged gap where the front window used to be. He saw the driver's determined expression.

'Quaid . . .'

The fast-moving vehicles closed in on each other with frightening speed. Metal charged at metal. Mason then flinched as Quaid wrenched on the wheel at the last minute, flicking them past to the right of the oncoming car, and then spun them half a circle to face its rear.

'All out!' he yelled. 'Take 'em down. Sally, stay here.'

Mason threw open the door and jumped out. There were five enemies in the other car. He saw both back doors crack open, brought his gun up and opened fire. To his right, Roxy did the same. Quaid and Hassell were also with them. As a team, they raced forward.

All four of the Range Rover's doors were now open. Mason's bullets hit inner door panels and shattered side windows. The mercenaries' problem was they were facing the wrong way. Mason fired through the rear window of the vehicle, the bullet travelling the length of the car and out the front, missing its target before thudding into a brick wall.

A merc popped up in the back seat, head visible and gun pointed at them. Mason didn't risk anything. He fired a bullet as he threw himself headlong and came up against the back of the black vehicle, so close he could feel the heat of the exhausts close to his face.

Roxy dived in next to him.

'We gotta maintain the advantage,' she said.

Mason knew she was right. He half rose and fired blindly through the back window. Quaid and Hassell were crouched metres away, using the angle for cover. He rolled and peered around the corner of the car.

He saw legs hanging out of the front passenger's side. A gun appeared, too. Mason fired a bullet at the legs.

The target crumpled to the ground, now fully revealed. Mason shot him in the chest.

Roxy peered around the other side of the car. Her first bullet missed the driver's legs and enabled him to dash around the front of the vehicle and shoot back blindly. Quaid positioned himself prone on the floor, face forward, so that he could see underneath the car all the way to the front. Mason assumed he saw a pair of ankles because he suddenly started firing.

'Got him,' Quaid whispered.

Right then, the surviving mercenaries either panicked or decided on a crazy course of action. They rose up and jumped out of the big back window one at a time, landing among Mason's team.

Mason didn't have time to react as a pair of boots stomped to the ground right next to him. A foot lashed out. Mason felt a blow to the side of the head. He rolled away, and managed to climb to his knees.

The mercenary dived at him, swinging a knife.

# Chapter 19

The knife slashed at Mason's arm, slicing into his jacket and drawing a thick line of blood. Mason flinched at the pain but ignored it. He wrapped his wounded arm around his adversary's throat from behind, pinning the knife to the man's chest and cutting off his air supply. And then, despite possibly being too close, Mason decided to bring the gun into play.

Bad move.

The mercenary lashed out, striking the gun from Mason's hand. The guy was strong. He heaved upward, bringing immense pressure on his own throat, but managed to heave Mason off his feet. As Mason stumbled away, he got a glimpse of Roxy tackling a second mercenary as Quaid and Hassell waded into a third.

It was chaos. Just a sphere of pain and groaning, blood and torn flesh. Mason took a blow to the face that would have sent him to the ground if he hadn't managed to half block it with a hand. He received a kick to the stomach, but the merc couldn't get the right angle so the blow barely bothered him. He flung out a leg that connected solidly with the mercenary's chest.

The man grunted. He dived at Mason. The world contracted to a desperate, sweating melee of strength and

131

struggle, but Mason was good at close quarters. He'd practised close-quarter boxing for days on end. He wriggled left and right to create a little space, brought his fists close to his chest and then delivered vicious uppercuts as fast as he was able. He used his elbows as the gap between himself and his adversary grew larger.

Blows connected with the man's chin and then his eyes. His head jerked back. Mason gained more space, but he could tell how strong and resilient this man was. Face stretched in a rictus of pain, the man blocked Mason's blows.

Mason switched his attention to the ribs and the spleen, delivering quick, stunning blows learned from years of training. The man's thick jacket protected him from the worst of the impact, but some of Mason's punches got through. When the man brought his arms down for cover, Mason started back on the face.

Taking a breath, Mason used the split second to glimpse his surroundings. Roxy was on her knees, delivering blows to her opponent whilst trying to dodge a knife. Quaid and Hassell were still attempting to subdue the third mercenary. Quaid had wrestled the man's gun away as Hassell targeted his body with kicks and punches. None of them wanted to shoot a man unless they were shot at. As a soldier, Mason would have found the tactic hard to accept. But, as a civilian, as the man he was now, he understood it and clung to the ideal. They couldn't sink lower than their enemies.

Mason had fallen to the ground. Now, he reared up and raised both elbows, aiming to bring them down onto his assailant's skull, but the man rose with him, struggled to his feet and kneed Mason in the face. Mason rolled back and jumped up, clutching the back of the Range Rover. The merc still had hold of his knife. He thrust now, a little left and then a little right, making Mason dance to each side to avoid the thrusts. He forced Mason around the side of the car.

When the man attacked again, Mason used a new tactic, knowing he was superior. He closed down the space they operated in by jumping into the back seat of the Range Rover. When the man followed, knife first, Mason clamped down on the arm and twisted it. The merc yelled out in pain and then followed Mason further into the back seat. Mason punched with both fists, landing solid blows. The other man's face grew bloodied and bruised. His shoulders slumped. Mason leaned in but the merc rose up, heaving Mason into the roof of the car. Mason's right shoulder hit hard, sending a shockwave of pain through him. He fell face first onto the back seat. The merc drove forward with elbows, battering the top of Mason's head. Mason struck out with a jab to the throat, following up with stiffened fingers to the eyes. The merc, blinded momentarily but situationally aware, changed tactics, leaning back and swinging his legs up off the floor, plunging his boots into Mason's midriff.

The back seats were already slick with blood. Mason slid further inside, away from the punishment. He used the grab handle to lift himself and deliver a kick of his own, one that connected solidly with his opponent's face and made him stagger and fall into the footwell. Mason spent two seconds taking a breather and then fell on the man, pummelling and punching and taking care to evade the ever more desperate slashes of the knife.

Mason made sure the guy was crushed down into the footwell and targeted his ribs and head. His knuckles ached, his fists were bruised and bloody. By the time the merc finally lapsed into unconsciousness, Mason was spent. He slumped over the man's body for several seconds before forcing himself back out of the car.

Onto the concrete. Knees first.

Pain swept through his nervous system. The first thing he saw was his discarded gun. He shuffled towards it, still on his knees, hoping to use it as a deterrent to stop the fighting.

Roxy had relieved her opponent of his knife and then given it straight back, only instead of delivering it to his hand she had shoved it to the hilt into his stomach. The merc was staggering and clutching the handle now, wavering on his feet. Roxy performed a spin kick that connected with his forehead and sent him flying back to land hard on his spine, the knife still sticking from his stomach.

Quaid and Hassell circled their opponent, who appeared to have a broken arm. The good arm held a black-handled blade, the kind the military might use, and the guy clearly knew how to use it. Quaid's arms were bloody and Hassell winced every time he used his right leg. Both men were injured. Mason scooped up his Glock and aimed it at the merc.

'Give up,' he said. 'Stand down now.' The fact that Johann was not among the mercenaries both surprised and pleased him. Their enemies had to be using numerous teams.

The merc threw a quick glance at him, and then seemed to take in the entirety of the scene for the first time. His eyes registered that he was alone.

Two of his compatriots were dead. The others were unconscious. Clearly sensing he was in trouble, the merc backed away.

'Hands up.' Quaid found his gun. 'Turn around.'

The merc glared at them. 'You guys aren't gonna shoot me,' he grated. 'You woulda done it already. You want me, old man, come and get me.' He brandished the knife.

But Quaid had had enough. Aiming carefully, he shot the man in the meat of his thigh. Mason recalled enough of his training to know he'd purposely missed everything vital and that the merc would be okay with medical treatment. The man crashed to the ground, yelling.

Hassell kicked the knife away. Mason took a moment to review the scene, which brightened his demeanour considerably. They had dealt fairly and fully with men who were trying to kill them.

Mason made his way to the merc with the thigh wound. 'Who do you work for?' he asked.

'Go to hell.'

'It's no skin off your nose,' Mason said. 'I'm not gonna tell anyone you grassed. Hey, we'll leave you alive too. Just say that you lost us, not that we beat you. Save face, maybe save your job. Just tell me who you work for.'

The merc's expression changed, taking on a speculative aspect. 'The guy who hired us . . .' the merc said. 'He's crazy. A first-class psycho. I wouldn't cross him. Name's McCloud. Everyone knows it. He wants it that way. You don't impede him, don't resist. If you do . . . Well, you vanish.'

'Vanish?' Mason was jolted out of the moment.

'Yeah, gone for ever. This McCloud, he's a madman. A rich fuck with a serial killer complex. He's the god of death, man.'

'Sounds very scary.' Roxy wandered over. 'I'm shaking in my boots. You say his name's McCloud. But who does he work for?'

'McCloud don't work for anyone, you bitch. He is the boss. Don't you listen? I'm giving you prime meat here.'

'Bitch?' Roxy grated and as her hands flexed. Mason knew they were just aching to lock around the man's throat.

'Big mistake,' Hassell said. 'The only person who can call Roxy a bitch is Roxy.'

Mason stepped in quickly. 'This McCloud's working alone?'

'No, no, he's with some other sick fucks too. A dozen of them. They're untouchables. Call themselves the Guild of—'

The sudden roar of an engine froze the words in his throat. Mason spun to see the second Range Rover powering into the car park, men hanging out on all sides, guns in hand, the dented front grille charging towards them.

'Scatter!' he yelled.

# Chapter 20

The black Range Rover bellowed as it bounced up the irregular slope into the car park. Its underside scraped against the concrete. The men hanging out of the windows were thrown up and down, at least one of them dropping his weapon.

Mason pulled out his gun and ran for cover. The nearest was the first Range Rover, which was parked askew to the entrance. Mason positioned himself behind the rear tyre and sighted on the newcomers.

Roxy had had the same idea and hunkered down next to him. Sally was still huddled in the back seat of their car. Quaid and Hassell ran forward and ducked behind the rear wheel.

The big car's tyres came to a crunching stop in the gravel that was scattered atop the car park's surface. The mercenaries didn't give any warning shots; they fired as soon as they were able. Bullets punched into metal to the side of Mason's head and at least two flew around the front and back of the car, narrowly missing their own men.

There were angry shouts and violent threats as the men exited their vehicle.

'They're tired of chasing us,' Quaid said. 'Poor souls. Probably want to get back to their diets of red meat.'

'And baby oil,' Hassell said.

Mason didn't let them settle. As soon as their vehicle was stationary, he let loose several rounds. He didn't pop his head up though. There was entirely too much lead flying around.

'We have as much firepower as they do,' Roxy said. 'And we're four to their five. We need to pick them off fast.'

Mason agreed. But the mercs were covering his team's ability to advance with unending gunfire. The sound of their bullets split the evening. Mason, sitting on his haunches with his back to the wheel, could see the last crimson streaks of the setting sun across the far horizon.

He took a quick look along the stoic line his team made. 'We all go together,' he said. 'On three.' He knew they couldn't let the mercs approach their car unchallenged. They'd just pour around the front and back, firing as they came, giving their enemies no chance at all.

'One, two, three.'

Into the heat of their own gunfire Mason and his team went, the action reminding Mason of years past in the army. He stayed low, coming around the bonnet of the car. Directly in front, he saw two pairs of running legs. Mason knew the owners' aim would be on the vehicle. He opened fire quickly, and was surprised when Roxy appeared below him, at full stretch, on her stomach, also shooting.

Their bullets thudded into the mercenaries. They were big men, and took the bullets in the chest, the force of the impact knocking them down. Quaid and Hassell must have had a similar effect at the back of the car because, abruptly, all the gunfire stopped.

A heavy silence filled the air.

Mason watched his enemies collapse. Roxy scrambled to her knees, still aiming. The men hit the concrete with a thud, their guns flying from their nerveless fingers. It was that fact above all else that convinced Mason they were down for good.

He stepped around the car. Roxy was at his side. Towards the back, two men lay groaning, shot through the stomach, with Quaid and Hassell approaching them. The only man standing was the driver, who had exited his vehicle a few seconds later than the others and saved himself from getting shot.

'Hands in the air,' Mason said.

The driver complied. Mason didn't lower his gun. He waited for Hassell to walk over and frisk the man, relieving him of a concealed handgun and a knife.

'There's no time to waste,' Sally said over their ear-based comms system. 'We still have to check out the little round church.'

Mason knew exactly what she was getting at.

'You,' he said to the driver. 'You idiots created a lot of noise, which means the police forces from three bloody counties are gonna be converging on us. We're going to leave you free, so that you can clean it up.'

Roxy grasped his shoulder. 'Is that wise?'

'What else can we do? Some are wounded, some are dead. We can't stay here. At worst, these guys can delay the police. At best, they can clear up and leave nothing for the police to find. It's in their interest to do so.'

'And we leave without having to explain.' Roxy sounded impressed. 'I like it.'

If he was being honest, Mason wasn't sure he agreed with his own plan. He didn't like leaving the mercs free for the police to find, even the ones that were wounded. Too many variables. But what else could he do? Sally was right. The round church was their priority, and they couldn't kill their enemies on the spot.

'I'd love to interrogate them,' Roxy said, looking over the downed men.

'I bet. But we don't have time. We squeezed some info from the other guy. That'll have to do.'

Quaid's voice came over the comms. 'We should move.'

Mason made them collect all the discarded guns and throw them into their boot. He then urged the mercenary driver to get on with rounding up his men and getting the hell out of there. Quaid jumped behind the wheel of their car.

Sally was ready in the back seat.

'To the church,' she said.

Mason slammed his door closed and tapped the dashboard. 'Quickly.'

# Chapter 21

They exited the car park at a steady speed, turned left and followed the road back to the little round church. It took them just a few minutes. Mason used the time to clean up as best he could and to examine his aching knuckles. A quick look at his teammates showed a bedraggled bunch with ripped clothing. They were covered in cuts and bruises, their eyes wide, expressions almost wild.

'Smarten yourselves up,' he said. 'We don't want the vicar to suspect anything.'

'It's gone six-thirty,' Sally said with disappointment in her voice. 'He won't let us in.'

'Then don't park too close,' Hassell said quietly. 'You know my speciality.'

Mason nodded. Quaid passed the church and pulled in as soon as he was able. Together, they left the car, smoothed down their clothes and started walking towards their destination.

'Good job back there,' Mason said as they walked. 'We worked as a team. Worked well.'

'It was shoot or be shot,' Roxy said. 'No choice.'

'You don't have to convince yourself,' Mason said, ears still ringing from the recent gunfire. 'We did the right thing.'

'I know.'

'Sorry. It sounded like you were wallpapering over a few cracks.'

'With all the old bodies and kills in my head, it'd need a superstore full of the stuff,' Roxy said without any sense of exaggeration. 'But I believe that, today, we did the right thing.'

'Kill or be killed,' Quaid said. 'No choice. I'm just shocked I remembered my training and managed not to kill anyone.'

'You always will,' Mason said. 'Like it or not. But it worries me that Johann didn't turn up.'

'How so?' Roxy turned to him.

'Because it means they have numerous teams working on this,' Mason said. 'I don't think that's a good sign.'

'There was a time I thought I was James Bond,' Quaid reflected as they walked and smelled the cool night air. 'Long time ago, mind you. I had this glorified image in my head as I walked and talked army life, completed my missions. It was everything I wanted. Wasn't until I became a leader that I saw all the bullshit unfolding. Realised that it's all just a terrible game of power, wealth, brinkmanship and manipulation. They'll let a hundred men die to gain an inch of ground on a positive bluff, a thousand to politick their way into some higher form of office. They have no scruples, these men in power. No sense of real right and wrong. They are flesh-eaters and they do not care what form of carrion they consume.'

Mason knew that Quaid's profound words deserved more than a quick offhand answer. Quaid had joined them through a sense of purpose and a desire to help people in need. He needed to forget the events that happened whilst he was in the army, the unspeakable orders he'd followed, but also to realise it wasn't his fault – it was the fault of the higher-ups and their self-motivating agendas. Mason fought for the right words, but just then the little round church came into view to their left. The whole group fell silent. Mason was reminded that it was medieval, dating back to the fourteenth century. The circular nave fronted a low oblong building and, Mason saw, the front door was currently wide open.

'No.' He felt a sense of doom and started to run.

Sally had seen it too. Together, they crossed the road with the others behind and ran towards the property's main gate. The main street that ran through Little Maplestead was currently clear of traffic. Mason pushed through the little gate and ran up the path that led to the front of the church.

He slowed at the entrance, once more plucking his gun from his waistband. He felt like he'd done it entirely too much today, but this mission was becoming more dangerous by the hour. What had started off as a monotonous journey and then a fist fight had fast turned into a lethal encounter.

'These basins are hot bloody property,' he said quietly.

'Doesn't that prove their worth?' Sally commented.

Mason didn't answer, now crossing the threshold into the church's interior. He slowed to let his eyes adjust; the gathering darkness outside wasn't as intense as the shadow-land that held sway inside the ancient building.

Mason stayed close to the entrance, staring into the darkness. It was utterly silent inside. Unidentified hulks stood on all sides, unmoving. He waited until he was sure they weren't about to be ambushed, and he could discern at least most of the shapes that stood ahead.

'Going in,' he said for the sake of the others.

He entered the nave, seeing pews to either side and an altar at the far end. White walls supported a timber-beamed ceiling. There were no steps leading up to the altar, but there was a bulk of blackness lying before it, an outline that made Mason's heart leap.

He rushed forward down the aisle. He reached the unmoving figure seconds later and reached out. His left hand encountered a still warm body but a quick check for a pulse showed him that the man was dead.

'Is that the vicar?' Sally's voice was strained behind him. 'Oh, no. They killed him?'

Mason had suspected it as soon as he saw the figure. That was where the second Range Rover and its occupants had been. They'd been here, checking out the church.

And murdering its vicar.

'I'm so glad we shot them,' Hassell said earnestly.

'Shit,' Roxy said. 'All the guy wanted was to walk his little dog.'

Mason bowed his head and, even though he wasn't religious, said a quick prayer for the vicar. Seeing the sacrifice and blood of innocents never failed to infuriate him. Something he'd seen far too often in his army days. But there was nothing he could do here. The vicar's killers had already been dealt with . . .

. . . and some let go.

Mason couldn't dwell on that now. He rose, turned around and grabbed Sally's shoulders. 'We're here for the painting,' he said, aiming to divert her thoughts. 'Search for that.'

Sally let out a shuddering breath, turned and started scanning the walls. It wasn't a difficult process. Mason saw only three hanging pieces running down the length of the nave.

'It's not here,' she said quickly.

'Would they have taken it with them?' Hassell said with anger in his voice. 'Was it inside one of the cars we've just left behind?'

Mason cursed silently at that irony. 'It's the most likely scenario,' he said.

What now?

Sally hadn't given up. 'There has to be a storeroom,' she said. 'Maybe a vestry.' She ran the length of the nave, stepped past the vicar and checked the far side. She walked back to the front and scanned the walls there, her body language becoming more fraught by the minute.

'They could have destroyed it,' Quaid said. 'Maybe we should check the grounds too.'

Mason thought that a good idea and was about to respond when Sally spoke up.

'They didn't destroy it,' she said. 'They left it right here.'

She stood staring up at a wall. Mason left the vicar's side and walked over to her. There, just above head height, was a rectangular painting with a frame made of stained oak. The wooden border was lap jointed in the style of the earliest frames, with its sides overlapping at the corners.

'What is that?' Roxy peered over Mason's shoulder.

Sally took out her phone and started taking photos. She roved around the painting, trying every angle, clicking away. Mason stared at the old canvas.

'Is that a monastery?' he asked.

It was a dim representation; a tall building surrounded by a wreath of fog. Some indistinct shapes that might have been trees, a winding river, a battered fence. It had a high central tower with other wings and annexes all around it, but nothing was clear-cut. It was as though the artist wanted his depiction to be vague.

'Maybe a convent? An abbey? A priory?' Sally said as she continued to take her pictures. 'Who knows? That's for us to figure out. I don't know why the mercenaries left it here, but I'm grateful that they did. Just a couple more shots.'

Mason thought about her words. 'Remember the Amori?' he said. 'They were almost as conscientious as us about not destroying or stealing history, at least at the beginning. They deteriorated rapidly, I guess, but did respect relics.'

'You believe this is the Amori again?' Quaid asked.

'It better not be,' Hassell said. 'It'd mean Marduk escaped.'

'He could do that,' Roxy said.

Mason shook his head. 'No, I don't believe it's the Amori. We stopped them. Marduk's in prison. The only person not accounted for is Cassadaga, but this isn't him either. And you all heard what that merc said. It all leads back to some psycho called McCloud.'

'I used to enjoy a bit of McCloud back in the old days,' Quaid reminisced. 'TV programme about a cop who used to ride a horse.'

'Well, I really don't think you're gonna enjoy this McCloud,' Roxy said. 'He sounds like a riot, in the worst sense of the word.'

Sally finished taking photos. Mason led them back outside. He paused to take a last look at the forlorn shape that lay before the round church's altar, shaking his head at the waste, the cold violence of it all. He wondered briefly if some men and women were born without a conscience – or was it life's events that altered them?

Outside, darkness had finally fallen. The sky was a shroud that blanketed the village. Silence stretched from horizon to horizon. Mason imagined guiltily how many mercenaries had survived and if any police had turned up, but he couldn't dwell on that now. His whole team was striding forward, moving into the next phase, ready to take on whatever challenges came their way.

Mason hurried to catch them up.

# Chapter 22

Waiting to die, Murdock McCloud thought. They're all waiting to die, just waiting to join the others under the greensward . . .

He enjoyed gloating over the dead. Loved it, actually. There was nothing more exciting than staring out of your bedroom window across your own lands knowing that an unknown quantity – even he'd lost count – of corpses, cut down by his own hands, lay under those well-preserved lawns. His property. Never laid to rest, never at peace. His to gloat over and rejoice in for as long as he lived.

McCloud was standing at the far end of his tower bedroom where a corner window looked both north and east. He was three storeys up, the impressive castle battlements below. And though nicely insulated in here he could practically feel the Highland winds, the chill bite of the air as it scoured the rolling lands. His greensward lay beyond the gates and to the east, locked in by fences and low stone walls and, if you knew exactly where to look, you could see countless small depressions where the ground had sunk after holes had been filled in.

McCloud's mind turned to the living. There were three more already waiting, just chained in his dungeons and at his leisure, living in utter desolation, terror and filth. He preferred them to be as terrorised as possible; loved to feel the wretched fear radiating off them as he approached. They were now at what he called 'the marinating stage'. On thinking that, his craggy face broke out into a grin and his heart started beating faster. Don't worry, friends, he thought. I will be with you soon. Oh, and you will shudder to see me. The bloody things we will do together . . .

The chime of a precious two-hundred-year-old floor-standing clock snapped him out of the reverie. The real world was intruding. The real world hadn't been this intrusive for years. McCloud took a deep breath, turned away from his window and leapt right into that world. He exited his room and made his way down several twisting, narrow sets of rocky stairs to a ground-floor study. As he walked, he mulled several important issues over in his mind.

The Guild of Night, McCloud and his eleven partners, were chasing the greatest treasure of all. And they appeared to be in competition with a third party. As he pondered this, McCloud tried to still all the emotions he felt – the anger, the frustration – at being made to wait for news of the basins. Emotions clouded the mind. He would not give in to them. Even now, beset with demanding concerns, he sought the cold dark centre of his soul.

'Sir, I have laid your breakfast out in the study.'

McCloud barely noticed the servant, one of four that were bound to him. He hurried on past the well-dressed man, breathing steadily and seeking the dispassion that dwelled within him to chase away the shadows of frustration that crouched over him like a large, predatory bird.

And he found it.

Calm once more, McCloud considered what the Guild of Night knew about the others who appeared to be chasing the Ark.

Since they were a small anonymous chapter within the larger organisation of the Freemasons, the Guild had access to a wealth of information and resources without having to stretch themselves too much. Since their inception in the eighteenth century, they had vowed only to communicate by coded message delivered by courier or face to face and, since they lived all over the United Kingdom, face to face was out of the question. The outmoded way of communication was proving troublesome for McCloud now. It just wasn't fast enough.

Special handshakes if they ever came face to face. Passwords and coded messages if they didn't. They had even developed their own version of the secret Templar alphabet, something only the twelve main members could ever know. McCloud knew that they were a very careful group – he just feared their care was currently harming them.

Be that as it may, he thought. It didn't detract from the fact that an ingenious and capable team were competing with them.

Surely the initial description of them – a company called Quest Investigations, concerned with safely transporting relics between locales – was incomplete? He knew their names, knew their business, but he didn't know a lot more. A mercenary named Johann claimed he knew one of the men. A man named Joe Mason. Apparently, this Mason had been some kind of hot-shot in the army until an IED explosion had taken out two of his friends, an event Mason thought he was responsible for. Mason had frazzled up after that. He quit the army and went to work at a private security firm. That was when Johann lost track of him. Investigations were continuing.

McCloud reached his study, and considered the breakfast that lay spread out on the oblong table at the centre of the room. It was perfect, as expected. The coffee smelled good, and the sight of freshly buttered toast made him feel hungry. McCloud pulled out a chair and sat down.

The Guild of Night were an old and immensely powerful organisation. Always looking to get ahead by twisting information to their own purposes. This is what they used the wider group for. They all lived in large houses scattered across England and Scotland.

*All this wealth, all these resources and might, and yet we use travelling men and women to communicate. There must be a better way.* It hadn't been a significant hindrance until now, McCloud reflected. He took a moment to think about the other eleven members and wondered who might follow him if he asked for a policy change.

Michael Sallow, an Englishman, and McCloud's second in command, would agree. Sallow had always been supportive of McCloud. McCloud also believed he could count on the support of Campbell, a Scotsman, and Barrow, another Englishman but beyond that . . . it was all a bit vague.

A real leader didn't ask for a change unless he knew he could win the vote. Failure was seriously undermining, and McCloud was under no illusions that his position, whilst traditional, was always under threat.

At least, that was how he saw it. McCloud was constantly at war, whether psychologically or actually. It was why he needed those infrequent moments of peace. He had once discussed the issue with Michael Sallow.

'Do you not worry that you will one day get caught? Lose everything?' Sallow had asked him.

'I worry about everything,' McCloud had said. 'But when I feel emotion, deep emotion, I am forced to follow where it leads me. Killing helps soothe the roar in my mind, the loudness of all that emotion.'

'Killing calms you,' Sallow had said with nice insight. 'It brings you peace. I understand that.'

'Do you? Have you partaken?' McCloud sensed a kindred spirit.

'No, no, but we all need a . . . a . . . hobby.'

149

McCloud felt disappointment. 'I see. I see it more of a lifestyle choice. Without murder, I would not be the man you see today.' It was liberating to debate his blood-spattered way of life. McCloud knew that his fellow principal Guild of Night colleague would never discuss it with anyone. 'Without murder,' he said, 'there would be no point.'

That had been years ago. McCloud had progressed to better killings since then. Masterpieces that pacified his raging soul. If it weren't for the everyday business of the Guild consuming him, he would pursue that life full time.

But the Guild distracted him in its way. Look at the issue facing him now as he buttered more of the toast and poured another cup of coffee. Look at the issue of the Molten Sea basins and this new ingredient – this Mason.

It had been a whirlwind few days since the importance of the basins had been realised. After the first two had been discovered in the possession of a wealthy, recently dead couple in a coveted and guarded secret collection that they'd jealously kept for their own pleasure, McCloud had worried that other parties might have also realised their significance. But no red flags had gone up.

However, when those basins had been examined more closely, by learned members in the field, the word had spread like a forest fire that they were a significant find. That they might be worth something. And when their connection to the Temple of Solomon was mooted . . .

The Guild was all over it. They could trace their roots back to the Knights Templar and Saladin. To certain crusades. Indeed, it was the Templars who had survived the dreadful attacks of Friday, 13 October 1307, that created an early form of the Guild, a rogue branch, out of the need for pure vengeance. The Guild was formed from the worst kind of acrimony long ago and it was still run that way at the behest of its ancestors.

It was said that the Knights Templar had looted many treasures. And it was true. Even their own legends spoke of it. They seized temples throughout Christendom and converted the churches of their enemies. They appropriated the Holy Grail and found the Ark of the Covenant. They were the keepers of holy faiths the world over. The greatest soldiers of Christ that ever walked the Earth.

If the basins led to the Tabernacle and then the Temple of Solomon, McCloud had to believe that they would then find the long-lost Ark. But the basins were proving tricky to find. Not least because of the attention they were drawing.

Which brought the name Mason once again to mind. That name was starting to worm its way more and more into his consciousness, much like a virus. Maybe – and here was a thought – just maybe, he could personally kill Mason. Would that work? Would that banish the growing infection that was Mason's name from his thoughts?

McCloud decided right then and there, with coffee staining his lips and the butter knife in hand. He resolved to send a message to his eleven colleagues, one shaped around finding all the Molten Sea basins and sending a huge force to utterly destroy the other team. The thought made him bite his lips until they bled, then made him slowly lick the blood away. It was spine-tingling. They had the wealth and the resources to find anything and make anyone disappear. It was a godly power. And any mercenaries they used couldn't be traced back to them.

And we murder them. We murder the other team. McCloud debated with himself, wondered if he might demand video footage of the murders, but decided the process would be too risky. He was better sticking with what he was good at, what he intimately knew.

Close up, silent and bloody kills that could take days on end.

McCloud summoned an aide by pressing a button on his phone. The man, immaculately dressed, appeared seconds later.

'I want a message sent to the Guild,' he said. 'As fast as possible.'

'Using the Footmen, sir?'

'Yes, yes, tell them to get in their cars and drive to the premium members' dwellings. Use the Alpha handshake along with the code that I will give you. This is top secret and requires an expeditious reply.' McCloud was about to utter the words 'Suggest we take out other team with all prejudice,' but felt that was a little watery. The Guild was sometimes slow to act. He needed to shock them and force them into action. Sitting back, he wiped his lips with a large napkin and said: 'Recommend we obliterate competing entity with utmost prejudice.' That hit the right note.

'Now,' he said after speaking. 'Do my bidding at once. Nothing is more urgent. Do you understand?'

'Yes, sir.'

McCloud poured his third coffee of the morning and took it over to the half-dead hearth where he set about raking the glowing coals. The old castle was cold when the sun cowered behind dark banks of cloud as it did today. McCloud poked and prodded the fire with tongs and a shovel, getting them red-hot and glowing. In his thoughts was an image of a strapped-down figure, a mewling victim whom he could torment for as long as he wished. But, right now, his mind was calm. He didn't crave the release of murder. The message he'd sent to the Guild had temporarily stilled any turbulent feelings.

The only problem was the amount of time it would take his equals to reply. They would lose days. And in days . . . there was no telling how much the other team could accomplish.

McCloud let go of the bittersweet emotion. It did him no good. His mind turned to the seven basins and the great treasure that they might yet reveal.

The Ark of the Covenant.

McCloud ran through the story . . .

# Chapter 23

The Guild of Night, in all its forms, had hated the Church since the events of 1307. Finding and flaunting the Ark would hurt the Church badly because it was so indelibly entwined with their history, their literature, their law. Of course, the Templars had taken possession of the Ark in earlier centuries, but the Church had been aware of that. And the Church had tortured many Templars to learn of the Ark's location.

The Tabernacle was the dwelling place of God, a portable tent constructed by Moses. Inside this sanctuary were kept many valuable items. The Tabernacle ultimately made its way to the Temple of Solomon, the new incarnation of God's presence, and resided there until the physical temple's destruction around 586 BC. Of course, the great treasures that the temple held would have been spirited away far in advance of its downfall.

Which brought McCloud's thoughts around to the Molten Sea basins. The tangible pair had now been found and they would lead to the five not so tangible ones – the ones that existed as pictures or paintings or carvings. All of them carried clues to a specific location.

But to where? Where was the most likely resting place of the Ark of the Covenant? McCloud longed to know. But he was getting ahead of himself.

In the fourteenth century the Templars had smuggled the Ark away from the violence and volatility along with many other treasures. Some said it had been brought here, to Scotland, others to Europe or further afield. One thing was for sure – the Templars had known about and revered the Ark for more than a century.

McCloud tried to imagine a scenario where the greatest Templar treasures would finally be in the possession of the Guild of Night. This was the closest they had come in six hundred years. The trail of clues that led to the Ark had been conjured up in the fifteenth century, an elaborate enigma-blazed path that would lead to their holy of holies. The Grand Master of the time, a man named William Baillie, had decided that weighty and crucial secrets were best kept hidden, for even among the Templars, the Freemasons and the Guild, there were those who might be swayed or forced to betray their brethren. William Baillie knew that flesh was weak – it could be persuaded in many ways.

Baillie was also a liberal – he couldn't decide if the Guild should have access to the treasures, but couldn't take it away from them either. After all, it was their forefathers who had wrested it away from the Holy Land and all its bloodshed; brave and desperate men who had walked dark and dangerous byways to bring these valuables home.

So Baillie concocted an elegant shadow trail using the Molten Sea basins, the idea being that if someone could solve the puzzle then they would deserve the treasures, but first he concealed the Ark and all the riches of Solomon's Temple. Baillie was a great historical figure in the Freemasons but, more importantly, he was the greatest Grand Master of the Guild of Night.

Of course, Baillie could never have imagined that the two main basins would end up in the hands of a pair of covetous old collectors, people that shunned the outside world. Their premature deaths had been a stroke of luck.

McCloud left his study and decided to take a wander down to the dungeons. It wouldn't hurt to whet his appetite for future killings. What else did he have to do right now? The latest reports had come in – those telling of the presence of the skilful, hostile team set against them in the search for the basins.

Which left time to . . . kill.

McCloud paced out of the study, along a freezing corridor and through the main hall. He steered his way towards the kitchens but stopped before a metal-strapped wooden door set into an old block wall. He produced a black key, unlocked it and took out a torch. The door opened to reveal a narrow twisting stairway leading into dark depths.

McCloud negotiated his way down the nausea-inducing stairs, twisting back on himself three times before reaching the bottom. The flags down here were damp, slicked with water. They were irregular too, their joints full of moss. The walls were also damp, and black, the ceiling sharply angled as if struggling under the weight of the castle above. There was the constant drip of water echoing through the place, the smell of mould and the taste of fear in the air.

McCloud loved it. Silence reigned, yet he knew three people cowered in the shadows behind their wrought-iron cell doors. He knew they knew he was here – and every one of them longed to be overlooked.

'Don't worry,' he said, feeding their terror. 'I am only here for one of you.'

McCloud guffawed, loving every moment of it. Adrenalin flooded his veins, making him feel alive. The dungeons were currently the abode of three drifters who had been plucked from the streets of Glasgow – two men and one woman. These people would not be missed. They were rarely noticed by the general public despite being in their faces almost every day. The public preferred to believe they were not there – so when they went missing nobody noticed. At least, nobody who mattered.

McCloud came close to the first cell. The stink was almost tangible – a mix of nervous sweat, filth and disease. McCloud drank it in deeply as he set eyes on a man with long white hair and a sunken face, a man who shivered under old rags in the frozen dark. McCloud chuckled. There would be no easing up on the wretch – not until he drew his last agonised breath.

McCloud moved on to the second cell, and then the third. The occupants of both were kneeling, holding out beseeching hands in silence. The vision was odd, but appealing. McCloud loved the sight of the man and woman begging him for a reprieve. They could not know that the sight of them pleading made his blood run hot.

He rattled the second cage, as though preparing to enter, and enjoyed the terrified whimpers of its occupant. He crossed over to a far wall where several torture instruments hung, all in plain sight of the cells. He produced a whetstone then pulled down the axe and spent a few moments sharpening the edge.

Is it time to break some rules?

The Guild operated well by following its ancient guidelines. McCloud had just set in motion a new method of communication – but was that going to be good enough? The modern age demanded faster messaging, immediate back-and-forth contact. Perhaps a new mode of exchange needed to be put in place. He was certain that the Church, even the Pope, sent a text message now and then.

Where had it all gone wrong?

The French persecution of 1307 had destroyed all the bonds that existed between the Templars and the Church. The horrible confessions the Church had extracted under torture were designed to meet a list of false charges and relied on recruited so-called witnesses, most of whom had been expelled from the Templar order for serious wrong-doing. Even Vatican scholars in later years admitted that the confessions were contradictory and the fact that they were venerated later, in 1308, by papal decree did not help those thousands who had died in disbelief and agony.

The Guild of Night were far from the initial godfearing manifestation of the Knights Templar.

There were no prayers, no meditation. No metaphorical nourishment of the so-called 'meat from God'. Spiritual discipline became a whole different regulation that involved swords, chanting and bloodletting. An order that had once embodied classical Christianity became something else altogether.

There was an old slogan, McCloud recalled, used by early crusading Templars in the eleventh and twelfth centuries: 'We shall slay for God's love.' McCloud thought how that simple sentence now seemed incredibly twisted and profound when you related it to Templar history. It was deep, deeper than bedrock, embedded in their philosophy.

McCloud threw the axe down. His mood had changed. It was cold down here in the dungeons, too cold for a man as consequential as he.

It was time to take hold of this new quest with both hands and properly wring its neck. Time to take charge. The Guild of Night would come out of this either wreathed in glory or teeming with condemnation.

McCloud determined it would be the former. Any action could be taken. There were no limits. The Ark must come back to the Guild. It was their birthright, a part of their history. McCloud could only imagine how hard the Church would fight for it once the actual graft of finding it was done.

Not while I'm alive, he thought. I promise to slay for my God's love. To assassinate, to massacre, to remove every obstacle.

There could be no other outcome to this pursuit than the complete victory of the Guild of Night.

# Chapter 24

Their car journey through the night was, at first, as sombre as a wake. Mason couldn't get an image of Little Maplestead's dead vicar out of his head, the senseless loss of life, the brute force that these mercenaries employed just because they could, with no thought for consequence or innocence or lifelong trauma. Everyone else stayed silent too, as if they were all stuck in the same sorrowful loop.

Quaid drove aimlessly at first, but eventually started making his way across to the A1, one of England's main arteries. They had been on the go all day – bruised, aching and bloody – and needed to recuperate.

Quaid found a hotel as the evening deepened and a light squall swept the land. The team stepped out of the car onto a crunchy, gravel-strewn driveway, bent their heads against the weather and made their way to the revolving front doors. Mason made sure to take his backpack that contained the golden basin with him.

Eight minutes later they were alone in their rooms.

Mason locked the door, wedged a chair against the doorknob, dropped his backpack on the floor and then stretched out across the crisp white sheets. He closed his eyes, letting the events of the last few hours wash on through. His mind reverberated, but it also yearned for peace. He recalled the feeling of burnout after his friends had been killed in Mosul, the event that changed his life and took him out of the army and into the security job for Patricia. Mason was still trying to believe in himself after that long-ago day's failure.

And the quiet moments fed the voices of irrationality that still resonated through his mind.

Mason sat up, tired, aching, but not yet ready to quit. He reversed his action of a few moments ago, hefted the backpack and headed down to the hotel bar. The sign on the door told him it'd be closing in about thirty minutes, but that was okay. Mason had never been a heavy drinker, but a big day and a reproving conscience affirmed that he might need something to take the edge off.

There was only one other person at the bar. He walked over and sat next to the raven-headed woman, who was drinking rum.

'Bad day?' he asked.

'They're all bad,' she said. 'But some go quicker than others.'

'You seen your room yet?'

'Nah. Figured I'd get to that later.'

Mason thought it was typical of Roxy to drink first and rest later, but said nothing. 'We never spoke much about that episode in the cemetery,' he said. 'Wanna talk now?'

'Back in London? We only have half an hour, Joe. I doubt that's long enough to dissect all my evils.'

'Your own self-analysis put you off your game,' he said. 'In a deadly situation. I don't want that to happen again.'

Roxy turned to him, raising her glass towards her lips. 'I was distracted,' she said. 'By the one issue that consumes me. I can't promise you anything.'

'Then we'll have to help you through it,' he said, ordering a double whisky. 'What's the next step?'

160

'I don't measure it that way.' She shrugged. 'I can't quantify my inner demons, Joe. I only wish that I could.'

It made sense. Roxy was raising her barriers slowly, day by day, fencing off the past. You couldn't attach a calculation to that.

'We'll get through it together.' He raised his glass and clinked hers. The bar was warm and dark, and threw shadows across her face. He couldn't tell whether she smiled or grimaced.

'Or die trying,' she said quietly.

Mason drank his whisky and, later, drifted away, leaving Roxy with her elbows resting on the bar. Returning to his room, he put the chair back in place, dumped the backpack and turned out the lights.

Mason was worn out, but sleep was still a long time coming.

Breakfast found them scooping up platefuls of fried food at the buffet, toasting bread and drinking endless cups of coffee. Mason made sure the backpack was resting against his right shin before taking his attention off it and examining the team. Despite getting sleep the night before, they were all tired. Quaid hadn't shaved yet, and sported a face full of greying bristles. Hassell sat with his head down, speaking even less than usual. Sally looked like she wanted to shovel the whole breakfast into her mouth quickly and get started on her research.

Only Roxy seemed comparatively unfazed, sitting with her usual aplomb, looking as hard as they came. It was difficult to reconcile that Roxy with the one who was searching for the softness of youth that she'd never known, the woman she might have been. The quest consumed her.

Mason decided to open the conversation. 'How about' – he started carefully – 'we stop driving around aimlessly? We take the day, or days, here and let Sally decipher the new clues in relative peace?'

'Should we stay in one place for too long?' Roxy asked.

Hassell nodded his agreement with Mason. 'As far as I can tell, they aren't hunting us. They're enmeshed in their own quest. Of course, we'll take the usual precautions, but I think we'll be safe.'

'Hours,' Sally said.

Mason frowned at her. 'What?'

'You said deciphering the clues would take me a day . . . or days. I'm telling you it will take hours.'

'Which should give Quaid time to get that grey out of his bristles,' Hassell said, trying to lighten the mood.

Quaid fixed him with narrow eyes. 'What grey?'

But Sally's words settled it for Mason. They would remain at the hotel, maybe book for an extra night just in case. He was also aware that the longer they took to crack the clue, the less chance there was of finding all seven basins first.

'No grey?' Hassell asked Quaid around a mouthful of toast.

'No grey.' Quaid frowned back at him.

'Which reminds me,' Mason said out of nowhere. 'Those mercenaries killed the vicar, but they didn't vandalise the painting in Little Maplestead.'

Sally thought about that and then nodded. 'We had a similar thing with the Amori,' she said.

'Are we talking the Freemasons here?' Quaid ventured. 'So far, the Knights Templar have featured quite heavily from the Temple of Solomon to the church in Baldock. Is the Little Maplestead painting a piece of Freemason history?'

'As I said before,' Sally replied, shaking her head, 'the Freemasons these days are a benign and charitable organisation—'

'But that doesn't mean they don't harbour a few bad eggs,' Mason put in.

Sally shrugged. 'I guess that's possible. But I do hope they keep leaving the clues in situ.'

162

'We have two clues to decipher now,' Quaid said. 'The painting and the one from the original basin that Roger Beat was working on.'

'Then let's get to work.' Sally pushed away from the table, reached down and picked up her laptop bag. Then she exited the restaurant and started looking for a quiet place to sit down in the lobby where she wouldn't be interrupted. Three minutes later, she was ready.

Mason lingered at the table a moment. 'I just wanted to check,' he said, catching their attention, 'that you're all all right with this. It wasn't what we expected from our first job.' He saw them as family and valued their opinions deeply.

'They tried to kill us,' Hassell said simply.

'Whatever works,' Roxy answered. 'The deeper we go the better.'

'It's not what we expected,' Quaid agreed. 'But it is still the job. We're doing the right thing here. These people are killers, and they don't care who they walk over to get the job done. I'm in all the way, a team player.'

Mason was glad to hear their opinions, even happier to know they harmonised with his own. He nodded and left the table after asking Quaid and Hassell to reconnoitre their perimeter. They would stay in touch using the comms system.

'I'm starting with the earlier clue,' Sally told him as he approached. 'The one that was written around the rim of the basin. We'll save the painting clue for later.'

Mason watched her log into her account and bring up the Rusk Notes. They were seated in a corner of the lobby with wraparound windows to their right and their backs, large potted plants to their left. The plush blue seats were comfortable if a little threadbare. The large lobby bustled with activity as people came and went for breakfast, and then started to quieten as ten a.m. approached.

Roxy sat beside Sally, not watching her but keeping a close eye on the passing people. Sally plucked a notebook out of her pocket and consulted the writings inside.

'I believe it is an example of the secret Templar alphabet,' she said excitedly after some time. 'Look – these are the symbols that circumvent the lip of the basin.'

◁▽▷ ◁◊▷▽◁ △▽▷△▷

◁▽▷ ◁◊◊▷△▽▷✕ ▷▷▽◊

Mason studied the odd markings. 'Can you translate?'

'There is a key,' Sally said. 'Reverse engineered, so to speak, from the only three texts of the secret Templar alphabet known to exist. My father studied it briefly when he visited Paris, the home of at least one of the texts. Now, I believe the key is public knowledge. But I also have it here on a secure server that I can access remotely.' She tapped on the keys of her laptop. 'Yes, here it is. Now, let's see what I can do.'

Sally started comparing the photographs of the symbols that Roger Beat's staff had sent them to the secret alphabet's key.

'It's a comparatively simple alphabet,' she mused aloud as she worked. 'Each symbol is a piece of the cross of the Order of the Temple. It is the cross of eight points, or eight beatitudes. The letters are represented in compliance with angles and points determined by the cross. Do you see?'

Sally turned her computer screen around to face Mason who saw little more than an ordered jumble of pointed diagrams, all drawn in blue. When Sally spun the laptop around once more, he was none the wiser.

'Here we go,' she said, leaning forward. 'Now listen: The First Lodge. The Timeworn Desk.' She sat back. 'That's it. The next clue.'

Mason blinked at her. 'The first lodge? The timeworn desk? What the hell does any of that mean?'

'A hint towards the Freemasons?' Roxy asked.

'Technically, the Freemasons meet *as* a lodge, not in a lodge,' Sally said. 'But the term is commonly used to mean any building, too.'

'You mentioned that the Freemasons are a good, honourable organisation these days,' Mason said. 'But everything continues to point at them.'

'To be a mason you must be of good morals and reputation and be able to financially support your family,' Sally told them. 'Be able to pass interviews and inquiries. You must be able to come of your own free will and believe in some kind of supreme being.'

Mason frowned at the last. 'You mean God?'

'Not necessarily,' Sally said without looking up. 'God, or the Supreme Being, could also be interpreted as the hidden answer to the mystery of existence. If you don't believe in God, you surely still believe in the mystery. There has to be something beyond the reaches of the material world, right?'

Mason couldn't say that he'd ever truly contemplated such an idea. For a soldier, life was like a bullet. It either passed you by, left a nasty scrape or hit you head on. There wasn't a lot to see beyond what was in front of you.

'You're saying that human existence is still a mystery despite scientific progress?' Roxy said. 'That's the supreme being?'

'It could be,' Sally said. 'A Freemason has the freedom to choose which supreme being he believes in. But, as we have already said, we're not up against the Freemasons. Perhaps a splinter group.'

Mason brought them back to the point. 'We're looking for the first lodge,' he said. 'And a timeworn desk. That must mean something to somebody.'

'If only we knew a Freemason,' Sally said.

'Don't you?' Mason ventured. 'One of your father's old friends?'

'Joe.' Sally let out a long, frustrated breath. 'You know I won't speak to them. They inhabit a world I've never wanted to be a part of. Privilege, mutual benefit and narrow-mindedness have never sat well with me.'

'Of course,' Mason muttered. 'Sorry.'

'No worries, but you're right. We are looking for the first lodge, and I think I might know how to find it.'

Mason sat back. Roxy wandered off to grab them coffees. Quaid and Hassell reported in that the coast was clear, but they were continuing to monitor the situation. Mason remembered to book their rooms for another night. By the time they all sat back down again, Sally was starting to look pleased with herself. Her fingers flew across the keyboard. 'It seems I don't even need the Rusk Notes for this,' she said. 'The oldest masonic lodge in the world is, comparatively, not that far away from here.'

'How far?' Roxy asked.

'And can you be sure it's the right place?' Mason added.

'I'll get to that,' Sally said. 'But don't worry too much about that. Worry about getting us to Edinburgh as fast as you can.'

# Chapter 25

'Edinburgh?' Mason said. 'That's a helluva long drive.'

'Especially if it turns out to be the wrong building,' Roxy said, only half-joking.

Sally gave her a tight stare. 'The oldest masonic lodge in the world is the Lodge of Edinburgh No.1, called the Grand Lodge of Scotland. It possesses the oldest minute of any masonic lodge in existence, dated to 1599. It operates out of a building in New Town, which dates to 1820. There's no doubt, Roxy.'

'And the Timeworn Desk?' Roxy asked.

'I haven't found any reference to that yet,' Sally admitted. 'I'll keep digging.'

Mason knew Quaid and Hassell were listening in on the open comms and asked for input. After a moment of reflection Quaid spoke up.

'There's always the train,' he said.

'You want to go on a train?' Sally asked in a high-pitched voice. 'A train? We're chasing one of the greatest treasures of all time? And we're taking the train?'

'It is the fastest way,' Mason said. 'And we're travelling light. And you can work in comfort whilst we're on the move.'

'You sound like an advert,' Sally grumbled.

'What's wrong with the train?' Quaid asked.

'Nothing at all. It's just, considering our quest, it doesn't seem right turning up to Edinburgh on a train, that's all.'

'I don't think it matters how we turn up,' Mason said. 'It's what we do when we get there that counts.'

Edinburgh is a city resplendent with contrasts. Old cobbled streets full of lingering mystery stand alongside wide thoroughfares bristling with boutique shops and chain restaurants. Ancient city skylines of old monuments and an impressive craggy castle, if studied closely, also contain modern stadiums and shopping centres. The old rock of Edinburgh vies ferociously with the new foundations as the city modernises but clings hard to its roots. Part of its charm is its unending battle with change, a transformation it embraced in the past when New Town was built, adjustments it neither accepts nor impedes.

Their train pulled into Waverley Station, rattling along the tracks as it approached the platform. Mason was sitting in an aisle seat, the backpack on the luggage shelf above his head. The trip up had been both relaxing and picturesque; some of the scenery they passed around Holy Island was stunning and, for miles, the train had run alongside cliffs and beaches. Mason had been sat beside Hassell for the duration, and made good use of their downtime to confirm his colleague's state of mind.

'How you holding up?' he asked.

Hassell ran a finger down the two narrow tramlines that crossed his right cheek. 'Considering I was in an explosion, not bad.'

'I'm talking about Gido.'

'Oh . . . well, I killed him, didn't I, so I'm better off than he is. Vengeance is sweet.'

'I don't believe that.'

'Gido had Chloe killed, and then manipulated me into

168

working for him for years. You don't think getting revenge for that level of savagery is gonna feel sweet?'

Mason had turned away. 'I don't know.'

'I miss Chloe, I blame myself,' Hassell said. 'I blame the killers. But most of all I blamed Gido. Now, there's a hole where my hatred for him was. I don't know how to fill it. The hatred hasn't fizzled out, the blame hasn't decreased. And let's not forget I'm on the run for the rest of my life.'

'Because of whom you pissed off during your time working for Gido.'

Hassell nodded. 'What would you do, Joe? I know what happened in Mosul. You nurture blame of your own.'

'Nurture?' Mason repeated. 'That's an odd word. Is that how you see it?'

'We tend to hold it close to our hearts, so . . . yeah.'

Mason hadn't thought about it that way. Guilt was such a powerful, debilitating, all-encompassing emotion. It gnawed through your soul like a hungry rodent. 'I'm still struggling,' he admitted. 'I should have done better. But, after, at first all I wanted was to be left alone. To be . . . quiet, you know? I let people down, I failed. I'm trying to come to terms with all that by doing better now.'

'I helped kill the men who killed Chloe,' Hassell said. 'And now I've killed the man who orchestrated her murder to recruit me, a man I worked for. That's some complex shit, man. My head's not big enough to make it all fit.'

Mason nodded. 'So what the hell do you do with all that?'

'Well, you don't bury it,' Hassell said to Mason's relief. 'Maybe I should sneak up on it, a bit at a time.'

Mason wasn't sure if Hassell was joking, but this didn't seem like the time. 'Maybe that's all you can do,' he said. 'But Gido deserved everything he got. And you acted in self-defence. We're not killers in the same way that our enemies are. They have no heart. We don't kill innocent people or non-combatants.'

169

'Is that the key?'

'You're asking the wrong person. I think we're all a bit broken if I'm being honest. Adulthood breaks everyone, sooner or later. You just never stop trying.'

Hassell had nodded and turned to the window. Now, as they stopped in Waverley Station, Mason rose, shrugged into his leather jacket, and pulled the backpack down from the rack. People were already moving along the aisle, heading for the train doors. Mason watched as Roxy got in front of the steady flow to open some space for her friends to get out. Seconds later, they were climbing off the train.

It was a long, windy platform, crammed with commuters, from people carrying large suitcases to others wheeling little trolleys behind them, the rumble of their solid wheels loud on the concrete. Single travellers, couples and families filled the space, forcing Mason and the others to take a steady walk to the exit. As they came out into the station proper, Mason almost immediately saw a long ramp that led to Waverley Bridge, away from the worst of the bustle.

'Follow me.'

Sally had booked them into a hotel room. Mason turned right at the top of the ramp, heading for the New Town. To their left, Old Town stood at a higher perspective, promising narrow alleyways, sharp slopes and seemingly endless flights of steps. Mason walked towards Princes Street, slowing as a noisy tram trundled by.

'Hurry,' Sally said in their midst. 'You might not believe this, but I've fielded three calls today for new jobs. This is taking up all our time.'

'What other jobs?' Quaid asked. 'Anything local?' He smiled to show he was joking.

'Doesn't matter. We can't take on any other jobs. The stakes are too high. We have no choice but to keep pressing forward for the sake of the basins, but more importantly to make sure they don't fall into the wrong hands. That could have terrible consequences.'

Mason had had the luxury of turning jobs away before – he'd tasked Patricia to give him only assignments he thought he could handle, which was how he ended up in the bowels of the Vatican in the first place – but never as part of a team.

'If nothing else,' he said, 'we're gonna be kept busy.'

They crossed Princes Street, walked for a while and then turned right to start up a long slope that led to George Street. Sally announced that their hotel was close. Mason checked the time. Their train journey had taken over four hours, so he wasn't surprised to see that it was mid-afternoon.

'How far is the lodge?' he asked.

'Three minutes,' Sally said. 'Walking.'

He stared at her. 'That close?'

'Yeah, it's literally around the corner.'

'I suggest we do this properly,' Quaid said. 'Check in, leave our bags and then head out to the lodge together.'

Mason agreed. They found their hotel and spent a few minutes in their rooms before meeting down in the lobby. Quaid, as usual, was the last to arrive.

'Am I last?' he said. 'I got busy with my ablutions.'

Roxy frowned. 'Crap, I don't know what that means, and I don't want to know. Shall we go?'

They exited their hotel and found themselves on George Street, which was a wide thoroughfare that stretched east to west as far as Mason could see. Cars were parked along an island in the centre of the street. An open-top bus rumbled by, filled with tourists. Black taxis dropped people off up and down the street. Mason waited for Sally to get her bearings, taking in the atmosphere, the contented, expectant buzz that seemed to fill the Edinburgh air.

'It's this way,' she said, pointing north. 'We're looking for Hill Street.'

171

Mason checked for any signs of their enemies as they walked, noting that Hassell was doing the same. Quaid was quizzing Sally.

'This lodge,' he said. 'Is it open to the public?'

'It was,' Sally said. 'Infrequently. At the moment, however, it's closed.'

'That could prove a little tricky.'

'For whom?' Hassell said. 'Not for us.'

'I'd rather not break into a masonic lodge if we don't have to,' Quaid said. 'And what do we know of this desk?'

'The Timeworn Desk,' Sally said. 'It was the second part of the riddle. I couldn't find any mention of it. Not in the Rusk Notes, not among any old scribblings that my father left, not online. It feels like a dead end.'

'Then why are we here?' Roxy asked.

'Well, it's not that much of a dead end,' Sally said. 'But it is worrying.'

'Are you saying that we could be in the wrong place?' Mason asked.

Sally shrugged. 'Hey, I'm not perfect. I work with what I have. The Rusk Notes are not perfect. There's a lot of guesswork.'

'A long way to come on a guess,' Hassell said. 'A lot of time lost if we're wrong.'

'There will always be a misstep along the way,' Sally said. 'It's the way of hunting for relics. Obviously, it's an imperfect science. We're dealing with clues that were left hundreds of years ago, sometimes by desperate people. Following their logic isn't always possible.'

Their mood darkened so that even the lively buzz that surrounded them failed to invigorate them.

'I'm just pointing out that we can't rely on everything being solved through research,' Sally said. 'Sometimes you just have to get lucky or delve much deeper.

'Freemasons,' she went on, 'are used to keeping their work close to their chests. Now, Freemasonry's guiding principle is the skill of stonemasonry: styling itself upon fraternities of medieval stonemasons who used secret words and symbols to identify each other and protect their work from outsiders. These symbols can be carvings in buildings, seemingly obscure. In fact, the more obscure the better. They can come in the form of secret codes or even hand-shakes.' Sally paused as she waited to cross the road, looking out for traffic.

'How does that help?' Quaid asked.

'It got me thinking that maybe the Timeworn Desk is a Freemason secret. It would date back to the time of the Templars, so maybe it's a Knights Templar secret too. Something kept through the centuries. It turns out that the Timeworn Desk is the original desk on which the minutes of 1599 were written – but more than that. It was used by the first Templars that came to Scotland in the fourteenth century, those who fled here to escape the persecution. It's the oldest-known desk in Templar history.'

'Because all the others were destroyed,' Quaid said.

'Most probably. I found references first in ancient Freemason minutes, in cross-references to Edinburgh and especially when the 1820 building was first used to house the old lodge. It was moved there, you see, in a very reverent ceremony. The ancestors of the old Templars must have venerated it, knowing its history and its worth. Before that, the Templar histories tell of a valued desk that came from the Holy Lands, but give no name for it. I guess that came later.'

'Edinburgh has big ties to Freemasonry,' Quaid said. 'Even I know that. There are buildings everywhere dedicated to the order, even shops. Ask a taxi driver to show you Freemason Edinburgh and he'll know exactly where to go.'

'It's understandable if the order began here,' Sally said. 'We're right where we should be.'

'More than that,' Roxy said, slowing. 'This is Hill Street.' She pointed to her right.

Mason rolled his shoulders and took a slow look around. 'Be ready,' he said.

# Chapter 26

Hill Street was a narrow, cobbled road with cars parked along its right-hand kerb. A white van drove between the brick buildings that loomed on both sides as Mason watched, its red lights flashing constantly as it took extra care passing the parked vehicles. A blue car tried and failed twice to reverse into one of the empty parking spots.

Hill Street was a one-way, nondescript path to another basin, the hidden way that led to the Ark. It had already occurred to Mason that since Freemasonry was so deeply rooted in Edinburgh's past it would make a good hiding place for the Ark.

Sally set off down the street, counting numbers along an unrelenting, varied façade of windows and doors. The ground beneath their feet was a little slick, the air cold. Mason felt the odd flick of drizzle on his face and pulled his leather jacket tighter. They went single file along the pavement as a woman walking a dog rushed by. Mason wrestled with an odd feeling – maybe it was the way they'd arrived here or how they'd been unexpectedly thrown into the midst of all this chaos, but searching for this treasure felt most unlike their previous missions. Ever since they'd arrived in Edinburgh he'd felt a sense of mystery in the air, a sensation of something ancient bearing down on them that wasn't just the perpetual, lofty castle. Could it be more than the weight of history?

'This is it,' Sally said.

Mason stopped on the narrow pavement. His back to a nearby house, he looked across the road and saw a brown double door between two dirty pillars. A lintel ran along the top of the door bearing the words 'The Lodge of Edinburgh' and, below that, '(Mary's Chapel No.1)'. The door looked old, the blockwork dusted with soot and pitted. The entrance fitted in well with the ones that stood to each side and, indeed all along the row, the double pillars barely standing out. The façade consisted of four storeys. Sally motioned to a six-pointed masonic symbol between the upper two windows. An ornament hanging beside the first-floor window was also adorned with subtle masonic symbology.

'There's even a doorbell.' Roxy nodded at a fitting to the right of the door. 'Shall we press it?'

'We're just tourists,' Sally said quietly. 'Just tourists.'

Mason looked further along the street. 'There's no entry this side,' he said. 'It's too public.'

'A dead end,' Roxy grumbled. 'As we feared.'

'Shall we see if there's a way around the back?' Mason ventured.

'My thoughts exactly.' Hassell was already moving.

They traversed the road a little further, passing people left and right, feeling hemmed in by the narrow thoroughfare and its tall buildings, eventually reaching an unremarkable little side street that cut between the houses. Hassell whistled his appreciation.

'Follow me.'

They walked down the road between double yellow lines and then turned left at a gym, reversing their journey, now parallel to Hill Street. The backs of all the buildings were just as forbidding as the front but, where the masonic building was, Mason saw a black wrought-iron fire escape leading from top to bottom that caught Hassell's eye immediately.

'I can make that work,' Hassell said.

Mason immediately turned away, not wanting to draw attention to themselves. He fell in alongside Hassell.

'What are you suggesting?' he asked.

'That I do what I'm good at,' Hassell said, with a rare grin.

A little after four a.m. Mason and his colleagues took the short walk back to Hill Street. The night was damp and cold and windswept. Fittings and signs rattled above the doors of shops and restaurants. Plastic bottles and carrier bags flew up and down George Street which was – unfortunately for them – well lit throughout the night. Hassell led the way as they hurried across the road.

They walked as quickly and as quietly as possible, sticking to any shadow they could find, wanting to attract no attention or the eyes of those who lurked around the streets at this hour. They had dressed in dark clothing and carried masks that they would don later. Hassell had brought a backpack with him.

Behind Hill Street they stopped and once more stared up at the black fire escape. The skies were starry, the moon half full, giving them a little light to work with.

Hassell didn't waste time. He climbed over the spiked iron railings and first tested and then started up the fire escape. He stayed low, hunching as he passed windows where he might cast a shadow inside. Because they were so close, Mason could hear Hassell's boots ringing out gently on the iron risers he made his way higher and higher. The whole staircase consisted of two flights and two platforms, one at the third floor near the central chimney that ran through the building and one at the fourth. The top floor of windows appeared to be bricked up. Hassell kept moving until he reached the first platform.

He leaned over the rails and beckoned the rest of the team to follow him up.

Mason climbed cautiously. Clouds obscured the moon for the length of their climb. Soon, they were all crouched along the fire escape below Hassell as the New Yorker reached into his pocket and produced a set of carbon fibre lock picks.

'Trusty old set,' he said. 'Last used at Notre-Dame. First used four years ago. Never let me down.'

Mason watched him fiddle with the lock. Hassell worked soundlessly and rapidly, his face pressed to the glass of the door so that he could see inside. In seconds, the door clicked. Hassell pushed it inward quickly, held up his home-made digital alarm code reader and prepared to connect it to the alarm. After a moment, Hassell turned to them with a shrug.

'Alarm isn't switched on,' he whispered. 'Stay silent. Somebody might be still inside.'

Mason inched forward behind Roxy. The only sound was their light breathing. They stood at the beginning of a hallway. Mason could see the outline of paintings or photographs on the wall but couldn't discern anything. The last man in, Quaid, closed the door.

Hassell indicated that they should start moving forward. They took out their torches but didn't turn them on yet. The natural light was enough for them to see where they were going. Hassell put his lock picks away and readjusted his backpack before moving forward.

Mason followed him cautiously, thankful for the carpeted corridor but still taking care to tread with a light step. The corridor continued all the way from the back of the house to the front. Hassell stopped at the first room and peered inside. He beckoned Sally forward.

'Looks like a study,' he whispered directly into her ear.

Sally nodded. Since darkness prevailed on this floor, they could be reasonably sure that they were alone. Hassell entered the room first, followed by Sally. Mason, Roxy and Quaid stayed outside.

'I'm not used to being this quiet,' Roxy whispered into the dark.

'I know,' Mason said.

'Do we need to gag you?' Quaid asked with half a smile.

'You could try.'

Roxy turned to Mason then with a serious look, about to say more, but at that moment Sally reappeared shaking her head. Hassell stepped around her and led the way further along the corridor. Mason heard a floorboard squeak despite the carpet and quickly turned to Quaid.

'Stop.'

Everyone froze, listening intently. For the first time, Mason heard the old masonic building creaking and groaning around them as if possessed of a living entity. Odd shadows were cast everywhere. It was a spooky old dwelling, mired deep in history, carrying the ghostly presences of times gone by. Windows rattled at the front of the building, buffeted by flurries of wind. Something whistled occasionally and gently below them, maybe a hole in the wall that needed regrouting. A loose tile jangled on the roof above. Above it all, Mason didn't think a squeaky floorboard should make much of a difference.

Hassell moved on. They paced along the corridor a step at a time. A squall of rain struck a window ahead, splattering across the glass. Hassell stopped outside another room and peered in.

'Office,' he said, beckoning Sally forward.

Two minutes later, Sally was back outside and shaking her head. 'The desks just aren't old enough,' she whispered to them. 'We're talking circa Fifties at best.'

Mason trusted her every word. They turned to the next room, but it was a large closet full of dust and cobwebs. The final room on the third floor was a kitchenette. Hassell

179

proceeded to the main staircase, passing by a window that looked out over Hill Street as he did so. The window was unshaded and revealed an empty, windswept, drab-looking scene outside.

Together, the five of them started up the carpeted risers.

Mason looked up into the fog of darkness ahead. Hassell switched on a torch, cupping the end. Mason didn't blame the man; the sheer darkness at the top of the stairs told them that the area was empty.

Hassell made it up and headed for the nearest room. It was a large space, possibly a meeting room. Mason soon followed him inside and by the dim light of the stars and Hassell's faint torch made out a few scattered chairs, a low table and several glass cabinets. There was also a mini-bar built into one corner of the room.

Hassell pulled Sally out, shaking his head. They moved along the new corridor. Although it was gloomy, Mason could make out another three rooms on this floor. As Hassell slowed in front of the first, he heard the faintest of noises: a scuffing sound. Possibly a shoe against a wooden floor or a piece of fabric scraping a surface.

It came from one of the rooms ahead.

Mason had come armed but didn't reach for his gun. Any loud noises here at this time of night would surely bring the police, especially considering the building was in the middle of two rows of houses. As one, the team froze.

Hassell turned and silently told them to wait with a wave of his hand. He crept forward, inching to the nearest door. A quick glance inside revealed nothing. He moved on to the next. It was at this door that he stiffened and pulled back sharply.

Mason's heart sank. He'd been hoping the scuff was something other than man-made. Hassell pressed himself against the corridor wall. Mason and the others crouched lower in the shadows, hoping the shorter stance would help shield them from anyone who emerged from the room.

It happened seconds later. Mason saw four people step into the corridor, the first an older man who appeared to be in his sixties, the other three much younger and fitter. One of the men turned in their direction and saw Hassell almost immediately.

'What the fu—'

In silence, Mason and Roxy sprang at them.

# Chapter 27

Mason flew across three feet of corridor at the first man, striking him in the midriff and driving him back into the wall. The man grunted, but remained otherwise silent, obviously also aware that they should keep the noise down. When the man bounced back purposefully, Mason was ready for him, delivering a jab to the ribs and then an uppercut that struck just underneath his chin.

The man's head snapped back.

Mason wasn't finished with him. Just as the back of the man's skull made a dent in the plaster wall, Mason delivered two blows in quick succession to his solar plexus. The man sank to the floor soundlessly.

To Mason's right, Roxy struck the next younger man in line, driving him back into the room. Inside, he collapsed over a desk. Roxy used his vulnerable landing to step in and knee him hard in the groin, then watched as he slithered down to the carpeted floor.

The third man was being targeted by Hassell, who had stepped around Roxy. Quaid was tackling the older man, grabbing him by his tie and forcing him to his knees.

'Please don't hit me,' the man was saying. 'I'm just a guide.'

Hassell grunted as his opponent came at him with

blows that caught him on the side of the face and temple. He staggered, his left leg folding. Mason dashed across the corridor and sent a crushing blow to the attacker's ribs, then grabbed hold of his head and brought it down against his knee. The man's nose broke, blood gushing, but he wasn't done yet. He slumped so that he was sitting on the floor with his back to the wall, and kicked out hard and high.

Mason fell as the man's boot collided with his own knee. Pain exploded in his right leg. The seated man kicked out again, catching Mason across the chest. Hassell stepped hard on the man's thigh, eliciting a groan of pain.

'Did they beat us here?' Sally hissed at the older man. 'Hey, hey, how did you beat us here?'

'I am a guide,' the man insisted. He had a distinctive Scottish accent. 'Just a guide.'

'Don't be an ass.' Quaid shook him by his tie.

Sally leaned in. 'What exactly are you here for?'

Mason blocked another kick from the seated man. Hassell again tried to step on him. Their breath was loud in the enclosed space, sweat running into their eyes. It was Roxy who ended the fight, clattering in from the side with no finesse at all and just kneeing the guy in the side of the face. The guy's head hit the plaster wall. He keeled over and didn't get back up.

Mason rubbed his chest where the man's boots had struck hard.

'You okay, baby?' Roxy asked. 'Need some cream for that?'

Mason ignored her. He slipped his backpack off. He rummaged inside, coming up with a set of zip ties. They had no tape for their victim's mouths but hopefully shouldn't need any. It was clear they'd wanted to remain as quiet as Mason's team.

'Tie them,' he directed Roxy and Hassell.

He crawled closer to the guide, who became loquacious.

'Those three men, they didn't say who they were or where they were from. Just offered me a thousand pounds cash to help them find an old desk. I mean, that's some serious money. And it's not like we're stealing anything.'

'You know where you are?' Sally asked.

'Of course I do. I'm a member here. This is the Lodge of Scotland. Didn't you know that?'

Sally ignored his prattle. 'What exactly did they tell you to look for?'

'The Timeworn Desk,' he said. 'They told me to find something called the Timeworn Desk. I mean, I've been a member here for the last decade and I've never actually heard of it. But I had to take a look. The money was—'

'Yes, we heard. And what have you found so far?'

'Nothing. Nothing at all. We've covered all four floors and all the rooms barring the three at the end of this corridor. There are no desks here older than fifty, sixty years.'

The man's words deflated Mason. In this chase, the last thing they needed to hit was a dead end.

'Wouldn't you have known that already?' Roxy said, rubbing her knee. 'Being a member here?'

'They don't let us in every room. Usually just the first and second floors. Our meetings are largely conducted there.'

Sally looked away from the guide towards the final three rooms. 'For now,' she said, 'we take his word for it. We check up here.'

Mason agreed. If these men had disabled the security system, then they had been prowling through the house for a while, and if they'd found the desk already there was no reason for them to be up here.

'Tie him too,' he said.

The guide protested but Roxy soon had him trussed up, relishing her task. Hassell helped line their enemies up along the hallway and then looked at Mason.

'What are we gonna do with them?'

184

'Wait until we leave,' Mason said. 'Then call the cops.'

'We can't waste time talking,' Sally said urgently.

'She's right,' Quaid said. 'For all we know, they have friends outside.'

The thought sent Mason dashing towards the first room. The others were close to his heels. He reached the entrance, looked inside and saw a rectangular space filled with bookshelves. There was a rolling ladder, a table and several chairs but no desk. Mason quickly moved on to the next room.

He darted through the entrance. This was a storeroom; there were unlabelled boxes piled high, bottles of wine and piles of clothing. Dust sifted through the air, thin shafts of moonlight causing it to appear to ripple as it drifted in wayward patterns. Mason felt his nose starting to tickle and backed out of the room.

Looked up the corridor.

'Last room,' he said.

Sally was already on it, peering hopefully around the doorframe. When Mason saw her step purposefully inside he knew they had a chance.

'Watch them,' he told Hassell, pointing at the trussed-up foursome before racing after Sally.

The final room was a study-cum-library. There were floor-to-ceiling gilt-edged bookcases lining the walls, and the floor was covered by a plush red carpet. The bookshelves were filled with leatherbound volumes, the ceiling a slight dome with a masonic symbol in the centre. To one side of the room there sat a desk.

Sally was already approaching it. Mason stepped around her so he could see the desk properly. It was dark, most probably constructed of thick oak, and looked steadfast in its position by the rear window. Mason could imagine men trying to move it, and failing. Sally approached it from the side.

'Early style chest of drawers,' she said. 'Herringbone inlay, stringing and cross banding.' She looked back with a smile. 'This is a very old desk.'

'The Timeworn Desk?' Quaid asked.

'Let's see, shall we? Now, show respect. If we're right Freemasons have used this desk to sign important documents on for centuries. It's integral to their history. It could date back to before desks as we know them were actually constructed.'

Mason frowned. 'How so?'

'The Knights Templar may have used them first, before everyone else. In case you didn't know, they invented the world's first banking system. Do you know Temple Church in London? It stands on Fleet Street opposite Chancery Lane.'

Mason shook his head.

'Temple Church was the world's first bank. They figured out how a pilgrim who needed to travel many miles and safeguard his cash could deposit his money in London and withdraw it in Jerusalem. Instead of cash, he carried a letter of credit. The Templar bank was a private bank.'

Mason knelt before the desk. 'First one to find a basin gets a free watch,' he said, already studying the rear lip for carvings.

Sally shook her head at him, muttered something about respect and knelt to one side of the large desk. Both pulled out their torches, shielded the tips and let light spear onto the desk alone, moving in close. Mason's study revealed only a lightly scarred block of wood that made up the entire back support.

'Maybe it's on the surface,' he said.

Quaid was quickly surveying the whole thing. 'It has pigeonholes,' he said. 'Two on the writing surface. And a couple of pull-out slides. Maybe there's something on one of those.' He knelt down to check.

Sally was studying the right-hand side of the desk. 'There are definitely carvings here,' she said. 'Just none that represent a basin.'

Mason crawled across the carpet, heading for the desk's left side, shivering as the heat of the battle wore off, and the room's penetrating chill pierced his clothing. This side was harder to reach. There was only twelve inches of space between the wood and the wall. Mason struggled to fit his head in the gap and angle the torch adequately.

Sally appeared at the other side, her torch blinding his eyes. 'You see anything?'

'Not with that light in my eyes.'

'Sorry.' She angled the torch towards the desk.

'Truth is,' he said. 'We don't have enough space.'

'We need to make it work,' Sally said. 'Because there's no way we're about to move this lump of wood.'

'You think it's the Timeworn Desk?' Mason asked.

'It certainly could be. It's the only candidate here. It appears to be of the right era. Wait . . . Do you see that?'

Mason, with his head close to the floor, looked up. Sally's torch was illuminating a round carving close to the top edge of the desk but the glare of light off the wood was blinding. He waited for her to angle the torch correctly, at the same time ensuring it didn't betray their presence to the world outside.

'Hard to make out,' he said.

'It's not a basin,' Sally said, disappointed. 'It's a pentagram.'

Mason studied her. 'Could that mean anything?'

Sally's voice was breathy in the enclosed space. 'It's associated with initiation in masonic iconography,' she said. 'It has no real application, but many medieval cathedrals have the pentagram as the stonemason's mark, and we know stonemasons used symbology to validate each other back in the old days. But . . .' She suddenly stopped speaking and bit her lip.

Mason leaned forward. 'Yes?'

'One notable use of the pentagram was in the seventeenth century, when Sir Robert Moray used it in his signature to the minutes of the Lodge of Edinburgh, Mary's Chapel. He called it his mason's mark.'

Mason felt a shiver pass through him. 'Right here?'

'Yes, probably on this very desk. The history all around us is quite remarkable.'

'But it's not what we're looking for.' Quaid's disembodied voice floated around them.

'Unfortunately not,' Sally said. 'But it does prove we're in—'

'No,' Quaid interrupted. 'I mean I've found what we're looking for.'

Mason quickly backed out of the space, rose to his feet and crossed over to where Quaid was bent double. 'As you can see,' Quaid said. 'The legs are thick. There's a carving on the inside . . . here.'

Mason crawled underneath the desk alongside Sally. They aimed their torches upward. At first, all Mason could see was the scarred and pocked underside. But then he turned his torch towards the leg.

It was a carved depiction of one of the seven Molten Sea basins, set into the wood about halfway up the leg. The craftsmanship was exquisite, the markings perfectly made. The basin covered the whole width of the leg. Sally used her mobile phone to take several photographs.

'All right,' she said. 'I'm convinced we got what we came for. Let's get the hell out of this place. I feel like I'm robbing history, or something.'

'Whoever carved these basins knew that someday, someone would come searching,' Quaid said. 'The physical basin led us to this place. Who do you think it was?'

'Someone who couldn't let a secret lie buried,' Sally said with a shrug. 'Or such an amazing treasure be lost for ever.'

Roxy had been surreptitiously checking both the front and back windows. 'I think we need to move, people,' she said. 'It's after five, and people are starting to stir out there. Well, some curtains are at least.'

Mason agreed and crawled out from under the desk before climbing to his feet. Quaid and Roxy were already leaving the room. Mason waited for Sally and then followed. Out in the corridor they made their way back to Hassell.

'Were they good boys?' Roxy asked, eyeing the trussed-up men, who were still where they had left them.

'Barely a squeak,' Hassell said. 'It feels as if they're waiting for something.'

Mason frowned at him. 'Care to explain?'

'I can't. But Roxy's right. We need to move.'

'And call the cops.' Roxy waved at their captives.

'You got some good photos?' Mason asked Sally as they reached the staircase. 'There's no chance we'll be getting back in here.'

Sally nodded. 'Of the basin and everything around it. We should have everything we need, Mason.'

The team retraced their steps, descending the stairs to the third floor before traversing the corridor to the unlocked exit door. Hassell led the way and cracked it open slightly, taking a look outside and a glance across the alleyway below.

'Clear,' he said.

Silently, they exited the masonic building onto the fire escape and started making their way down. They took their time, still conscious of making noise. From its height, Mason was able to see all the way down both sides of the street below. There was no sign of other people. He wondered what time the gym might open – knowing they kept early hours – and urged the others to greater speed.

'Move,' he said. 'If we can make it back to the hotel without being seen we'll have pulled this off perfectly.'

And that was when it all went wrong.

## Chapter 28

They emerged from the shadows at the top of the alleyway and started running towards them. They weren't carrying weapons, but looked like they knew how to use them. They wore big jackets, dark jeans and many donned masks to hide their identities. There were at least fifteen of them, men and women.

Hassell had already dismounted the staircase. Quaid was close behind him. Mason paused near the bottom as Roxy turned.

'There's too many of them,' he said. 'And we can't start a gunfight. Not here.'

'That's probably what they're thinking,' Sally said.

Roxy eyed him closely. 'You got a plan?'

'Yeah, but it's pretty desperate.'

'Why the hell does that not surprise me?'

Mason took another look up the fire escape. The highest platform ended just a few feet below the roofline. The line of windows up there would make for good hand- and footholds.

'Divide our forces,' he said. 'It's the only way.'

'And which way are you going?'

'Up.'

'Up?'

'The roof,' he said. 'You three take that alley to the left, draw some of them with you. Sally and I will take the high road.'

Roxy grimaced but then set her features. Mason saw immediately that she was up for it. Every second brought the running, silent bunch closer.

'They were waiting for us,' Sally said.

'Maybe. Or for our friends inside,' Mason said. 'Follow me.'

Mason whirled and started ascending once more. This time, he didn't remain cautious, but raced up the iron risers as fast as he could. 'You're a champion fell runner, right? I remember. How's your balance?'

Sally grimaced. 'Haven't done any running for months. Fell running is great for balance though. Why do you ask?'

'Because up there . . . you're gonna need it.'

Sally didn't look fazed. 'Actually, I tell a lie about the running,' she said. 'But I recall running around half of Rome chasing the Book of Secrets. I think I'll be okay.'

'Stay with me.'

Mason reached the top of the stairs, pausing on the square platform. Looking up, he saw the top of the roof with its black iron guttering and, above that, a stone chimney. He climbed onto the three-inch windowsill, taking care to avoid the jagged glass somebody had embedded into the grouting. He reached up, balancing himself by pressing his fingertips into the top part of the window. Now, he was three feet above the platform and another three from the top of the roof. He decided to take a chance and test the guttering – it looked like cast iron and he could see that it was held in place with thick iron bolts. Mason jumped up a little, grasped the edge of the guttering and held on. His boots swung in mid-air. Below, he could hear the approach of his enemy, but nobody had arrived at the fire escape yet.

191

Mason hauled himself up, using the guttering. The piece where his fingers gripped twisted in place. His fingertips hurt; one started to bleed. The edge of the guttering was sharp. Mason pulled harder until he managed to clear the guttering and roll onto the roof.

Up here, a cold wind blew. Mason could see across a wide span of dark rooftops. More importantly, he made out a way forward. Although the roof was slightly inclined there was enough room to make their way along on the inside of the chimneys. Without wasting any more time, he prostrated himself and reached down a hand to Sally.

'Grab hold.'

Sally was looking up, the blue tips of her hair hanging back due to the angle. Beyond her, Mason could see that five figures were closing in fast on the fire escape. The other ten or so were giving chase to Roxy and the others.

'Hurry,' he said as she came up.

One man was moving much faster than the others, hopping from rung to rung and then from the platform's guardrail to the window and roof in just three bounds. Mason was in no doubt that he couldn't be outpaced and would have to be dealt with.

The rooftop formed a narrow but gentle slope. Chimney stacks stood to their left, close to the edge. There were Velux windows built into the roof at varying intervals, their white frames standing out against the black rooftops. The sharp wind bit a little more up here and tugged at Mason's clothing and he could hear himself panting as he rushed along in Sally's wake.

Mason slowed and glanced back. The fastest of their pursuers was only yards behind, while the rest were still negotiating the platform to the roof. Mason stopped abruptly, crouched and dropped a shoulder, hoping to hurl his attacker over him, but the man was too wily. He pulled up suddenly as if he had air brakes, his boots skidding slightly across the slick roof.

'Who are you?' Mason asked.

'I'm Walter fucking Scott, pleased to meet you,' the man said in a Scottish accent. 'Now stop running, you pair of arseholes.'

Mason doubted that somehow this was the famous Scottish writer come back to life but decided not to pursue the issue. 'Stop chasing us,' he said equably. 'You won't like what you find.'

'Oh, really?' The man lunged, feinting with his right hand, and then kicked out.

Mason caught the boot in one hand and twisted, throwing the man off balance, letting him fall to the roof. Then he turned and motioned at Sally.

'Run.'

Mason followed her, trying to get some distance between them and their enemies. The trick of staying alive in this situation was living through one dangerous moment and then another . . . and then another. Mason hurried along as fast as he could. Sally treated the roof like a field or a forest; she was used to the uneven ground and obstacles and started to pull away from him.

Mason's right boot slipped. He grabbed hold of a chimney breast, steadied himself, then turned.

Walter Scott hit him hard, diving at his midriff. The man was a reckless fool. Mason employed every ounce of strength to hold his ground but was driven backward. Somehow, he managed to angle his body so that they slammed into the chimney. Scott ended up on top of Mason, his hands around Mason's throat.

Mason struck out, aiming for the throat, face, ears. Any vulnerable area would do. Scott pressed down on him. Mason's head was pushed against the rough stone, the pain in his throat unbearable.

One of his punches caught Scott across the left temple, temporarily dazing him. The grip eased slightly. Mason struggled to rise, but Scott's weight was still on him, and he found it hard to move. Scott took a few deep breaths and managed to refocus his eyes.

'Bastard,' he grated.

Mason struck upward time and again. Scott flinched and grunted and took the punches, even the better-aimed ones. At one point Mason smashed him across the eye, closing it immediately, but still Scott held on.

Mason felt the strength starting to leave his body. He couldn't dislodge the man above him, couldn't pummel him into unconsciousness either. The pain was lessening, his vision narrowing, a numbness starting to move through all his limbs.

Something shifted above him. Mason took a moment to focus. There were hands across Scott's face, female hands. They were targeting the eyes and the windpipe. Mason knew instantly what was happening. The hands had left his throat. The space above him was clear. It didn't look right somehow. Where the hell was Scott?

Mason focused further. Now he saw Sally to his left, holding a length of timber in her hands. It seemed that she had pulled Scott away and then smashed him over the head with the plank of wood.

'Thanks,' he grated.

'Just as you taught me,' she said. 'Eyes and throat. It felt disgusting though.'

Mason breathed deeply. The fog started to clear. Sally held out a hand. Mason took it, climbing to his knees. He gripped his bruised throat and massaged it, taking several gulps of air.

'I'm so glad you listened to my lessons,' he managed.

Sally looked pleased. 'No worries. It's the others we have to worry about now.'

Mason turned his head. The four other pursuers were on the roof and starting towards them. Mason used the chimney to lever himself upright and then pointed to the far end of the roof.

'Go.'

Sally didn't drop her length of wood. Mason ran after her, gauging that they were little more than a minute ahead of their attackers. That fact was bad enough. The other fact – that he didn't know what waited them at the end of the line of roofs – was much worse.

Where the hell could they go next?

At first, Roxy thought she, Quaid and Hassell could outdistance their pursuers. They were all pretty spry. However, it turned out their pursuers were equally agile, if not more so.

Roxy angled left towards an alley as eight men and two women came for them. They had less than twenty yards advantage. Quaid and Hassell were to either side. Ahead, the alley was blocked by a fence.

'Crap,' Roxy said.

They hit it at dead run, leaping at the last second. Roxy caught hold of the top and hauled herself up. For a moment she balanced on the top edge, hands out, and then leapt down to the other side. Hassell was a moment behind her. Quaid waited for just a second, assessing their attackers, before joining them.

'All carrying guns,' he said. 'But keeping them concealed for now.'

Roxy turned to run. 'Gunfire would bring every cop from here to Glasgow down on us.'

The alley was wide and filled with wheelie bins and recycling crates. The backs of homes stood to both sides, reached through gated archways. Roxy stayed in the centre, conscious of the lightening skies and at least two early risers, judging by the lit windows to her right.

'We're gonna have to escape them,' she said. 'A mass brawl isn't going to work either.'

Hassell ran harder at her side. 'Follow me.'

'You got a plan?'

'No. But I'm happy to make it up as I go along.'

'Dude.' Roxy jogged at his side. 'That's all I ever do.'

Their pursuers had now also negotiated the fence. Roxy saw an end to the alley ahead where a wide road crisscrossed it. As she reached it a strong crosswind blasted her face.

'This way,' Hassell said.

They cut right, running hard. They couldn't hear their followers, but a quick glance behind assured them that nothing had changed. The men and women were bunched into a group, some talking into handheld radios, most just keeping track of Roxy and her friends.

'They're too close to shake,' Roxy knew.

'Then let's thin the herd,' Hassell said.

Roxy liked the sound of that.

# Chapter 29

Mason slowed as Sally negotiated a pair of chimney breasts. The gap through them was narrow. Sally pushed through, scraping her jacket. Mason was a step behind. A quick glance back told him that their pursuers were closing slowly, taking chances. Walter Scott hadn't moved since Sally smashed him across the head with her plank of wood.

Mason kept running. The view across rooftops up here was spectacular, but all he was aware of was the piercing wind and droplets of hail. His boots echoed, his breath came in short bursts and his throat still ached, but he kept up the pace.

Sally slowed as the end of the long line of rooftops drew nearer. Mason was already looking for options. There was a small gap in the roof ahead, where one rooftop was lower than the other. Sally jumped down into it, travelling only about four feet, landing sure-footed. Mason was a step behind her.

'What next?' Sally asked.

'I'm working on it.'

Mason ran to the furthest edge of the roof, the one that looked over the alley. There was what looked like a brick-built lean-to below, a small annexe on the back of a house.

It was a good eight-foot drop, but there was also a window directly below them.

'C'mon,' Mason said.

He showed Sally the way down, knowing he should go last. Sally didn't hesitate, but crouched near the cast-iron guttering, grabbed hold of it and then lowered her body off the edge of the roof. Her feet sought the window ledge, found it and got some purchase. Now, Sally was hanging from her fingertips, facing the wall. She reached down, grabbed the top of the window and started to ease her body down further.

It was a process that couldn't be rushed. Mason stood above her, keeping an eye on the roof.

Their pursuers arrived forty seconds later. Sally jumped two feet to the top of the lean-to, then slithered down its slightly angled surface to the edge. She caught herself six feet above the ground. Below her, to the left, was a bright blue wheelie bin which she jumped onto and then leapt off.

Mason was already following, but had no time to take extra care. He grabbed the guttering and held on, flinging his body off the roof. At first, his boots flew through thin air, brushing past the window ledge and failing to gain purchase. Their enemies jumped down to the lower roof. Mason's eyes saw only their shoes running towards him.

A man came close, lifting a foot and bringing it crushing down on Mason's fingers. Mason let go a split second before impact and, in one fluid movement, reached down to grab the top sill. The guttering clattered above his head. The aggressor then tried to bring his shoe down onto the top of Mason's skull. Mason bent as quickly as he was able, grabbing the windowsill carefully before letting go and then hitting the top of the lean-to. He flapped his arms, seeking balance.

Above, two men were already lowering themselves in the same way. Mason wondered briefly how long the guttering would hold out. Even bolted to the wall he didn't think it would resist all of them.

Mason steadied himself and sought the wheelie bin. Sally was waiting for him, ready to run. She didn't even look out of breath. Mason hit the top of the wheelie bin, landed heavily and slipped to the left, smashing into the ground with his shoulder. A savage blast of pain bombarded his senses.

Gritting his teeth, he pulled himself to his feet. Above, the four men were stuck in various stages of descent, easy targets but not this morning. Mason wouldn't have used his gun even if he'd been able. Shooting men down so callously wasn't something he would stoop to.

Sally checked on him, laying a hand on his shoulder. Mason was more conscious of the urgency of their situation and urged her to run. She set off fast, Mason loping after her. They retraced their steps of earlier. The pain in Mason's shoulder started to subside.

'Now what?' Sally asked.

'Anywhere,' Mason said. 'Just run.'

They flew back up the alley, away from the point where Roxy, Quaid and Hassell had led the larger force of pursuers. They passed the still-closed gym and back to Hill Street. At the small junction, Sally turned left.

'Hurry,' Mason said.

Hassell led the other two along a main road where a few early commuters were already driving through Edinburgh's eclectic mix of old and new streets. He didn't slow the pace and neither did their pursuers. Large stone-clad buildings stood to their right, some with steps leading up to the front doors. Hassell took them to another junction and then turned right.

'A park,' he said. 'It'll be deserted at this time.'

Roxy wasn't convinced about them being led into a park. 'Do you have a plan?' she asked.

'We have to thin them out, give them something to worry about. I think we can survive one encounter, don't you?'

Roxy thought it was risky. 'I guess we can't run for ever.'

'Exactly. And those smug bastards need to be taught a lesson.'

Hassell led them across the road towards an open area. 'You know I always study the map,' he said. 'This is St Andrew Square.'

Roxy saw a large area, with a well-tended garden and a tall Roman column at its centre. A mansion dominated the east end and she saw a tram passing to its far side. The team went in through one of the entrance gates and started to follow a curving path. Ahead of them was a small café pavilion.

Hassell led them around the side of the café where he stopped and started counting. Roxy used the respite to take three deep breaths.

'Now,' Hassell said.

They stepped from around the corner. Their pursuers were metres away. Roxy set off at a sprint, led with an elbow and sent one man flying. The next she kicked in the chest, knocking him to the ground and herself off balance.

She staggered sideways.

Another man swung at her. Roxy took the blow across the face, tasted blood in her mouth and then leapt at him, grabbing his jacket with both hands and planting her forehead into the centre of his nose. He grunted, flung his hands up to protect his face and fell back.

Hassell had already incapacitated one man and one woman, and was now face to face with a much larger opponent. No way he could easily take this guy down with one punch. He started to dance around the man, throwing punches, staying mobile. Quaid went low, kicking out at two pairs of legs and tripping two attackers.

Roxy knew their window of opportunity was closing.

They had taken out a few but there were still too many to fight. She flung out a fist as another man confronted her.

'Go!' she shouted.

Hassell and Quaid immediately turned and started to run, surprising their opponents. Roxy followed suit. They had downed five of their pursuers with the surprise attack. Hassell led the way out of the square, across the tramlines, and turned right up the next street.

'Did that work?' Quaid asked.

'I think so,' Hassell said. 'We're alive, aren't we?'

Roxy touched her forehead where she'd headbutted the enemy. A bruise was definitely forming. Blood slicked her face. But they were free and clear, their enemies only just emerging from the square.

'A few twists and turns and we could lose them,' she said.

'Don't worry,' Hassell said. 'I know exactly where I'm going.'

'You keep all that shit in your head?' Roxy meant his knowledge of maps, streets and alleys and roads and every little byway that made up towns and cities.

'I always study the places we visit very closely,' Hassell said. 'It's good mind exercise – helps me focus and keeps the guilty voices from taking over my brain.'

Roxy could understand that. It was thin, stony ground for Hassell. She swung left in the other man's wake, making sure Quaid was keeping up.

'Like your style back there,' she told him. 'Tripping them up.'

Quaid tapped his head. 'This is for thinking,' he said and then pointed to his legs. 'These are for dancing.'

Roxy blinked. 'Aren't those old song lyrics?'

'No, they bloody aren't. It's something I used to say to my daughter.'

Roxy hadn't even known Quaid had a daughter, and realised then just how little she knew of her companions beyond what was necessary to know. She thought the weeks they'd spent in Sally's house had brought them closer together, but it was clear some gulfs still existed.

But now wasn't the time. Hassell was twisting between buildings and through alleys in an effort to lose their pursuers.

The new problem was: where the hell were Mason and Sally?

# Chapter 30

Mason sprinted along Hill Street, Sally at his side. Within seconds, they were heading back towards the wide thoroughfare of Princes Street. Mason breathed easily; Sally looked like she was out for a stroll. A quick look back revealed that the four men were gaining on them.

Mason turned left at the junction, now running past closed restaurants, banks and cafés in the direction of St Andrew Square. A thread of worry coiled through his mind like a poisonous snake – worry for Roxy and the others. The fact that he hadn't heard any gunfire was a slight comfort. It was only then that he remembered the communications system lodged deep in his right ear.

'Roxy?' he asked. 'Quaid? Hassell? Can you hear me?'

There was no sound other than a faint crackling.

'Nobody can hear me,' he said absently.

'I can hear you,' Sally said. 'They're just out of range.'

Mason couldn't force the worry from his mind. He hadn't wanted the team dynamic, hadn't wanted to be part of that again after Mosul but – somehow – it had found him. In the end, he hadn't been able to resist it. The five of them just fell in naturally together. They weren't blood brothers constantly beset by the trials of war, but they were a new family that worked well together and watched each other's backs.

Family?

Mason didn't have time to dwell on that thought. The men at their backs were less than thirty seconds away. The road ahead was wide and open and offered no hiding places. To Mason's mind there was just one solution.

'Sorry,' he said.

The man who'd just climbed off his motorbike looked surprised when Mason plucked his ignition keys from his hand and shoved him backwards. Before the expression had changed Mason was across the bike and had the machine switched on. Sally leapt across the seat behind him.

'Hold on tight,' he shouted.

Her hands looped around his waist. Mason twisted the throttle, but not quite quickly enough. One of the men was beside them, reaching, so close Mason could hear his heavy breathing. Mason kicked out, catching the man on the knee. The man fell against the bike. Mason managed to keep it upright as the man's face smashed against his shoulder. With a twist of the throttle, he sent it forwards, then turned right and gunned it along George Street.

There was cursing in his wake, the four men not happy. Mason didn't need to drive at a high speed to escape them so slowed after the initial getaway and looked back with the engine still roaring in his ears. The machine he'd appropriated wasn't a powerful superbike, it was more like a brawny lawnmower with a really shouty engine.

The four men were standing, looking after them, consternation and anger clearly plastered across their features. One of the men was shouting furiously as if the weight of his cursing would make them turn around. Mason felt a moment's relief . . .

. . . but it was only a moment.

As he watched, glancing forwards and now behind him, a blue Mazda drove along George Street. One of the men stepped out into the road, flagging it down. Mason saw the driver roughly pulled out, and the men jumped into the car.

'Hold on tighter,' he said.

He gunned the engine, instinctively knowing the car would be faster. The road became a blur beneath their wheels. Sally's arms were tight round his waist, her face looking over his shoulder. Mason steeled himself against the fresh breeze that tugged his jacket and scoured his face and bent forwards over the tiny windscreen.

The car was already roaring behind them, coming at speed. Mason flung the bike to the left, heading downhill, and saw a tram idling across the road in front of them. Quickly, he swerved to the right, now travelling the wrong way down Princes Street.

Sally's words of warning slammed through his ears. Mason ignored them. The road was empty. He travelled around the front of the tram and then switched lanes. The road stretched straight ahead, giving the car the advantage.

Mason flung the bike right this time, heading back towards New Town and the narrower roads. Heading up the first hill he spied a little offshoot to their left and took it. High concrete walls and the fronts of cafés stood on both sides, their proximity throwing the exhaust note of the bike back at them, making it rowdier. Mason opened the throttle, seeing nobody ahead, flying along the narrow pathway.

The car was suddenly behind them, coming at a reckless pace and only just fitting through the channel. When Mason chanced a look back, he saw two grinning faces in the front seat. Mason pulled on the brakes as they approached another road.

He turned right, now once more on George Street. The road was wide open and quiet. He let the bike drift slowly as he flung it to the left and then opened the throttle to the limit, making the engine squeal. The car fell back slightly.

They were headed for Charlotte Square, at the end of George Street. Mason turned right past Las Iguanas, the restaurant reminding him that life wasn't all about being chased through the barely lit streets of Edinburgh by a mix of madmen and mercenaries. A quick blast along the road brought them to another junction.

Mason slowed, aware that he needed to find as many corners as he could. He turned right and then right again, flew along that road until he could swing left, realising he was headed right back to Hill Street. Before he got there, he took another left and saw a wide street at the bottom of another long hill.

'It's working,' Sally said in his ear.

Mason saw that the car was falling back. He didn't waste time, urging the bike forward with a twist of the throttle. The little engine complained, but did as he urged. Soon, he saw Queen Street Gardens before him.

'Get off when I stop again,' he said. 'Go where we saw the Hard Rock on George Street. I'll meet you there.'

Sally's arms tightened around his waist again. 'What are you going to do?'

'Nothing that'll work with you on the bike,' he said. 'I need to take them out of play.'

Mason raced along Queen Street, then swung the bike in several directions, negotiating street corners at speed. As soon as he lost sight of the car in the rear-view mirror, he pulled up and waited for Sally to slide off before watching her edge her way into the shadows. A second later, he opened the throttle once more.

The car roared around a corner in pursuit. Mason spurred the bike as fast as he dared, negotiating more corners until he was lost deep in the New Town. The cold had long since numbed his face; the wind blasted in his ears. Mason saw only blurs as he raced past homes and eateries and shops.

The blue Mazda was a street behind, keeping him in sight. Mason had to get the distance perfect. If the car was too close, or too far away, it wouldn't work. He kept an eye on the rear view as he negotiated even more corners.

At last, he was ready. The Mazda was pouring on the speed.

Mason slowed to a dead stop as fast as he dared, jumped off the bike and tried to ignore the strange feeling in his head that came with the sudden loss of speed and mobility. He turned the bike around, jumped back on and opened the throttle fully. The small bike shot forward, straight at the oncoming Mazda.

As expected, the men in the front seat started to grin.

Mason stayed with the bike until seconds before impact. He aimed it on a dead straight line with the front of the car. At the last moment, he jumped away, hit the pavement and rolled, crashing into the front of a house with his body tightly compressed.

The loose bike smashed into the front of the Mazda with a resounding crunch, travelled up the bonnet and struck the windscreen with its front tyre. The glass smashed instantly and the bike flew up over the roof, the men in the car all instinctively ducking out of the way.

The car was still traveling at speed and, as the driver dipped his head and lost control, its front wheels slammed into the far kerb, making it slew wildly. From then on it was under its own momentum, slewing in the road, twisting until its back end crashed into a shop frontage and shattered the framework. The noise was tremendous, the sound of a bomb exploding.

Mason wasted no time. Despite his aching, bruised limbs he struggled to his feet and shuffled away from the scene. The car's engine still roared, although it was wedged in the shop front, and going nowhere. Glass and metal framework, bricks and mortar fell onto its roof and broken windscreen. At least two doors were badly buckled. Mason saw a flash of blood on one of the side windows.

But people were now looking out of their windows; he saw curtains twitching. Some exited their front doors and started towards the apparent accident. The bike was nowhere to be seen, probably wedged further inside the shop.

Mason kept his head down and kept going. The aches in his body subsided the more he walked. After a minute, he dug into his pocket to fetch out his phone and call up a navigation app. It took only a moment to find his bearings and start heading back to George Street.

Where, he hoped, Sally would be waiting.

# Chapter 31

Back in Sally's hotel room, the team were lying low.

Mason was caught between the necessity of getting out of Edinburgh quickly and the desire to maintain their secrecy. For the moment, however, nobody knew they were here, and they still had research to carry out. Sally had a new clue to decipher.

Mason spent some time in the bathroom, sponging away his aches and pains and wiping blood from several scratches whilst Roxy stood outside the doorway, watching.

'So you jumped off a moving bike onto the sidewalk and rolled straight into a house?' the American said with a hint of reproval in her tone. 'And before that you abandoned Sally? See what happens when I'm not there?'

Mason winced as he touched his right side. 'Do you really need to be standing right there?'

Roxy clicked her tongue. 'Give me a break,' she said. 'You're the first decent specimen I've seen with his top off in weeks.'

'Decent specimen? Thanks.'

'Don't let it go to your head. Options are limited.'

Mason twisted so that he could better see his ribs and the red welt that crisscrossed them. He sponged the area and then reached for a towel. Roxy had already regaled him with her tale of how they escaped their pursuers.

'So what's next?' Roxy changed the subject, leaning back against the open door.

'Sally,' Mason said. 'See what she can come up with.'

He threw the sponge in the sink, dried his body and then shrugged back into his T-shirt. He followed Roxy out of the room, noting that she sank into an armchair that already had two miniature rums balanced on its leather-backed arm.

'Did you notice,' Quaid said as Mason appeared, 'that the mercenaries – if that's what they were – targeted us directly? As if they wanted us out of the way just as much as they wanted to get inside that lodge.'

Mason nodded. It was clear that whoever opposed them, whoever else was also searching for the seven Molten Sea basins, didn't want anyone interfering with their quest. It was also clear that they were ruthless.

'All it does is cement the fact that what we're searching for is incredibly valuable,' Sally said. 'They're desperate.'

Mason took a moment to catch her eye. 'Thanks for your help back there,' he said.

Sally almost blushed. 'I was just doing as you taught me,' she replied.

Quaid was looking out of their second-floor window, peeking through the curtains and taking his time. He didn't report anything suspect, which Mason took as a good sign. Hassell was seated on the bottom of the bed, bolt upright, with that faraway look of pain still bright in his eyes. Sally sat at the top of the bed, the laptop on her knees. Her head was bowed as she stared at the screen. Mason saw the team dynamic at work but thought they were all still very distinct and separate parts of the whole, each with their own profound challenges to overcome. But he had to talk to someone. He decided on Hassell.

'Did you get hurt, mate?' He knew the man was fine, but wanted to open a dialogue.

'Me? Nah. I'm good.'

'So it's the Devil calling?'

Hassell looked up at him with a tight smile. 'I guess you could say that, if the Devil looks like a truckful of guilt.'

'Still feeling guilty for killing Gido?' he asked carefully.

'Of course. Killing that lunatic changed nothing from my past. I still worked for him. I still gullibly ducked under his wing.' Hassell shuddered. 'It makes me feel so unclean.'

'In the end,' Mason said, 'we're both trying to push through something. It's the way you do it that matters.'

'And that's what I'm trying to do,' Hassell said. 'But the weight of the past keeps on dragging me down. It's like I'm trying to escape a grave, but something keeps on rising up behind me, pulling me back.'

'Ghosts of the past,' Roxy said quietly. 'They cling hard.'

Hassell nodded. 'I think appeasement is working slowly,' he said. 'Accept their power, learn to live with their influence. The only way forward is to live in tandem with them.'

'And what is forward?' Mason asked. 'Where do you go next?'

'Well, there's no living easy with my past,' Hassell said. 'I know already that I'm gonna have to fight it every day. Every hour. The only time I feel calm is when I'm working. Ironic that that work is illegal, isn't it?' He tried to smile but managed only a grimace.

'You're going to throw yourself into work?'

'It's a start.' Hassell shrugged and went silent, still thinking.

'With us?'

'I want to . . . but we'll see where we go from here.'

Mason thought about the way both Zach and Harry had died in Mosul, on his watch. For a long moment, he was thrown back into that desert – not just the desert of Iraq but the desert of his emotions in the wake of the explosion.

211

The buildings were dry and dusty, the sun high and blinding. Sweat had been stinging his eyes. He'd emerged from a house after checking it for IEDs, alone when he should have had backup, but the platoon was stretched. Two minutes later Zach and Harry entered the house and stumbled across a bomb he'd missed.

Mason could never later fully describe the feeling of shock and horror that gripped his heart and mind. It was overwhelming, a tangible squirming thing that sent him to his knees and wiped away all chance of thought. As the soil and debris fell around him, Mason knew that his friends were dead and that he'd never be able to trust himself again.

Now, years later, he was in a place where trust, belief and confidence ran in tandem. It worked as part of the new team dynamic. And the more it functioned seamlessly, the more self-assured Mason felt.

'Build barriers,' Roxy said, swigging a miniature rum. 'That's what I do.'

'Does it work?' Hassell asked.

'It's slow,' Roxy admitted. 'But when I feel the barriers strengthening, there's no better feeling in the world. I can be the person I want to be.'

'I wish I could feel that way,' Hassell said. 'But I can't get past the fact that I worked for this man for years.'

Mason nodded. 'But you can find a way to cope with it,' he said. 'You are doing. You're stronger now than when we first met you. Gido had you back then. Now, you're free. You're saving lives. You're part of a team . . . working . . .'

'The past will always cling to you,' Quaid spoke up then. 'It's inescapable. You war with it like it's a living, breathing animal. A predator. I think Roxy's right – it has to live, but inside a cage.'

Mason refrained from commenting, struck by how like-minded they all were. But then they had all suffered terrible traumas through the years.

'Better to be that animal,' Roxy said with half a smile, 'than to succumb to it.'

'A maxim that you embrace,' Quaid said, turning.

'You can be my role model.' Hassell almost grinned.

Roxy choked. 'Yeah, well, steady on, boy. You don't wanna end up like me.'

'I've got the new clue on screen,' Sally put in then, drawing them all back to reality and the hotel room. 'If you want to take a look?'

Mason shook the past away as if sloughing off a dead skin. It would never leave him, but he could step out from under its influence now and then. He crossed over to Sally and leaned in so that he could see the laptop's screen.

'Is that a photo of the desk carving?'

'Yes. As you recall, we took a lot of pictures, trying to get the best angle in the cramped space. This is the best of the bunch.'

Mason squinted. It took him a moment to realise that he was looking at one of the Molten Sea basins, slightly raised from the desk. The carving was accurate in every way and there was some writing around the edge.

'Can you read it?' Mason asked, peering closely.

'I can with this,' Sally showed him a magnification app and proceeded to apply it to the image. 'Okay, here we go. The town of the warriors, the church of the Templars, follow the cross.' She sat back, smiling.

'You know what that means?' Quaid asked.

'Not a clue. I'm just happy we've found another clue.'

Mason agreed with a sharp nod. 'Although it does appear to be a bit of an ambiguous clue,' he said.

'On the surface, maybe,' Sally was already looking for her notes. 'Leave it with me.'

They did just that. Quaid left the room and went in search of sandwiches. Hassell returned to his own room to take a break. Roxy decided she needed a proper shower and also departed. Mason was left with his aches and pains and a decidedly quiet Sally Rusk.

He tried to put together what they'd achieved so far. The basins were undoubtedly the way forward and they'd found five, one of which consisted only of photographs. But the number five suggested they were getting close to the end of their quest.

Which was?

Solomon's Temple? The Ark of the Covenant? A sprawling mass of Knights Templar treasure?

The question of who was chasing them around the country still hadn't been answered but Mason knew there were hundreds of shadow entities abroad in the world that would stop at nothing to amass great wealth and power, that thought themselves entitled to privilege such as this. He had no doubt they'd show their hand again shortly.

And how was their first job in the field of relic protection going?

He smiled to himself. Not as expected. Somehow, they'd managed to stumble onto something incredibly important, something mind-blowing. Where it would lead them, Mason didn't know, but he was sure about one thing.

It would lead them there together.

Mason felt the team had been growing and maturing ever since it met. At the beginning there were issues, most of them centred around himself and his reluctance to recreate the team dynamic. It was understandable. He'd lost almost everything to his time as a soldier, including a marriage. But slowly, Roxy and the others had grown into a team of friends. He still wasn't sure how he felt about it. Not entirely. The past and all its associated feelings would never die . . . but the future might hold some promise.

Quaid returned with a bag full of sandwiches. Mason grabbed a tuna mayo, ripped it open and sat down on the bed to eat. Roxy returned looking fresh and, typically, upended the sandwich bag on the bed, letting everything fall out in chaos so she could sort through more easily. Hassell reappeared, looking sadder than when he'd left.

'How are we doing, Sally?' Mason asked after several moments of silence.

'As you know,' she said absently without looking up, 'Freemasonry and the Templars are inextricably linked to our quest. The Templars brought the treasure from Europe and then morphed into the masons. Now, Freemasonry in Scotland is older than anywhere else in the British Isles.' She paused, thinking.

'So, what does "the town of the warriors, the church of the Templars, follow the cross" have to do with any of it?' Quaid asked.

'Scotland is the epicentre,' Sally said. 'That's what I'm saying. We know for a fact that many Templars settled here after the persecution. I wouldn't be at all surprised to find the Ark buried right here.'

'Don't get ahead of yourself,' Mason chided gently.

Sally looked up. 'I guess you're right. Well, identifying the church of the Templars is tricky, I'll grant you. Just look at the UK and you'll see dozens of them. It needs narrowing down.'

'Which you've done? Right?' Mason prompted.

'I think so.'

'We're all ears.' Hassell sat down with a smile.

'There's a little village south of Edinburgh called Temple. It's a civil parish that lies along the east bank of the river South Esk. The name "Temple" denotes its ancient association with the Knights Templar.'

'I believe there are hundreds of places and buildings throughout the UK associated with the Templars in the same way,' Quaid said.

'Of course,' Sally said. 'But Temple wasn't always called

215

Temple. When the Knights founded the village in 1237, it was called Ballentrodoch.'

As Sally paused to rustle her notes a little more, checking on something, Mason knitted his forehead in confusion. 'I'm not seeing a connection.'

'We're in Scotland, right? Well, in old Scottish Gaelic, Baile Nan Trodach means "town of the warriors". It's what the Templars named their new town.'

'And is there a church in Temple?' Hassell asked.

'Not only that,' Sally said. 'Its name is Temple Church, and it has several legends associated with it. One of those legends states that the treasure of the Knights Templar was removed secretly from Paris to be hidden in Temple. There's a saying: "Twixt the oak and the elm tree, you will find buried the millions free." That's a hybridised quote from French legends that also state the treasure was taken to Scotland.'

'So south it is,' Mason said, gathering up his discarded sandwich wrapper and then his backpack, which he'd stored in Sally's room. 'I guess we need to hire a car.'

'You think the next clue's inside this Temple Church?' Roxy asked.

'It's where the basin leads us,' Sally said, her eyes glowing with excitement. 'We're almost at the end of our quest.'

Mason, knowing they would face heavy opposition, made them all pause to clean and check their weapons. 'We don't know how many we'll be up against,' he said. 'But what we do know . . . is that they're deadly serious. And they'll be gunning for us.'

'Sounds like a normal day at the office,' Roxy said. 'I'm in.'

# Chapter 32

The ruins of Temple Church stood in a beautiful location in the rural village of Temple. As they drove along country lanes and winding roads towards it, Sally explained a little of the history that had wrapped Temple in its ancient shroud.

'In the twelfth century the very first Grand Master of the Knights, Hugues de Payens, was gifted the lands around Ballentrodoch by David I, King of Scotland. It became their prime Templar seat in Scotland until the persecution happened. At the time, the lands were owned by England. The knights were all prosecuted, but not all were found guilty. In addition, those who survived found a powerful ally to their north – Robert the Bruce had been excommunicated and was not required to follow papal commands and would have welcomed them with open arms.'

'What happened to Temple after that?' Roxy had asked.

'Many knights integrated with the Hospitallers,' Sally said. 'Others moved, changing the name of their order to the Order of Saint John and the Temple. It wasn't until 1618 that Ballentrodoch took the name Temple.'

With no obvious parking available they pulled into a clearing close to an attractive wooded dell by the South Esk river, a little way from the heart of the village. They climbed out of the car, donned backpacks and checked weapons, and walked up a quiet road in the direction of Templar Church. Mason saw trees to the left, standing silent in the windless day, and, on their right, an old dry-stone wall that ran along the road, with green fields on the other side. The sun was still rising, about halfway to its zenith, and the skies were blue and clear. A deep, earthy smell reached his nostrils as he walked, emanating from the trees. The only sounds that penetrated this broad wilderness were of their boots echoing off the hard tarmac.

They came upon Templar Church after five minutes of walking. The building was a distinctive but roofless ruin standing in a graveyard and fenced off to the general public. Sally cited some warnings she'd read online about the building being dangerous. Mason thought the people who wrote that really had no idea.

The whole area was quiet. As they walked around and peered through the wire fencing Mason saw that many of the gravestones bore images of the skull and crossbones and masonic symbols. It was a short walk around the site and Sally stopped opposite what appeared to be the rear of the ruined church.

'Are we climbing over?' Hassell asked.

'We've only solved two-thirds of the clue,' Sally said, waiting with her hand on the fence. 'What does "follow the cross" mean?'

Mason knew her question was rhetorical but considered it anyway. 'I guess we need to look for a cross,' he said.

'In a churchyard?' Sally regarded him with an arched expression. 'Really?'

'Okay, okay, I get your point. There's bound to be a few. But what else could it mean? Maybe we'll see something we recognise.'

'What else could it mean?' Quaid echoed.

218

After checking that all was clear, the five of them began to scale the metal-link fence. It was made up of large rectangles, each bolted to the next, and felt rickety and unsafe, especially to Mason as he perched on top. They all jumped down to the other side, Mason landing awkwardly on the soft grass. As he got back to his feet, he said, lightly, 'Well, that wasn't clumsy at all.'

Roxy's boots had been inches from his face when he landed. 'Perfectly fine,' she said, dusting herself off.

Sally crossed the uncut grass towards the church's rear window, which at some point in the distant past had no doubt held thick panes of impressive glass. It was empty now, its skeletal frame part of this ancient stone carcass that history appeared to have forgotten. Mason thought it a sad sight. Time marches on, but it was your past that defined your future. That very fact was what defined him. Maybe there was a lesson here – let your past crumble away to dust.

Sally took her time, aware that the building had been designated as dangerous. It was a four-walled stone shell with empty window apertures, vacant doorways and a steeple. The ground inside was earth and grass, at least on the surface, and mould clung to several walls. Sally's eyes shifted carefully from side to side.

'Just below the steeple,' she said. 'There's a round depression. I don't see a cross, but it might have held something once.'

Mason ventured to the left. Apart from discoloration the stone was bare, old and worn. It didn't take long to walk the length of the building. Around the back, he met up with Quaid, who'd walked the other side.

'Some of those blocks are so badly pitted a cross could have been chipped off,' Quaid said. 'But I saw no sign of recent activity, to be honest.'

Mason agreed. He stopped and looked through an empty

rear window. Sally was standing in the centre of the roof-less church, staring up at the walls.

'Any luck?'

'All of it bad,' she said, sniffing. 'There are no symbols on these walls.'

They took another look around, taking their time and getting closer to the walls. The sun crested above them, throwing out rays of warmth. Mason was struck by the absolute quiet that hung over the site, which seemed wrapped in haunting beauty.

Half an hour later they met by the front entrance.

'I'm sorry to say we've drawn a blank,' Quaid said.

Sally nodded her agreement. 'Which means . . .' she said.

'The cemetery,' Roxy said a little gloomily. 'My life lately appears to have been a long line of crypts, mausoleums and cemeteries.'

They climbed back over the fence with a little more aplomb this time, landing softly on the other side and then making their way to the graveyard. It was a small plot of land that held maybe twenty gravestones. Mason saw imme-diately that there were several carvings adorning the concrete markers.

As the sun beat down, the team dropped to their knees in the grass, checking every stone.

Mason studied a marker closely, identifying an hourglass and a skull and crossbones. Checking that marker off, he moved to the next as Sally spoke up.

'I'm seeing several masonic carvings,' she said, 'that possibly date back to the Templars, or shortly after.'

Mason examined another marker, this one depicting a woman and two children but no cross. Quaid and Hassell appeared to be having no luck also, and Roxy was busying herself checking their perimeter.

Sally insisted on checking all the grave markers herself. When she was finished, she straightened and let out a long sigh. 'I'm not liking this,' she said. 'Could we have read it all wrong?'

'But Temple is an ancient Templar village. It was Ballentrodoch, town of the warriors,' Quaid said. 'I can't believe we can't find one cross.'

Sally narrowed her eyes at him. 'That's a point,' she said. 'In a church. No crosses. I wonder . . .' She turned on her heel and made her way across to a gravestone that stood close to the chain-link fence that surrounded the church. Mason watched her bend down and start scrutinising it more closely.

'I wonder . . .' she repeated.

Roxy appeared at Mason's side. 'What's she wondering?'

'I have no idea.'

'She's in research mode?'

'You make her sound like a robot. But, yeah, she's in research mode.'

Roxy sent a look around the churchyard. 'You think we're alone out here?'

'It's a good question. The good news is that we seem to be dealing with mercenaries so far who don't have a whole lot of subtlety.'

'So far?'

'Obviously there's somebody else behind all this. Maybe even the Freemasons. They must know we're closing in on the end of our mission.'

'You think they'll get desperate?'

'I think it's a given.'

Sally was rooting around in the weeds at the bottom of her headstone. Now, she upended a bottle of water over it and started to scrub it clean with her hands and coat sleeves. Mason started walking towards her along with Roxy.

'Have you found something?'

Sally sat back. 'I think so.' She sounded short of breath. 'The clue was "follow the cross", right? Well, what if we're not looking for a crucifix?'

'What else could it mean?' Mason asked.

'Exactly what it says. Follow the cross. Do you remember how we found the Templars' secret alphabet on the clue that was written on an earlier basin?'

Mason nodded. 'A collection of symbols,' he said.

'That's right. And do you remember what I said? Each symbol is a piece of the cross of the Order of the Temple. It is the cross of eight points, or eight beatitudes. The letters are represented in compliance with angles and points determined by the cross.'

'Have you found the symbols?' Mason asked.

'Yes, at the foot of this grave. Half buried among the weeds. I noticed them on my first look. They rang a bell, but we were searching for a cross. Of course, the cross is the Templar alphabet.'

'What does it say?' Roxy asked.

Sally placed her backpack on the ground, unzipped it and reached in for her notes. Mason crouched down to look. The headstone bore a row of symbols close to its base, mostly triangles pointed in different directions, some with circles at their centre. He waited patiently for Sally to work out what they meant.

She worked with a pencil and a notepad, eventually looking up to say: 'It's short and sweet. It just says: to the crypt.'

Roxy groaned. Mason bent down to look. 'Is that it? Surely there's more to it?'

Sally checked again, her expression slightly confused. 'No,' she said after a while. 'You can see here' – she rubbed the headstone – 'that no markings have been removed or worn off. This is the full clue.'

'To the crypt?' Roxy said, worried. 'What crypt?'

'I'm thinking it's literal,' Sally said, standing and looking down at the grave.

Quaid and Hassell came over to them. Quaid overheard her last comment. 'You think this stone marks the entrance to a crypt? Something that runs under the church?'

'It'd make sense,' Sally said. 'Remember that the legend says that the Templars brought their treasure here. Twixt the oak and the elm tree, you will find buried the millions free. I think that they were once buried here at Temple Church.'

Mason agreed with her. It would make sense, and the short clue was nothing if it wasn't literal.

'When we drove through the village,' he said. 'I noticed a little farm and supply shop. Let's hope they sell shovels.'

# Chapter 33

Mason plunged his shovel into the earth, leaning in and then pressing down with his boot. The others followed suit. Mason felt uncomfortable – gravedigging was not exactly how he'd imagined spending the afternoon – but continued because of the faith he had in Sally.

The day had turned wild again, strong winds gusting through the trees, rustling the branches in torrid waves. Torn foliage and twigs battered their faces and jackets. Mason bent to the task, trying to shrug off the uneasiness. The top layer of sod came off easily, leaving the bare earth. Mason thrust his shovel in again, lifting up another pile of soil and depositing it behind his back. Together, they dug deeper into the grave.

'Well, I never saw myself as a gravedigger,' Roxy said after a few minutes. 'How wrong does this feel, guys?'

'I have to admit,' Quaid said, 'I'm regretting starting this.'

Sally was digging furiously. 'Keep going. We'll break through, I just know we will.'

Mason was afraid to ask, 'Into what?' and kept at it. Sweat was beading his brow. His mouth was dry. As a team they stuck together, excavating the grave shovel by shovel, trusting in Sally's instincts.

They were four feet down near to the top end when Sally's shovel broke right through the dirt and hit nothing but empty space.

Mason leapt forward as Sally teetered on the edge of a void. He caught her round the waist and steadied her, pulling her backward. His boots hit soil but, a few feet to his left, he made out a hole.

It was surrounded with overhanging earth, long roots hanging down like dreadlocks. Mason got down onto his knees and shuffled forward, testing the firmness of the ground.

'I think we've found something,' he said, not without a little incredulity in his voice.

'Out here in the middle of nowhere,' Quaid said. 'Who'd have thought it?'

'Not me.' Roxy flung her shovel down and strode to Mason's side. 'I'm guessing it's another damn crypt?'

Mason picked up Sally's shovel and started hacking at the edges of the earth. Huge clumps fell away. Sally drew a torch from her bag and knelt at his side.

'Let me see.'

Mason drew back. Sally switched the torch on and aimed it into the black hole below. The first thing Mason saw illuminated was a set of stone steps, now covered in debris. He found their apex and sliced at the earth that covered them. Soon, he saw the first step, an oblong concrete platform from which they could begin their descent.

Roxy and the others crowded around.

'Torches,' Mason said. 'And take a couple of good breaths. It'll be the last fresh air you breathe for a while.' He turned to Roxy. 'I'm sorry you have to go through this.'

The American bit her bottom lip. 'I guess I'll be facing my fears once again. Don't worry, I'm a big girl.'

Sally inched her way towards the hole. Mason was about to go in front of her but then remembered they'd just unearthed a centuries-old passageway and that the dangers ahead wouldn't be any worse than those behind. And, of course, she knew better than any of them what to expect.

Sally bent low and started inching her way down the stone steps. Mason fell in at her back. Roxy took the rear after taking a last long look around. The narrow staircase was slippery with dirt and gravel. A fetid smell reached their nostrils. Mason shone his torch on the steps and then the walls but saw nothing except damp stone and a wall of earth. The only sound was the soft tread of their boots, and the soft exhale-inhale of their breathing.

Sally descended twelve steps before she reached the soft floor of a tunnel. Mason noticed that each step was bowed in the middle, as if – at some point in the distant past – this had been an active passageway. There was debris everywhere and the roots of trees and a few rocks jutting out into the tunnel. Sally inched her way along.

Mason followed carefully. Already, he felt claustrophobic. The others were crowded close to his back. Around them, tiny cascades of earth fell from above, spattering across the floor. Sally and Mason shone their torches ahead, but made out only a narrow passage in the earth shored up sporadically by wooden ceiling braces. Beyond that lay utter darkness.

As they picked their way forward, Roxy's voice rose from the back of the group. 'I don't like the feel of this. It's not safe.'

'Not far now,' Sally said.

'How can you possibly know that?'

Sally didn't answer, just kept on creeping forward. All their backs were bent and at one point they were forced to crawl. Mason felt a trickle of soil hit the nape of his neck and then fall across his hair. It was cool under the earth, but they were all sweating.

He scrambled to keep up with Sally. She was smaller and, with her fell running, possibly fitter. She wasn't hanging around either, just pushing ahead. Mason slowed to inch his way past an outcrop of rock and realised that she was way ahead.

'Hey,' he said. 'Stay together.'

A network of roots hung down to the right. Mason was forced to crawl under them, snagging his backpack and having to pull it free. He didn't pull too hard. He wasn't sure what would happen. Ahead, a rotten wooden door hung askew to reveal another passage, even narrower, that branched off to the right.

Sally turned around and waited. Mason made sure the others were with them before waving her on. The passage continued straight, an unwavering man-made pathway built beneath the Scottish countryside. The wooden ceiling supports they passed creaked gently as if reminding them of the immense weight resting on top. The floor was over-grown with weeds and roots and littered with rocks.

Mason ignored the oppressive feeling, concentrating instead on the passageway. It ran unerringly towards . . . something. Maybe it was a bolt-hole and would come up somewhere in the woods, maybe it would be a dead end, but the clue had definitely read: to the crypt.

Sally forged on. Mason hurried to keep up with her. He figured they'd been walking slowly for about eight minutes when the end of the passage came up quite abruptly.

The back wall was high, semi-circular in shape. Stone ledges that had once been dug into the earth wall lay on their sides or edges where they'd fallen. Mason counted at least eight of them as Sally rushed forward.

'Slow down,' said Roxy, eyeing the walls nervously.

Mason joined Sally as she dropped to her knees in the dirt and focused her torch on the ground where the ledges lay. He spotted several objects lying around. One in particular was bulky, wrapped in old brown cloth. Sally removed it from its ancient resting place and brought it more into the light.

Everyone crowded around. 'What is it?' Quaid whispered.

Carefully, Sally unwrapped the object, which, as the cloth came apart, turned into several smaller items. 'Pottery,' she said. 'Probably from the old church. A bowl, a plate and a chalice.'

Quaid leaned over. 'It's not the Holy Grail, is it?' he asked gruffly.

Sally shook her head seriously. 'Unfortunately not. What else do we have?'

Mason helped, picking up the smaller wrapped items that had fallen at the same time as the shelves, whilst the others illuminated the scene. Mason heard nothing but their breathing and some indefinite rustling, probably some unknown creature in the darkness.

'Plates,' Sally said, unwrapping items. 'One incredibly old crucifix, and another that can be worn like a pendant.'

'I have a brooch,' Mason said. 'The clasp is broken.' Somehow, it felt incredibly sad, finding someone's piece of ancient, damaged jewellery all this way underground.

Sally shuffled forward, reaching into the darkness under the broken shelves. 'This fell the furthest,' she said. 'And it's heavy.'

She dragged out a large object wrapped in the same rough brown cloth and deposited it between her knees. Mason watched as she uncovered it.

'Now what the hell is that?' he asked.

Sally bent closer, studying it carefully. She shone her light on it, turning it in her hands. Mason straightened up for a moment, easing his aching back.

'It's the ancient seal of Templar Church,' she said. 'The one that's missing from the front. They buried it down here, maybe to preserve it, I'm not sure. The seal is like a coat of arms, bearing religious symbols and words significant to the specific church.'

'I don't recall seeing a church seal before,' Quaid said.

'Just take a look at any English church to see a surfeit of seals and arms – so many, to be honest, that almost everyone passes them by without a second thought. I guess they worked like a corporate logo does today. The arms were immediately recognisable and covered our churches at the time. The Church also assigned them a spiritual function: the arms reproduced the glory of God. Interestingly the actual coat of arms is depicted in code.'

Mason was getting fidgety. 'Is it what we're looking for?'

Sally stared closely at the seal. 'There's script around the sides,' she said. 'And, right in the middle, a carving of a small basin. A Molten Sea basin. This seal is exactly what we're looking for.'

Mason watched as she took photos from every angle, in all kinds of light, and then gently rewrapped the seal before putting it back into place.

'We're not taking it with us?' Hassell asked.

'This is a sacred place,' Sally said. 'We don't have the equipment yet to remove these artefacts in the correct manner. We can organise someone to do that at a later date.'

It seemed the correct thing to do and Sally was obviously determined to do it. Mason stopped her wrapping and took a few pictures of his own. 'Just in case,' he said.

'In case?' she asked

'If you lose your phone down here, I'm not coming back to get it,' Roxy clarified. 'Can we go now?'

Mason saw no other reason to stay. They turned around in the space without checking any further and made their way into the narrow passage. Steadily, they started back towards the exit. Mason shivered. They'd been down here in the cold for a while now. He'd be glad to see sunlight and the open sky even if it was chilly up there. Roxy was a step behind him, also anxious to escape the tunnel. Sally came next and then Quaid and Hassell. Together, they retraced their steps of earlier.

Six minutes passed. Mason was squeezing past a protruding boulder when the sound of whispered conversation reached his ears. It travelled down the passage from somewhere ahead. Mason instantly stopped and crouched, waving at the others to do the same.

'What is it?' Sally whispered.

'Company,' he said.

With nowhere to go, Mason felt a touch of despair. The passage ran only one way; it was narrow and overgrown and dangerous. Even as he listened the sound of creaking support timbers reached his ears.

'What are we going to do?' Sally asked.

Mason turned to her. 'We're gonna have to fight our way out,' he said.

What choice did they have?

# Chapter 34

Sally moved to the back of the line. Mason made sure their torches were switched off and a swathe of darkness enveloped them. They removed their backpacks and crouched behind the jutting-out rock. Roxy tried to move to his side, but Mason held her back.

'I'll do this,' he said.

'It's what I'm good at,' she said.

'Me too,' he said. 'And you have more than enough to overcome. I don't want to force you to kill and set you back on your road to recovery.'

Roxy sighed but let him stay in place. 'They will be trying to kill us, so it hardly matters,' she said. 'It's not like this is a dark-ops mission, and I've been told to target someone I can't be sure deserves it.'

Mason steadied himself. The whispered conversation came closer. He could hear the shuffling of feet now too, although he couldn't guess at the enemies' number. This would take skill, and it would need luck. The first thing he saw was a handgun entering his field of vision from around a corner, and then the arm that held it. He'd been half expecting a crusty old professor to be leading the way.

Mason rose, grabbed the arm and yanked it hard

231

towards him. The owner staggered in shock, dropping the gun to the floor and falling to his knees. Mason delivered a throat punch and then a hard blow to the nose that rendered him unconscious.

Already, the second man was in sight.

His torch was focused on the passage ahead rather than on what had just occurred. Quickly, Mason delivered another throat punch, this time shoving the shocked mercenary in Roxy's direction as a third man came around the corner. The third man's eyes widened. Mason noted his stunned expression and wasted no time grabbing his collar, pulling him forward and off his feet.

The man crashed to the floor, stirring up a fog of dust. Mason kicked him in the ribs. Roxy disarmed her opponent, rendered him unconscious and took Mason's place beside the rock.

'Doug?' someone was whispering from around the rock. 'Doug? Are you okay there?' The heavily accented eastern European voice carried a thick hint of suspicion.

Roxy turned to Hassell, who read her mind and grunted an affirmative. Roxy shrugged. A surprise attack was worth a try. The next man came around the rock, exercising extreme caution.

'Hey,' he started to say, seeing his own man on the ground being pummelled by Mason.

Roxy, hidden behind the rock, struck out like a snake, jabbing his throat and eyes. The man jerked back into the wall, stumbled and tried to bring his gun up.

Roxy shot him in the stomach.

Hassell and Quaid were at her side. Hassell had his own gun drawn. 'Warning them that we have weapons too?' he asked.

Roxy nodded. She could already see the next man coming around the rock, dashing low and fast. His gun was aimed towards Mason.

Roxy put a bullet in him too, and now both men's bodies were blocking access around the rock. It was a moment before she realised it would be easier to actually crawl underneath the rock.

She gritted her teeth. It was the last thing she wanted to do but the situation called for extreme measures. She dropped to her knees and then the floor, taking a good look under the rock. There was about two feet of space. The ground was strewn with grit and small rocks. She started shuffling forward, increasingly aware of the heavy jagged abutment above her.

Mason ran back to Hassell, dripping with sweat. His knuckles ached but other than that he'd escaped without injury. He took a quick look at the men Roxy had shot.

'No alternative,' Hassell said.

Mason nodded. At his feet, he could see Roxy's legs wriggling as she forced her way under the rock. To his right, he could also see the two men plugging the gap were being moved from the other side. As their bodies fell to the floor, Mason grabbed the first hand he saw and yanked it forward. A burly man wearing a denim jacket lashed out with his left fist and caught Mason a blow across the right cheek. Mason ducked and fired in several more punches before falling to his knees in the dirt as the man crashed down alongside him.

Above, another mercenary crowded past the rock. Hassell jumped at him.

Mason scuffled and traded blows in the dirt, crawling from left to right and landing on top of his opponent. Already there was another pushing past the rock. Quaid couldn't quite reach him because of Hassell. The man had a gun but seemed uncertain where he needed to aim. Quaid brought his own gun up and fired at the rock beside the man's head before pushing past Hassell and smashing the gun from his hand. Mason grabbed the jacket of his

233

opponent and hauled himself along until they were face to face. Then he headbutted the guy, causing him to gasp. Taking advantage of the man's momentary confusion, Mason drove his fists into the guy's ribs, tight and fast, not doing much damage but enough to retain his advantage and keep the guy off balance.

Roxy forced her way under the rock. It was slow going. The heavy weight bore down on her, but she put it out of her mind as much as she was able. At last, her head emerged from the other side, and she was able to take in the sight beyond.

There were four mercenaries still waiting, all with their guns drawn. They were focused on the rock and the chaos unfolding around it. Roxy shuffled forward an inch at a time, taking care to make no noise. The men were holding torches in front of their faces, all focused on the rock, helping her remain in the shadows.

The space was confined. Roxy shuffled and swayed back and forth to force her body out from under the rock and then into the gap between it and the narrow passage. Her trousers tore at the knee, her jacket bunched across her shoulders. She held on to her gun tightly, crouched and gathered herself.

She took the opportunity to absorb more details. At the back of the party were the professors they'd encountered at Baldock church. She couldn't remember their names and, to be ruthlessly honest, they didn't matter right now. The men with guns were the sole focus of her attention.

Roxy sneaked in as close as she dared, then rose to a standing position, gun in hand. She shot the first man in the chest, turned to the second and fired again.

As expected, the third man had already drawn a bead on her.

Roxy ducked, rolled and came up behind him, firing at the fourth man and tagging him in the thigh. Then, she was running, a handful of dirt clasped in a fist. She threw it at the third man as he fired, the bullet whizzing past so close to her skull she felt the heat of its passage. The dirt hit him in the face, making him cover up. Roxy launched herself at him, tackling him at the waist and driving him against the big rock. His spine hit hard, making him grunt in pain. Roxy focused on the gun, pinning the arm to the rock with the hand she held her own gun in.

Which left her other arm free.

Roxy hooked it around the man's neck, cutting his air supply off. He fought, lashing out and jerking wildly but she held on.

Her other big issue was the two professors, who were stood back, looking at each other in shock. One of them glanced at the weapon that had fallen to the ground near their feet.

'Do it and you die,' she growled.

Her opponent bucked back and forth. Roxy used her body to pin him to the rock. She kept his gun pointed at the ground, letting it go off twice in the enclosed passage as she steadily choked the life from him.

At last, his body slumped. At that moment one of the two professors darted for the gun. Roxy had two lightning-fast breakthrough moments. One – he was called Justin, and two, if he turned that gun on her she was going to have to kill him.

Justin picked the gun up, holding it in his hand still pointed at the ground. His eyes turned to her, speculative.

'Don't be a fool,' she said. 'I don't want to kill you.'

'You killed them,' Julian, the other tetchy professor, said.

'They were armed. And they're not all dead. Put the gun down.'

Justin wavered. He didn't want to act, she could tell. It was his ego taunting him, the image he wanted to portray. There was a moment stretching between them, something as unpredictable and volatile as explosive. Justin's eyes bored into hers. If he twisted that gun in her direction, she would shoot him, and she would hate herself for being forced to do so.

Julian put a hand on his colleague's shoulder. 'Leave it,' he said. 'Our work is not their work.' He nodded at the downed men.

'Then we won't get in your way,' Roxy said. 'But I see you as enemy combatants. If you don't do as I say, or if you try to run, I will shoot you.'

Justin dropped the gun with a clatter. Roxy closed them down in double-time, taking any temptation to use firearms away, and ordered them to stand to the side. After that, she returned to the rock.

On the other side of the rock, Mason had used his elbows to subdue his opponent. Quaid had knocked his opponent to the ground and Hassell was struggling with the last man standing, the two men caught between the rock and the earth wall. Mason noticed Hassell and the last man crashing into one of the timber stanchions, and winced as he saw the wood splinter. As he watched, his own opponent seemed to wake up, then started to buck and rear, trying to throw Mason off. He slid to the left and tried to hold on. His torch fell to one side. Both he and Hassell were forced into a chaotic, bloody and dusty scramble inside the crypt, their rolling torches throwing light and shadow across the walls. Mason caught a blow across the face. In darkness, he fought. Behind him, Sally switched on her own light and tried to illuminate the scene, but her grip was shaky. Quaid leapt to Hassell's aid.

Mason struggled in the shadows. A blow landed on the top of his head. Mason saw dark spots. He felt the other man gaining the upper hand. He gripped clothing hard, forced his way back from his adversary, trying to create room. He swung with two fast hooks just like he'd been taught in the gym, catching his adversary on the side of the jaw with both. The other man slumped, still struggling but weaker than before. Mason knelt on his chest and then grabbed his own gun and struck the other man's temples with the butt.

The fight finally went out of his opponent. Mason collected the man's gun and then patted his clothing for other weapons. Ahead, Hassell and Quaid had grabbed hold of their foe, and were banging his forehead into the rock. Mason went on to collect more weapons and shove them into his pockets. They wouldn't kill if they didn't have to, and one way to stop the killing on both sides was to remove the guns.

'Hey, guys, don't shoot me.'

Mason was relieved to hear Roxy's voice. 'Are you okay?'

'Yeah, had to tag a few but they'll live with medical attention, I think. I've got two professors over here too.'

Mason recalled the two men from Baldock. 'See what you can get out of them.'

'I'll try.'

Mason thought that Roxy sounded a little subdued. Of course, working on civilians wasn't something she'd be comfortable with.

He berated himself. Of course, none of them were comfortable with it. But they could at least try to some degree.

A few minutes later they pushed around the rock to see Roxy with an arm draped around one of the professors' shoulders. Mason saw it as more of a cajoling gesture than anything else. Typical of Roxy to use it as part of her threats.

Sally and Mason approached the odd scene.

'What do you want to know?' the other professor asked.

'Happy to help,' the one with Roxy's arm hanging across his neck managed.

'Who hired you?' Mason asked quickly, talking to the other man.

'"Who hired . . ."? Don't you even know who you're up against?'

Mason shook his head. 'Not really.'

As they spoke, Sally, unable to wait in her excitement, had started to flick through the photos on her phone. She began to study the seal and the words upon it carefully.

'I can read this . . .' she said softly.

'Listen, Justin, just tell them,' the one with Roxy's arm around his neck said. 'Please.'

'All right, all right, stop bleating about it.' Justin turned to Mason. 'Now, listen, I don't know a lot, so you'll have to make do. They didn't tell us much, but they told us more than the grunts over there.' Justin flicked a disdainful hand towards the fallen mercs.

'Grunts?' These men were the enemy but that didn't mean Mason liked the way Justin dismissed them.

'Not a whiff of a brain cell between them,' Justin snorted. 'Anyway, let me continue.'

Mason took a deep breath, realising how incredibly out of his depth Justin must feel. The way he was talking . . . almost as if he was lecturing. And, despite appearances, he had to be scared.

'Get on with it,' Roxy growled.

'They call themselves the Guild of Night,' Justin said, his voice low in the tunnel as if smothered by the dust and dirt and sheer weight of the ground above them. 'They're . . . like a secret organisation within a secret organisation. So . . . the Guild operate inside the Freemasons. I don't know how big they are, how far they can reach. I'm not privy to their ambitions or their motivations. All I know is a man called Murdock McCloud is the boss and he's a very bad individual. Comes from this neck of the woods . . . I believe.'

Mason blinked at him. 'Right here? This village?'

'No, no. Scotland, I mean. He owns a castle in Scotland.'

'Well, that narrows it down,' Quaid said drily. 'There's only about one every twenty miles.'

'It's not just him,' Justin went on, shuffling his feet nervously. 'They're a group. The Guild is spread all over England and Scotland and they never use modern technology to meet. It's all envoys and ambassadors, that kind of crap.'

Mason wondered if Justin knew what he was talking about. It sounded as if he was plucking facts out of the air and weaving them into a tall tale. Having said that, they'd heard the name Murdock McCloud before.

'When you say McCloud's bad, what do you mean?' he asked.

'The worst kind of bad,' Justin said immediately. 'A clever nutjob with power and influence. No conscience. Of course, it's all just stories until . . . well, until it isn't.'

'If they're so secretive where do the stories come from?' Hassell asked.

'Stories always get out,' Justin said. 'It's the human way. Each tale resonates, like the toll of a bell. Light or dark. Soft or loud. They come from workers, from staff, from the eager mouths of trolls. The stories can't help but spread.'

'And get embellished along the way,' Quaid said. 'I know the sort. Christ, I heard more than a few of my own in the army. When I was the boss, I was either Hitler or Churchill depending on who you spoke to and what time of day it was.'

Justin shrugged. 'You hear something once, twice,' he said, 'yeah, it's hearsay. You hear it from every source . . . maybe not so much.'

'We're getting off track,' Roxy said, tightening her arm a little more around Justin's neck. 'What else do you know about this Guild of Night? Why do they hire mercs? Why do they want the basins? How many do you people have?'

Justin squirmed a little, as if he'd been caught deliberately misleading them. 'They're insular, secretive,' he reiterated. 'Established a long time ago, back in the eighteenth century and directly from the Templars. Or what was left of them. And you have to imagine that what was left of them . . . was a pretty acrimonious, hostile order.'

'Because of the persecution,' Quaid said.

'Yes. And as to why they want the basins – that's pretty obvious. They hate the Church. They blame the Vatican for their oppression, and with good reason, may I add. If they can find a way to hurt the Church, they will stop at nothing to accomplish that aim.'

'Are we all searching for the Temple of Solomon? The Ark?' Mason asked.

Justin shrugged. 'The Templar treasure is vast. It could be all those things and more. And they hire these goons to do their dirty work' – Justin pointed at the injured men – 'because it helps maintain a secrecy they enjoy. It's not like they have an army of their own.'

Mason had heard enough. Clearly, the Guild of Night needed investigating, in particular this Murdock McCloud. And he certainly wasn't enjoying Justin's low-key arrogance. He was about to speak up when Sally beat him to it.

'Of course,' she said, still examining the photos. 'Of course. It's all here.' She looked up. 'I know where we have to go next.'

Mason put a hand to his lips. 'Not now. Too many ears. Roxy, tie them up and let's get the hell out of here.'

Hassell stepped over to help her. Sally rose to her feet and faced them with a satisfied smile on her face.

'It's clever,' she said, unable to help herself. 'But I think I've cracked it.'

'Can't wait to hear,' Quaid said.

Mason didn't speak. He was conscious of the two professors. Of the quiet moans of the injured men. And of the fact that the way back through the tunnel was now a lot more dangerous than it had been.

'Hurry,' he said.

# Chapter 35

As they made their way back through the tunnel, they were forced to crawl on their stomachs, occasionally holding their breath as they squeezed through a particularly tight spot. At one point, Mason worried he was stuck as he forced his way through a narrow gap, his clothes catching on rocky outcrops, his skin scraping against rough stone. The tunnel was cold and smelled of dank earth, the soft roof raining down trickles of dirt that caught in their hair and pattered across their necks.

Mason was sweating hard as he reached the base of the stone steps that led up to daylight, delighted to see the way out at last.

Roxy sighed in relief as she emerged from the darkness just behind him. 'Bring me that sunshine.'

There was a light drizzle falling, the rain dropping through the underground entrance in sparkling droplets, spattering the stone steps and making them slick. Mason put one boot on the first step and then started up.

Roxy pushed past him on the stairs, almost unbalancing him, but he let it go. He was surprised when she stopped halfway up the flight. 'Shit,' she said.

Mason hesitated with feet on two stairs. 'What is it?'

'Cars,' she said. 'Same make that chased us a few days ago. There's three more of 'em lined up along the road outside the church. I see four men, all armed.'

'How far away are they?' Mason asked.

'Too far.' Roxy knew what he was thinking. 'We'd never reach them without being spotted.'

'Could we take them all at once?' Hassell asked, referring to their own firepower.

'Risky, very risky. We can only pop up one at a time due to the restricted exit.'

'What alternative do we have?' Quaid asked.

Mason took Roxy's place on the flight of stairs and carefully raised his head so that he could study the scenario. The four men were wearing jackets that didn't conceal their weapons, and hats that didn't conceal their hard faces. They lounged stiffly against the cars, throwing the odd glance in Mason's general direction. 'They look bored,' he said. 'You think they're connected to those we left below?'

It was a rhetorical question. Hassell answered with the obvious reply. 'No chance. They'd be on us by now.'

'So what do we do next?' Sally asked fretfully. 'The next clue won't wait around for ever.'

Mason backed down the steps and turned to Hassell. 'This is a major setback,' he said. 'But you're the expert. How do we exfil a situation like this?'

Hassell smiled grimly. 'It's gonna be hard to conjure up a distraction down here,' he said. 'And leaving all at once is – as Roxy said – risky. They couldn't fail to see us.' He looked around, thinking hard. 'The only way out, I'm afraid . . . is back down.'

Mason frowned. 'How is that gonna help? We'd be trapping ourselves down there.'

'Maybe not. Do you remember there was another passage-way? We could hopefully use that to escape.'

Mason remembered that it had been smaller still. 'How can we be sure it's a way out?'

'We can't. But consider this: if we're quiet, the guys already down there won't know we've returned. And the passage branches off before we reach them. They won't know which way we went.'

'And once they find the seal, they won't care.' Sally nodded. 'It's a great idea.'

Roxy didn't look like she agreed and, to be fair, Mason thought, it was still a major setback. They were effectively trapped down here with no obvious way to reach their cars. Mason turned to follow Hassell back down into the earth. They walked carefully and quietly as they started to renegotiate the passageway. What worried him most was the creaking ceiling supports. They might have survived intact for hundreds of years down here, but today's influx of new elements was bound to make things shift. He kept his thoughts to himself.

Hassell crept at a slow pace until he reached the low thorny tangle of brush and then dropped to his stomach to crawl underneath. Roxy went next, followed by Mason. The earth was quite smooth by now, since the journey had been made recently several times. On the other side of the tangle, Mason saw the rotten door that hung askew.

Hassell was squeezing into the new passage.

Mason struggled to remain quiet, as he started squeezing into the passage himself. Its tightness made him want to gasp and grunt. It was an odd sensation, and the sudden narrowing of the tunnel surprised him.

The earth walls were shored up by wooden stanchions at regular intervals. The ground was thick dirt and rock with the occasional boulder. Mason barked his shin several times. Moving forward, he thought to shine his torch carefully backwards to make sure they were all inside the tunnel.

'All here,' he whispered to Roxy. 'Let's go.'

Mason cursed at himself in silence. They hadn't thought this through at all, and had left Sally at the back of the line. If someone followed them, she wouldn't be able to fight back.

Shaking his head at his mistake, Mason bade them all back out of the tunnel and switched positions. He put himself at the rear of the pack. Long minutes passed. Mason could hear the groaning conversation taking place further along the tunnel as the mercs they'd shot tried to figure a way out. They were getting closer.

'Move,' Mason whispered.

In the dark, they shuffled through the narrow offshoot. They crawled at first, then squirmed on their stomachs as the passage constricted. Whoever had cut the original tunnel hadn't paid as much attention to this one, barely making enough space for a normal-sized person to crawl through. And in here, the air was thinner. Mason's chest started heaving.

Together, the five of them scrambled over piles of rocks that snagged their clothes and scraped their skin. They scrabbled aside loose earth that hampered their progress. It was slow going as they negotiated the medieval tunnel, wishing their predecessors had made a better job of it.

Mason's knuckles and right arm were aching from the effort. It had been a painful, vicious battle back there. He tried to ignore the pain as always, but the conditions down here and the way he had to constantly pull himself forward didn't help.

'I think this is a bad idea,' Roxy said at one point, her voice travelling back to Mason, who read all kinds of emotions in her tone. Frustration, anger, even some fear. This was not Roxy's forte. Nobody answered, but whether it was because they agreed with her or they wanted to stay quiet, Mason didn't know.

They continued to drag themselves along the tunnel. Again, Mason wondered why the designers couldn't have built it a little larger. If it was an escape route, it was hardly a quick one. His clothes were damp from the moist earth, his breathing laboured and his eyes barely able to pick out the man ahead.

Eventually, they came to a length of pure rock. The ancient builders had had their work cut out here, having been forced to dig through the rock if they wanted to continue. Luckily, it only ran for about four feet and then formed a hard slope to lower ground beyond. Mason found that he could slither to the edge of it and then slide for several feet, ending up at the bottom. It was a brief but comfortable relief after so long wriggling through dirt.

Hassell was still at the front of the line. Mason imagined Roxy, who was following, would be filling the air with off-colour comments as she hauled herself along.

As the minutes passed, Mason began to feel as if he'd never reach the end of this tunnel. The cloying restrictiveness of it overwhelmed him. They'd be stuck here for ever, crawling until they ran out of breath or just gave up. He couldn't imagine having to somehow crawl backwards the way they'd already come.

A moment later he heard an unbelievable noise behind them. Someone else was coming along the passage, crawling at a far faster rate than he was.

Mason swore to himself. If they were armed, he was well and truly fucked. He pressed himself into the earth wall close to a wooden support, and brought his knees up to his chest. Then, he swivelled around, using the loose dirt to help him move. He used the timber as a prop to help him turn around in the cramped tunnel. His body protested as he tried to turn. The rocks ripped at his skin. He could feel the top of his head scrape against something hard and ungiving, and then the trickling sensation of blood on his scalp. But he did it. He turned around. He was ready to face whoever was following them – head on. His enemy was coming closer, a tunnel rat of the highest order. Mason tucked his legs in and then pushed off hard with his knees, forcing his whole body to swivel until it faced the wrong way down the tunnel. The top of his head scraped earth and then rock and started to leak more blood.

But he was facing his adversary.

Mason could hear movement, but there was no torch-light. The other guy was crawling blind. Maybe he enjoyed this kind of shit and had volunteered for it. Mason waited, hearing the quick shuffling approach. He saw a dark shape first, a huddle of blackness, and then the figure was in his face, almost knocking their heads together. Mason lashed out as best he could with a right, the rasp of his breath loud, echoing in the confined walls. His already aching knuckles connected hard with a cheekbone. There was a gasp and a grunt of surprise. Mason drove forward his advantage.

He grabbed his opponent's head, and drove it face first into the ground. Then, as the man raised his head back up, Mason drove his forehead into the man's nose. It was a solid connection. Gave him the chance to grab the man's head once more and drive it into the ground again even as he was hit multiple times by a weakly jabbing left. Seeing that, Mason only had to worry about the man's right hand.

It came fast, and it held a knife.

Mason squirmed to the side, but the passage barely allowed him any movement. The knife missed, glancing off rock. Mason clamped the man's wrist against the side of the passage.

He heard scrambling behind him. Mason clasped the man's wrists as his opponent tried to find a way to bring any strength to bear. A light fell across them, shone by Quaid. At first, even though flooding from behind, it blinded Mason, but then it helped him assess the options.

They weren't good.

On the plus side, he couldn't see anyone following his opponent. Probably, then, the guy had volunteered to check the passage quickly on his own. But holstered at his side was a handgun, which he'd been moving too quickly to carry in his hand. If Mason let go of the man, there was a chance he'd reach down and try to draw it even in the cramped conditions.

They struggled hard. Mason was bleeding, the blood trickling down across one cheek. As he flung his head to the right a red mist filled his vision. Light spun before his eyes. He fastened onto his adversary's wrists as best he could. All he knew in the crazy melee was darkness and bright blasts of light, cobwebs that clung to them, the rising of dust and the sharp shortness of breath. He twisted the wrist that held the knife until his opponent screamed, his voice filling the passageway, but there was no alternative. They rolled left and right, crashing into the supports that helped prop up the roof, until they splintered.

Mason finally broke the guy's left wrist, twisting it hard until he heard a snap. The knife fell to the floor. He held on firmly to the man's right wrist, giving him no chance to reach for his gun, then he scrabbled for the knife, grabbing it by the blade, the sharp edge cutting into his flesh. He dropped it again, then grabbed the handle this time and tried to jam it into his opponent's neck. The knife struck flesh and tore clothing as the man raised his free arm to defend himself. The knife slashed the back of the man's hand. Mason tried again. This time his opponent was too slow. The knife's blade entered the man's neck. The man stopped struggling. He seemed almost surprised. Then his head flopped forward and his breathing slowed.

Mason relaxed. He was panting hard, trying to deal with the flood of adrenalin that was now starting to dissipate.

'Take a moment,' Quaid said behind him. 'Hassell kept going. I think he's found a way out.'

'Well done,' Mason puffed. 'Well done, Hassell. I knew he could do it.'

The news galvanised him. All he wanted now was to see a big sky, to feel unobstructed and free. He paused as more noises reached his ears. On listening, he concluded that they emanated from further back in the tunnel.

'Crap,' he breathed. 'There's more of them. They're gonna have to find a way around their dead friend, but I guess it won't take them too long. Go, just go.'

Mason gathered his strength and squirmed his way around once more until he was facing the right way. The same wounds on the top of his head hit even more spiky rock, increasing the flow of blood. He gritted his teeth, closing his eyes until he was the correct way around, and then grabbing hold of two clods of earth to propel him forward.

Quaid was already out of sight.

Behind him, more mercenaries crawled closer.

And to his right, the wooden roof support shattered.

# Chapter 36

Mason moved fast, desperate to escape the cracked support before it gave way completely. Soil was already cascading from above, and it was only a matter of time before the whole tunnel caved in around him. He fought to catch up to Quaid.

'Move it,' Hassell's voice came from the darkness ahead. 'There's no easy way out here.'

Mason's heart sank. At that point the tunnel dipped again, sending him forward on his stomach. Mason hit the bottom of the passage face first and took in a mouthful of soil.

Spluttering, he looked up. Quaid's torch illuminated the way ahead. It widened here, much like the other space had enlarged where they'd found the seal. Mason was able to climb to his feet and they could stand three abreast. He put a hand to his head that came away slick with blood.

'They're coming,' he said. 'An indeterminate number, but they're right behind us. Why have we stopped?'

Hassell nodded to the right. A solid wooden door was built into the rock and earth, its hinges carved into the stone. The wood was strong and had aged far better than anything else down here.

'We were waiting for you,' Hassell said. 'But now let me do the honours.'

The American turned, dropped his shoulder and barged into the wooden door. The hinges grated, stone on stone, and the timber shuddered, but the door held.

'Put your damn back into it,' Roxy said. 'Here, let me.'

But Hassell tried again. Mason wished he knew what was beyond the door. Hassell grunted as his shoulder hit an unyielding surface yet again.

From behind, Mason heard a noise in the tunnel and stepped back. Quaid and Sally both turned off their torches. A blackness deeper than night enveloped them. Mason closed his eyes briefly to enable them to adjust to the new darkness faster.

As the impenetrable gloom fell, Mason found his other senses became more attuned. He heard at least one man grunting as he pulled himself forward and then heard him start whispering to a colleague. All movement stopped for a while. When it started up again, it was more cautious.

Mason was aware of Roxy at his side.

'Out of the way,' she said.

Mason frowned, but allowed her to cautiously move in front of him. He saw immediately that there was a niche in the wall between two wooden spars, a space where she could hide without being seen.

Mason dropped to the floor.

The first man appeared, cautiously, sweeping his torch left and right. The beam passed right over Mason, who noticed that the man held a gun in his other hand.

The first man stepped clear. A second followed a moment later.

In that instant, Roxy struck. She shot the first man in the thigh and, too close to the second to fire, smashed the gun from his hands with a downward strike. This man was trained. He didn't immediately go for the fallen gun, but spun and struck at her, catching her across the temple. Roxy swayed and reeled to the side. Her head struck a wooden stanchion. The support wobbled. A chunk of earth fell from the wall and rolled over her feet. The mercenary she'd attacked pressed his advantage, forcing her back into the side wall so that earth cascaded down over her face. Roxy tried to bring her knees up, but the guy twisted away and punched her in the gut.

Roxy ignored it. The guy appeared surprised when she came back with a flurry of blows. They fell backwards, their figures picked out by two discarded torches that had fallen to the ground, a kaleidoscope of chaotic images passing in and out of shadow and light. They fought across the width of the cave, Roxy finally beating the man to the ground with a devastating flurry of attacks.

Mason found the first man had fallen right alongside him, clutching his leg. He scrambled atop the figure and kicked his gun away into the darkness. Then he kneed the damaged leg and throat-punched the guy, conscious that Roxy might need his help. In just a few seconds, the man was out of action.

Mason rose to his knees, approached another man, who was shrouded in darkness, and struck out with his boot. The blow connected with the guy's left knee. The joint popped and he fell to the ground with a scream.

Roxy pounced atop him in the chaos.

Mason whirled. Another man had emerged from the tunnel. That meant there were four of them – the same number he'd seen left behind at the SUVs earlier. Clearly, they had realised their compatriots had been put out of action.

Mason was six feet away from the new arrival.

And that was way too far. The man carried a torch in one hand and a gun in the other and was emerging cautiously. There was no way Mason could close the gap in time.

He stared down the barrel of the gun as its holder pointed it at his forehead. The man's face, cast in shadow, was like the face of the Grim Reaper.

'How many of you are there?' the man asked.

Hassell's gun resounded loudly in the underground space. The newcomer flew backwards as a bullet smashed into his chest.

'More than enough,' Roxy answered the man's question.

The area was a muddle of light and shadow, fallen torches aimed erratically. Sally's own torch swept their faces and then the tunnel entrance. Her gun was drawn though she didn't yet have the confidence to use it. Mason stayed absolutely silent, which enabled him to listen.

'I think we're alone,' Roxy said.

Mason thought so too, unable to pick out the sound of anyone approaching. He found his torch and pointed it at Hassell, who stood with his gun still levelled.

'Did you get that door open, mate?'

As Mason spoke, Hassell blinked and lowered the weapon.

'No,' he said. 'Not yet.'

'I think it needs a proper English shoulder,' Quaid said, walking across. 'You Americans eat too many hamburgers.'

Hassell glared at him. 'And you eat too many fish and chips, my friend.'

Mason saw Roxy about to join in the banter and gestured for her to guard the tunnel and walked over to the thick wooden door, joining Quaid. The first idea that came to mind was to shoot the hinges but that could lead to an unfortunate ricochet. The second thing that came to mind was brute force.

Mason struck it with a shoulder. The door shuddered. Timbers bent. It continued to hold.

Which was more than could be said for the ceiling supports.

The stanchion that had been damaged in the fight earlier broke with a snapping of timbers that sounded like gunfire, making Mason and Roxy dive headlong and reach for weapons. It was only when Mason checked on Sally that he saw her staring at the left wall.

'The stanchions broke,' she said. 'That's not good.'

Mason followed her gaze. Both ceiling supports now stuck out from the wall at forty-five-degree angles. The thick planks that ran overhead were held in place only by time. Mason imagined the weight that was bearing down on them.

'Time to go,' he said.

Hassell pushed again at the obstinate door, to no avail. Quaid manoeuvred him out of the way and ran at it shoulder first. Again, the whole thing juddered but didn't give. Mason decided to put his boot to it.

They were making enough noise now to wake the dead. Roxy was close to the tunnel, still listening. Sally shone two torches onto the door, illuminating the area. It could only be a matter of time before they escaped.

Another snapping of timbers shot through their senses. Mason saw a second ceiling support break, its timbers shattering along their length and, because he was staring directly at it, noticed a large chunk of ceiling shift.

'It's coming down,' he said 'We have to—'

The rest of his words were lost as he charged the door. His right shoulder crashed into it. Pain shot through his arm and ribs. The wood cracked this time and one of the hinges skewed. As Mason pulled away, gasping, Hassell and Quaid got their fingers behind the wood and started to heave it backwards and forwards.

A lump of soil fell from the ceiling and crashed to the ground.

Mason's heart leapt as he saw it. The threat of being buried alive shot through his brain. Roxy returned from her place by the tunnel and joined Hassell and Quaid as they yanked hard at the obstinate door.

It came open inch by inch. It had opened about half a body's width when another portion of ceiling crashed to the ground.

Mason wanted to help but couldn't get in. Instead, he stood beside Sally and watched the state of the roof as pieces of it kept collapsing.

'Hurry!' he urged the others.

Roxy heaved with all her strength as Hassell pulled and Quaid wrenched at the timber structure. It flew away from its moorings with a suddenness that sent them all sprawling. At that moment another support timber snapped, and Mason saw a mass of ceiling move ominously right above their heads.

'Run,' he cried. 'Just fucking run.'

The ceiling came down. Chunks of earth and rocks rained in a lethal hail. Mason was struck on the shoulder and felt soil cascade over his head. His vision was blocked. He grabbed Sally's hand and urged her along with him. Ahead, Roxy was already through the door with Hassell and Quaid following. A large boulder plummeted between them, so big Mason had to leap over it as he ran. There was a roaring, crashing, booming sound as the ceiling collapsed. In front of his eyes was nothing but a wall of earth. His mouth was full of it.

He crossed to the door and urged Sally forward, straight after Hassell. His boots were bogged down by falling earth. The stench was cloying; the whole place smelled of death. His shoulders, arms and hands were pinball machines for large clods of soil and rocks. The weight of the cave-in pushed him down, bowing his back and bending his knees.

Mason felt like he was slogging towards safety, like a man knee-deep in sand running away from a tidal wave. The weight was all too much, slowing him to the point of walking. All that was left was for him to grab the half-open door and . . . pull.

Mason grasped the horizontal timbers and pulled with all his strength, now praying that the door wouldn't break free of its hinges. It helped propel him through six inches of earth and then another six. A rock glanced off his left shoulder, punishing the bone but helping remind him he was still alive.

Mason heaved his body past the door and a stone step. There was debris here but, because the steps led straight up to a hole in the ground, not much of it. Hassell was at the top, scraping at the earth that covered the gap above them.

Roxy was looking down. 'You took your time, Joe.'

Mason gasped and fell to his knees, then began brushing the soil from his shoulders and arms. He couldn't answer her. The roar of the roof collapse still filled their ears. Displaced air rushed past them.

'And now we have a new problem,' Hassell muttered from above. 'How the hell do we dig our way out?'

# Chapter 37

Hassell, Quaid and Roxy crowded around the top of the steps and clawed the earth downwards. They stepped out of the way of minor cave-ins every so often. The unspoken fear was that the way out had been hidden beneath a coffin or something similar, but Mason tried to stay upbeat. The way in had been a simple gravesite. The way out would hopefully be something just as simple.

Ten minutes passed, and then another ten. Mason stayed near the bottom of the steps. Soil from the cave-in below started pushing its way up, first one, then two and then three steps, worrying Mason that the staircase was filling up and they were going to be buried here as it rapidly filled with soil, but, after a few moments, an ominous silence fell.

'I wonder how far it extends,' Sally said. 'I hope the main tunnel isn't compromised, there's so much history down there.'

For a moment, Mason felt sorry for the mercenaries who'd perished down below in the cave-in, but then reminded himself that they'd tried to kill him. Still, buried alive was no way to go.

In a strange, surreal moment, he pondered in disbelief how far he'd come since working for Patricia and her security firm. The security firm had offered steady, simple work. At the time, it had been everything he needed, offering a way of being left alone and working unaccompanied. After Zach and Harry died, he hadn't wanted to hurt anyone else and being part of a team was out of the question.

Now . . . he was stuck underground in Scotland with a group of people he considered family, trusting his life to them as he waited below. The spectre of Iraq had receded – but Mason knew it would rightfully never leave his thoughts. He didn't want it to. That horror was part of the mould that had made the man he was today.

Above, clods of earth were tumbling downwards to be deposited on the stairs. There were two wooden roof supports he could see, neither of which appeared compromised by the collapse below.

Half an hour after they'd started digging and pulling, Hassell turned and grinned down the long flight of stairs. Behind him, a shaft of sunlight pierced a hole and washed across his shoulders.

'We're free,' he whispered.

Mason's heart leapt. Roxy and Quaid reached up and widened the hole. A gush of fresh air wafted across them. Mason breathed deeply. Hassell fell to his knees above and then cautiously raised his head to peer out. He took his time, surveying the whole area. After a few minutes he rose and waved them up.

Mason emerged into the day feeling drained, but the sunshine and the brisk wind helped revitalise him. They were standing, covered in dirt, in a clearing in the woods, surrounded on four sides by trees. The first thing Sally did was take out her phone and plot a way back to their car.

The first thing the others did was to swipe dust and soil from their heads and shoulders and knees.

'That way,' Sally said after a while, nodding. 'East.'

Mason imagined they were still relatively close to Temple Church. He was sure the tunnels hadn't run for miles.

'Stay wary,' he said, still brushing himself off. 'If any of them escaped the main tunnel, they could be looking for us.'

'If the main tunnel is still intact, they'll be searching for the clue,' Sally said. 'I guarantee it.'

They took their time, allowing their bodies to recover from the trauma of almost being buried alive just as much as the physical combat they'd endured. Mason ached all over. His shoulders throbbed and his shins were bruised. The short walk through the trees was pleasant enough – they threaded a course between sun-spangled greenery and negotiated a meandering stream where they stopped to clean their hands and faces – but Mason breathed a sigh of relief when they spied their car.

They drove away quickly. There was no point risking a confrontation with Murdock McCloud's men now.

Sally settled herself in the back seat with her laptop open and her notes to her side. She took out her phone and started scrolling through photographs.

'You said you'd cracked the clue,' Roxy said.

'I know, but I want to make doubly sure.'

Mason relaxed, taking a moment to close his eyes. It had been an arduous day so far and, judging by the low position of the sun, they'd been inside those tunnels for some considerable time.

'Just find a hotel,' he said. 'We can discuss the basins later.'

Roxy leaned forward, draping her arms across his seat, reminding Mason that her body was crisscrossed with old scars. It was another reminder of the life she'd led, a reminder she could never ignore.

'The more I seek to raise barriers,' she said softly. 'The more those barriers turn into ordeals of their own. Just once' – she smiled – 'why can't they be good.'

'Focus on the positives,' Mason said. 'We're alive. We fought and we won. We came away with the prize.'

'Sure,' Roxy said. 'But I feel like it's more like . . . we live to fight another day. We fight. That's all we do.'

'We're doing good work,' Sally spoke up. 'Great work, in fact. The Ark of the Covenant and Solomon's Temple have been sought for years. If this McCloud guy gets it what's he going to do? Gain wealth and power from it? Flaunt it? Preen over it? I don't know . . . but he's certainly not going to hand it over to a museum.'

'Reminds me,' Mason said. 'We have to start looking into this Guild of Night. It's always best to know your enemy, and we know shit about this one.'

'We know McCloud wants to kill us,' Roxy said. 'So we must be pissing him off. That's something.'

Quaid found a hotel about thirty minutes from the village of Temple and parked up. Ten minutes later they were alone in their rooms. Mason took a while to shower and dry, though he had to pull his dirty clothes back on. He was going to have to buy a new pair of jeans and maybe some boots. Remembering to bring along a change of clothes for this mission hadn't exactly been a high priority.

They met for a meal and then retired to a quiet corner of the hotel bar, where a plush L-shaped sofa welcomed them with luxurious, leather-covered arms. Mason ordered a beer and sank into repose with a deep sigh.

'I've heard it said' – Roxy took a seat beside him – 'that those who make noises when they sit down are getting old.'

'I'm thirty-four,' Mason said indignantly. 'Thirty-five in June. I'm guessing you're older.'

Roxy punched his thigh, striking a recently bruised area and making him groan. 'Take that back,' she said. 'I can punch you all night if I have to.'

Mason held up a hand in defeat. Using the other, he raised

his beer to his lips. Quaid was staring at them. 'Try being fifty-one,' he said. 'Aches and pains just pop up for fun.'

Mason tried not to think about it. He already felt older than his years. After a moment he sat forward and turned to Sally.

'What do you have? You haven't stopped researching since we got here.'

Sally glared at him. 'Do I stink?'

'I didn't mean that . . .'

'Oh, Joe's doing really well with the ladies tonight,' Roxy laughed. 'Insults everywhere.'

'I didn't mean—'

'To be fair, you're right,' Sally went on. 'I can take a shower later. The Ark won't wait. And neither will our enemies. Let me run this past you.'

Mason sat back, listening. Around them the hotel bar bustled with activity. A five-strong group of women to their right were getting louder with every sip of their drinks whilst a barely legal trio of teens ignored each other at the bar in favour of their smartphones. Mason pitied the hassled-looking waitress flitting between tables.

Sally drew their attention and said:

'A Warrior King of Kings,
A Victory Everlasting,
Hic Jacet invictus Robertus Rex Benedictus.'

'I salute you,' Roxy said, raising her pint. 'Because that means jack shit to me.'

'The real clue is in the last line,' Sally said. 'It's Latin. Once you know that, you can decipher the first two lines quite easily. They're all about the Battle of Bannockburn and the so-called Outlaw King.'

'And what does it have to do with the Molten Sea basins and the Ark?' Quaid asked.

'In case you don't know, the fabled Battle of Bannockburn was a turning point in Scottish history. The English king, Edward II – the same man who tortured William Wallace to death – assembled an army of a hundred thousand men – knights and papal mercenaries – to eliminate the Scots. These armed knights and battle-hardened mercenaries all marched north to Bannockburn. The Scots were only able to gather eight thousand lightly armed men to face the hundred thousand. Once the slaughter had begun there was a sudden lull in the fighting. The enemy froze as the battle trumpets rang out, and the sound of seven hundred experienced, enraged Knights Templar bearing down on them threw the English army into chaos. The Knights were infuriated at the massacre of their fellow Templars. They came down the valley, battle flags flying, their swords raised, and fell among the enemy with ruthless precision. It is said the English army broke and fled that day.'

'Is it true?' Quaid asked carefully.

'There are other versions,' Sally said, 'that refute the presence of the Templars. Indeed, a true Scottish nationalist would shout you down if you even suggested that their outlaw king, the great Robert the Bruce, needed their help to win the Battle of Bannockburn in 1314. Yes, it's seven years after the persecution, but the facts tell us that many of the Templars did indeed flee to Scotland. And wouldn't they want to help defend their newfound land? Of course. In the dead of night, they came to Scotland, their ships weighed down with treasure, bullion and sacred objects carried from Jerusalem and other places. They were taken in, welcomed, allowed to continue their lifestyle. Some say that only about fifty Templars were at Bannockburn but, whatever it was, and even if they weren't there, they assuredly knew Robert the Bruce.'

'The warrior king?' Mason ventured.

'Exactly. The warrior King of Kings, a Victory Everlasting,

relates directly to Robert and Bannockburn. The last line reveals all.'

'And they wrote it in Latin because . . .' Quaid said.

'Because it is written in Latin,' Sally said. 'In real life. It's a single line from the epitaph on Robert the Bruce's tomb.'

'And what does it mean?' Roxy asked.

'Here lies the invincible, blessed King Robert,' Sally said.

'You're saying the clue points us to Robert's tomb?' Mason said. 'And where is that?'

'I haven't actually gotten that far yet,' Sally said, starting to tap her keyboard again. 'Give me a minute.'

Mason downed half of his beer, and let out a long sigh. It had been a rough day. He'd never come close to being buried before. All the fighting that came before paled in significance to almost being covered by tonnes of earth whilst you still lived. Mason shuddered at the very thought of it.

'I've got it,' Sally said.

'Where are we going next?' Quaid asked.

'Robert the Bruce is buried at Dunfermline Abbey,' Sally said with a smile. 'And maybe the Ark of the Covenant is too.'

Mason looked over at her. 'You think Dunfermline Abbey might be the end of the road?'

'It could be. The Ark and the Temple will both lie somewhere of high importance, of great significance. I'd say Robert covers all that, wouldn't you?'

'There's one other thing,' Quaid said, looking over at Sally's computer. 'Is that Dunfermline Abbey?'

'Yes.' Sally swivelled the screen around so that they could all see it. 'The first image that came up.'

'Doesn't it remind you of something?'

Mason squinted, vaguely recognising the shape . . . the contours . . . the angular features. It did remind him of something he'd seen in the recent past.

'We've already seen that shape,' he said.

Quaid smiled. 'Exactly.'

Now Sally took a moment to study the picture more closely. It took only a few seconds for recognition to register in her eyes.

'Oh, of course,' she said. 'How did I not see that? It's the painting from Little Maplestead, isn't it?'

Mason nodded. The painting they'd discovered back in Little Maplestead had contained a dim representation of a tall old building sitting in a wreath of fog, surrounded by indistinct shapes that might have been trees, a winding river and a battered fence. It had had a high central tower with other wings and annexes all around it, but nothing was clear-cut. It appeared that the artist had wanted to keep his depiction deliberately vague.

'Two clues are pointing us towards Dunfermline Abbey,' Quaid said quietly. 'I'd say that's pretty clear-cut.'

'I'd agree,' Sally said, excitement in her voice. 'I can't wait . . .'

'Have you found anything relating to the Guild of Night?' Mason sought to ground her a little.

Sally chewed on her bottom lip. 'I tried,' she said. 'But they're like ghosts. They don't exist. If you remember, our informants told us they don't even communicate by conventional means. They leave no trail, nothing to grab hold of. I fear the only way to investigate them is to talk to people who know them.'

'The two professors knew very little,' Mason said.

'Yes, we need somebody far more notable, an influential member. The trouble is . . . they never show themselves.'

Mason nodded, disappointed that they had no clear idea of the nature of their enemy. All he knew was that they were ruthless.

'I just hope they never found that clue under Temple Church,' Hassell said.

Mason thought about their trip to Dunfermline Abbey. 'I guess we'll find out tomorrow,' he said.

# Chapter 38

Murdock McCloud was livid. Not for the first time, he bemoaned the Guild's propensity for using hired help. Yes, it helped maintain their cover, but you never knew what calibre of person you would be getting. Dealing with the mercenary muscle was getting harder and more dangerous every day.

But McCloud wasn't the only one taking risks. All twelve of the Guild's key members were contributing to their current endeavours in recovering the basins and the Ark. His second, Michael Sallow, was entrenched in the historical research side of things. Barrow and Parke, both English, were helping him. From Scotland, Douglas and Mclean were helping out with transport and weapons and even the clean-up of bodies. McCloud didn't feel alone.

His brotherhood stood by him.

But now that the mercenaries had failed to kill Joe Mason's group once again, McCloud was no longer able to contain his anger. It was a seething creature that curled and twisted around his body and blocked his airways so that he could barely breathe. It was a bloody knife searching for fleshy leverage. Joe Mason had fast turned from little more than a name, uttered by an obscure mercenary called

Johann, to a particularly large fly crawling around the edge of his wine glass. Mason was going to have to die.

McCloud paced the length of his office. He stopped at the window, again looking out over his kingdom and the countless graves that lay at the edge of his land. Although he was leader of the Guild of Night, other proclivities often grabbed his attention and stayed in the forefront of his mind until he assuaged them.

I need to kill. Mostly I need to kill Joe Mason, but he's not here right now.

There were subjects waiting below. Subjects already tenderised and chained down in the dungeon. Could he take the time to attend to them? The chase to find the Ark and the temple was a close-run thing. Even so, he felt confident that he would be triumphant.

His phone rang. The Guild of Night had never communicated directly by anything other than emissary in their centuries-old existence, but McCloud had now chosen to break that rule. It was the only way to stay ahead.

'Sallow?' he answered on the second ring.

'Grand Master,' came the reply. 'I have news.'

McCloud took a seat. 'Go ahead.'

'Firstly, our professors have retrieved the latest clue from Temple. We lost many mercenaries though . . .'

'I don't care,' McCloud said.

'I understand, of course. It depletes our ranks, that's all. The professors are alive and working on the next clue even as we speak.'

'Tell them to work faster.'

'Of course, Grand Master. In other news, as you know, our rivals escaped once more. We do not know where they are right now.'

'You mean Mason and his team? Do we know where they are going?'

'As soon as the professors' work is done, we will find

out. Am I to instruct Douglas and Mclean to procure greater quantities of mercenaries?'

'The more the better. This idiocy with Mason has gone on long enough. I want him dead. I want his motley crew dead. I want information, Sallow, information that tells us what they've done, how they tick, what they're likely to do next. Do you understand?'

'To put it into perspective, Mason is ex-army. When he left, he had thirteen years in. He's no soft target, but he left under a cloud. Something to do with an IED. That's his weakness, where we can destroy him. One of his crew, Roxy Banks, is some kind of ex-American agent. It's hard to get intel on her. Another of them served as a British army officer for years. They're no pushovers.'

'I want them eliminated from the face of the Earth.'

'Of course, Grand Master.'

'I've begun to think it might be better if you brought at least one of them to me.'

'Grand Master?'

McCloud knew that he was fixating on Mason, that the man was getting under his skin. But he was becoming more and more determined that he would be the one to kill Mason. It was what he did. Mason was a new challenger.

'Killing Mason would be good for me,' he said quietly.

'Then the Guild will try to make that happen,' Sallow said.

McCloud took a deep breath, trying to force Mason from his mind for just a moment. It was no easy task. 'And how will you contact the others?'

Sallow was quiet for a long moment. 'I think it is time to drop the old ways and adopt something new,' he said. 'As you and I have done.'

McCloud knew it was a roundabout way of asking permission. 'I agree,' he said shortly. 'But do stress we are in a time of emergency.'

'Understood. The old ways will always be the best.'

And McCloud knew it was more than just idle comment or someone wanting to ingratiate himself. The Guild of Night had stayed off every radar for centuries by being careful. Was it his obsession with Mason that was inducing this new cavalier attitude?

'I always have this phone with me,' he said. 'I want to know immediately when anything changes.'

Sallow agreed and hung up. McCloud sat for a moment, contemplating all that had been said. Changing the careful habits of several lifetimes was never something to take lightly but he still believed the situation warranted it. For the next few minutes, he tapped at his computer screen, brought up a picture of Joe Mason and stared at it, the sight making his anger boil over, making him seethe and conjure visions of blood-soaked nights where men and women screamed under his touch. It would be invigorating and righteous to kill this man.

After a while, McCloud rose and started to make his way down to the dungeons. It was cold out in the castle, and the wind keened as it forced its way through old gaps and crevices. McCloud wrapped his thick jacket more tightly around him. As he walked though, he started to warm up inside.

Death, and the smell of blood. The sweet taste of their fear, their desperate pleas and gasps . . . It was the honeyed music of his most gratifying dreams.

He paused at the door that led to the dungeons, checking to make sure he wasn't being followed. The staff were very discreet in this castle, sometimes too discreet and, even though they were told to retire at nine p.m. he'd often caught them trailing him as if, in some way, that might curry favour.

Tonight, he was alone.

McCloud opened the door to the dungeon and paused. Riding on the air was the terrified whisper he loved so much, a muted murmur of pure fear escaping a clenched throat. Who should he choose tonight?

Already, he could feel the burdens of the day sloughing off like some onerous skin. Already, he stepped and breathed lighter, his head full of positivity.

Tonight, he would use the old Templar weapons.

McCloud crossed the dungeon floor without looking once at his prisoners. Through experience he knew they'd be watching him through their rank mops of filthy hair, their hands gripping the bars of their cells, wondering who was going to suffer tonight. McCloud breathed it all in deeply. As above, so below. McCloud was the Grand Master of both realms.

The far side of the dungeon was home to countless weapons and instruments of torture. McCloud had enjoyed testing them all. There was a marble tiled piece of wall that stood in pride of place and upon it were hung several swords and daggers, and a mace. There was also a shield and a helmet that had once belonged to Gilbert de Chartres, a Knight Templar of the thirteenth century.

McCloud stood silently in a moment in respect. Then, he reached out a hand and plucked the helmet off a wide marble shelf.

The helmet was heavy, cold and almost alien in design. It fitted snugly over McCloud's head and narrowed his vision to a rectangular visor. Once in place, he felt top heavy, but the peace it brought him was like nothing else. McCloud now thought about how he should unleash the wrath of the old Templars this evening.

It had been a brutal day, hours full of bad news. McCloud decided not to toy with his prey; a cruel, inhuman end would be quite fitting. He turned to the cells.

They were there – the pitiful. There were four of them, rejects of humanity, wretched specimens that would not be missed. Their white faces stood out like small moons in the dark, their pathetic sobs rode the air like restful music to McCloud's ears.

He plucked the shield and a steel gauntlet from the shelf. He fitted both of these over his left arm. Next, took one of the daggers – the one with a blade about eight inches long.

McCloud paced over to the cells. He loved this bit. The choice. Choosing as they knelt and suffered and pleaded. It swept all his troubles away, the sensation sweeping like warm nectar through his veins. He laughed, low and spiteful, a great historical figure viewing his prey.

They were his vanquished enemy, his direct rivals. He would be the great knight of old with all the power in his hands. He would prove his prowess.

McCloud played the part, walking in front of all the cells and back again in sweeping movements. He viewed the rabble as they sat in their filth, listening to their doleful overtures with a grim smile stretched across his face. He gripped his long dagger and shield, sometimes banging them together, enjoying the terror his vision wrought in their minds.

Some time after midnight, McCloud stopped outside the second cell from the eastern wall. He unlocked it, stepped inside and grabbed his victim by the hair. He pulled hard, forcing the man to squirm across the floor in his wake. The man struggled but was no match for Murdock McCloud, who was great and knightly and overflowed with sacred purpose.

The man rose up to his knees and tried to strike McCloud.

McCloud turned, using his shield to block the blows, then yanked the man's hair as hard as he could. The man screamed.

Man?

McCloud revised his thinking. This was no man. This thing was a pathetic animal, an insect that crawled upon the world foraging only for itself, and deserved nothing better than a boot stamped down upon its back. McCloud's boot. He resumed walking, dragging the mewling thing in his incredible wake.

Outside the cell, McCloud made it kneel. He forced its head down. He stepped away and gripped the dagger more tightly.

He looked to the other cells.

They were watching. As he wanted them to, the soon to be dead. They couldn't look away from the spectacle. And what a grand spectacle he was – Murdock McCloud and his Templar accoutrements, the Grand Master of the Guild of Night who exterminated whenever he pleased.

McCloud raised his dagger.

'Do you have any last words?'

He always gave them the chance to speak, mostly because they used the moment to beseech him even more, to look up with their wet eyes and red faces and implore him to spare their lives. He loved generating this one-minute-to-midnight moment for them, mostly because it often aroused him.

This man dared not even lift his eyes. McCloud was disappointed. Maybe the long captivity had broken this one. Either way, it didn't matter. The end would be the same. McCloud would get everything he wanted.

He gripped the dagger tightly and flexed his muscles. McCloud was a broad, strong man and wore knightly armour well. He worked out every day, often pushing his muscles beyond their limits. Creating sinew was another thing he loved. Sinew was the tight bond that held the world together. It helped make him the great man he was today.

Without another word, McCloud plunged the dagger down into the top of the thing's head. The knife's tip sank right through the cranium, passing into the brain. First

271

the sharp-edged blade, and then the hilt cracked against the top of the insect's head. McCloud could push no more; the dagger had sunk all the way in. He let go and stood back. The victim swayed for a moment, blood flying from between its lips. McCloud was fascinated to watch its death throes, taking it all in. The way it shuddered, the way its bare feet tapped the ground, the way it eventually collapsed face first, the impact making the top of the dagger's handle strike noisily on the concrete floor.

Mason will die this way.

McCloud knelt down and withdrew the dagger with one powerful heave. It came free wetly, covered in blood. He quickly crossed to the sink and cleansed the metal of the insect's fluids, hating the fact that he was forced to do so. This was what servants were for. But moments like these were McCloud's zenith, the pinnacle of his existence. He wouldn't share them with anyone.

Even the clean-up was gratifying. McCloud replaced the weapons, shield and gauntlet reverently in their places.

When he was finished, he placed a quick call to a man connected to the Scottish underworld. A man who could procure him another insect. Then, he warmed up his muscles and proceeded to stuff the dead thing into a large suitcase. This was a tried and tested operation. The suitcase was on wheels. McCloud filled it and then wheeled it out of the room. He climbed the dark stone stairs in blackness, loving the dull thump of the staircase hitting every step on its way up. At the top, he paused and listened to the stillness of the castle.

The obscurity of midnight and the early hours held sway. McCloud wheeled the suitcase across a shadowy hallway to a side door that opened onto grounds. He laid it flat, unzipped it and then tugged out the dead weight, hefting it over his shoulders and then opening the door.

The moon was high and full tonight. It illuminated

Murdock McCloud creeping across his castle fields with a fresh dead body draped across his shoulders, a dark sneaking hulk carrying a flaccid sack of flesh through shadow and gloom. If anyone saw from their bedroom window, they knew better than to break the peace.

# Chapter 39

Dunfermline Abbey sits at the heart of Scotland's ancient capital, bordering an extensive park and within walking distance of the high street, its history stretching almost as far back as Scotland itself. The mausoleum of this nine-hundred-year-old abbey houses some of the most renowned kings and queens, but the building's exterior architecture is almost as impressive: enormous buttresses surrounding the outside, immense Romanesque pillars inside. Above the nave is a wondrous collection of pillars and columns, and, all around, striking stained-glass windows look out across the sprawling grounds where tombs and gravestones lie in abundance.

Mason and his team arrived mid-morning with a relatively simple clue – Robert the Bruce. The obvious answer was that the riches they were seeking were stowed somewhere around the old king's tomb. Sally was the first to caution them against over-confidence.

'Study everything,' she said. 'As a historian I've learned that nothing should be overlooked. The Molten Sea basin symbol could be anywhere. Its location might have nothing to do with Robert's tomb.'

'You guys look out for ancient relics,' Roxy said. 'I'll watch our backs.'

They entered through the front gate and meandered across the grounds, eventually arriving at the front door of the abbey, which was open wide, inviting them inside. Mason saw fields of tombstones to left and right, several rambling, leafless trees, and rows of houses further away. The group were fresh after a night in the hotel and had managed to buy some new clothes on the outskirts of Dunfermline. Mason had decided to leave his backpack in the car this time, as had the others, but they all carried their Glocks and what was left of their ammo. They also had their Bluetooth earbuds with them.

Roxy stayed behind as they entered the abbey. Mason found himself in an airy nave with a large window at the far end above the altar. He placed a note in the collection tray and ventured further inside. Sally was at his side.

'Check everywhere,' she reiterated.

They split up. Mason saw flags on many of the painted walls, coats of arms in ceremonial colours. Carved columns marched to left and right, all the way to the end of the nave. Mason studied every surface, every column, searching for something that resembled the Molten Sea basins.

'I'm seeing plenty of carvings,' Quaid said. 'A few indeterminate sculptures. A whole lot of brick, block and mortar. Nothing useful.'

'Keep looking,' Sally said.

They threaded their way through the abbey's interior, careful not to get in each other's way. Mason wondered if Sally would be able to give up the need to check everything herself this time but, judging by the size of the abbey, she was most likely going to have to. Ten minutes quickly turned into thirty.

Mason avoided those few people he met along the way: two people carrying cameras who were clearly tourists, two more who were helping clean the interior. Muted music filtered in from somewhere. Mason kept his eyes peeled for the prize.

Roxy's voice lit up the comms. 'Have you found anything?'

'Still searching,' Sally said. 'I'm approaching the tomb of Robert the Bruce.'

'Well, get a move on.'

'Why?'

'They're here.'

Mason clenched his fist. 'How many?'

'More than enough, believe me. They sent the full force this time.'

Mason knew Roxy couldn't hope to survive alone outside. 'Get in here,' he said. 'Don't engage them out there.'

'I have no intention of engaging anything,' Roxy replied. 'On my way.'

Mason's eyes swept across the inside of the abbey. There were places to hide, but only among the pews and behind altars. Did their enemies know they were here? Would they conduct a search anyway? Of course, they too would be seeking the next clue.

'Scatter,' he said.

Quaid and Hassell lost themselves among the pews. Sally was already out of sight and probably examining Robert's tomb. Mason waited for Roxy and then pointed to the nearest alcove.

'Hurry.'

They took cover behind a low-slung coffin. Mason peered around the edge. They stayed low, breathing shallowly.

Seconds later, three men wearing leather jackets walked through the door, quickly spreading out. Mason counted another nine following them. They all wore jeans and boots and held themselves with a military bearing, and all their eyes were as hard as obsidian. Mason barely breathed as three men walked towards his hiding place.

His gun was in his right hand.

'Get ready for contact,' he said.

He didn't see where they went next. Hassell's voice came

over the comms. 'I'm watching,' he whispered. 'They're spreading down the main nave and along both aisles. I see Justin and Julian at the back.'

He stopped speaking. Mason imagined the enemy closing in on him and Quaid. He could hear low footfalls now, the sound of boots coming closer. Roxy was staring at him from just a few metres away.

'This doesn't work for me,' she said.

Mason stared at her for a second, unsure what she meant. It was then he recalled the incident in the graveyard in London, when he'd thought she'd lost it from too much introspection, too many barriers being raised between her past and her present. Roxy had been frozen for several dangerous minutes that day. Now, she wanted to attack first to stop that from happening.

'Don't do this now,' he said, gripping his gun.

'Like I said before, I shoot. I ambush. I don't get waylaid. It's like it was back then. I can't stand waiting to be fired upon.'

Mason understood to a degree. Roxy was a proactive character; she never took a back seat. Waiting to be attacked would distress her. She needed to be active. She needed to be in control. He grabbed her arm. 'You with me?'

'We should attack.'

'I need you with me, Roxy.'

'Then follow my fucking lead.' Roxy started to lift her head.

Mason gripped her arm even tighter, urging her to stay covered. 'Not yet,' he said. 'Please. Not now.'

'I'm ready to fight, to raise another barrier. Don't try to stop me now.'

Mason gritted his teeth and readied himself. He recalled Roxy saying that her head was full of dead bodies and old kills. He knew she was still trying to find the young woman she'd once been.

And now he knew the desperate need hit her in tense confrontation, when she held back. Back when he'd worked for Patricia the people around the office had called her a loose cannon.

But she wasn't loose.

She was wound tighter than a coiled spring.

Roxy, wound up to the max, let out a roar as she rose above the lip of the coffin. Mason knew he had to rise with her. He was a second behind, gun poised, finger on the trigger.

The three leather-jacketed mercenaries were approaching them, just eight feet distant, and now gaping open-mouthed in shock. Mason was glad to see that Roxy didn't open fire immediately – she waited to see their hands dart towards their weapons. As soon as fingers touched guns, she opened fire.

Four rapid shots. Two double-taps. Two men flew backwards and hit the wooden pews, collapsing amid the timbers. Mason sighted on the third man and shot him once through the skull.

Seconds later, Quaid and Hassell popped up with their own guns sighted and let off two shots each. The bullets flew among the nine remaining mercenaries, winging one and killing another. There were shouts and curses and then the mercs were dropping to the floor and pulling out their own weapons.

Mason dragged Roxy down behind the coffin as lead flew their way.

'You're not bloody invincible,' he said.

'I'm good, now.'

'Now we've blown our cover, you're good?' He shook his head. 'The first time I thought it was because you missed the ambush. I can understand that. Now . . .' He paused as bullets pounded the coffin they were sheltering behind. 'Now . . . I see it's because you can't hold back.'

'I don't wait to be shot in the face, Joe.'

He was starting to see that. Roxy was a great part of his team, but this was something they were going to have to work on.

Assuming they lived through this, of course.

'They'd have discovered us anyway,' Roxy said. 'I got three of them without risk.'

'Two,' he said quickly. But that didn't matter now. Mason peered cautiously around the side of the stone coffin. A bullet impacted and sent flecks of stone at his face. Mason sighted on a merc hiding among the pews and fired back, seeing his bullet shatter timber.

Roxy rose and fired three times, using the distraction Mason had caused to lay down a volley of her own. But the mercs were well and truly dug in beneath and behind the pews now and suffered no casualties.

Mason checked his pockets. 'I'm down to my last two mags,' he said. 'How about you?'

'Three,' Roxy said.

Quaid and Hassell both had three mags left as well. When Sally didn't speak up Mason grew worried.

'Sally?'

'I'm sheltering near Robert's tomb. I think I've found something.'

'Inside?'

'No, silly, I'm not that quick. It's really interesting actually. And shocking. I just wish I could explain it all to you.'

'Take your gun out of your pocket,' Quaid said, reminding them all that Sally was still a novice when it came to the action side of things. 'Protect yourself.'

Mason had other things to worry about right now. Sally's commentary was distracting, but the sound of renewed gunfire soon overrode it.

Mason waited for the shooting to stop, then peered around his stone coffin and fired two quick shots, targeting the places he already knew the mercenaries to be. His first bullet shot through the pews and hit the far wall, his second killed a man.

Seven left.

Mason knew that lack of movement would eventually get them killed. They had to stay mobile. The chapel around them was bare apart from the stone coffin but the one next door offered a coffin, an altar and a wide niche. As he studied the terrain, he caught sight of Quaid and Hassell sheltering amid the pews, their bodies protected only by the thick chair legs. Quickly, he turned to Roxy.

'Cover me,' he said.

The raven-haired woman nodded. Mason took a breath and then scrambled past her into the next alcove, temporarily out in the open. At this point Roxy unleashed half a dozen quick shots that kept the enemy pinned down.

Mason ran and then twisted his body to the right, jumping into the next chapel along. He hid in the wide niche and addressed Roxy through the comms.

'Your turn,' he said. 'On the count of three.'

'Ready.'

Mason raised his gun, took a deep breath and started to count. On three, he leaned out, loosing off four rounds as Roxy crawled out from behind the coffin, and ran to new cover. The mercs tried returning fire but their aim was off due to being fired upon. Quaid and Hassell added to the confusion.

Mason saw Hassell crawling among the pews, trying to find a better vantage point. Some of their enemies spotted him and tried to pick him off. Quaid kept them at bay with a hail of gunfire.

Mason, focusing on the firefight, found it hard when Sally kept breaking in on them.

'I'm shocked,' she said suddenly. 'I'm now doubting that this is the final resting place of the Templar treasures. Robert the Bruce is but a guardian, not the final protector.'

'What have you found?' Quaid asked.

'Another carving, and a very revealing one.'

'Take photos,' Mason said, leaning out to check the lie of the land.

'Oh, I am. When will you be finished?'

Mason cursed. 'It's not like we're baking bread here,' he muttered, squeezing his trigger once more.

The mercenaries were moving too. Mason ducked back as a stream of gunfire pocked the niche wall he was hiding behind. Roxy was crouched behind a small altar and saw one of the arms of a cross break off.

She turned to Mason. 'We're trapped,' she said. 'What the hell are we gonna do?'

Mason spread his arms. 'You tell me,' he said. 'They have us pinned down.'

Nowhere to run, very few places to hide. And they were outnumbered. Roxy was itching for a fight. Mason could see it in her face.

He tried to remain calm. 'I have an idea,' he said.

# Chapter 40

Mason raised his gun and opened fire

The stream of bullets was aimed way above the heads of the sheltering mercs, at one of the big pendant lights that hung above them. One bullet nicked the wire that secured it and then another severed it.

The light came crashing down among the pews.

The noise was tremendous, dozens of glass bulbs shattering down among the wooden seats and smashing to the concrete floor. Mercs dived out of the way or rose and started to run. Mason and Roxy were already on their feet, targeting individuals. Mason shot one man in the leg, another in the shoulder as they darted away. He stepped out of hiding. A stray bullet struck the plaster pillar to his left.

Quaid and Hassell ran to the end of their row, towards the mercenaries.

The noise of gunfire filled the abbey. Shots echoed back and forth between high walls and towering ceilings. Mercenaries scrambled to run clear of the destruction and the bullets. Mason followed them and targeted them as best he could.

Some men dived clear, rolled and returned fire from a kneeling position.

Mason was forced to drop, too, using what remained of the pews for cover. As he targeted a denim-jacketed man a voice exploded in his ear.

'Who are you? Leave me alone? Get away from me!'

Sally.

Mason cursed loudly. Roxy was already turning towards him.

'Hassell, Quaid,' he said. 'Stay and finish the job. Roxy! With me.'

Mason and Roxy crab-walked as fast as they could towards the end of the nave and the church altar. In their ears, they could hear Sally's protests. They had no idea where the tomb of Robert the Bruce was actually located, but knew it wasn't too far away. Sally couldn't have walked that far since she'd entered the main doors.

Crossing where the nave met the altar, they saw Sally's back. Beyond her were two men, both large and waving their handguns in her face. Mason pressed as close as possible to the nearest wall, still walking forward and trying to remain concealed.

They didn't slow. There was no time. They came upon Sally's back from the right, hidden behind an outcropping.

'What have you found?' one of the men was asking.

'I'm just a tourist,' Sally said. 'Please don't hurt me.'

'You are not a tourist. We saw you searching that tomb. Now, tell me the truth or I will shoot you in the stomach and question you whilst you bleed to death.'

Mason wasn't about to give them a chance. He stepped out, coming from around Sally's back with his gun extended. Without hesitation, he fired twice, taking out both men. Sally screamed to hear the gunshots loud in her left ear.

'Th . . . thank you,' she said. 'I wasn't sure what to do.'

'You did fine.' Mason checked the fallen men and made sure they were out of action. He searched their bodies for magazines, found six and threw three to Roxy.

'Eyes, throat, balls,' the American was telling Sally. 'You know the holy trinity.'

'I know, I know.' Sally hung her head. 'Putting training into practice is harder than you think.'

'These will fit the Glocks,' Mason said of the mags he'd found.

'Perfect.' Roxy pocketed the spare mags.

Sally turned to them, a fresh eagerness in her eyes. 'Let me show you what I've found.'

Mason put a hand on her shoulder. 'First,' he said, 'we have to help Quaid and Hassell.'

'Don't worry. We're coming to you.' The words barked out in his ear. 'This is too close for comfort.'

Seconds later, Quaid and Hassell came into sight, running with their backs bent. Quaid was carrying four more spare magazines that he'd taken from fallen men in the nave. Hassell reached them first.

'Run,' he said simply.

They were outgunned by a stronger mercenary force. Mason and Roxy were the only well-trained individuals. Mason nodded, turned and pointed to a far exit. Together, the five of them raced for the door, hoping it would lead them outside. Quaid fired two shots behind them for good measure, wincing as the bullets pockmarked the walls but intent on guarding their exit.

'Six or seven back there,' he said. 'And they're well dug in. Did you get photos of the basin?'

Sally nodded. 'I did.'

Mason led them to the far door, slowed and cracked it open, ready to start shooting. Outside, a field filled with endless rows of tombstones greeted them, shadow-strewn in the red-hued sunset. Mason eased his way out.

The area was empty, quiet. He ran to one large tombstone and crouched behind it, waiting for the others to do the same. Seconds later, he peered around the side.

'Clear.' Roxy was already checking it out. 'All the way to the front gate.'

'Let's not risk it.' Mason had spotted a smaller gate set into the hedge about three hundred yards to the west. 'I don't fancy another confrontation, and I hear sirens.'

Hassell led them towards the side gate, staying low. 'I'll get us out of here,' he said.

Mason fell in behind the New Yorker without hesitation, thinking how well they were starting to blend and work as a team. Even under fire inside the abbey they had functioned well as a unit. It was an important and interesting new dynamic that was improving every day.

'Get us back to the car as fast as you can,' Sally told him. 'We're about a forty-minute drive from Solomon's Temple.'

As they drove south-east from Dunfermline, Sally handed her phone around, showing off the photographs she'd taken inside the abbey. Mason squinted hard, trying to make out the carving and the words that arced above it.

'It's not much,' he said.

The gilded white marble tomb of Robert the Bruce lay in splendour, overseen by what appeared to be a wooden altar. The altar contained a crest, and several other carvings. But, set into its side, was a large, round etching that drew the team's attention. It showed a Molten Sea basin, rendered very small, near the top. The sculpture itself depicted what appeared to be a procession of men holding chests and stars and other treasures above their heads. At the front, one man held up the Ark of the Covenant.

Around the sculpture were the words 'ad crypta'.

'I see it,' Mason said. 'But I don't understand it.'

'Look closer,' Sally said.

Mason closed his eyes and then searched the image again. 'I see the Ark,' he said. 'And the treasures held aloft which I presume imply Solomon's Temple. The procession of men.

They could be Knights Templar, I guess, but the resolution makes it hard to be sure . . .'

'But where are they going?' Sally said. 'Their procession is leading to somewhere.'

Mason squinted even harder. There, at the far edge of the carving, stood a castle high up on a craggy pile of rock. The identity of the castle was unmistakable.

'No way,' he said. 'Even I know where that is.'

Sally took her phone back. '"Ad crypta" means "to the vaults". It's Latin. I think we've just discovered the location of Solomon's Temple and the Ark of the Covenant.'

Mason couldn't get the image of the castle out of his mind. It was iconic, the perfect representation of a formidable fortress. 'How far is it?' he asked.

'Satnav says another thirty minutes,' Quaid said. 'We'll be there by tonight.'

Mason thought back to their enemies at Dunfermline Abbey. 'And so will they,' he said. 'But I think we got the drop on them.'

'Couldn't bear to destroy it?' Roxy asked Sally with a smile. 'The carving, I mean, not the abbey.'

'Of course not. We are defined by our history, by the rights and wrongs that we do. I always seek the high road.'

Mason hoped he did the same. His moral compass helped him do the right thing. Did his soldier's instinct make him stray off course? Mason wasn't sure, but certainly hoped not. The two impulses could be seen as mutually beneficial.

'I'll get us there as fast as I can,' Quaid said. 'But it depends on those two professors back there and how quick they are.'

'Justin and Julian are no slouches,' Sally said. 'Unfortunately.'

'It makes sense that they hid the treasures at Scotland's most recognisable symbol,' Quaid said. 'Though I suppose they didn't know it at the time.'

'Edinburgh Castle,' Mason said. 'All this time it was Edinburgh Castle.'

Roxy sighed gloomily. 'The words "ad crypta" sound a little ominous,' she said. 'Though we should probably expect that by now.'

Mason determined to take stock of their ammo, their provisions and anything else that might matter before they arrived. If they could end this tonight, so much the better. If they could find the treasure and then alert the authorities . . .

Why not do that first? a voice in his head asked.

Because they wouldn't believe us. They'd question us too, losing valuable time. Time in which the Guild of Night might ensure those treasures would never be found. And, additionally, who knew how far embedded the Guild was inside the Scottish system? Freemason lodges were often headed by high-flying policemen. Perhaps the Guild had a similar structure.

'Twenty minutes,' Quaid said.

# Chapter 41

Edinburgh Castle stood atop Castle Rock, occupied by humankind since at least the Iron Age. Through the years it had been a military fortress, a royal residence and a prison of war, and the very sight of the structure brooding over the city below evoked visions of soldiers, of kings and queens. The castle's great defences were known to have presided over some of the grandest moments in history and, tonight, they would inevitably try to do so again.

Darkness lay across the streets as they returned to the city. They drove up Lawnmarket, approaching the castle, which tonight was backlit with a dark blue radiance that picked out the walls and battlements. The parking area sat before them, cast in shadow and surrounded on two sides by chest-high castle walls that overlooked the city. Quaid started to drive through the car park but then slowed, turned around and headed back for the exit.

'Bad news,' he said. 'We're too bloody late.'

Mason had seen it too. Four large SUVs were parked as close to the front gates as they could get. Nothing subtle there. Mason felt temporarily at a loss, seeing that they had arrived in second place.

288

'They beat us,' he said. 'Now that puts the cat among the pigeons.'

'And they're here in force,' Roxy said. 'Four cars mean there's at least fifteen. Maybe twenty.'

Mason waited as Quaid pulled up as far away from the SUVs as he could. A moment later he turned the car off. Mason listened to the engine ticking in the sudden stillness.

'We can still do this,' Roxy said. 'Hitting an enemy from behind is often more effective.'

Mason agreed with her reasoning. Plus, the mercenaries were unlikely to have left many guards behind – they might be expecting Mason's team to already be inside the castle. He exited the car and waited for the others to join him.

'Nice and easy,' he said.

Together, they first sauntered over to the left side and stared out over the walls. Grassmarket lay below them, a wide street with a good selection of hotels, cafés and pubs. As they pretended to sightsee, they made their way closer to the SUVs, keeping their eyes on the windows.

Nothing moved inside the vehicles.

Mason turned his gaze to the castle itself. A path ran from the edge of the parking area through a round, arched entrance above which was hung a coat of arms. Mason saw that a closed gate that barred off the entrance was standing slightly ajar.

'Already inside,' he said. 'And probably taken out the security.'

It was a fair assumption. These were ex-soldiers and should be able to handle any local security measures.

'Or this Murdock McCloud guy made a call,' Sally said. 'The Guild is very well connected.'

Also a good point. Mason hadn't thought about it that way. 'Fair enough,' he said. 'Could have said he wanted to use it for himself and a few friends for the night. Easy.'

They stood by the SUVs, watching the open gate. There was still no movement. Mason checked to make sure his gun was nestled at the small of his back and then turned to the others.

'Ready to end this?' he said.

'Ready to find the Ark of the Covenant,' Sally said.

'Well, hang on there, Indiana,' Roxy said. 'This is gonna get a lot more dangerous before we reach that point. You stay at the back.'

Mason turned from tourist to soldier in a heartbeat. He spun away from the car and dashed up the pathway towards the open gate. He paused for a second as the others caught up, surveying beyond the gate and inside the castle grounds. The path continued inside, winding past the brooding castle walls. Still, there was no one around. Mason prepared to run again as a brisk wind picked up, stabbing at his exposed flesh with icy specks of sleet. They were exposed up here on this great craggy rock, subjected to the elements.

Mason touched the wooden gate and pushed it further open. He slipped inside the castle, making no sound, and hugged the nearest wall, followed by his companions. They started cautiously around a curving wall. Slowly, ahead, the upper part of the castle grounds came into view.

Mason saw several cannons aimed to the north, and a wider road behind them, leading deeper into the castle. He paced softly, looking for any anomalies.

The first thing he saw was the red-hot glowing tip of a cigarette. It belonged to a shadow that lounged among the battlements, a guard left behind. Mason waited a while, eyes seeking clarification, and eventually figured that the guy was staring out over the battlements whilst having a smoke.

Mason and Roxy ventured forward, using the row of cannons to shield them from the figure. The darkness was thick inside the castle, the security lighting barely adequate.

Mason and Roxy were able to sneak under three cannon barrels before pausing to check on their quarry.

Mason saw a wreath of smoke plume into the air from the man's mouth. The guy was wearing all black and there was a gun holstered at his waist. He didn't move much, just appeared to be staring over the tops of the buildings towards the distant Firth of Forth.

Mason sneaked up behind the bulky figure. For a moment, he considered the easy route which would be to simply heave the guy off the battlements. That thought, however, went against his code of ethics. The fall would probably kill the man. Yes, the guy would turn on him and kill him in an instant, but Mason's moral compass was better than that. He would kill, but only if he was absolutely forced to. Instead, he slid his right arm around the man's throat in a choke hold, almost lifting him off his feet. Roxy removed his handgun and shoved it into the waistband of her jeans. Mason throttled the man until his body went limp.

The cigarette fluttered to the floor and went out. The body slithered half under a cannon. Mason was about to frisk the fallen man but then stopped. Something else had caught his eye.

Ahead, half hidden by the castle wall, there was another man, a figure leaning back, appearing half asleep. Mason signalled quickly to the others. He crouched, listening. It seemed their activity hadn't disturbed the relaxed individual.

Mason stayed low and crept up on him. As he approached, he saw the man stir and spend a few seconds wrapping his leather jacket more tightly around his frame.

It was then that Mason recognised him
Johann.

This was bad, the worst possible time. They couldn't proceed and leave a mercenary at their backs, especially one as capable as Johann. At this moment, Johann was anything but capable. Mason wondered if he could sneak up and take the man out without any complications.

Emotions warred like evil demigods inside him. How did he feel about taking on Johann? How was Johann feeling, giving their enemies information on Mason? Because that had happened, Mason was sure of it. The dynamic that existed between ex-soldiers should be unwavering, it should be sacred. But their missions had clashed. It occurred to Mason, briefly, that if his own life had taken a bad turn, he might have ended up just like Johann. PTSD could make your dark moments turn into your worst nightmares.

He crept closer. He flexed his muscles, making ready. This close he could see Johann's closed eyes and half-open mouth. He manoeuvred himself into the right position, just to the left of Johann so that he could hook a big arm around the man's throat.

Mason struck. At the same time Johann must have sensed something – perhaps it was a soldier's instinct – but his eyes flew open, and he saw Mason's move. Johann threw himself forward into a roll and then leapt to his feet.

'Mason,' he breathed, trying to shrug off the shock. 'Don't be a fool.'

Mason approached him, keeping his voice to a whisper. 'Why are you doing this, Johann? You're better than this. We kicked ass together, fought in the same dustbowl and shed the same blood. You were one of the good guys.'

Johann sneered. 'Good guys? You have to be kidding. You think any of the top brass care about us? You see them looking out for us? They send us off to war, mate, and they don't give a shit. I told McCloud as little as I could, protected you. I can't help that he turned you into an obsession.'

Mason hesitated. 'An obsession?'

'Guy's got the hots for you, and in all the wrong ways. Wants to drink your blood out of your skull, man.'

Mason knew he had to try to steer Johann away from this nightmare path that he was on. 'Join us now,' he said. 'Leave the Guild, or whoever you're working for. You stay with them, you're gonna end up dead.'

'Is that a threat?' Johann, typically, took it the wrong way.

'Of course it's bloody not. I'm trying to help you here, pal.'

'No. You just want to get past me.'

Johann leapt at Mason. He was a big guy, and replete with muscle. His first blow shook Mason's frame to the bones, his second made him gasp. Mason covered up and, close to Johann, tried to reason with the guy.

'Please,' he said. 'Don't make me do this. Not to an old friend. We fought together. We saw the best and worst of humanity. We share too much history.'

'We shared nothing except death,' Johann spat at him, striking out again. 'I remember what happened to your crew. The bomb. Two men died in that blast.'

Mason was hit mentally, struck with a hammer blow. The events in Mosul were always just a hair's breadth from his thoughts. Fighting with Johann was bringing the whole nightmare flooding back. The way he checked the house; the way Zach and Harry went back in afterwards and never came out.

The sound of the blast.

And, afterwards, the sight of the blood.

Mason staggered, not sure why until he returned to the present and felt the blows Johann was raining down on him. He threw up a hand and then struck out, determined not to take any more punishment – not physically or mentally. He had succumbed once, lost his career and his wife, but recent times had proven to him that you couldn't blame yourself for bad circumstance and there was new life after your friends' deaths.

Mason smashed a fist into Johann's face, saw blood spout from the man's nose. He threw a gut punch in low, felt it take the wind out of Johann. The other man gasped and stumbled. Mason delivered a stiff elbow, smashing Johann's cheekbone. And then, suddenly, Johann was on his knees in front of Mason.

'I didn't want to do this,' he said.

Johann grabbed his legs, tried to unbalance him. Mason punched Johann in the back of the neck, one, twice, three times. When Johann's grip loosened, Mason kneed him point blank in the face.

Johann fell back, his face a mask of blood, teeth falling out.

Mason knelt down so that he was at the same level and started throwing his fists as if he was striking a punchbag. Johann rocked back and forth. In the end he slithered to the floor, comatose, leaving Mason kneeling over him with bloody fists and a distressed expression on his face. Mason breathed heavily.

Roxy checked the unconscious figure for any more weapons, relieved it of some communications gear and then signalled to the others.

'All clear.'

Mason climbed to his feet, wiped his hands and breathed deeply. He tried to quell the surge of self-hatred and guilt that had flooded him, tried to rein it all in. The memories flew through his mind like predatory birds. But it had been Johann's memory, Johann's truth. That didn't mean it was real or even relevant. Mason took several deep breaths and studied the terrain ahead. It was time to move forward. 'Which way?'

'Underneath the Great Hall are three layers of vaults,' Sally said. 'Some of them make up the old prisoners' quarters which you can still visit to this day. The Latin clue read "to the vaults". So I guess we go forward and then left.'

The route was wide open and contained little cover. Mason stayed close to a low wall as he made his way around. There was a tall building to the right, its dark, undraped windows giving the impression that it was abandoned. Mason stayed close to the grim edifice.

The entrance to the vaults lay through a single door at the end of a wide courtyard. There were no signs of guards anywhere, so Mason made his way across and paused outside. He stayed low, listening, but all he could hear was the castle's overwhelming, ancient silence and some distant sounds from the city – the roar of an engine, a rumbling truck, the drunken squeal of a tourist. None of the sounds raised his suspicions.

'My turn,' Roxy said.

The raven-haired woman placed a hand on the door handle. As expected, it opened easily. Roxy pushed inward with Mason at her back, taking her time. Inside, was a kind of reception room. A short flight of stone stairs stood to the left.

But what struck Mason immediately was the presence of light. Someone had been this way quite recently, someone with sufficient clout to leave all the lights on in their wake.

They advanced carefully down the stairs. At the bottom, they turned to face another flight leading down. Roxy's shoulders stiffened. Mason peered over her shoulder to see what had unnerved her.

Seated at the bottom of the stairs, resting in a plastic chair, was a man wearing a thick jacket over a bulletproof vest. His head was down as he flicked through his phone, clearly absorbed in whatever he was reading.

Mason reckoned there were eight steps separating them.

The team remained absolutely still. Though Mason couldn't actually see a gun he expected the man to be armed.

Mason waved Roxy back. Roxy spread her arms in protest, took a steady step down, closing the gap between them to seven steps.

Mason's heart leapt into his mouth. 'Too risky,' he whispered over the comms system.

Roxy descended another step.

'If he looks up . . .' Quaid said.

Mason knew the answer. Roxy was currently too far away to reach him before he could draw his gun. A second later she'd descended to the fifth step up from the bottom.

Still, the guard flicked through his phone, head down. Roxy was now four steps away from him.

And then everything changed. The guard sniffed and looked up. His eyes locked with Roxy's. They were mere feet away from each other. The man's lower jaw fell comically. Mason saw his lips form a curse even as he reached for his gun.

Roxy launched herself at the guard, knocking him off his chair. Mason was already running after her but didn't draw his gun. They couldn't risk the noise of a bullet being fired down here.

Roxy grappled for the man's gun arm, locking it in a tight fist. His free hand swept around, striking her right ear. Roxy concentrated on the gun. She took another blow to the face but shrugged it off, barely flinching. The two struggled powerfully, both wrestling for the upper hand. Roxy kept the guard's more dangerous arm pinned beneath her body.

Mason leapt down the stairs and reached them seconds later. He knelt, delivering a roundhouse to the man's face and then another. A third knocked him unconscious. Roxy disarmed him and then sat back, sighing.

'Too close,' she said.

'A little reckless,' Mason said.

'Ya think? He never stood a chance.'

As ever, Mason had to admire her confidence. He passed the guard's gun to Hassell and then surveyed the area. They were in a narrow stone passageway that led deeper underground, the way ahead lit by discreet lights that reflected greyly off the walls. Mason took a long moment to listen.

'I think we're good,' he said. 'But what happens when these guys start to wake up?' He was also referring to the guard they'd taken out by the cannons.

'You go ahead,' Roxy said quickly. 'I'll take care of them all. I'll catch up when I'm done.'

Unhappy at his lack of foresight with the guards, Mason nodded, knowing Roxy would do a swift, reliable job. Of course, he knew nothing ever went absolutely perfectly. Mistakes were often made. Ahead, the empty passage beckoned. He started down it with Hassell at his back.

'We're in the vaults now,' Sally whispered. 'Where the old cells are.'

Mason saw the first cell just a few steps ahead, and passed that information back to Roxy via the Bluetooth communicators. He didn't know what she had in mind for the guards, but it might help.

The four of them then continued slowly along the rock-lined passage. The narrow path soon opened out into a wide area where rows of hammocks hung to either side of a walkway. Timber beams lined the walls and the ceiling. Oak barrels rested on the floor at sporadic intervals. Mason saw bars on the windows on both sides. They walked past the hammocks until they reached a wrought-iron gate at the far side. The gate stood open, revealing another flight of stairs.

'Down to level two,' Sally said breathlessly.

'Be ready for anything,' Mason told them. And started to descend.

# Chapter 42

A second, spacious set of prisoners' quarters led to another gateway, this one also leading further underground. The next would be a third set of vaults under the great castle.

The last set of vaults.

Mason felt a peculiar sensation in his chest, a mixture of high excitement and profound stress. They were close to their goal, but a small army stood in their way.

Exercising extreme caution, Mason eased his way around a wall so that he could see the whole of the third vault chamber. It was wide, arched, with a series of niches at intervals along the wall. There were no prisoners' quarters here, just a wide space that appeared to be used for storage. Several old boxes stood in one corner whilst a stack of green plastic crates occupied the centre. Mason also saw a pile of old computer paper that appeared to have been chewed around the edges, probably by mice.

'Where are they?' Sally whispered.

'Maybe they cracked the clue,' Mason said. 'We haven't checked all the way down, have we? They probably have enough men to investigate as they go along, every wall, the floor, the timber supports.'

'You must be right,' Sally examined the large chamber with wide eyes. 'But, still . . . where are they now?'

Mason walked out into the centre of the room, feeling exposed. He was searching for anything that felt or looked out of place. It occurred to him then that they could already have passed the very thing they were searching for.

'What's that?' Hassell asked.

Mason followed his gaze to the room's far western corner. The man had good eyes. It appeared that a slab had been moved and placed on top of the one beside it. Mason started towards it but was soon overtaken by Sally.

'Hold back,' he said, but his words fell on deaf ears. Sally was in research mode.

'Here,' she said, bending down with her head in the corner. 'The wall joins here and right there is a Molten Sea carving.'

Mason squinted. Despite the light, the corner was still doused in relative shadow. One half of a round carving had been cut into each wall. If he stared hard enough Mason could just perceive a basin, recognisable only because he knew what he was looking for. There were some other carvings on the wall too, a portcullis, a sword that might have belonged to a Knight Templar, a crucifix and a lock and key.

Sally rocked back on her haunches. 'They're pretty faint,' she said. 'And probably attributed to the prisoners who used to dwell down here. It feels random. But that portcullis . . .' She went quiet.

Mason glanced over to where the slab was missing. The gap was about three feet square and, below it, a shadowy flight of steps led deep underground. The edges of the surrounding slabs were rough and cracked, as if someone had exerted a lot of pressure to lever the slab up. Mason now saw that it was cracked from end to end too, as if that same person had gotten frustrated and started hitting it with a crowbar. It also occurred to him now that all the surrounding slabs were cracked and fractured, as if they too had been subjected to massive force.

Sally crawled over to him. 'It's a hidden mechanism,' she said. 'The portcullis. The sign signifies a hidden gate, or something. See how they've tested every slab within a few yards' radius? They knew the passage was here, but couldn't figure out which slab was hiding it.'

'So they attacked them all,' Hassell said, shaking his head. 'Amateurs.'

'How would you have done it?' Sally asked.

'Well, I wouldn't have smashed the floor to bits.'

'See the latticework of the portcullis?' Sally said. 'It has four spikes. That takes us four slabs from the corner which' – she looked down into the hole – 'brings us here.'

'You cracked it,' Mason agreed. 'Now, shall we get down there?'

Again exercising extreme caution, they descended the stone stairway. Mason went first, climbing down twelve steps before reaching a slimy stone floor. A chill greeted him, the bone-deep chill of a place that had never felt heat. The passage was about four feet wide, the rough ceiling a foot above his head. Mason waited for the others to join him.

It was pitch-black inside the passage.

Mason plucked his torch from his pocket and switched it on, first cupping the bulb. A faint glow illuminated the way ahead. The passage ran for ten feet before a bend took it out of view. They traversed it slowly and, when they came to the bend, slowed.

'You hear something?' Mason said.

It wasn't a question. They could all hear faint voices now, travelling back along the passage. Mason took a cautious glance around the corner.

The voices were distant, maybe thirty feet ahead. He could see lights from a dozen or more torches playing around the walls of the tunnel. The group was so far distant and so quiet Mason imagined they could be from a different time, ghosts of the past that travelled Edinburgh's underworld on a quest for vengeance.

But he knew only too well what they were.

'A lot of mercs,' he said. 'A fair way ahead. If we're quiet, we can creep up in the dark.'

'And then what?' Sally asked.

'Then . . .' Mason said. 'We'll see about taking them out, finding the Ark and getting the hell out of here.'

'We'll need Roxy for that,' Hassell said.

It was a fair point. It had been over ten minutes since they'd parted. Mason imagined the raven-haired American wouldn't be much longer.

'I hope she's okay,' Sally fretted.

Mason couldn't imagine anything alive that would take down Roxy Banks.


The first guy Roxy tried to move was a heavy oaf. Roxy had been hoping he'd be conscious by the time she set about him, but that wasn't the case. She considered dragging him up the stairs so that she could hide both men in the same place but then decided she couldn't be bothered to expend the energy. There was a small room just off the corridor, somewhere she could imagine staff leaving personal possessions and coats, so she dragged him using his belt. The idiot got his leg stuck in the doorway and made Roxy lose her grip. Then the door closed on his knee. He'd feel that one in the morning. Roxy stooped down, kicked the door in and grabbed the man's belt once more, hauling him inside the small room. Then, she smacked him across the head for good measure, making sure he remained unconscious.

'Don't you dare wake up, asshole.'

Her guess about the room had been close enough. She found some coat hooks, a pile of belongings and a desk with a computer on it. The computer was up and running, the screen showing four different scenes in low resolution. Sally had been right. Whoever this Murdock McCloud was, he'd paid to be alone tonight.

Or maybe he'd threatened. Or cajoled. Or maybe even asked nicely. Roxy wasn't sure. She'd come across so many small men who believed themselves to be powerful dictators lately, she was starting to lose count. The trouble was – these small men always caused irreparable harm before they got exactly what was coming to them.

Roxy found Sellotape in a desk drawer and used half a roll to bind her captive's hands and feet. Then she laid him on his back, shoved a glove in his mouth and sellotaped that closed too. She wasn't too bothered about his safety. He could still breathe, which Roxy wasn't sure he really deserved to be doing at this stage. He'd been ready to shoot them in cold blood. He'd known exactly what he was getting into.

Roxy found the key to the door on a hook, locked it after her and then threw it away. After that, she climbed the stairs and ventured back out into the night. A wintry gust of wind hit her, scouring her face. Roxy took a deep breath. She put her head down and ran over to the northern wall where she saw the cannons. She could already see her prey, the previously downed Johann, with his legs sticking out from under one of the big guns. She took a quick glance to all sides, expecting to find nothing untoward and not being disappointed. She ran up to Johann, grabbed his legs and started to drag him out into the open, wincing slightly as the back of his head bounced on the cobbles. She consoled herself with the knowledge that this asshole had been ready to kill them all too.

Roxy looked for a place to stash him, seeing nothing close by. The courtyard ran in a slight curve to the west, so she dragged him that way. The ground sloped at a nice angle, easing the pressure on her muscles. At the bottom of the slope, she found the National War Museum and, beside it, a welcome sight.

The prisoners' latrines.

Quite a fitting place for her prisoner to end up, she thought. The door was painted black and looked old. It wouldn't stand up to Roxy's boot. She kicked it hard near the handle, saw it fly back against an internal wall and then proceeded to tie her captive up with the rest of the roll of Sellotape–before dragging him inside the latrine. Roxy gagged him and then left him there, head propped up against the far wall.

Roxy closed the door behind her. Time to get back to Mason and the others. As she paused for a moment, breathing heavily after dragging the man so far, she heard a noise on the wind. It was the sound of several people, walking and talking. She stayed close to the curve of the wall and walked back up the slope towards the main courtyard before falling to her knees to help stay out of sight.

There, walking through the courtyard in the direction of the prisoners' cells, was a very strange procession.

She counted ten men and two women. They were dressed strangely for a frosty night out at the castle – the men wearing expensive bespoke suits and the women long, flowing dresses. They held their heads regally, smoked cigarettes and cigars and took their time as they walked past Roxy's hiding place.

Twelve? She thought. Could this be the Guild of Night? Was this their victory procession?

Roxy tried to hold back instincts that told her to take these people out. She didn't usually hold back, didn't avoid confrontation. Her muscles coiled, ready for an attack.

Joe Mason's voice cut through the red mist in her head. Don't blow your cover.

Her response: I should get the drop on them now.

Roxy rose, but then forced herself back down. Despite her instincts, she knew Mason was right. It didn't stop her fingers twitching, didn't help her impulse control. She rose again, desperately close to being seen, but then managed to force herself back to her knees.

By now, the odd procession had passed her by. She was staring at the back of it, the men walking in twos and threes, the women aloof and seemingly unapproachable. Roxy waited for the last man to pass and then crept out of hiding.

She keyed the mic that nestled in her ear. 'Can you hear me, Joe?'

'Barely. Where are you? Stopped for coffee?'

'Yeah, sure, there's a nice café here. You have company.'

'Say that . . . again.'

The line was breaking up, the reception deteriorating. Roxy realised she didn't have a clue where Mason and the others had gone and determined that her best course of action was to follow the Guild of Night.

If that's who they were.

And not get seen.

That doesn't matter. If I get seen, I'll go through them all.

That was what she really wanted.

Roxy watched as the group started entering the castle through the door that led to the prisoners' cells. She would hold back as long as she could. She would try hard to let the procession find its way underground.

After that, she wasn't promising anything.

# Chapter 43

Mason heard someone approaching from the rear. At first, he thought it was Roxy but then realised he could hear several men talking as they got closer.

'Shit,' he said. 'We're exposed here.'

They were right in the middle of the tunnel, halfway towards the light. There was no turning back.

Torchlight speared the darkness from behind them.

Hassell hissed, 'Follow me, quickly.'

The New Yorker ran back five steps and then disappeared. Mason followed him, surprised to find a small niche in the passage. He hadn't even noticed it on the way past but Hassell, always observant for alternative routes, had. The four of them squeezed inside and held their breath.

As Mason waited, he counted twelve dark, shadowy figures pass along the tunnel. He couldn't see very much but they appeared to be older men and women and dressed in their Sunday best. They didn't fit down here, not one bit.

'The Guild,' Sally whispered as the last man vanished.

'I thought they never met in person,' Mason said.

'Who knows?' Sally said. 'The Ark of the bloody Covenant is a good excuse to ditch the habit of a lifetime.'

Mason counted to ten, then poked his head back out into the tunnel. The procession had reached the main body of men and women by now. There was quite a lot of conversation, some of which drifted back down the passageway.

'I see everything I've ever wanted, Jacqueline.'

'And I. And to think, it's been down here all along.'

They laughed. They shrugged off centuries of historical significance with a chuckle. The men sounded equally blasé about what was happening.

'How on earth will we ever divide it all up?' one asked with a guffaw.

The others joined in with the laughter.

Mason stepped back out into the passageway then, just as a shadow came up on the right. His instinct took over. He ducked, spun towards the shape and struck out. The shadow caught his first blow on an upraised arm and deftly prevented his second from striking its ribs. There was no noise, and they were up close. Mason could hear the breath escaping the other figure's lips.

'Stop trying to dance with me,' Roxy whispered. 'Behave.'

Mason pulled back and heaved a sigh of relief. In the dark, he barely managed to make out Roxy's features.

'You were lucky,' he said.

'Yeah, right. I was just about to take you out.'

'Will you two stop wittering,' Sally said. 'We need to move now, whilst they're distracted.'

Mason knew she was right. The five of them remained in the main passageway and started towards the torchlight that illuminated the space ahead. They moved without sound, coming up on the backs of three men. Mason slowed, breathing easily, as he came within touching distance of them.

He knew there were at least thirty people ahead, all crowded into a relatively small space. At first, he couldn't see what they were looking at, and struggled to find a gap to see through. He didn't think they would notice an extra body, so he pretended that he was one of their number. There were so many people down here – not just the Guild members, but countless mercenaries – that it was hard to know who was who.

Sally, at his side, was also trying to see into the room.

This was the same kind of large-vaulted chamber, four storeys below Edinburgh Castle, that Mason had seen earlier. The dust motes that danced in the air told him it hadn't been visited in a long, long time.

And then the whole assemblage moved forward. Gaps opened as people advanced into the great chamber. Mason moved with them, knowing he and the others were dressed similarly to the mercenaries and that the Guild wouldn't be able to tell one person from another.

'My God,' Sally whispered, now seeing what lay inside the chamber.

Mason was stunned by what he saw and found himself unable to move. Ahead, there was a substantial platform. Then, the floor fell away in a sharp, wide slope. Littering that slope was all manner of golden treasure, its gleaming surface illuminated by a dozen torches. Mason saw four immense golden pillars that would have held the tent of the Tabernacle up. He saw candlesticks and lampstands and two wide tables. He saw oil lamps lying in a heap. Beyond the first pile, lower down, stood a gilded altar, clearly covered in dust and grime but returning the light of the torches with a flash of gilt. Other luminous accoutrements stood in front of and around the altar. Several large partitions that might have been room dividers were stacked to the right whilst breastplates and headplates stood to the left.

But this was only the slope that led to the main floor of the chamber.

Seeing what was further down there took Mason's breath away. On a wide rock plateau stood all the trappings of

Solomon's Temple, from a stack of the very blocks from which it had been built to endless rows of incredible golden objects, bowls and basins, candelabrum and altars. It was all too much to take in with a single glance.

'It shines,' Sally said softly, 'like nothing I've ever seen.'

Mason found that the reflected light from the lustrous regalia left dark spots on the backs of his eyes. It was strong enough to be blinding. He tried to centre himself in the moment, ignore the splendour and focus on the real world. To the left, a group of eighteen mercenaries stood in reverent silence, their drawn guns pointing at the floor. The Guild of Night – if that's what they were – stood at the edge of the platform, all gazing down in a big group.

'The Ark,' Sally said. 'I can't see it.'

Mason wasn't surprised. 'It was part of the temple,' he said. 'It should be down there somewhere.'

'I've never seen so much gold,' Roxy said. 'These biblical boys certainly knew how to treat themselves.'

Mason was about to answer when a broad figure at the head of the entourage turned around. He stood well over six feet and looked like he knew how to handle himself. Mason didn't have to wait long to find out who the man was.

'Did I, Murdock McCloud, not promise you greatness?' the man said in a Scottish accent. 'Did I not assure you that we would prevail?'

'You also promised us anonymity,' someone said a little sourly. 'I don't see any of that around here.'

'But are you not glad to be here?' the question was clearly rhetorical as McCloud went on. 'Standing here, right now, with this incredible motherlode before you. We have found it, my friends, the Tabernacle, Solomon's Temple, the holy Ark. We have found it. We made the sacrifices, the contributions, and yes, everything paid off.'

'It's incredible . . .' someone said.

'The best moment of my life . . .' another said.

But there was animosity in McCloud's ranks. Mason could sense it and he could hear it. He stood behind the largest man there with Sally at his side, but further back so the shadows that lined the tunnel helped conceal him. The others were to the rear, cloaked in darkness.

'And now that we have revealed ourselves?' someone grunted. 'Do we reveal all? Tell them who we are? Tell the world at large that it was us, the Guild of Night, who found the Temple and the Ark? I believe that we should.'

There were several murmurs of agreement.

McCloud's eyes narrowed and his face turned blank. 'That,' he said, 'would be a deadly decision.'

# Chapter 44

One of the men completely misunderstood the threat behind McCloud's words. 'Not for us,' he said. 'We would stand apart. The great Guild. We have now been revealed to each other and, now that we are, why not announce our presence to the world?'

McCloud attempted to leave them in no doubt as to what he meant. 'The Guild is a powerful group,' he said. 'Old. Established in the eighteenth century. Do you know the calibre of men who preceded us?'

'They were knights,' someone said.

'Thank you, Sallow. Yes, knights. Our predecessors fought hand-to-hand on the battlefield. They struck down their enemies with sharp iron; they didn't make war with words or through social media. They were real men and women, with real vision. Take-charge killers. I see the Guild that way. I always will.'

'We spared no expense and no lives tracking down the Ark,' Sallow said.

'I didn't condone any form of killing,' one man said.

'The world deserves to see the Ark of the Covenant,' a woman said. 'To see Solomon's Temple. I believe it deserves—'

'Deserves?' McCloud spat. 'The world is a cesspool run by fools and the super-rich. Only in isolation do we steer clear of the madness. Tell me, everyone, that this is not your preference?'

Mason watched, identifying six cynics. These men and one woman drifted to the right, separating themselves from the others as if they couldn't bear to stand at their side. For a moment, McCloud appeared stunned.

'Tell me this is not your preference?' he roared, colouring.

All those gathered before him jumped. Sallow stepped back. McCloud seemed unaware that saliva was running from his lips.

'We are the powerful owners of ancient secrets,' he snarled. 'We are better than they are. And by they, I mean everyone. We corrupt those we want to, own others, influence hundreds. We cannot simply reveal ourselves.'

'Honestly,' a man said, 'I don't see why not. What's wrong with operating in the light and being universally acknowledged? What's wrong with real fame? I propose we put this to a vote.'

McCloud, seething, took one small pace forward. 'You think the Guild is a democracy?' he spat. 'I see. All right, then. Here's my vote.'

There was a moment of stillness. Mason was aware of the confusion that rippled through the crowd. A moment later, McCloud struck.

His right hand emerged from his pocket holding a long dagger. It flashed through the air, its steel blade bright, and sliced through the jugular of the man closest to him. It arced further still, slipping through the neck of the next in line.

And then McCloud was moving. He grabbed one individual by the throat and thrust his knife into another's jaw. Blood fountained through the air, painting the scene with gore. McCloud moved amid the chaos with precision,

311

slipping from one aghast doubter to the next, slashing and stabbing. He finished by plunging his dagger into a woman's right eye. He let her fall with the dagger still inside her skull.

Mason had already dragged Sally back into the shadows. They watched as McCloud, panting, dripping blood that wasn't his own, turned to the five still-living members of the Guild of Night.

'Does anyone else want to reveal the Guild to the whole world? To share this treasure with billions?'

'Not me,' someone said.

'Idiots,' another spoke up. 'They deserved to die.'

McCloud bent down, retrieved his knife and wiped the blade on the clothes of the dead woman. 'I hope you see the severity with which I view betrayal,' he said. 'The—'

A man was still stirring. Mason saw it and winced. This wouldn't end well. The man was climbing to his knees, eyes wild, blood dripping from a fresh hole in his right cheek. His head turned towards the tunnel.

'Shit,' Mason said.

'We are now officially fucked,' Roxy said.

McCloud may have read something in one of his confidantes' eyes, he may have heard the wounded man move, he may even have sensed the shift behind his back, but at that moment he turned, saw the still-breathing man and roared.

The man bolted for the tunnel.

Straight towards Mason. There was nowhere to turn for the man, nowhere to run. The passage was pitch-black, but now illuminated as a dozen mercenaries turned their torches towards it.

McCloud sprang after the running man, reaching out and catching him by the back of the jacket. For one hopeful moment Mason thought he might haul the man back before he reached the tunnel, but that didn't happen. Instead, the terrified individual squirmed out of his jacket on the run, leaving it dangling in McCloud's hands.

'Come here, bastard,' the Scotsman said.

Mason tried to shrink as the lights illuminated him.

McCloud and his prey were now steps away. McCloud's knife plunged down into the man's spine, bearing him to the floor. The pair hit hard, crashing into the concrete.

Mason was left staring into the torchlight.

'That's Joe Mason,' Sallow suddenly cried. 'Kill him. Kill them all!'

'Don't use your guns,' McCloud roared above the sudden tumult. 'Protect the treasure.'

And even as Mason cursed his bad luck, Roxy stepped around him to confront their attackers.

'Come get some,' she said.

# Chapter 45

Roxy opened fire. McCloud's warning about firearms meant nothing to her. She shot three mercenaries in the chest and kicked another in the stomach. The man grunted and fell back into one of his colleagues. The two men dropped to the floor. She whirled around, kicked out low and broke the knee of another man close by.

Mason was a step behind her, targeting men on the left. It went against his nature to use his handgun, since he knew his enemy had been ordered not to use theirs, but because they were so badly outnumbered, he fired off two shots before engaging with his fists. Two mercs went down, groaning in agony.

Quaid and Hassell were ready to open fire, but forced to hesitate in case they clipped Roxy or Mason. Hassell moved close to an opponent and shot the man through the stomach. Quaid smashed another in the side of the skull with his Glock. Another mercenary leapt at Quaid and knocked him to the floor. Quaid managed to raise his gun and shoot the man point blank through the chest.

Roxy's every blow was designed to debilitate, whether it be to throat, eyes, trunk or between the legs. Two mercs didn't listen to McCloud's order and opened fire anyway, their bullets passing dangerously close to the fast-moving American.

Mason leapt at his next adversary, grabbing his shoulders and propelling both of them down the sharp slope where the Tabernacle treasure was stacked. Mason rolled, trying to stay his momentum, scattering the riches, his head glancing off a pile of bowls, his body striking a golden altar. When his momentum was arrested by a gilded box he sat up.

Surrounded by the treasure they'd been seeking for so long, he locked eyes with his opponent.

The man sprang for him. To the right, Hassell also rolled down the slope, grappling with an opponent. The two crashed their way through a gleaming fortune. From the platform above, McCloud's roaring voice could be heard – commanding his men to take care amid the treasure.

Mason lifted a golden vase and smashed his assailant across the face with it. The vase was solid, and the man slumped immediately. Mason threw it at the next attacker, hitting him in the forehead, then rose quickly and tackled him around the waist like a rugby player.

Roxy was knee-deep in candlesticks, bowls and small tables. She'd lost her gun on the roll down here. She met an attack with two upraised fists and lost her balance. The man forced her onto her back and then climbed on top, raining punches down at her face. Roxy's hands were free, but she didn't try to cover up. Instead, she sought a weapon with her hands. First, she found a bowl, brought it up and clouted her attacker across the face with it. He grunted, blinked, but kept on striking her, saliva running between his clenched lips and through his thick beard. Roxy grabbed a small table and slammed the edge of it into his left ear, confident it would knock him for six. The man flinched but still didn't budge, though his punches stopped raining down for a few seconds. Still searching, Roxy's fingers found the edge of a candelabrum.

Who could keep fighting with a candelabrum sticking out of their face?

Working fast, Roxy picked up the weapon, turned it and jammed the candlesticks hard into the bearded man's cheek. He yelped and brought his hands up to protect himself. Roxy rolled, heaved him off and found herself facing the other man's boots.

Instantly, she grabbed hold and yanked him off his feet, then rolled to her right into the legs of another man. Two attackers fell hard.

Quaid and Hassell fought together. They slipped down the slope boots first and then chose to attack the mercs who were doubling up on Mason and Roxy. Hassell struck one in the ribs and got his attention, and then Quaid bashed him over the head with a heavy brass bell. As it struck, the bell reverberated, adding a surreal element to the chaos, but that didn't stop Quaid using it again ten seconds later to render another man unconscious.

The fight was going their way. The sudden assault, the use of guns, the onslaught of Roxy; it had all thinned their opponents out. Mason guessed there were seven dead, most of the others either unconscious or coming to. They had to press their advantage.

Mason was hurting but tried to ignore the pain. He saw a man lying close to his feet. The man was trying to get back up. Mason kicked him in the head.

There was a sharp pain in his arm. Mason turned and saw a man with a knife beside him. The man flashed the blade again. This time, Mason stepped back, but the blade sliced at the material of his jacket and penetrated, drawing a red line across the flesh of the right side of his stomach. The pain centred him, making him focus on the deadly blade.

The man struck again. Mason angled his body out of the way at the very last second, letting the blade thrust past his ribs, then trapped the arm that held it with his right arm.

Using his left hand, he punched the man in the face sharply, three times. There was the crack of cartilage. The man threw up an arm to ward Mason off. They fought face to face, inches apart. Mason could smell the guy's garlic-laced breath, could feel spittle flying between them. The man's eyes were wide, his face stretched in exertion. Mason threw well-rehearsed punches, sometimes at the ribs, sometimes at the face, weakening his opponent with every blow.

Another mercenary stepped towards them. Mason waited for the right moment. He kicked out at the man's legs, striking his shins hard and sending him face first to the ground. As he landed, Mason kicked him in the head.

This distraction allowed Mason's opponent to yank the knife free from under Mason's arm. It didn't intend to stay free for long. The guy thrust it straight back towards Mason's ribs.

This time, Mason chopped down with his right hand, striking the wrist and changing the direction of the blade. It struck the rocky floor, drawing sparks that showered across the top of Mason's hand and made him flinch. The blade snapped. Mason saw it happen first. He now concentrated both fists on his opponent's face, driving him off his heels and back to the floor.

Mason punched him into oblivion.

Roxy's opponent also wielded a knife. They stood at the bottom of the slope, their boots deep in treasure, the riches of Solomon's Temple laid out to their right.

The merc jabbed his blade at Roxy, circling her, trying to find a way in.

The interior of the chamber was a flashing jumble of light and shadow, like a kaleidoscope. Some of the mercs had dropped their flashlights, others still held torches as they fought. Beams of light speared the darkness from where they lay either propped up by urns and vases and tables or sinking steadily into a pile of golden jewellery. The shafts of light were random, wavering and erratic, painting the treasure chamber with an almost supernatural ambiance, a ghostly and otherworldly illumination.

Roxy stumbled over a large sword and fell to her knees. The knife whistled past her left ear, nicking the flesh and causing blood to flow. The attack had been swift and concise, but it left the man's underbelly wide open.

Roxy delivered three devastating punches, breaking ribs and other bones. Blood seeped from the man's mouth as he slithered to the floor, the knife falling from nerveless fingers.

Mason took a moment to observe the way the battle was going. As he'd already noticed, their initial onslaught had taken half their adversaries away. Now, the unconscious outnumbered the still standing, and those who fought were being beaten. Mason allowed his eyes to travel back up the slope, to where the Guild of Night had been standing.

Surprisingly, they still lined the platform, all six of them observing the battle. Mason saw Murdock McCloud at their head, an enraged expression plastered across his face.

'Kill them!' he was screaming. He had bitten through his lips, and blood ran down his chin. 'Kill, kill, kill!'

There was something terrible about the way McCloud shrieked the words; something both passionate and evil. The other five members of the Guild standing with him had sensed it too and had stepped away, creating space between them. McCloud shouted and gesticulated at the mercenaries, oblivious.

Mason spent a few moments crawling through the mass of treasure, visiting two half-conscious ex-soldiers and punching them until they passed out. To his right, Quaid and Hassell circled two opponents. On the left, Roxy was climbing up off a motionless man.

The chamber and the gold slid between light and shadow as Mason moved forward. Men were picking themselves up off the floor all around him.

'You five,' McCloud shouted. 'Up here now. Guard our exit.'

Mason clenched his fists as three able-bodied men and two of the mercs who'd barely recovered started scrambling up the slope to McCloud's side. There seemed to be an air of furious resignation hanging around McCloud, a sense of failure and anger and murderous intent.

And Mason believed he knew why.

'Now you can shoot the bastards,' McCloud said. 'I want this gold glazed with their blood.'

The mercenaries reached for their weapons. Mason was already in motion. There wasn't time to yell out a warning. He just hoped his colleagues shared a similar sense of self-preservation to his.

Mason threw himself to the floor and crawled behind the nearest unconscious merc, dragging the man's bulk across his own. Roxy ducked behind a wide golden altar. Quaid and Hassell, thinking quickly, crawled under the golden partitions that had helped make up the great Tabernacle itself.

Gunfire filled the air. Mason felt bullets strike the merc he was hiding behind. Heard the man groan and breathe his last. Felt the trickle of blood as the man bled out. Impact after impact hit the dead body. Mason felt one bullet pass right through, mercifully missing his own bulk and denting a bowl to his left. The great cave echoed back and forth as its riches trembled under the thunder, as the torches were displaced and sent their beams shaking fitfully, as treasure rolled and spun and revolved left and right. The deadly roar filled the air until McCloud let out a stentorian howl.

'Enough! You're ruining everything. The Guild must live to fight another day. Get us out of here.'

McCloud was choosing survival over unlimited wealth. Over the glistening hoard he considered his birthright. Something was wrong. Mason felt this behaviour didn't fit

319

with the entity that had pursued the path to the Ark right across the United Kingdom.

But then . . . he had just seen McCloud kill six of his own colleagues in cold blood. Clearly, not all of the guy's dogs were barking. The Guild was a punitive dictatorship whether the six remaining members understood it or not.

'Hurry,' McCloud shouted as the mercs surrounded him.

Mason pushed away the dead body of the merc that had fallen on top of him. He climbed to his knees. He had no idea where his gun had gone. He looked first to Roxy, and then Quaid and Hassell. Above them, at the top of the steps, the Guild and their remaining mercenaries were preparing to leave the chamber.

Roxy scrambled forward, face livid. She scooped up her own gun from where it lay, raised it and targeted McCloud. She fired. The bullet struck a mercenary just as the man moved in front of the Guild's leader, taking away most of the back of the guy's head.

Blood spattered McCloud and his cronies.

Quaid and Hassell pushed the heavy partitions away, letting the rectangular sheets slide down their legs.

Mason rose to follow, but the fight wasn't done yet. There were still three or four able-bodied mercs down here, rising now that their colleagues had departed, and closing in on them. Two held guns of their own. Though Mason and his team had fought hard, they hadn't obliterated their enemy.

Mason saw a gun sighted on him.

He was helpless, standing in the line of fire. The mercenary took the time to smirk. In that instant, Roxy threw her gun to Mason, the black weapon spinning through both light and shadow. Mason lifted his hand, caught the gun and squeezed the trigger all in the blink of an eye.

The merc appeared surprised as blood started to blossom over his heart. He blinked and then fell dead.

Mason threw himself at the next opponent.

Roxy started wading through the masses of gold.

'Hassell,' she said. 'With me.'

She started to give chase to the Guild of Night.

## Chapter 46

Roxy refused to give McCloud and his cronies a free ride. She couldn't let them leave so easily. With Hassell, she climbed the slope back up to the platform, stumbling through the treasures.

She found Sally hiding in the niche part way along the tunnel.

'Relatively safe back there,' she said. 'Did you see the Guild pass?'

'Yeah, running with their bodyguards,' Sally said. 'Don't tell me you're thinking of chasing them?'

'We can't let those murderous bastards escape. They'll only come back stronger.'

Roxy still held her gun. Hassell carried a knife. They could hear running footsteps ahead, further down the tunnel. They could see waving flashlights. Roxy waited for them to vanish, not wanting to risk a bullet being fired down the narrow passageway, and then set off after them.

The tunnel was tight and treacherous, the ground uneven and more noticeably so as they ran in the dark. Roxy kept her goal firmly in her mind. They couldn't let the Guild – and especially McCloud – escape. Only four mercenaries were with them. She and Hassell would pose them a serious problem.

She ran with caution, glad the passage was just one long push forward. She couldn't see her adversaries. Couldn't hear them either. Had they already escaped?

Soon, a square rectangle of light appeared in the ceiling ahead. Roxy had known the exit couldn't be re-covered because the mercs had broken the slab trying to get it open.

She slowed, conscious that they might be lying in wait for her. She let Hassell boost her so that she could grip the square hole's sides and then used her body strength to lift herself up. The wide room above was empty of people. She lifted herself over the edge and then reached down for Hassell, using one hand to help pull him up. Soon, they were running through the vault.

A flight of stairs lay ahead. Roxy hit it at speed, doubling back on herself and then climbing a second. They reached the second-floor vault, where the prisoners' old quarters were. No sounds reached her ears. She checked Hassell was a step behind her and kept running, soon reaching the flight of stairs that led to the first vault.

She paused, hearing the sound of running feet echoing back down to her. She used their noise to mask her own. Cautiously, she climbed the stairs steadily up to the first vault.

Another set of prisoners' quarters, well lit. Hassell whispered to her as they ran.

'What's the plan?'

'We catch them out in the open. We stay in cover. I have my gun. They don't stand a chance.'

Roxy knew that once they exited the castle there was a wide-open courtyard to negotiate before they reached the esplanade, where the parking area was. That would be where she and her friends would attack.

The chase went on. They negotiated the top vault and then rose again, coming up to ground level. Roxy saw that the main exit door was standing wide open. Their prey had already left.

Perfect.

She preceded Hassell outside, taking care. A cold blast of wind struck her face. To her left, ranged along the roadway, was a fast-moving procession – the six members of the Guild and their four bodyguards. Roxy saw one of the guards look back but had had the presence of mind to stay mostly hidden. The guy didn't see her.

Roxy waited, angry because she couldn't pursue immediately but making herself hold back. She smelled the sea on the air and could hear the odd rumble of distant traffic. Hassell waited by her side.

'What you intending to do with that knife?' she asked, mostly to take her mind off the pressure of waiting around.

'It was all I could find.' Hassell shrugged. 'Don't worry. It'll find a home.'

Roxy smiled grimly. She chanced another look around the open doorway, saw that their quarry was far enough away to risk moving. They were already halfway to the parking area. Roxy stepped outside and started running, heading over to the curving castle walls first and using them to help conceal her sprint.

They rounded the castle in pursuit of the Guild.

It was clear ahead. Roxy ran until she saw the walkway that led out of the castle to the esplanade where the Guild members had left their transport. It was easier to hide here, more curving walls and flights of steps up to the castle's heights, the corner of a shop and a ticket office. Roxy paused near the portcullis and peered around the corner.

'There,' she said.

They were going to have to be quick. Already, the Guild were climbing into two cars with a merc each, the other two mercs jumping into a third. Roxy guessed they would be the honour guard.

She turned to Hassell. 'Now we stop them.'

The car's engines roared to life. Roxy ran under the

portcullis and into the open, making for the nearest vehicle: a dark blue SUV. The two mercenaries on board were too busy talking to their colleagues via Bluetooth to see her coming.

Both cars containing the Guild were already moving slowly, swinging around to face the exit. Roxy ran up to the SUV, grabbed the door handle and pulled. Because it hadn't set off yet, the internal locking mechanism hadn't engaged. The door flew open, revealing a surprised mercenary who had shoved his gun between the seats.

Roxy grabbed his arm and hauled him out. The man fell sideways and down, tumbling to the ground. Roxy had already sighted her firearm on the second man, the one in the passenger seat.

'Don't do it.'

He didn't listen. He didn't reach for his gun. Roxy could see it nestling in the door's side pocket. He flung the door open and leapt outside, hiding on the other side of the car. Hassell landed on the man who'd been dragged out of the car. Roxy dashed around the front, chasing her new prey, gun up. She could hear the other cars manoeuvring. It was essential they didn't get away.

The merc was on his knees, hands in the air. Roxy was surprised. It wasn't often you came across a sensible merc. She strode up to him and smashed her gun twice across his temple, rendering him unconscious. He fell to the hard ground. Roxy continued around the car and came back to Hassell.

The New Yorker was tussling with his opponent but had cut him twice. One of the wounds was bleeding quite badly, so badly in fact that the merc was concentrating more on staunching the flow than fighting Hassell. Roxy kicked him in the face and climbed into the driver's seat.

'Get in,' she told Hassell.

The other two cars were now facing the right way. Their drivers stepped on their accelerator pedals. Roxy's car was

325

already running. She didn't hesitate, just rammed the gear selector into reverse and sent the car speeding backwards. It hit the side door of the first car, crumpling the metal and turning it half around. She ducked as someone opened fire through the glass, shards spraying outward in a deadly shower. The bullet missed. Roxy drove her foot to the floor, scraping past the first car and heading towards the second. This one she hit hard in the rear, striking the left side so that it spun around.

Hassell held on tightly to his seat belt. He hadn't had time to strap in.

Roxy now engaged drive, sending her car leaping forward. She struck the first car once more, this time at the front, creasing the bonnet. Then, with complaining sounds coming from her own SUV, she reversed and drove into the side of the second car.

Both remained stationary.

She saw the heads and shoulders of the Guild members, who had been thrown around, now resting against the glass. They would be groggy. Roxy saw steam rising from her own engine. She flung open the door, raised her gun and stalked out.

Hassell ran to the first car as she dashed towards the second. There would be one mercenary inside each car. Roxy stayed low, under the line of fire. She shot through the back window, careful to angle her bullet so that it wouldn't kill anyone, at least not yet. She wanted the Guild captured and in custody. The glass exploded, shattering inward. She saw the heads of two men suddenly duck out of sight. Doors opened on the far side.

Roxy slid in on her knees, hugging the back of the car. She took a quick look underneath, couldn't tell the difference between Guild and mercenary shoes. She stayed low and crawled to the side of the car.

Glanced around. The mercenary was coming straight at

her, too fast to shoot. She rose up like a force of nature, the top of her head smashing underneath the man's jawbone. He grunted and collapsed to the floor, largely unaware of what had happened and mostly comatose. Roxy kicked him in the face for good measure.

Hassell pulled on the door handles of the first car, but it had locked. He ducked as the merc inside targeted him with his gun through the window. The safety glass blew apart, and the bullet passed harmlessly through the air above Hassell's head. Hassell reached inside, grabbed the merc by the gun arm and pulled. The gun wavered between them. Hassell ran with the forward momentum of the car, grappling through the broken window. He smashed the other man's head against the inner frame of the car. The Guild members shouted or screamed, some urging the driver to go faster. Hassell's fingers slipped off the merc's jacket due to the amount of blood that was splashing down on to it.

The gun came up again. Hassell was ready. He ducked out of the way, leaping to the rear of the car. The gun discharged into the air. Its owner became somewhat disorientated as his face smashed into the bulkhead several times.

Hassell kept pace with the car. He couldn't reach through the window anymore, due to the gun's presence. Instead, he raced around the back and came up on the other side.

The driver's side.

He plucked the knife from his waistband, reversed it and smashed the window to the side of the driver's face. The man cursed and picked up speed, making Hassell sprint alongside. The car park exit was just ahead, narrowing sharply as it led out into one of Edinburgh's city streets.

Roxy yelled out a warning as the occupants of the car she was targeting decided to follow suit. She chased after the car as it swept through the wide parking area.

'Hassell!' she cried. 'Get down!'

# Chapter 47

Deep underneath Edinburgh Castle, Mason surveyed a scene of carnage and chaos. Many of the mercenaries had been shot and were dead, but some still struggled back from unconsciousness. Quaid was with him, standing amid the gold. Sally was still up in the passage, looking down.

The best way forward was to make sure nobody was capable of giving chase, Mason thought. He counted four mercs in various stages of recovery and made his way across to the first. The man, on his knees, swung a haymaker that connected with Mason's thigh. The muscle went dead and Mason staggered. The merc swung again, but Mason was out of reach of this second attack. The merc fell forward on to his face. His head connected solidly with a golden table, knocking him unconscious.

One down, three to go.

Quaid had cottoned on to Mason's intentions. He made his way over to another merc who was currently on his knees struggling to stand. Quaid pummelled him around the head until he collapsed back down to the ground.

Mason was already engaged with the third. This man wore a denim jacket and sported a thick bushy beard. He was a huge man, bald, with eyes that looked too small in his fleshy face. He snarled at Mason as the two engaged and then produced a knife from the small of his back. The blade was short, but it would still leave a nasty wound.

The bearded man thrust forward twice but Mason evaded the attacks. The second time, he stepped in and delivered an elbow to the face. His adversary, already groggy, collapsed to one knee. Mason was forced to retreat when the man started swinging his blade blindly.

Mason backed up further as the man lumbered to his feet once more. He was breathing heavily, hanging his head and bleeding from his mouth so badly that the blood fell to the floor in a steady trickle. Now, his eyes locked with Mason's.

'Last chance,' he said thickly.

Mason said nothing, just waited warily for an attack. When it came, low towards his waist, he stepped out of range and prepared to lunge in for a final flurry of elbow and knee strikes. The moment his foot came down however, he knew he was in trouble.

Something shifted under his boot. A bowl? A pot maybe? It slid out from under him and sent his left foot skidding. Mason felt his legs go out underneath him.

He hit the floor, landing heavily on his right side. The man mountain with the beard was already in motion, clumping forwards heavily to close the gap. Mason groaned as the pain arrowed through him. His head struck a candlestick, drawing blood; his hip came down on something solid and sharp. When he looked up, focusing, his enemy stood over him.

'No mercy,' the man said as if repeating a mantra.

Clumsily, he fell to his knees over Mason, his bulk blocking out whatever flashlights were still illuminating them. Mason was forced into a world of darkness. The man's body heat enveloped him, along with droplets of sweat. Mason struck up at the jowly face, striking flesh but barely inconveniencing the man.

The knife was gone. The man's big hands wrapped around Mason's throat. He didn't even try to stop Mason hitting him, just started to squeeze. Mason felt the pain instantly and tried to focus – recalling every boxing move he'd ever been taught.

He concentrated on the ribs, the side of the head. He used his training. The other man groaned and stiffened and even whimpered once, but didn't once allow his hold to lessen.

Mason felt the life being choked out of him.

Darkness started to invade the edges of his vision. His blows became weaker. He found that he couldn't grip the wrists above him tight enough. The face was twisted with effort, hanging about twelve inches above him.

Mason saw only blackness.

He didn't see what happened, but suddenly the enormous bulk collapsed on top of him. The hands around his throat relaxed and fell away. Mason still couldn't breathe for a few seconds but then, painfully, all sensation started to return.

Someone was tugging on the big bulk that lay across him, but without success. Mason brought a knee up and helped roll the unconscious mass off him.

The dubious light that illuminated the chamber revealed Sally's face now hanging above him. In her right hand, Sally held a large oblong chest. The events of a few seconds ago started to make sense. Sally had made use of her new training to get involved in the fight.

'Thanks,' he murmured. 'I see you found the Ark of the Covenant.'

Sally winced and put the chest down gently. Even in his groggy state, Mason could see that the most sacred relic of the Israelites was a gold-plated wooden chest about fifty inches in length, thirty inches in height and thirty in depth. A crown moulding of gold had been fitted around the top. A golden ring hung from each side.

Dismissing the Ark, his brain kicked into high gear and he turned to check on Quaid. The older man was standing over a recently felled opponent, sucking on his bruised knuckles. Quaid looked tired. He was barely standing. Mason rose unsteadily to his feet.

'Is that all of them?'

'I wish we could tie them up,' Quaid said.

Mason's only thought was to help Roxy. The task was complete down here. No enemy at their backs. He took several deep breaths and gingerly massaged his throat, willing the deep ache to go away.

It didn't.

Mason climbed back up the long slope to the platform above. Sally and Quaid were with him. He collected a discarded flashlight, considered looking for his gun, but then decided they didn't have the time. At least ten minutes had passed since Roxy and Hassell set out on their own in pursuit of McCloud.

They traversed the long tunnel at pace, moving as fast as Mason's woozy head would allow. They helped each other up through the ragged hole at the end, and then ran through the lower vault.

Mason's head was clearing with every step. The fresh air probably helped, and it got fresher as they emerged into the second vault. Another quick run and they were crossing the topmost prisoners' quarters, climbing the flight of stairs that would lead them outside the castle.

Mason stepped out into the night, looking left and right. His throat still throbbed but his head was clear. Sally and Quaid were at his side.

And on the wind, he heard the roar of car engines.

'Car park,' he said.

They raced around the castle grounds, just in time to see two cars roaring away from Roxy. Her cry, stentorian, swept across the esplanade.

'Hassell! Get down!'

Roxy opened fire.

# Chapter 48

The Guild's cars roared towards the exit, coming together where the road narrowed.

Roxy stood with her legs apart, gun held out in front of her. She targeted the tyres. Four shots blew two tyres out, one for each car. The vehicles swerved and crashed into each other, then veered off and struck the stone wall that encircled the parking area. There was a screech and a clash of metal and then the sound of two engines roaring.

Mason yelled out a warning to Roxy – to stop her from turning and firing on him – and then ran to her side. Hassell, ahead, picked himself up off the ground. There was a long moment of silence as they studied the crashed cars.

'I'll take the one on the left,' Roxy said.

Mason nodded, heading to the right. They ran through the blustery darkness, their progress illuminated only by streetlights and the deep blue nightlights that illuminated the castle. It was shadowy and cold up here. Mason rolled his shoulders as he ran, trying to ease the ache there too. The car's doors opened as he approached.

The civilians exited the vehicle, undeterred by the crash. Mason saw three Guild members including Murdock McCloud and one mercenary. He didn't slow, just vaulted around the car's rear and targeted the most dangerous man there.

The merc looked surprised. McCloud shouted orders. Mason jammed the merc back against the wall, right where the car had struck, and punched him across the face. The man's head whipped to the left. Mason followed up with a stunning jab to the nose. The mercenary spat blood and fought back, peppering Mason with a flurry of blows from clenched fists.

Mason was having none of it. He bent his knees, grabbed the merc around the waist and then hurled him over the wall. The merc's face broke into an expression of shock and then disappeared, his scream cutting through the air.

Mason spun. McCloud was running along with two of his cronies. On the other side of the esplanade, Roxy and Hassell were dealing with the other three. Sally stood to one side, a phone to her ear.

Mason heard sirens approaching.

Someone must have reported the gunshots. It was a fair assumption. Mason took off after McCloud and the others, reaching an older man first. Mason didn't slow down, but instead smashed the man across the back of the neck with his elbow. The man sprawled, landing on his face and scraping across the ground for several feet. Mason didn't slow or let up, remembering that these people had been prepared to watch him murdered in cold blood. He reached the next running man seconds later, this time leaping and kicking out the legs.

He connected solidly. Bones snapped. The runner screamed and went down hard, skidding across the concrete.

Ahead, now stood Murdock McCloud.

Mason slowed. The leader of the Guild had seen what happened to his friends and clearly saw no point in running. He confronted Mason with a grin on his face.

'I can make you rich. Satisfy your every desire, good or bad. I can teach you how to be a killer and a king.'

Mason shook his head. 'You're finished, McCloud. Your so-called Guild is finished. Jail's too good a place for you.'

'Jail?' McCloud guffawed. 'As if? Don't you know who we are? If you did, you'd know how far our sphere of influence extends.'

Mason lunged forward. 'Fuck your sphere,' he said.

They came together at the top of a long flight of stone steps, one of the flights Mason knew Edinburgh was famous for. Black, steep concrete risers led all the way down to a street a hundred feet below. McCloud produced a wicked-looking knife with a curved blade and sliced it towards Mason's midriff.

Mason danced aside. The knife flashed under the street-light. There was already blood encrusted under the shaft. Mason backed away.

'What's wrong?' McCloud said. 'Didn't think I'd know how to use it?'

'Oh, I know all about you,' Mason said.

McCloud slashed at him. The moon chose that moment to make an appearance from behind scudding clouds. It emerged above the castle and sent bright, stark light down across the entire scene.

Mason was bathed in the glow. McCloud came at him again. Mason stepped inside the man's swings, face to face, and headbutted him back towards the top of the stairs.

McCloud wiped blood from his face. 'What's wrong with you?' he said. 'Don't want to be powerful? To have them eating out of your hand? Don't want formidable anonymity? I can give you everything. You and your crew.'

It started to rain, large heavy droplets that crashed down to the ground like bombs. Mason's view of McCloud grew obstructed. He leapt in, swung for the man's head.

The rain soaked the two men. The light of the moon lit them. From a distance, they could have been old ghosts battling in sight of the castle at the top of the long flight of steps.

Mason threw out an uppercut that sent McCloud stumbling. McCloud sliced open the skin on top of Mason's right hand. Blood sprayed through the rain, reflecting off the droplets. Mason blew water from between his lips. He flung a fist that dripped blood, struck out with another that almost broke bone. Falling water smashed the ground all around them as if it was trying to draw their attention. Mason grabbed McCloud's jacket and tried to wrench the knife away.

McCloud clawed and flapped, keeping Mason at bay with the sharp, gleaming blade that was now slick with crimson. Every time McCloud swung it, sparkling rain flew off the edge.

Mason breathed easily, fists raised. He ducked and then punched out, catching McCloud across the jaw. He put out a hand to ward off the inevitable knife thrust. He grabbed the wrist and twisted it.

'You may know knives,' he said softly. 'You may even know how to use them. But I was forged in war. You created yourself the coward's way, by terrorising people, intimidating them and then standing back to watch. There are others like you in this world, and they all lose in the end.'

Mason ignored the knife as it passed close enough to nick his cheek, took a step into McCloud and raised a boot before kicking out as hard as he could. The boot connected solidly with McCloud's midriff. McCloud flew through the air, clearing the top five steps and coming down hard on his spine. He rolled unstoppably down the concrete steps.

Mason followed, trying to keep pace, but McCloud's speed was unrelenting. The man picked up pace as he fell. Mason heard the crunching of bone, the distraught sounds of someone who couldn't help themselves.

It was fitting, in a way. Mason wasn't sure all the stories of murder, mayhem and bloodshed that surrounded McCloud were true but, having met the man, it was entirely possible.

McCloud was dying as he rolled helplessly.

Mason tried to catch him, to arrest his fall. It was a long way down the flight of steps. He descended so fast that he almost tripped headlong himself. He could only watch as McCloud crashed down the entire flight, hit the pavement below and then rolled out into the road. His arms and legs flapped as he finally came to a rest, his head lolling. Mason reached his side seconds later.

'McCloud,' he said softly. 'You still wanna fight?'

There was no reply. Murdock McCloud lay motionless. If he was still alive, he showed no obvious signs of it. Mason became aware that the comms still worked then as Roxy's voice blared through his skull.

'We can see you,' she said. 'We've got your back, Joe. And we're with you, in spirit at least. It's all clear up here. Guild zero, Roxy three.'

'They're all out of it,' Quaid said. 'No fight left in them.'

'McCloud is down,' Mason said. 'Umm, literally.'

'Did we just find Solomon's Temple?' Sally broke in. 'The Tabernacle. The Ark of the bloody—'

'Technically, we didn't,' Roxy said. 'And there were a lot of chests and things down there.'

Sally's intake of breath could be heard as she tried to deal with Roxy's blasé attitude. Mason brought their attention back to a harsher reality.

'Is that the police?' Looking back up the steps, he could now see flashing blue lights approaching the castle. They painted the old buildings up there in a lurid light.

'I called and started the explanation,' Sally said. 'Hopefully, it'll prevent our arrest.'

'And I,' Quaid said, 'have a few contacts in the area, strings that I can pull.'

'You'd best make it quick,' Roxy said. 'The boys in blue are almost here.'

Mason enjoyed hearing their interaction, even if it did sound a little weary. It was enough to have survived the battle, to have found the treasure and stayed alive. It was enough to know that they had disbanded what remained of the Guild of Night.

Murdock McCloud groaned at his feet.

Mason decided to remain at the man's side. Not that he assumed the fallen leader was able enough to crawl away. But he didn't want to move the man in case his injuries were more severe than they looked. And he didn't want him to get run over by a passing car – as satisfying as that might have been.

He wanted McCloud to pay the price for everything he'd done.

'I'll wait down here,' he said. 'Send the cops down when you get a chance.'

'The climb back up gonna be too much for you?' Roxy asked, amused.

'Yeah, it's the climb that'll hurt.' Mason stared back up the long flight of steps and admitted that might actually be the case.

But he wanted to remain with McCloud. Wanted to see the man surrounded by police, taken into custody. Wanted to see an end to this mission.

And a fresh way forward beyond their nightmare search for the Ark of the Covenant.

So Mason stayed under the bright moonlit sky, soaked by the rain and parted from his friends, wondering what the next few hours would bring. And the boundless treasure waited where it had lain for uncounted centuries beneath the great, craggy rock and the primordial, imposing castle that had always watched over it.


THE END

You've met Jack Reacher.
You've met Jason Bourne.
Now it's time to meet Joe Mason . . .

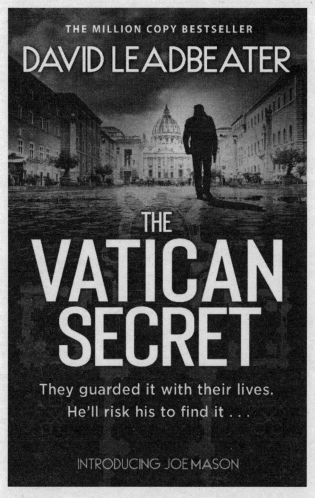

THE MILLION COPY BESTSELLER

DAVID LEADBEATER

THE
VATICAN
SECRET

They guarded it with their lives.
He'll risk his to find it . . .

INTRODUCING JOE MASON

Go back to where the adventure began with
*The Vatican Secret.*
Available now!

The adventure continues . . .

Don't miss the second action-packed
and adrenaline-filled instalment.
Available now!